THE PRINCESS
of the
IRON PALACE

THE PRINCESS
of the
IRON PALACE

by
Gustavo Sainz
Translated by Andrew Hurley

Grove Press
New York

Published by Grove Press, Inc.
920 Broadway
New York, N.Y. 10010

Library of Congress Cataloging-in-Publication Data

Sáinz, Gustavo, 1940-
The princess of the Iron Palace.

Translation of: Princesa del Palacio de Hierro.

I. Hurley, Andrew. II. Title.
PQ7298.29.A35P713   1987   863   86-33625
ISBN 0-394-56066-3

Manufactured in the United States of America
First Edition 1987

10 9 8 7 6 5 4 3 2 1

ACKNOWLEDGMENTS

The quotations at the end of each chapter are from the *Complete Works (Obras Completas)* of Oliverio Girondo (Buenos Aires: Editorial Losada, 1968). The titles of two chapters, 6 and 20, are also from Girondo. One or two quotations within the text, indicated by parentheses and quotation marks as well as by italics, also come from Girondo's work.

This book is dedicated to Brenda, who inspired it, and to my friend Arnaldo Coen, its first enthusiastic reader, and is for Alessandra and our Claudio.

CONTENTS

THE PRINCESS
of the
IRON PALACE

1

I don't know much about sick people

The girl belonged in an institution, I'm telling you. She never wore anything but men's clothes, with a hat and a tie and the whole works, you know?, and you know who she looked like? Do you remember Mercedes, my brother's old girlfriend, that used to run around on him? Uh-huh, that one—listen, you know something? There used to be this expression, you put horns on the guy. Well, he had such a pair of horns from Mercedes running around on him that he had to file them down every time he wanted to go through the door. I'm not kidding, they looked just alike, but it wasn't just that she looked like her—I mean she wore the same makeup, she combed her hair the same way, she dressed the same way, right?, smoked the same way, everything the same. And in her pocket, get this, where men carry their driver's licenses and credit cards and what have you and a handkerchief to wipe up their come with, she carried her little bottles of makeup and her compact and all. You won't believe this, but one day a traffic cop stopped her, and she stuck her hand in her pocket like she was going to pull out her business card or some citation from the mayor or something, to show him she was a big shot, like men do, right?, and she was saying No, oh no, I look awful, and *chíngale!*, shit, she pulls out this little tube, like a tube of toothpaste, right?, this tube with some kind of cream she had to put on herself, on her legs or whatever, because every time she got scared or a little shook up or got upset or nervous or something, right?, this red rash would come out on her, all over her, and she's got to take out this little tube of cream and pull up her pants leg and squeeze a little white worm of it out on the rash and rub it in, I mean massage it in, *caress* it in, work it in real good, and all the time this cop standing there saying Your license, please. And her dressed like a man, right? Anyway, she was a good friend of these two girls that lived next door to me, the Jalisco Sisters, and she was always at their house or talking to them on the telephone at all hours of the day and night or coming over to my house for a visit. Sometimes we'd go out together, you know? We'd almost always go out together.

The Jalisco Sisters were real real real *real* skinny, but they had these very pretty faces. They were jumpy, though, nervousy, you know?, like a couple of birds. The older one had a kind of decided look about her, she'd move her hands like she was swimming through us, like this, or walk along like she was beating a drum, and the other one was always laughing and opening her eyes like big O's and sputtering and flaring up like when you strike a match, and then bang!, *chíngale!*, all of a sudden she'd be depressed, and she'd look like some sad little canary with its feathers all droopy, or she'd shiver like she was cold, or about to fall off her perch and die, but then in a little while she'd be waving her bony hands around again, happy as a lark, and giving off these little pops and sputters, right?, and you'd swear it was fireworks going off. Next to those two, I'll tell you, Dressed Like a Man and I were a couple of papier-mâché dress dummies—mani, what do you call them?, manisomethings. Uh-huh, mannequins, right. . . .

So anyway, one of our favorite places to go, we went there all the time, was this place that was down in a basement, in the basement of this old house. It was called The Two Turtles, and the man that owned it was this really funny guy, a real character. I mean, just to give you an idea—he had the whole place decorated like a brothel, I mean a real whorehouse. I kid you not. In some of the rooms he put, in some of the rooms he had . . . A *base*ment—you know, a *base*ment, like they used to have in old houses to store stuff in. . . . In some of the rooms he had nets, and in this other room he'd painted stuff, but where the main room was, where there was supposed to be the biggest crowd—and there was always a crowd!—he had it all full of witches—yes, *witches,* on broomsticks and everything, right? Hanging all over. Little bitty, about so big, hanging all over the place. And this guy had twisted all their feet around, like this, so they'd look like me. What I mean is, all the witches *were* me, their feet were all turned in, like I walk, right?, like I stand. Pigeon-toed witches. And when my shoes wore out, he made this rule, he had this rule that like I couldn't break, right?, that I had to leave them there, because since I was always dancing, I mean I was the life of the party, always dancing. . . . Everybody knew me, can you imagine, and everybody liked me a lot . . . The bell of the ball, so to speak. . . . Besides, they didn't usually let people my age in, right? Sometimes I'd get there, and they wouldn't even let me in, because they had some pretty raunchy shows sometimes. So then they'd say No, you can't come in. I'd go with my brother, right? Never by myself. Or with the Jalisco Sisters from down Guadalajara way, or Dressed Like a Man, but never ever by myself. No, you can't come in, it's pretty raunchy right now. It's that they had women doing stripteases and stuff, but all kinds of people went, I mean *all* kinds. . . . They'd get out of parties, or the movies, or their hotel rooms, of course, and if they knew the owner, who was this tall, dark kid with a belly shaped like a pear . . . Prostitutes, these super well-dressed girls, Gabriel Infante went . . . He always wore white shoes and pants real real

pegged at the bottom and wide up here at the top. . . . So anyway, we went there to dance. It was a place you went to to dance,
the night people and the people who knew where to go went there,
the in people and the super in people. Anyway, this one night my
brother and I were leaving, and my brother says Kids, listen to
that, I think some poor jerk is getting his hubcaps stolen. And I
say God yes, I'll be damned if they're not. So we start looking
around the parking lot, through all the cars, all the cars parked
around there, and we start getting close to our car, and we saw it
was *ours*—three guys were practically dismantling our car. So my
brother says Oh shit, that's my car, and he takes off running,
trying to catch them, right? And so then, so then the guys saw
him running across the street after them, and they jumped into
this old Ford they had there double-parked, and they started to
take off. About then my brother the idiot, take my brother, *please*,
instead of letting them get away, he runs up to this old Ford, and
he grabs hold of the window—well, really, he was just trying to
get the door open, but they screeched off and there he was, hanging onto the window, so he hung on for dear life, with his feet
flying out behind him, like in the cartoons, right? He'd run a few
steps, but then he'd have to pick up his feet because the car was
going too fast, right? Run a few steps and fly a few steps. These
other guys were hitting him in the face, slapping him, trying to
pry his fingers loose, but he was hanging on, I mean there was no
way he was going to turn loose. But finally he had to turn loose,
right? So we ran back to The Two Turtles. Everybody says What
happened! Because we looked sick—we looked like we'd been
eating three-day-old enchiladas. My brother was puffing like the
bull at the bullfight. So anyway, there was this guy there that had
a job in something or other for the government, like a secret agent
or something. Imagine how secret he was if we all knew about
him! So anyway, my brother runs in like a maniac, over and over
saying Nine twenty-seven two forty-three, nine twenty-seven two
forty-three, nine twenty-seven two forty-three, over and over
again. The license plate, right?, those guys' license plate. So he
went over and gave the guy the number, and this guy says Don't
worry, I'll find out, I'll get 'em, not to worry and so on and so

forth. Of course, he never did anything, right? So we didn't have any hubcaps. But what I wanted to tell you was, there were about thirty pairs of my shoes hanging all around the dance floor. Or forty. I was Miss Popularity, right?

Sometime around then Dressed Like a Man called me up one day and really laid a number on me. Listen, she says, I'm dying no less, I've got this terrible pain in my gall bladder, no I mean my stomach. I think one of my ulcers just burst—and listen, I'm desperate, I don't know what to do, I'm dying. Please, find me a nurse, a cheap nurse, because I can't stay here by myself and my mother just left for Israel. And me, the eternal sucker here, Mother Superior says No, listen, no, come to my house and to-morrow, first thing in the morning, we'll go find a hospital. You can't just go to any old hospital, you never know how they are. Listen, just come over here, come to my place and tomorrow we'll find a good . . . And I swear I hadn't finished saying the word *good* yet, when she was knocking on the door. . . . I think the son of a bitch, I mean the bitch herself, the girl must have been calling from down on the corner, from the phone booth on the corner, because I mean there she was. And that's not the half of it! You know what else? She had all this *stuff* with her, her arms were full of ashtrays and pictures off the wall and these bottles of makeup, all her accoutrements, I'm serious, to come and stay. I can't tell you—when I saw her I almost fainted. I mean it was such a shock. My father, don't ask. My mother, forget it! She just comes in and takes over. First she takes over a bedroom, the next day the telephone, and in twelve days we were her maids and butler. Servants! . . .

Do you think she cared if every Saturday night she was going out with that weekend's Guest Celebrity? These guys, these real dreamboats, right?, would come in and wait for her to finish get-ting dressed and everything. My mother and father would just stand there with their mouths open. In shock. Then later on, for example, she started going out on weeknights too, and I'd say Come on now, please, come home early because we go to bed about twelve, so don't get home later than that because the house-keeper, I mean the maids and the houseboys and everybody go to bed, and there's nobody to let you in, so we have to get up ourselves, so please, come in early. Syphilitic bullfrogs! She'd come in at four or five o'clock in the morning. And picture my mother and me, having to get out of bed to let her in. My father was traveling a lot back then. I hated her. You've never seen anybody hate somebody so much. So then we put our heads together. We talked about a little conspiracy, to have her kidnapped you know, or insulting her or not talking to her, making her feel bad so she'd leave. So just about then Little Jalisco comes and says Listen, I want to see how this strikes you, uh, I asked your mother, and she said it was okay, huh? She said it was okay for you to come to Acapulco with us for a couple of weeks, because your mother said she was going to be going to San Antonio to buy some clothes, so she says instead of leaving you here all by yourself, um, she'd rather send you to Acapulco with us. So what do you think? Gosh, why terrific, sure, I mean great, and so on and so forth, because I was desperate too. And Dressed Like a Man listening to all this and looking very sad because she wasn't invited. And all the servants were going to get their vacation, so nobody would be in the house to take care of her. So anyway, I went off to Acapulco and my mother went to Texas. It was all to see if we could get her out, right? But she said she'd take care of the house for us while we were away, and she brainwashed my father. You know how long she stayed? For about five months! I was ready to pull my hair out. I was going crazy. You can't imagine. My mother hated the sight of her. She kept saying Well, if this young woman had at least said Can I live in your house?, but all she said was I'll just come for one night. . . .

Well but anyway, to make a long story short, Dressed Like a Man, one of the times we'd gone out together, one of the *countless* times we'd gone out together, she introduced me to this guy that talked a lot. He was from Guadalajara-*ándale!* too, and he looked like a monk. He had like three noses, one underneath the other, so you saw this great big huge nose, and he looked like he was always telling lies with that sweet innocent monk's face of his, or at least that's the way he looked to me. You know who I'm talking about? I've told you about him before, I'm pretty sure. He really

did look like a monk, or like a tourist without his luggage, one
of those guys you see in the airport standing there waiting for
the luggage cart to come with the luggage so he can go through
customs, just standing there, like this, like there was one bag still
missing, right?, and he was sort of halfway waiting for it to get
there and halfway not caring, and in the meantime, I'll just watch
these people's faces, thank you. I think you've seen him. He
worked for a while in the courts somewhere, and then he was
secretary to the minister of, uh-huh, that's him, the one that
dressed like, uh-huh, pale, pale pale pale, pale as an altar-boy's
ass.

Anyway, this guy asked me out to dinner, he started always
asking me out to eat. So finally, one day he called me, and the
four of us girls were all there, right? And the Jalisco Sisters were
hungry, and nobody had any money, so we decided we'd let him
take us out to dinner. On him. Or listen, to give you a better
idea, he was like a bishop and a camel at the same time, like the
Archbishop of Camels. . . .

The Two Turtles was closed on Mondays, so we went to this
other place, where the Astoria used to be? The owners of this
place thought they had this restaurant for pretty high-class people, but I'll tell you the truth, it was always full of lowlifes. Or
really, just common kinds of people, you know? But it was always
fun and it was close by, and there were always guys there, flirting
and trying to pick you up, and I liked that, right? I mean, we
kept going out with these zombies, right?, these guys that walked
like this. . . . So this place . . . Anyway, we were sitting there
minding our own business, never imagining in our wildest dreams
that one of us was going to wind up committing a crime and another one have four abortions and another one go crazy. We were
just sitting there listening to the mariachis. The Monk had kept
asking me out, so finally that night I couldn't say no anymore, so
we decided to sponge dinner off him, and I told him I'd go if I
could bring my girlfriends along. And so when he came to pick us
up, we told him we wanted to go to this one place because the
pâté and the French bread they gave you, and the crowd, and the
decoration really sent us, I mean we practically swooned—be-

cause they had these red tablecloths, you know, and soft chairs that you just sank into. They were warm, too . . . those chairs were like lovers.

So anyway, the maître d' comes over to the table. The maître d' comes over, and he says A glass of wine? He was asking us if we wanted a glass of wine, right? So one of the Jalisco Sisters puts her fingertips on her chest like this, and she chirps We'd like to have dinner. And No, thank you, no, nothing, nothing for me, I don't drink, The Monk says. The menu—can you picture this?— The menu, grunts one of the Guadalajara Girls. And the maître d' suggesting a vermouth, a nice port. He sort of runs down the list. Gin. And No, thank you, nothing, a duet, a trio, a quartet. His voice going Vermouth, port, gin, but he sounded like he was really saying something very different. His voice slid down our bodies like some mad tender waterfall arousing waves of sensual thrills . . . And his eyes were so intense they made your buttons want to jump off. . . . So what do you think happened next? He went to get the menu, he brought it back, and he stood there. He just stood there. He stood there next to us, right? The Monk's stomach was making noises like the heating was coming up in the radiator; he was starving. Dressed Like a Man was sitting next to him, her fingers going on the menu, like this, like she was typing a letter. And the Jalisco Sisters nodding and waving their hands and saying Oh this sounds good and Oh this sounds delicious and on and on, right?, like they talk. And the maître d' standing there, very attentive and distant. . . . So then we all decided what we wanted, and we ordered—I don't remember what, but I know in those days I loved Caesar salad, we'd just discovered Caesar salad. So the maître d' wrote it all down and snapped his fingers, and another waiter came and took the order off, and the maître d' just kept standing there next to us, between me and Little Jalisco, with his arms hanging down at his sides like all the strength had gone out of them, his face expressionless and harsh, innocent and carnal. At least so it looked to me, right? I said to myself, Funny, this guy standing here, just standing here doing nothing. I took out a cigarette and he jumped to light it, *zip!* I mean that was normal enough, right?, but then he just kept standing there. So then we started to eat, with these ay-yi-yi-yi songs in the background cheering up the place immensely. As you can imagine. . . . They'd brought some hors d'oeuvres by now, and we all leapt on them, like very neat, delicate vultures, like we were picking the parts out of a watch, especially the olives. Big Jalisco was going over the menu again like she was plucking through one of those big missals at some fancy wedding in the Guadalupe Cathedral. . . .

So then all of a sudden, this big group of like the Best-Dressed Men, or Eligible Bachelors, or Leading Men, comes in, a whole cast of Leading Men come running in. There were about nine or ten guys, and they come in like gangbusters and surround this other guy that was eating at this table over behind us. We thought it was a joke or something, or that they were getting back at him for some trick he'd played on them, or maybe a fight, something like that, right?, but the maître d' says It's nothing, but very insinuating, you know?, they're all friends of mine. . . . Meanwhile, they had this guy up against a pillar—pillar, is it?—up against this column. He was incredibly handsome too, and they all started kissing him on the mouth and taking off his clothes. . . . Men, right? All these men kissing him and dying laughing . . . The Jalisco Sisters had their faces down in their plates, and they were pecking at their food like hens. And The Monk and Dressed Like a Man I had forgotten about completely, in spite of the fact that the Queen of Cream was massaging herself anywhere she could reach by now. So then a bunch of girls started coming in . . . Classic streetwalker types! So anyway, I bend over to finish eating my soup, and the maître d' whisks it away from me. I mean did you ever! The soup is eaten hot, he says in this silky mandolin voice strumming insinuations, I will have it heated. . . . And I was so busy watching these street-walkers—this big cotton skirt, a Scotch-looking purse with a red fringe, these shoes with gold high heels—that I didn't say a word. . . . The soup is eaten hot. . . . Circumcised snake-handlers! That voice of his was his best part, if you know what I mean, and it didn't matter what words he said, his voice palpated you, it practically groped the bodies he liked, it was a tease. He attacked you with it, caressed you . . .

So then in a little while, right?, The Monk and I meanwhile making small talk, although I was so nervous I could hardly talk, in a little while the maître d' brought the soup back, and then he stood there again, staring at us, just staring, staring and then whoops! Eat your soup, like he was saying Vooly-voo cooshay avec mwa?—to *all* of us, The Monk included. Your soup . . . With this big hungry smile like The Big Bad Wolf. . . . Anyway, all of a sudden the mariachis stop, and all you can hear is Dressed Like a Man going scrtch scrtch scrtch. I take a big spoonful of soup then, right?, and all of a sudden we're surrounded—twelve or fifteen mariachis all over the place. Did I tell you the Jalisco Sisters are like chickens? Peck peck peck. They lived practically next door to me and they considered themselves the Classic Experienced Women, you know the type—they know a little bit about everything, right? Well, so, here come the mariachis, and they sort of hover over the table and ask us if there's not something we'd like to hear. Big Jalisco puts down her psalmbook, I mean the menu, and she turns, very very slowly, like she's inspecting her past, instantly the mistress of the situation, and she says No, thank you very much, no, thank you, really, no. . . . So then they regroup—they start tightening their chin straps and straightening those big huge sombreros, scraping their spurs on the brick floor and so on and so forth, but then in about two minutes they're back, bigger and darker than ever, and sticking out their bellies, those big bellies you know, that hang over their belts from all the pulque they drink all day. . . . Wouldn't we like them to play something for us. . . . So again we say No, we really don't, no, nothing, nothing, although over in the corner Dressed Like a Man is giggling and whispering and making those old jokes like "Hey Cisco, wait for me," you know . . . So they left again. But then The Monk shoves his nose practically into my lap and he says Really? Really? You really don't want to hear something? Really?

So a little later they're back again, but this time they talk to the maître d', still standing guard beside the Jalisco Girls, right? And he tilts his head over to them, and then he turns to me and under my girlfriends' chattering he says Señorita, tell us what song you would like to hear. . . . He clears his throat over the salad and swallows his drool. No, no song, really we don't want to hear any song. . . . So the maître d' says Oh. Then . . . but The Monk spurts out, like when you turn on the faucet and all of a sudden the water gushes out all over you, right?, The Monk says No, no, the señoritas don't want to hear any song. At that the maître d' sort of bows and looks down his nose like some kind of chessman, like this stern black castle bumping into a pawn that's on the wrong square. He bows very suavely and very very politely, very sweetly, with all the savoir faire in the world, and he says But no, señor, you are not to pay, I am the one who will pay. . . . And he turns and says to me, like we'd been friends since 1954 or something, I mean like since prehistoric times, he says Well? . . . Will you hear a song? Lascivious. And pissed off, too. . . . Dressed Like a Man started scratching again, and the Ándale Girls pretended to stay incredibly cool. . . . So, confused and everything, but like trying to get the situation under control, very condescendingly, but cornered, right?, because the guy was like very menacing if you know what I mean, I was almost scared, I took a little breath and I said Do they know "Consentida"? And *chíngale!*, bang!, right?, they break into "Consentida," chica-chica strumming and ay-yi-yi-ing for all they were worth. Bedlam! They sang me about five songs, can you imagine?, with the maître d' standing there at attention, so proud and full of himself, his chest all puffed out, and *libertine* at the same time, *calculating*. . . . I, when they exploded like that, I choked on a piece of lettuce, and for a second there I was desperate, gasping for air, but then I got it out and looked up like Does this bus go to Tlalpán? Even the teenagers that had come in, I mean even the *streetwalkers* all turned around and were looking at us.

So then anyway, they brought our dinner, and the maître d' says Let me cut your meat for you, and he stuck his hands in my plate. The vision of those hands touching my breasts made me sick and terrified and disgusted. I thought This night will never end. It was a nightmare! And the worst thing of all was that it all seemed so absolutely preordained. How can I explain it? . . . The maître d' leaning that Andalusian face of his over my hair. I could smell his warm breath . . . But a lot could happen between salad and dessert, right? For example, my girlfriends saw Loco Valdiosera over there with those guys that had come in. You cannot imagine how handsome he is. Incredibly handsome. Anyway, so when they saw him they said Look, that's Loco Valdiosera isn't it? Back then I didn't have the slightest idea who this Loco Valdiosera was. Picture me—Miss Sheltered, I could never even leave my house. My parents had to know the whole family tree— no, really, I mean the whole *pedi*gree, of every family we knew, because if they didn't, they wouldn't let me so much as speak to anybody—not Good morning or How are you. Not How . . . So I didn't have even the slightest idea. . . . So they started talking about this guy, about how he was a pimp, he was a smuggler, he was this drug addict, he'd killed some guy, he was a gunrunner, how he knew karate and he'd made a movie, he owned this whorehouse and he lived in Los Angeles, and so on and so forth—to make a long story short, he was this super sexy, super eligible, super sought-after guy who lived the life of, well, of a movie star. . . . And they were saying That's him that's him over there, right? So they asked the maître d' and he nodded, pretty ticked off but so so courtly at the same time, right? Grunted, really. And The Monk, you could tell, was terrified, but he acted like nothing was happening, with that provincial way he has of tucking his tail between his legs, right? But I was impressed. I was practically sitting there with my mouth open. Because if the truth be known, I'd never seen such a handsome guy in my life.

But then these girls, these streetwalker types I told you about, they start burping and coughing and screaming and throwing up all over the red tablecloth and the plates of food on the other table. And do you think the mariachis stopped singing? Or that the maître d' stirred a muscle? So how could we finish eating? I mean the agony we were going through. . . . The Monk was chain-smoking and my hands were shaking—I don't know if it was from being excited or scared. And between the chittering of the Jalisco Sisters and Dressed Like a Man's automassages and the waiters running back and forth changing all the stuff on the other table and the laughing of the Leading Men, it looked like the whole thing was sinking fast. All I wanted to do was escape, but Dressed Like a Man said I think we should stay, we need to calm down. . . . Everybody seemed to be of the same opinion. So we ordered coffee . . .

I started trying to take their minds off all this, right? Or maybe I was talking to relax, myself, to calm down, I don't know, but Dressed Like a Man was right with me. We started talking about the Abacosobatá. . . . There was this show back then, re- member?, it was at Balloons, it had come from Beautiful Cuba, it was one of the main shows—from Cuba, was it? Yes, from Havana, I'm sure. Anyway, we were so, but I mean so in love with this show that we went every day—the Jalisco Sisters, my brother, Dressed Like a Man, and I. Especially my brother and I, we went every day, every day. It just knocked us for a loop, this show, I'll tell you how crazy we were over it, one day at home we even picked up one of our maids and carried her around, you know like in that number they did, remember there was that one unbelievable dance number? When it opened they came in carry- ing this woman, right?, dancing carrying her, so that's the way we did it too, right? All of a sudden it just hit us, we couldn't help it, we grabbed up the feather duster and all the stuff for cleaning the house, and we danced and rolled around on the floor . . . Possessed! Shrieking like parrots . . . Everybody got the bug. We did the *whole thing*. Even the stuff that—well . . . we knew the songs they did with the chorus and everything, we knew thou- sands of songs. Some friend of ours would come over, and we'd sing and pretend we were pulling the microphone cord around, kick it off to one side, kick it with one foot, and move our hips around, and practically lick the microphone. We put on shows, with all the songs and dances, just like that show. Some friend of ours would come over, and the first thing we'd do was imitations of the show. When you come over sometime, we'll do the show for you, I told The Monk. Okay, he says, okay . . .

So anyway, one day in The Two Turtles, one day, oh my God!, everybody from the Abacosobatá comes in. I mean forget it, they were tops, they were our heroes, for us they were just the, well, and The Two Turtles had brought them in. So my brother and I got to be good friends with them. All Negroes . . . Ugly ugly ugly, right? But dynamite, just sensational. With a sense of rhythm, and a talent for music, I mean such talent, well, but you know exactly what I mean. . . . Anyway, one day at a dinner we had for my brother, because it was my brother's birthday . . . We told my parents, Listen, let's, we're going to have a dinner party. Okay, fine, they say, what do you want to do, what do you want to eat, so we can buy it, how many people. There'll be about twenty-three of us more or less and we want a sit-down dinner. We want *arroz con pollo* or *frijoles con cerdo*, either one. So then my father, who was really, I'm not kidding, he'd do anything for us, spare no expense, my father says But wait a minute—*arroz con pollo?* Uh-huh, that's what we want—*arroz con pollo*. But *why?* Because that's what we want to eat . . . That was what the Negroes ate, right? Especially in Cuba—that's one of the main dishes. So when they came in, well, anyway, we had this dinner party, just like we wanted, everything you can imagine. But then, oh God, my father comes down to see who was there and how everything was going and everything. There they were—one, two, three, twenty-one Negroes from the Abacosobatá, all the Negroes from the show at the Abacosobatá, and my brother and me the only white people, the only white faces at this dinner party at my house. When my father saw that, he went upstairs, and he said to my mother, There are Negroes in the house. As black as the ace of spades. My mother was scared practically to death. . . . She started yelling Come up here, come up here this minute. I barely got to the top of the stairs before she started—What is that pack of Negroes your father says is downstairs doing in this house? They're friends of ours . . . And we started laughing, right?, Dressed Like a Man and I are laughing our heads off. Little Jalisco smelled like oregano, her sister said the maître d' was muttering it sounded like we were making the whole thing up, to him, and The Monk was laughing so cute—I don't know exactly how he did it—his teeth squeaked. I kid you not, his teeth squeaked.

Well, anyway, poor Mother took the whole thing so hard . . . Because besides, listen, she had just found out that we had a dark room in the house, right? I mean not a darkroom like for cameras, it was this room that nobody was using. And since my mother never ever spied on us or anything, or noticed anything at all, because she's the absolute last word in distraction, I mean discretion, since she was so out of it, we took over this room and painted it black and put in all new light bulbs, red ones. And we kept it locked. We'd told my parents and everybody that it was our literary room. There was Dressed Like a Man and my brother and me. We were all living in my house, all three of us, and every day we took turns cleaning up and throwing out the cigarette butts and airing it out. Because at night, since my parents were in their bedroom, all our friends would come over and we'd go in there. My parents didn't know where we were, upstairs or downstairs—they really didn't care. We'd put in some couches, a record player, stuff like that. We'd turn on the red lights, and the whole gang of us would be in there. . . . In the morning we'd open the windows and air out the room and get some fresh air in, right? But we always left it locked up. . . . So anyway, one day, I don't know how it happened, but Dressed Like a Man was in charge of the ventilation as we called it, and she left the door unlocked. Oh yeah, I left it unlocked, she said. Well my mother just chanced by and just chanced to think of opening the door, so she opens the door, and she sees this black room with the floor painted black and all the furniture and stuff black, and the red lights and everything, and since she'd never noticed what color the room was before, she started screaming, like she was out of her mind, A brothel! A brothel! They've got a brothel in there!

So then the waiter brought coffee. A brothel! A brothel! As they're serving the coffee, right? They're running a brothel! First to the Jalisco Sisters, then to me, then Dressed Like a Man, and last to our host, with the maître d' with a patronizing little smile. We were drinking the coffee, right? Or well, really it was pretty hot, so I was waiting for it to cool off a little, or I was giggling, I'm not sure . . . You've got to see this literary room, Little Jalisco was saying. Oh no, I was telling them about the songs from Abacosobatá, that's what it was, and I was just bringing the coffee cup up to my mouth, and all of a sudden here comes the maître d' again, and he stops me with his hand. His big brown hairy hand. Brrrr . . . No no no no, allow me. And he takes the cup away from me, can you imagine, and he takes it away, just like with the soup. So I go Why did you take my coffee away, and he says Señorita, pardóng, but coffee must be drunk hot. The Monk is staring at all this with his eyes popping out of his head and his Pinocchio nose twitching. Noses, I mean. My girlfriends were about to fall out of their chairs laughing. But I'm letting it cool off a little, I said very meekly. Excuse me, señorita, but I will have it heated. And The Monk is holding onto his cup with both hands, just in case. But I'm letting it cool off!! No, no, don't be silly, coffee must be drunk hot, very very hot. Gelded devils! So, I didn't want to make too much of a scene, and especially not draw this handsome guy's attention that had come in and was looking over at me every now and then, so I finally just gave up, right? Anyway what else was there to say. I mean The stupid Monk should have said something, right? It was up to him, right?

So in just a few seconds here comes the coffee again. So I say to him, Listen. But instead of listening he says Will you have a cognac? No, thank you, no thank you v . . . Dinner without co-gnac is not dinner. I'm a teetotaler, says The Monk, all chirpy, I'm the Teetotaler of Valle Arizpe. Just one little moment, says the maître d', and he leaves us sitting there with our mouths as wide open as the lobby in the Palace of Fine Arts. And he brings back cognac. Courtesy of your servant, he says, all honey-tongued and rumba-ing, like this, right? Nymphomaniac snapping turtles! And The Camel there as serious as the Pope in Lent, right? Doesn't raise his head. . . .

So there we were trying to drink our coffee again, and he comes over with another big pot of coffee and fills up our cups all over again. I couldn't believe it. No, listen please, no more for us, no more for us now, thank you very much. . . . The harassing was starting again, right? We were absolutely dead serious now, but we didn't know what to do. There was this icky sticky feeling about everything. Ever since the before-dinner drinks we'd turned

down, there had been no hope. The situation just slipped right
out of hand. And the maître d' meanwhile going Oui, oui, a bit
more coffee, oh oui, with his eyes sparkling. You will find this
coffee is just the thing. . . . So we drank a little bit more, and he
fills up our cups again. I'm telling you, it looked like a decent
place, a good restaurant—and it was full of people. And of
course, as though this guy's attitude wasn't enough, they could've
put any kind of stuff in that coffee. The streetwalkers over there
were still at it, some of them by now on top of the table pawing
and getting pawed and making more racket than four mariachi
troupes at once. . . . So anyway, he filled up our coffee cups
again, and The Monk didn't try to stop him or ask for the check or
*any*thing. Handsome to the Maximum over there, and half his
horde disappeared into one of the bathrooms, and the conversation just died, once and for all. I mean all this time we'd been
talking, right? We'd been acting like this was all a little out-of-
the-ordinary, if you know what I mean, that we were in a kind of
a strange situation, but we could handle it, we'd all been around,
we were all experienced in the strange ways of the world, no big
deal for us, right? No big deal. But now we could never seem to
get to the bottom of those stupid cups of coffee, and my pulse was
up to about four hundred and twelve by this time. . . .

So in a little while, while The Monk was distracted watching
Dressed Like a Man put cream on the underside of one breast and
massage it in, I motioned to the maître d' and asked him to bring
me the check. . . . Just with my hand, like this, right?, making a
little squiggle in the air. Like this . . . The check, I said, just
with my lips. He was over there filling up the coffee pot again,
right? The Jalisco Sisters looked like sleepy pigeons. So the
maître d' whirls around and says very very slowly, very in-
tentionally, very politely—sort of elegant and stagey at the same
time, right?, like a movie maître d'—No, I would not consider it,
no. But I insist, yes, I said, nodding my head, motioning with my
hands, making my whole body plead for the stupid check. No. He
was firm about it. I was planning to plead with him right up to the
last minute and then kick him in the shins as hard as I could, to
see if I could break his leg for him. Hey, I say to the Montezuma

Monk, this guy won't bring us the check. So then Dressed Like a Man, who's covered with cream by now, cries *Oh, but why not?* So I say Who knows . . . So then one of the Jalisco Sisters stands up as thin as a stork but mad as hell, and she screams *Are you going to bring us that check or not!* In profile, right?, practically invisible she's so skinny, and you can't tell she's said a word. No, growled the maître d', not yet, walking over. The tables, the waiters, and all the customers turned around and stared ominously and kept moving their heads back and forth, like those Balinese dancers, right?, to get a good look. But things looked bad. So the Jalisco Sisters all of a sudden jump up like a couple of jack-in-the-boxes and say Let's get out of here, come on, quick. The Monk shoves his chair back and starts standing up. I didn't try to move. In spite of my disgust I was sort of curious to see what was going to happen next. Or was I so scared and stupefied I'd lost all my courage?

But anyway, the maître d' runs over and blocks the way—*zip!*, like that, and nobody could move. I suddenly shot off my launching pad. Dressed Like a Man bent over like she was fastening her shoe or rubbing some cream on her ankle, and then she just kept on bending down till she was on all fours crawling under the table to try to make a getaway. Even The Monk took this one step forward, with a jerky look on his face. You could see this diabolical inspiration descend on the hairy maître d' with all of us standing there not daring to do anything, I mean no way I was going to go up and slap him or something, right? And then we started to feel how hot it was getting . . . Like the inside of a tortilla factory, you can't imagine . . . And then we felt the sweat start. The maître d' was closer to me than to anybody else, so I got the full effect. He was stinking of wine, horns on his head, with these black hairs sticking straight up all over his groping, threatening hands, and his unreal tail hidden in his pants. Dressed Like a Man was still under the table, all confused and paranoid, and trying to crawl between Big Jalisco's legs, whose knees all of a sudden give out on her, so she goes Whoop and flaps her arms and crumples to the floor with this strange sound.

And the rest of us standing there like jerks with this very uncomfortable look on our heat-flushed faces . . .

So when we were finally getting into the car, The Monk says Boy, what was with that guy, anyway? The best line of the night, I mean that won the Nobel Prize for Commentary, right? Picture it—one of the Jalisco Sisters collapsing like a dropped napkin, me thinking they'd put something in our coffee, this other girl trapped between the table and a chair, and the maître d' standing there pointing a little plate with the check on it at us like it was a gun, blowing this smelly breath in our faces, lots of smoke in all this, lots of heat and noise, red tablecloths, and those half-naked streetwalker types cackling at this orgy at the next table. And we were standing there in a daze trying not to think of what came next! The girls and I, once we were outside, we broke out laughing. Had we conjured all this up? Boy, what was with that guy, huh? Stop talking and *move*, the Jalisco Sisters were yelling at him . . . He was coming on to us something awful, I said, as I closed the car door. . . . He started the car. You think that's what it was? he groaned. And he put it in reverse and backed out. I'm coming back to see about this, he said, scared to death, as he drove off. . . . We were relieved to get out of there, I'll tell you, and the farther away we got from the restaurant the more relieved we were. I opened the window, and to make a long story short, we realized we'd had it up to here with The Monk. We didn't care whether we ever saw him again as long as we lived. I'm going back to give that guy a piece of my mind, he yelled. . . .

If somebody had told me that night that I would wind up going to bed with him, and not only that but falling in love with him, I would've fallen over and floated away. I'd have turned blue. . . . He called me all the time on the telephone, right?, but frankly it was a *long time*, before we saw each other again. I never thought I'd go out with him again. . . .

(*"Believe it or not—these humiliations, this constant clamor is a thousand times more welcome than moments of calm and silence."*)

Entrapment and subsequent unpleasantnesses

One of those in-the-middle days—I mean one Tuesday like the ham in the sandwich between Monday and Wednesday, right?—this girlfriend of mine and I went downtown. We were walking along down Avenida Juárez, and I was telling her about Handsome to the Maximum, because that was all I could think about, us seeing each other in that obscure place. Because if I was ever sure about anything in my life, it was that he had been looking at me. And telling her about the captain or maître d' or whatever he was, right? Anyway, about that and seeing the guy all the other guys were kissing and the streetwalkers throwing up and everything. The day before, I'd found out that that hairy maître d' picked up all these really tough-looking hookers and took them who knows where. I think he had several apartments and they met men there, one of those kinds of things, right? So like hookers and Johns, Janes and hustlers, it was all the same. . . . Where was I? Oh, I remember, so I was walking down the street with this girlfriend of mine that was going to a psychoanalyst, right? I was going with her to the shrink's office . . . Women that go to shrinks, I don't know, it's like they don't have much to do, right? And this girl wasn't a bit more screwed up than I was, you know?, not a bit. . . . You know who it was? Mercedes, the one that had been my brother's girlfriend. And since her shrink didn't know telepathy, she had to go to see him, but all this prick did was make her talk about her sex life. He was married, of course, I mean naturally, right? And he's still married, to this girl he met in school and made her give up her education and even go with him when he went to Paris for his degree, right? But that didn't matter. He was interested—fascinated you might say—in masturbation techniques, in how her boyfriends touched her and how she felt and what she liked—and my girlfriend always spilled all the beans, all of them, and since she didn't have any other friend that would listen to her about her sex life, well, she gave in to this psychiatrist after twenty-four sessions of therapeutic gossip. So now she felt guilty, right?, but she didn't know whether to blame the shrink, for unprofessional conduct or whatever, you know, or go to another one, right? So we were saying that you can be one hundred percent sure this prick of a psychiatrist isn't going to tell or anything, for fear of making him*self* look bad, right?

Anyway, we were just walking along, when all of a sudden two guys start following us. When we realized it, I turn around and I see that one of them is Handsome to the Maximum. I almost died I was so scared! I'm not kidding—I almost died. I was so scared. . . . So the first thing that came to me was that we were right next to the Variedades movie theater—you know, the Variedades—which means right next to the office of this other girlfriend of mine. So we run upstairs to her office, and she's the first person we see, right there. I mean she was the receptionist, so I say You know what? You know what?, I say to her, Loco Valdiosera is following us—because back then everybody but everybody knew that Loco Valdiosera was actually crazy, he might do anything. I mean imagine—all *I* did was talk on the telephone, right?, and I knew. So I ran upstairs to hide, I was so capital S-C-A-R-E-D. We both ran upstairs.

We must have spent about four hours in that office—a little coffee, the latest gossip, all that, till we'd completely forgotten about this crazy, I mean loco *loco* Loco Valdiosera guy. Talking about first one thing and then another, mixing up all kinds of names and going nowhere, Mercedes told us about the love of her life, her true true love, extremely emotional as you can imagine, even punctuating her story with a tear now and then and finishing it all off with a little honk in her handkerchief. So then we go back downstairs after all this, and there they are, waiting for us by the door. It must have been six o'clock at night, and we'd gone up to my friend's office somewhere around three-thirty. And you can believe this or not, but there they were waiting for us by the door. . . . I don't think we had more than a peso between the two of us, right?, but we stopped this taxi. Señor, señor, we say to this taxi driver, get us out of here, please. And we got in without knowing how we were going to pay. Just jumped in the taxi, right? And we get away as fast as we can from Loco Valdiosera, who's surprised but still smiling, like losing that battle wasn't losing any big deal. A little contemptuous of the whole thing, maybe. And we still hadn't done any of the things we needed to do. I think we were looking for a dress or something, I forget. So we headed home, right?, we were going to go home. . . .

When we got there, I called the Jalisco Sisters to tell them the story, and they told us to come to a party. They were my neighbors, you already know that, right?, so we changed clothes, I let Mercedes wear one of my outfits, and we went. It was just your regular ordinary party, right?, with the same old people that came to our house too. That is to say, a nice normal conventional get-together, nothing extraordinary about it, if you know what I mean. Just a little party to have a drink and dance a little and *chat*, exactly like dozens of parties the Jalisco Girls and my brother and I would have every now and then, you know? This friend and that

friend and the punch bowl and some ice, how do you do, wanna
dance . . . You know. . . .

Anyway, we were at this party, and who should come in but
this friend of ours named Tito Caruso, leading this big pack of
like fifteen friends of his, counting men and women both. The
party was in one of those typical Pedregal houses—lots of glass
and potted palms and lights and soft couches and all that, real
close to where we lived, right? You've never seen my house? I
was dancing with—I don't remember who it was, but anyway,
they knocked on the door and somebody opened it. And Tito
Caruso and about fifteen friends of his came in, and in this horde
of people, you won't believe it, there was Handsome to the Maximum. Dazzling, I mean, and moving sort of like a 33 rpm record
played on 45, right?, sort of speeded up, but very very good-
looking, I'll tell you that for sure, very *very* good-looking, with a
trench coat and hat like that movie star—what's his name?, the
one in that gangster movie? Well anyway, he looked just like
that, with a London Fog trench coat with the collar turned up and
everything. . . . There were a lot of flies. It must have been
spring or summer, I mean in Mexico City who notices?, but it was
hot as hell, and Handsome to the Maximum bursts in with his
trench coat and hat on—very S/M looking. Somebody opened the
door and in he walked. I was so stunned I stopped dancing and
just stood there looking at him, because he really was something
to look at. Like a hot knife cutting through butter, everybody just
stood aside to let him walk in, or like a whore's cunt when she
wants to get it over with. Anyway, he walks over to me and says
Dance? Oh, I love to remember that! His smile lit up my entire
life. All of a sudden he was like giant-sized, and the house was
full of warm sheets, silk sheets, and all the silly things of my life
just slid right out of them. So anyway, I danced with him. My
head on his shoulder, trying to dive, ever so slowly, into his
smell, to glue myself to his smooth amorous muscles . . .

But just then, I don't know what brought it on, two of the guys
that were there started to fight. They started fighting, right?, and
all of a sudden everything got dangerous, but I mean *dang*erous,

because they were shoving each other through the glass doors and falling all over glass tables and crunching glasses—a disaster— and they smashed all the glass and everything reflected in it. Absolute chaos. They broke about a thousand mirrors and shelves, millions of things. They threw chairs at each other. And pretty soon some people started jumping in to help the guy that was losing, so all of a sudden there was this whole wave, I mean like an ocean of mean faces and backs and mouths spouting filthy stuff and spitting and roundhouse lefts and rights, punches and kicks and bodies making these incredible knots of arms and legs and buried heads—I don't know how to describe what that scene was like. Everybody jumped on the guy that was winning, this big animal about six feet four that stopped people in their tracks like a stop sign, and red-headed. Somebody was even beating on him with a leg they broke off a table. Me? Well where do you *think* I was? . . . Go ahead, ask me . . .

In all this confusion Handsome to the Maximum grabs me by the arm and yanks me out of the worst of it, and he says Come on, hide, hide. And he pushes me, into this bedroom? There was this crucifix in it that looked like it was made out of bleeding wood. And he says to me I'll go see what's happening, I'll be back in a minute and tell you, okay? And he's gone, whoosh. So there I am, scared out of my mind, praying—can you picture this?—praying to this crucifix. I didn't know which one was his friend, the one that was winning or the one that was losing. I mean by the look of him, by the image of him that I had painted for myself, I assumed he was going to go help the underdog, right?, I mean whether he knew the guy or not. So I yelled Don't go! No! Don't go! I was terrified. I was saying to myself, Well, I've finally met him, and now he's going to go get smashed. But then Handsome to the Maximum comes back all worked up, and he says Don't leave here because things are getting out of hand, I mean things are getting pretty ugly out there, they're wrecking the place—just stay here. And he leaves. I could hear the glass smashing and the cursing and screaming—and then he came back again, right?, to say Don't leave here, they're a bunch of animals—it's like the Huns, and he runs out of the bedroom again, like a shot. I was praying as hard as I could. I mean I was even worried about that crucifix getting broken to shit. And he was so good-looking, I mean he was so incredibly good-looking.

The noise never let up, and I could hear the Jalisco Sisters shrieking like macaws out there. Anyway, in a little while, I'll never know why, I decided to peek outside, right? I was dying to see whether they had pulled Mercedes' hair out or something, and I wanted to check on the Jalisco Girls, I mean they also owned the house, so imagine, and also I was just simply curious to say the least to know exactly what was going on out there. I was in there all closed up tight, right? So then anyway, I was just sticking my head out a little, and I see Handsome to the Maximum sticking his head out the door of the bedroom next door. Peeking out—like this—sticking just the end of his nose out, scared half to death, to find out how the brawl was going. Because picture this, he'd run out of the bedroom where I was and run into the bedroom next door, to hide, right? I mean they might mess up his face and then what? . . . Every once in a while he'd come out and run over to see how I was, the big fake. . . . When I think about it I could die laughing. Dismembered vampires!

The next day The Monk calls me. He thought he was this great detective, right?, and he had discovered that the girls we'd seen were prostitutes and the maître d' was like their bodyguard or chauffeur or Big Daddy—well, maybe he didn't go *that* far—but anyway When are we going out again? I don't remember what excuse I made—I never wanted to see him again, my liver spewed hot bile just thinking about him. I kid you not, I didn't want to see him. . . . That's why I say Sandwich Day, because first we had dinner at that place with the suggestive unctuous so-and-so, then I saw my adorable Handsome to the Maximum, and then here they are calling me about that awful greasy icky sticky yucky hairy maître d' again. Am I telling this all confused? I told you he had these big hairy hands, right? And don't even ask about the Jalisco Girls. They survived the Great War of the Cut Glass, so to speak, with the police at the end and the whole thing. Elephants' foreskins! If I told you that replacing the windows alone cost more than two hundred thousand pesos . . . Naturally, they never gave another party as long as they lived, and from that day on the get-togethers were all at my house, the first one eight days later. In my own house!

You can't imagine how excited I was! Handsome to the Maximum came with a very well-known girl. I mean she was one of the Ten Most-Loved Hookers in all of the Mexico City metropolitan area, you could read about her in the classifieds under Love for Sale, a real lady of the night, you know what I mean, and the only ones that didn't know that were my brother and me. We also didn't know—I mean how could we, right?—that they had agreed that this chick would throw herself at my brother while the other one seduced *me*, okay? I kid you not, this girl was the kinkiest thing since home permanents. . . .

So anyway, they said to us, Listen, we've got this apartment in this place named the Beverly. We'll go and you'll see. . . . Well, back then I didn't know what the Beverly was, I didn't even know what a hotel was for, okay? So anyway he says Listen a friend of mine's got this apartment there, and he's invited us all to a party. As time went on I found out what that place was, I mean I started going there a lot, right? It was the place they all got together, right? And they had such riots there that they had to have—you won't believe this—they had a carpenter on . . . retainer, do you call it? Something like that, anyway, they had this full-time carpenter to come in and fix the walls every morning. Or, I mean, there were a lot of apartments. And they had them all over the city, all of these guys. But anyway, that night, this night I'm talking about, I didn't know any of this yet. . . .

So anyway, he invited us out. And at the same time this girl starts flirting with my brother and throwing herself at him something awful, so we'd go to the party, right? And Handsome to the Maximum meantime is beanwashing—I mean brainwashing—my brother, saying like Hey, man, I can't believe it, man that chick is wild for you, Holy cow, brother, how do you do it, and What've you got that I ain't got, buddy, huh? And stuff like that, right? My brother must have been about sixteen years old back then, right? He was eleven months older than me, and I'm telling you this chick was making passes at him left and right. So anyway, he

finally says Okay, okay, brother, let's go, Jack. So I go to get my
coat to go to the party, all excited, I mean I had my hopes way
way way *way* up, you know?, I mean *delirious*. So my brother says
for me to go with him, in his car I mean. My sister and I will go
together, he says, we'll follow you. And Handsome to the Maximum says Perfect, kids, we'll see you at the Beverly.

We'd barely gotten in the car when my brother guns the engine
and leaves about forty feet of rubber and goes zooom down the
street, as fast as he can go, tires squealing and everything. Around
the block. As fast as the car can go, zip, around the block. We got
back to the garage before the doorman could close the door. I'm
telling you, home again after a truly dizzying spin around the
block. So my brother puts the car in the garage, and he starts
yelling at me that I'm an idiot and a stupid jerk, a retardo and a
stupid whore, and I don't know what all else. Do you mean you
don't know that Loco Valdiosera is a pimp? He's a drug addict, he's
. . . well, so on and so forth. My brother was frothing at the mouth.
And there I stood with my heart broken. And he wouldn't take me
to the party. We weren't going *any*where, and the party was still
going on at my house, but I went upstairs to my bedroom. I didn't
even know how to masturbate, so I just cried like an idiot, all gray
and sobbing and will-less and languid and snotty and pretty pessi-
mistic about the whole thing, I'll tell you. Orgiastic orangutans!

A few days later, Handsome to the Maximum shows up with
another girl at this other party. She was this girl with the funniest
hair, I mean to make you laugh, standing straight up like this,
and dyed. Not Only her Hairdresser, I mean anybody would know
it was dyed. Sticking straight up. So anyway, he comes in and
starts talking to me. All night long we were talking, him and
me . . . He and I . . . His friend walking around with her
hair sticking straight up, right? Oh, I already told you this girl's
story, didn't I? Incredible. When you met her, she'd say It's a
pleasure, I'm Carmelita Longlegs. I kid you not, that's how she
introduced herself. One brazen hussy, as they say, this Handsome to the Maximum was going out with. Anyway, we sat there
talking and talking, for a long time, I don't even know what we
were talking about, what he was doing I guess, what was "in" in

those days, I don't know. Oh I remember, I must have been talking to him about Ibero, because I talked about that all the time back then, I think I must have made guys' eyes glaze over about Ibero. . . .

See, I was at Iberoamerican University. Did you know that? I went to see Father Villaseñor, I think he died, didn't he? Anyway, listen, it was waiting room, waiting room, waiting room, trying to get in to see him, right? To get him to see me. Because he was supposedly my counsellor. I didn't know what I wanted to study or why in the hell do it or anything, you can imagine, but I wanted to go. Anyway when I finally talked to him and he says to me, Well, I recommend that you begin your studies in philosophy and letters, I said to him, Why philosophy and letters? Well, he says, because it's a very feminine thing to study, it removes you from any distractions you may be led into, it prevents you from being led astray, and it is a very nice course of study. So I signed up, and as you can well imagine, I couldn't understand a word of it, right? I went absolutely blank from one class to the next one, not knowing what in the world these people were talking about, just walking around like this. . . .

So I went to talk to the priest again. I went to explain to him that I was sorry, I didn't understand a thing, I couldn't study that. So he says to me, Well . . . look, let's talk turkey. I'll tell you what we'll do, but you have to do exactly what I say. So I said Sure, Father, perfect. Okay. I'll admit you to the university, but under one condition. So I said What. You take classes for one hour, and the other four you go to the cafeteria and give socials. If you promise me to spend four hours in the cafeteria every day, I'll accept you. Because he explained to me how inspiring it would be to the boys to go hear all the crazy stories I told, because I was a real clown in those days. So anyway, I said Okay, and so he says Good, but you have to look like you're really studying, you have to take some class. So he signed me up in cinematography, that was just starting. That was terrific, right? Because I mean what we did was watch movies all day. I had a great time, I never had so much fun. So I got in this movie class and, um . . . Wasn't I talking about something else? Oh yeah,

Handsome to the Maximum. That's all I talked about, back then.
I mean Handsome to the Maximum was absolutely staggered by
all my movies. . . .

So he started going to the university to see me . . . I'm serious!
I'm serious! He started going over there to see me, and he'd take
me to a Dairy Queen over by Ibero. We'd go have some ice cream
at the Dairy Queen and go back. The way he dressed was hilarious—everything green, with green corduroy pants and a green
sport coat and green socks and green shoes made out of antelope
skin . . .

One day we were going to go out with my whole family and
Gabriel Infante. I mean I'll mention names, but this is just between me and you, right? So that day Gabriel got flaming drunk,
and we didn't know alcohol was bad for him, right? Alcohol went
straight to his brain. He got so drunk we had to knock him out.
Not me, but Handsome to the Maximum had to punch him till he
knocked him out so we could get him in the car. But then all of a
sudden . . . Or anyway he *looked* unconscious, my brother and
Handsome to the Maximum sat him up in the car beside the steering wheel so somebody could drive him home. . . . My father was
rubbing his belly, and my mother couldn't do anything but keep
looking at her watch, I mean she couldn't believe the whole thing,
so my brother said why didn't they go on home and he'd take care
of Gabriel, right? We'd met him at The Two Turtles, and I wanted
to stay with Handsome to the Maximum a little while longer, so I
asked permission to go with my brother in case he needed any
help. So my parents said Okay, and they left, right? I mean, he-
he, they went home, right? So then my brother says Why don't
you two go together, and I'll take care of Gabriel. We were trying
to decide who was going to follow who when . . . Oh, I forgot.
Gabriel was the Hell Driver or the Infernal Driver or the Death
Driver or something like that. So what a combination, the Hell
Driver and drunk and crazy . . . Anyway, we got him in the car.
He was in the car, and while we were arguing about who was
going to follow who, he scoots over and turns the key and takes
off, driving like a madman. He just takes off. . . . For example,
we were going down this one avenue, following him, right?, and

he pulls over into the other side, where the cars were coming at him, against the traffic?, and he starts zigzagging through the cars, and dodging pedestrians at about ninety miles an hour. To hell with lanes and intersections and people standing on the corners. And the stupid asshole Handsome to the Maximum, instead of going down the right side and just watching him, there he went right behind him, right on his tail. . . .

So there we were, Handsome Asshole, my brother and me in the car behind, following him. Then Gabriel gets up on the median?, on the little like park in the middle, right?, and he starts driving like this through the light poles, up and down, up and down, sidewalk, street, sidewalk, street, and us right behind him. So anyway, to make a long story short, we went through some very risky and decidedly hair-raising adventures playing follow-the-leader with the Driver of Death. It was cops and robbers, you know, this great chase scene. And then there we were coming back to the glorieta with all those mushroom-things again, after making a circle for miles and miles. Candy-coated dildoes! We'd come back to almost exactly the place we'd started from!

Traffic was unbelievable. It was Saturday, so imagine, and we were all pale and scared-sick looking. You know the color of telegrams? That was us after an hour of zigzagging through the oncoming traffic on Insurgentes, Paseo de la Reforma, Rhin, and Gutenberg . . . Oh, I forgot, you know what he'd do? He'd open the car door and put his feet out, put his feet down outside and run alongside, run along while he steered the car, right? Out*side* the car. Then he'd jump back in. . . . One day Tito Caruso was so impressed with that, that we were riding along with him in his car, and he tried to do it. There was my brother, Tito, a girlfriend Tito had then, and me. And he tried to do it outside the Chapultepec movie theater. You know? He thought it was so neat that the Driver of Death did that that he said Hey, how hard can that be. So he opens the door of his brand-new car and starts running. And when he got back in he couldn't find the brake pedal, and *chíngale!* we wound up inside a truck, I mean *inside*, in the *middle* of a truck.

Anyway, so we came to the Plaza of the Mushrooms, don't ask

me how, pushing about fourteen trash cans and a newsstand in front of us. Like the cowcatcher on a train, right? So then Handsome to the Maximum says This is it, no drunk will run this light, he'll stop at the light and that'll be it—because so far, don't ask me how, we'd hit nothing but greens, right? And so I was going Red, red, like the stoplight was a mind reader, you know?, and I was sending these thought waves. But at the light, forget it, he just goes right through it. So listen, here comes this taxi, like a little Volkswagen, right?, across the intersection. And Gabriel's car runs right into the taxi, and the crash opens the car door, and Gabriel shoots out like the Man on the Flying Trapeze, you never saw anything like it, right?, like Shot from Guns through the air, and he lands on his head on the roof of the taxi he'd run into, and then he bounces off and lands on the street. On his head. A direct hit. I kid you not. You couldn't believe it. I swear, I swear on a stack of Bibles, just like this bang!, *chíngale!*, and then bang! again on the street. . . .

So we went from there to the Red Cross. It must have been about four o'clock in the morning by now, and about two o'clock that afternoon Gabriel finally came around, and you know the first thing he did? He called his lawyer. That famous lawyer, what's his name?, the one that's married to the movie star? And when Perry Mason, or whatever his name is, came in what do you think Gabriel said? He started saying it was all his fault, he was drunk, it was all his fault, all of it. The guy in the taxi was innocent. I couldn't believe it. Honest. That the taxi driver had had the right of way, and he'd been driving under the influence, and he was the one that banged into the other guy. Crazy, right? I mean did you ever hear of anything so crazy? . . .

So I was going out with Handsome to the Maximum. When I started going out with him, his business was going great guns. But then he started getting jealous, and he quit traveling to the border and stopped seeing a lot of his friends. So as not to leave me, right? Oh, I was such an imbecile, when I think of it, I would've married him. I mean I really loved him, you know?

So my family went to work. Quick. As soon as they saw I was going out with him, they started forbidding me to go out, forbidding me to set foot out of the house, I mean, a whole series of stuff. So I decided to get a job so I'd have an excuse to get out of the house. And that way I could see him, right? So I started working at this place where I would do these absolutely stupid things. Throw stuff. Knock stuff down. I knocked down every single vase, you can't imagine. I broke everything in the store. Because I got the job because of pull, right?, so they couldn't fire me. I worked in the boutique at the Palacio de Hierro. Oh, and that's funny too, when I was modeling, when I'd go to San Antonio sometimes to model, people would say Where are you from, or Where do you work or something, and I'd go At the Palacio de Hierro. And they'd go *Guat?*, that funny accent, *Guat?*, like What?, so I'd have to tell them, That's the name of the store, the Palacio de Hierro, it means the Iron Palace. So finally, I just started telling these Americans I work at the Iron Palace, and their eyes would get like this. . . . Who knows what they thought about a person like me working at a place with a name like that, right? Hilarious . . . Anyway, the Palacio de Hierro. Exclusive Gifts. Every gift in the place cost more than a thousand pesos. Much more, two thousand pesos up. So me, I was so sort of absentminded, right?, and every time somebody came in I'd say Hey! How's it going!, and I'd wave an arm at her, and *chíngale!*, I'd knock over a fourteen-thousand-peso pitcher. Oh, I'd do diabolical, terrible things. I mean, I think I grabbed that job as a way to open up, speak out, get out of myself, and tell people what was happening to me. I told my troubles to everybody that came in. I was the devil. Not a soul walked through the doors that I didn't tell about my trials and tribulations. Everybody, I told everybody. I was Miss Popularity, you know? I suffered like the very devil, too, because about that time they hired some detectives to follow us—my family, my uncle. There was one detective assigned to me and another one for Handsome to the Maximum. He was so good-looking . . . So they jumped to conclusions, right? These detectives turned in a report to my family where they said Loco Valdiosera lived off women, that such-and-such a woman kept him, that so-and-so gave him money, and that that wasn't all—he liked marijuana, all kinds of stuff like that, but I thought it was all a pack of lies, right? I mean, of course they seemed like these great huge made-up stories to me. . . .

Forget it, I never believed a word of it . . .

("They look at each other, feel each other's closeness, desire each other, caress each other, kiss each other, undress each other, breathe together, lie down together, sniff each other, penetrate each other, slurp at each other, excite each other, calm each other, doze off, wake up, turn on the lights, light each other, covet each other, touch each other, squeeze each other, fascinate each other, chew each other, like each other, drool on each other, mix, couple, separate, grow lethargic, die, are reborn, uncurl, arch, wiggle, twist and turn, stretch, warm each other, heat each other, strangle each other, clutch each other, shiver, rock, join, grow weak, push away, faint, then crave each other, attack each other, entwine each other, crash into each other, seize each other, press each other, dislocate each other, pierce each other, merge together, riddle each other, rivet each other, graft to each other, nail each other, faint, revive, glow, contemplate each other, inflame each other, madden each other, melt together, are soldered together, are calcined together, break apart, bite each other, murder each other, resuscitate each other, seek out each other, rub each other, shrink from each other, flee each other, and then surrender to each other.")

3

He had a Chivas Regal face

Gabriel Infante had been such a drunk, he'd been so drunk for so long that he even had a face like a bottle. And he started getting attached to me, you know, like hanging on me, he conceived this deep attachment for me, there was this whole dependence thing. Maybe because I'd listen to him . . .

Like this one time he was going to commit suicide. He called me on the telephone, and he told me to get a pencil and paper, he had something for me to write down. He was crying like crazy, right?, and it was raining cats and dogs outside. You know who was there visiting me for the first time? That was the first day Alexis Stamatis ever came to visit me. He came to visit me for the first time that night, and there was this rainstorm you wouldn't believe—torrents!—and what happened was, that the Jalisco

Monk had called me to tell me all about how the maître d' with those gorilla hands didn't work in the restaurant anymore, that he'd gone over there to tell him where to stick it, and he wasn't there, he'd run off or escaped or something with one of the whores, did you ever hear such a story?, but I didn't want to hear about it, although at the same time I was sort of interested, you know? But anyway, we got cut off. It was a terrible storm, like one of those ones in the Bible or something, so we got cut off, and then in about two seconds the telephone rings again, and I say to the other people, Oh, come with me, because on top of everything else, the lights had gone out. So I say to Alexis, to the maids, to everybody, Oh, come with me to answer the telephone. And Gabriel starts talking. I mean, it was Gabriel.

With him, well, there were a lot of things that kept us together. Not love, of course, not really love, but sort of the fact that he talked to me. Was it you that said that love is the wordiest of all passions? Because if that's true, then it was love. I let him talk to me when he was high as a kite on drugs, right? He talked and talked and talked. I even had problems because of that. I got into big trouble, because see he lived with these two women, these two women shared him, you might say. He was real in love with one of them, and he got a lot of money out of the other one. Anyway, the one he was so in love with—how can I put this delicately? She was a whore. I mean she was the biggest whore you could ever imagine in all your wildest dreams of whoredom. And he was madly in love with her, right?, but she told him, one day she said this wouldn't work, she couldn't live just for him, she liked to go out with other men. Other men . . . He suffered something awful. Just like the hairy maître d' I was telling you about, right?, that later on I found out his name was Tarcisio and he had run off with Carmelita Longlegs. He'd kidnapped her. And they lived together in hiding, from the gang, I mean, and since he couldn't go back to the restaurant he became a taxi driver. Anyway, that's what I heard, because they were hunting for him like he was Pancho Villa or somebody. Seems he had stolen a lot of money or some papers or something that was worth a lot of money to somebody. And whoever it was that told me also said that this

guy wanted to marry Carmelita, but she said 'Fraid not, I'm a
whore through and through, from my hormones to the tip of my
lower lips, man, woman, or tableleg, it's all the same to me, I'll
run around on you, and you won't be able to take it. She had a
tarantula tattooed on the inside of one of her thighs as big as your
hand. And Handsome to the Maximum told me once that whenever he went out with her, he put on spiked underwear, on top of
a chastity belt, because she'd eat you alive, a devow, de-
vowsomethingess, with teeth in her vagina and prehensile
lips . . . Uh . . .

So anyway, Gabriel was telling me that this woman that gave
him all this money, that they had had this big terrible scene, and
he'd hit her and practically blinded her in one eye. So she'd gone
to her mother and told her. This woman had run home and told
her mother, and her mother it turns out is the lover of some big
bigshot. Anyway, on and on like that. But I couldn't believe it
was Gabriel on the phone, because the last time he had called
me, I made him promise, he promised he'd never ever call me on
the telephone again, because I was like tortured by all these telephone calls, you know? So I had decided to cut him off, right?
I mean all the things he'd tell me about were making me sick,
literally. . . . Anyway, so this day with all the rain and the storm
to beat all storms, terrible, terrible rain and then on top of everything the blackout, who should call but him, and he just starts
talking. But meanwhile, my mother is on the phone upstairs,
right?, waiting for me to pick up the telephone downstairs for her
to hang up. So I answer the phone and it's him, so I go Gabriel,
you said you weren't going to call me anymore. So he goes Yes,
but listen, I've got to talk to you, I just had this big fight with
what's-her-name, do you know what what's-her-name did. And
then he told me all the gory details. And of course, my mother is
listening to all this stuff on the extension absolutely appalled, and
just about then my father comes home, and he yells Come up here
right this minute. So I went upstairs, right? My father had barely
taken off his raincoat, and he says to me, You tell me right now
who this Gabriel is. What Gabriel?, I say. The person that just
called you, he says, because I'm going to kill him. What do you

mean you're going to kill him? I mean just what I said—I'm going
to go find him and I'm going to kill him. *Now*, I'm going to kill
him right now, this instant, because you know as well as I do that
stained honor can only be washed in blood. It was just that simple, right? . . . He was good as gold, really he was, but he always swore he had Sicilian blood. So that's why stained honor had
to be washed in blood, because that's the way his ancestors
washed it, right?

What Gabriel was telling me was how this girl had run to her
mother and told her he was a drug addict, he was always on
something, plus all this other stuff, right? Like that she kept him,
she worked in a house of ill repute so she could keep him, so she
could give him the money he needed. And she's standing there
telling her mother all this with her face all banged up to boot,
from the beating he had given her. Terrible, right? So imagine
what this girl's family thought about all this—I mean it was a big-
deal family. Not to mention what *my* family thought. When they
heard all this stuff you can picture the fit they threw. So anyway,
he had called me to tell me all this stuff, right?, but also to leave
a message in case something happened to his other woman. But
mostly he called me to tell me all this stuff because his brain
was . . . He took cocaine and marijuana. He was this very, very
intelligent boy, too. Not to mention very handsome—he had this
great body, I mean has, and one time he won the national auto
racing championship. He won I don't know how much money. But
he was one of those Viva México! types, you know, he drove down
the road with his nose sucking up the white line. If he'd been
Japanese, he'd have been a kamikaze pilot, right? Couldn't care
less. I mean he'd say he'd rather live for five days on drugs than
twenty years as a jerk. He was just a drug addict at heart, that's
all there was to it. So anyway, my father, as soon as he found out
about Gabriel, my father swore he was going to kill him. Wild-
wigged urologists!

You know the type—as far as my father was concerned there
were two kinds of women, two count 'em two, kinds or classes or
types or categories—good girls and prostitutes. A good girl, like
me for example, could never have friends her family didn't know,

she had to go out solely and exclusively with one guy, from whom she had to remain aloof and, as the maids and one or another of my squarer friends would say, not get hot. They had to get to know my boyfriends in all these family get-togethers and stuff, and I was never supposed to go to the movies or bars or parties by myself. That's what my brother was for. To chaperone me? Even when I went on a date with a guy, my brother went with me, can you imagine? My father liked to listen to music like Agustín Lara, you know, Mexico's own Lawrence Welk, and before that he used to like to go out dancing with my mother to Ciro's. He also liked the idea of quote, purely masculine pursuits, unquote; so there'd be these nights, it didn't have to be Friday but it helped, when he'd take a night out with the boys, just whoosh! and he'd be gone, to some boxing match or a real Friday bash with some of his noisy friends—The Bad Boys . . . And then he has the gall to tell me he's going to go out and kill Gabriel. He swore up and down that he was going to kill him. So of course, I got real depressed, and really disappointed in my mother and father, right?, because on top of everything I never told who it was. They'd seen him a couple of times, we'd even all gone out together, but they were so forgetful about names, they could never seem to get faces and names together or anything, so these guys would always be my anonymous "friends," and that was that. So anyway, Alexis left and I never told. They knew his name was Gabriel Infante, but they had no idea where to find him, right? But by this time I felt so awful, so awful, I mean so depressed and awful, that I ran to my room and slammed the door and started to cry. I cried so hard, I cried so hard my tears were actually splashing, like this, I was crying with my breasts and my throat, torrents were running out my nose—tears even came out my navel. I kid you not. And nobody came in to check on me, so I just cried all night.

So then the next day, in the afternoon, I still didn't come out of my room or eat, all I did was cry, right? The floodgates of tears had opened, and I hadn't been able to go to sleep all night. So when I saw that everybody in my family had left the house, I decided to take a sleeping pill. . . . What I'm going to tell you I swear to God happened just like I'm going to tell you, okay? I'm not trying to hide anything or change anything around, I swear. This is how it was. . . . I took a phenobarbitol about three o'clock in the afternoon. Actually I took two, because I figured two of them would put me out till the next day, right? To just get some rest, to sleep. But then about two hours later this girlfriend of mine came by to bring me an invitation to her wedding. She came over, she gave it to me, and we cried for a while. Because this girl was, well I'd practically been sisters with her for years and years and years, and we'd lost touch with each other because we'd made all these new friends. When I became friends with Handsome to the Maximum and Tito Caruso and those people, she lost touch with me, right? So when she left, I thought the effect had worn off, I decided the effect of the phenobarbitol had worn off, so I popped in two more and went back to bed. . . .

In fact . . . I'll tell you, this girl, you know who it was? Mercedes, the one that had been my brother's girlfriend . . . And one day she was driving up the Acapulco highway, coming to Mexico City, right? She had two beautiful little twin boys, about five years old, all smiling and pretty, right?, with little rabbit teeth. And all of a sudden, a trailer truck is coming the wrong, this big huge truck comes down the highway the wrong way and there's no way to get out of its way. It runs right over them and it doesn't even slow down. She had this sports car, a little tiny thing, about this high off the ground, you know?, I don't know the name of it, and their heads were cut off. Decapitated? Decapitated, her and the two little boys. It was tragic. I didn't want to go to the funeral or the funeral home or anything. It was so horrible that they buried all three of them in the same coffin and welded the coffin shut. They screwed on the top, they closed up the coffin, and then on top of that they welded it closed. . . . Why do people like to look at dead people? Why do they leave this hole in their memory, this peephole in their memory? . . .

So anyway, a little while later I woke up. I felt great, I was happy, I felt fine. It was like everything was over, the problem had passed. Gabriel Infante was behind me, Alexis Stamatis was behind me, Handsome to the Maximum was behind me. So I got in the shower, took a shower, put on a new nightgown, I put on the best nightgown I owned. Of course, also always thinking, thinking, thinking, about all these things that were happening. But I wanted to snap out of it completely, be just fine. When my parents came home I planned for everything to be okeydokey, hunky-dory, terrific, because I thought No problem, right? What's the problem? But then I saw these four pills lying beside the bottle. There were four of them. And I didn't even give it a second thought, didn't bat an eye, I just picked them up and popped them in my mouth and swallowed them. Like you're walking by and you see this piece of candy, and you pick it up and pop it in your mouth and eat it, and you never think it might be bad for you, you know? I mean, later I found out about a lot of stuff there was no way I could know back then, right? But anyway, I took these pills and just went on as happy and calm as anybody could be . . . And I went back to sleep.

While I was asleep, then, one of the Jalisco Sisters called, and they told her I was asleep. But she knew that if I was asleep, all you had to do was scratch at the door and I'd wake up, right? I mean I was an *extremely* light sleeper. So the maid goes and tells her The señorita is asleep, she must be very tired, because I knocked on the door and she didn't answer. So she figures, I mean by intuition, that something's wrong, right? So she went and got this guy she was going out with at the time. He was a doctor, a pediatrician I think. Anyway, he was hilarious because he kept trying to brainwash my girlfriend. You're not the kind to go out with just one man, he'd tell her, no, not you, you have to go out with lots of men, that's in your personality. And he'd make her dates with other men himself, so she'd go out with two men at the same time. I mean even with one of his brothers, right? But Big Jalisco was a real bitch, I'm telling you, and I'm not real sure what happened exactly, but she'd do very weird things to these people. For example, she tried to get all these relationships to turn out so the guy would ask her to marry him. Then when he did, she'd calmly tell the guy to go screw himself. It was like a bet she had with herself, right? Well, so in those days she was going out with this doctor and with this friend of Handsome to the Maximum's named Andrés. . . . While you were having one drink, he'd have three. Or anyway that's what she said all the time. . . .

So, uh . . . Where was I? Oh yeah, so she ran to get these two guys, and they all came to my house. The first thing I knew about them being there, we were all in the living room, and they were trying to wake me up. They'd tried to get into the bedroom through this big window, they thought they could get in from the pool, the garden side, you know?, but they finally gave up and broke in the door. Andrés and this doctor dragged me out of the bedroom, holding me up like this, and they walked me past my parents' bedroom, who were watching some program on television and hadn't even realized that any of this was going on. They were dragging me out of my bedroom and everything, breaking down the door. So then Alberto, or whatever his name was, started giving me coffee and helping me walk. He'd ask me my name and all, right? So then he started trying to find out, with me dead asleep, find out how many pills I'd taken. Big Jalisco was terribly worried and she kept shrieking like a bluejay, Aiee baby, you're *soooo* asleep. That's the way they were treating me, right, like a lost cause or something, right? How many pills did you take? And I'd say One. Then they'd say Oh no, we think you took more than one. So then I went Two. So then a little time went by, and finally they said Listen sweetheart, listen kiddo, we think you probably took quite a few more than that . . . Three, at least, you must have taken. And I shook my finger at them, like this, right?, saying No, more than three, more than four. Then things sort of started making sense to me, right?, and it turned out I'd taken I don't know how many, but a lot. They were really scared now, because, or anyway that's what I remember, the mortal or lethal or whatever it is dosage is ten pills. *Ten* is the number that poisons you, and I'd taken I think eight. So then they made me swear that when they left I'd go get into bed and not get out again till the next day. They said I had to stay as calm as possible, and rest, and I ought to read something. So of course, I said Okay, right? So I went right to my bedroom. I was pretty sleepy anyway . . . As you can imagine . . .

So now I'd been in my room for two days already, two days,

and all of a sudden my mother comes in. She hadn't noticed that I'd been in my room or that Andrés, Alberto, and Big Jalisco had come over. Incredible, but she hadn't noticed a thing. So she comes into my bedroom. It was strange as everything for her, because she was so tough, so hard-hearted I mean that, for example, when she saw the headless corpses of my friend and her little boys and all, all she said was Look how innocent they look. And I mean they were still a little burned-looking, right?, but How nice that they'll all go to heaven together, my mother says. And the corpses without any heads, okay? . . . She was so hard-hearted she could see you lying there in the middle of the street and not blink an eyelash. A strong character, horrible, *cold*, right? So anyway, I was lying there in my room, and she comes in to tell me I should have a glass of milk. Well, she wasn't quite so hard-hearted in those days, right? The lights were off, and I said No, Mama, listen, I don't, . . . no, thanks. So then she says Why are you talking like that? And I go How? I'm talking all right, I say to her . . . in the dark . . . She says No you aren't. . . . So she flips on the light, and she yells, in horror, I mean she lets out such a scream—AAAAAGGGGGHHHHH! Like that, more or less, and she shoots out of the room in absolute terror. So I got scared myself, then, you know?, I got really really scared. . . .

Am I dragging this out too long?

So instead of staying in bed I went downstairs. I thought I'd watch television, see my father and mother, be a little sociable, you know? That'll cheer me up, I said to myself. So I walked in the TV room, and the two of them were sitting there, sitting there like . . . I mean they just sat there like a ghost had walked in. My own mother and father. So I say Well, okay, hey, everything's okay, don't get upset, I'm going to go lie down, I'm real sleepy. And my mother walks along behind me and helps me get into bed, right? And so then she told me about the glass of milk again. And I go No thanks again. So then she starts crying and moaning. Oh please drink a glass of milk! Just one glass of milk, for all you hold dearest! I mean there was my mother kneeling beside the bed crying and begging me to drink just a little something, if I loved her. I beg you, as you love me! She was so *servile* about the

whole thing, you know, and this was such an old-fashioned way to
. . . well. Drink a glass of milk! Please! So finally to make her
happy I said Okay, and in less than three minutes she was back
with the glass of milk. I drank it slowly, until she finally gave this
sigh of relief, because while I was drinking the milk she had been
holding her breath. You don't know how much I thank you, she
said, reaching for the glass automatically. Now sleep.

As soon as she was out of the room, I got up and looked at
myself in the mirror, first just to see why they were all so
shocked, but second to splash a little water on my face. Because
they'd looked at me, and like that!, they'd started screaming to
high heaven and acting like I was this horrible-looking monster or
something, and that worried me, you know? So I'm standing there
looking at myself, and I see these spots on my face. Because I'd
gotten poisoned, right? My face was practically completely deformed, all swollen up, like this, and there were these huge
blotches like bruises, purple and white and all different colors. I
was a rainbow all to myself. I looked like I'd bumped into a
clown. . . . You could hear the voices from the television 'way
off, so I went to bed, right? I just went to bed and nobody ever
mentioned the subject again. . . .

But all the razor blades disappeared from my house, all the
kitchen knives disappeared, all the sleeping pills, the bottles of
strychnine, everything. *Every*thing. Because I think they thought
I'd tried to commit suicide, which was not what it was at all,
right? I was just trying to get some sleep and forget some of the
things I was going through, you know, forget your troubles. But
mostly just sleep. Afterwards this doctor guy explained it all to
me. He said I got a little under the influence, you know, from
those first phenobarbitols, and then I got so drunk it was like I'd
drunk a whole bottle of whisky all by myself. So what happened
to me then was, that I lost consciousness. It was like *snap!*, and I
was out. So then you don't know what's good for you and what's
not. They say when I got up and took those four phenobarbitols,
when I got out of bed to take a shower, when I tell you I felt like a
million dollars, well . . . They say that when I went to the
bathroom I had to hold on to the walls, that I must have had to

work myself along like this, against the wall?, because I'd taken such a bunch of pills that I must have been completely, completely drunk, right? So anyway, that went away. I was okay in no time . . . I was sort of stupid and blah for two or three days, but I didn't have any trouble, I mean I don't have any complexes or anything or any psychological hang-ups or frustrations or maladjustments because I wanted to kill myself and didn't—no, none of that stuff, forget it. I mean, I didn't want to poison myself at all, right? All I wanted to do was sleep it off, rest, just sleep for a while. . . .

("From that moment on, even the most remote figures suggested the idea of death so violently, so urgently, that a can of sardines— for example—brought up the memory of the lining of a coffin, or the stones in a sidewalk, noticed for the first time, revealed their kinship to the marble markers of a vault. In the thrall of this macabre vision, one's eyes simply saw that the plaster of façades was of the very color and texture of bones, and at last, just as stepping into a bath, sinking into the waters of a bath inescapably led to the posture one would adopt in a coffin, likewise not a person buried his body between the sheets without brooding on the pattern which the folds and creases of his shroud would take.")

The palpable, the morbid

My parents had these Jewish friends. Or really, he was Jewish and she was Mexican. They lived in Acapulco and they were their best friends. By the way, you know how they died? I don't know if you remember this, but in the first big bomb the Arabs put in a Jewish airplane, in this airplane that was headed for Israel. They were going to buy clothes, because he had the biggest store in Acapulco . . . I mean, it's still the biggest store, you know, but . . . A sensational store, really neat. His kids took it over and they run it now. What a shame, you know? They're taking off from the airport and *chíngale!*, the plane blows up. I mean it's surreal, right? It's like you can't imagine what it's like to know people that something like that happens to, I mean, you practically lived with them your whole life and a thing like that happens to them. . . .

Anyway, they had a whole string of nightclubs, cabarets like, you know, in Acapulco, and bars, all kinds of businesses. And Carlos Stamatis, the skiing champion?, lived right across the street from them. He lived with his brother, who was married and was twenty-seven years old. Imagine, I was fifteen, and when I met Alexis, he was married to this girl from there. I didn't know who he was or anything, and then one day they invite us over. One day my mother and I are going to Acapulco, I mean we're *in* Acapulco, and they take us over to meet them. They lived right across the street. And since Carlos Stamatis was single, of course everybody thought he was this great catch, he was worth waiting for, blah blah blah, so they took me over to introduce me to him so while I was in Acapulco I'd have somebody to go out with. So they introduced me to him and to Alexis both, but listen, Alexis was the one *I* liked, I mean he was *extremely* good-looking. Not that Carlos wasn't good-looking, don't misunderstand me, but not as *extremely* good-looking. I mean his brother, married and all, was the kind of man that, I don't know, that really gets to me, like uh, I'll tell you who, like Louie Jordán . . . Uh-huh, like Louie Jordán. They were Greek. So anyway, guess what happens. I started going out with Carlos like I told you, but Alexis decided it was too dangerous, you know, that I'd better go out with his wife and Carlos and him. Because I was so young, right? So I started going out with all of them. All four of us would go out, and if Alexis couldn't go out with us for some reason, then he'd catch up with us later. Wherever we were, he'd show up. Like Dracula. So then my mother, who was not exactly the most naive woman in the world, or even close, noticed.

We were in this nightclub. We were sitting in one of Jacobo's nightclubs. Did I tell you his name was Jacobo? Jacobo and Sarita, right?, those were the names of these friends of my parents I told you about. We were watching the dancing and all, and Alexis shows up. Hey, hey, what happened? Nothing, here we are. And what do you think he did? . . . He says Listen, I was just out driving around, I just left the, uh, and I thought I'd have a drink, fancy running into you here. So then he says Come dance, come on. With your permission, señora? To my mother, right? And I go Okay, let's dance. And it was like the guy shot up like a Coahuila cornstalk, he was out of his seat so fast. So we started dancing on this dance floor about three feet square, that's how big this dance floor was—forget it, you couldn't move, we were practically dancing on top of the table.

So anyway, we were dancing, and he says to me, we just start talking, you know, and he says to me, What do you wish you were doing right now, this second, what would you like to be doing? Oh wow, I said, I'd like to be on the beach. . . . I always want to be on the beach . . . Just lie in the sun, really, that's what came into my mind. So I say What about you? So then he says Not me, I'd like to be doing something a whole lot easier and more fun. So I go What? Why, kissing you. And I go Oh, ha ha ha . . . And *chíngale!*, he kisses me. Right on the mouth! I was fifteen years old, so you can imagine. He tasted like spearmint, and I almost wet my panties I was so scared, like when you don't know what to do, right? I didn't know whether to run back to mommy or take off running or what. And my mother was a holy terror. . . . I didn't know whether to run or faint or what. Of course, about two minutes later my mother says Let's go, I'm very tired. And she never, to this day, has ever said a word to me, never mentioned that night, to this day, but two hours later we're headed back to Mexico City, and we get here that night. We'd been in Acapulco about two weeks when all this happened, and every afternoon when I knew it was time for Alexis to be getting home, I'd go out into the yard, right across the street from his house, remember?, and when he came home I'd go hello with my hand, like this, hello, hi, wave, you know, and he'd go in his house and I'd go in mine. It was this crush, right?, this platonic love. . . .

So then about two months go by, and one day he calls me on the phone. Hey, hey, how are you? I came to Mexico City, to visit you, I'm here in Mexico City. Around then, meanwhile I'd found out all about who he was. Jacobo had made him out to be the

biggest gangster ever, a quote, gangster among gangsters, unquote, Jacobo said. And he was, too, okay? He really is . . . The
biggest gangster in the world, a real son of a gangster. And you
know what they called him? Mister I Give a Shit. Behind his back
of course, but that's what all his friends called him, and I'll tell
you, things I saw with my own eyes, things you would not believe . . . I mean once I thought I was dead, I thought Good-bye
world, my lifeless body will be found next to his . . . I
swear. . . .

He was a really wonderful guy, though. I've never figured out,
never. . . . One day I asked one of his best friends, I said Do me
a favor, tell me about Alexis. What's he really like? . . . I went
out with him for nine years! Tell me what he's like with people,
explain what he's like to me. . . . You know when this was? Fifteen days, exactly, before I got married! Because even when I
was married I still went out with him. My husband knew about it.
He couldn't pry me loose, I mean I idolized the man. So I didn't
want to stop seeing him. . . . I took a trip with Alexis before I got
married, by the Church I mean. Then I came back. I went to the
United States to work as a model, and he went to get me. So but
anyway, we were with this best friend of his in all the world, and
I begged the guy, Tell me what he's really like. And he said
You've seen what he's like, the way you've seen him with people,
that's the way he is. Great winged chancre-sores! I don't have to
spell it out for you, do I? Because he was, he was terrifying. . . .

One time he had this nightclub named The Dwellings of the
Soul or The Interior Castle. It was really a nice nightclub. And
every day, before he went to this nightclub of his, we'd go have a
drink at his best friend's house, a great guy, I mean he seemed
like a great guy. He was a smuggler and all but he kept up ap-
pearances if you know what I mean, he had lots and lots of money
and a chain of car dealerships. It looked like he lived this perfectly normal life, right?, but everybody knew what he was, you
know? One of those nice guys, very good manners and everything.
Or really good manners and gross at the same time, he had the
filthiest mouth, he was always saying stuff.

So this one time we went to his house for a drink and a whole lot of people came in, the mayor of Manzanillo and two or three land commissioners or county commissioners or some kind of commissioners like that. And they were all going to Las Vegas. Everybody but Alexis, right? So we were sitting there drinking our drinks, and the man whose house it was gave me some champagne glasses, or really these I think he said goblets, is that right?, silver goblets, and eighteen Nancy Wilson tapes. He liked me, right? So he just gave me all this stuff like for a gift, right?, and Alexis and I went off to the nightclub. He'd been okay, just fine, talking to everybody and smiling, very friendly and polite, and we left . . . to go to The Interior Castle. . . .

We were having dinner and the doorman, who's dressed like a friar or whatever in that long habit-thing, comes over and says Somebody wants to talk to you, sir, outside, a Sr. Chirrión. He's with Sr. Hernández. Herminio Hernández I think it was . . . A lawyer, you know. The governor's son. We'd just left him not two minutes ago, we'd just had a drink with him . . . He asks if you will do him the favor of allowing him to come in, they missed the plane, they couldn't board the plane, could they come in please, the plane took off and left them. . . . No, tell them no, Alexis says . . . But . . . He knows he's not allowed to so much as step into this place. . . . This Chirrión guy was this guy that in Acapulco had been, well, he was way up there. And he was president of Manzanillo. He was the city president of Manzanillo. Mayor, I guess I mean. So the doorman leaves, and here comes the municipal president of Manzanillo himself, with the guy we'd just left, I mean not forty-five minutes ago. And he says Hey Alexis, don't be that way, let Herminio come in, he'll behave himself, I promise, I'll take the responsibility. But Alexis says No—very very serious Alexis was—He can't come in here, tell him he knows that. And this other guy says Come on, Alexis, be a buddy, forgive and forget, right? Hyenas in heat! Alexis spins around, like this!, and in front of God and everybody in the place he picks up a bottle of whisky and smashes it on the floor! He was furious! And he yells *Chingá!* You tell that motherfucker he'll rot in hell before he comes begging me to let him in here, because he's never going to show his fucking balls in this place again as long as I live! To the mayor, right? And the mayor says Okay, Alexis, whoa, okay, sorry I bothered you. . . . And he left. He said to me then, Alexis, right?, Forgive the intrusion, love. Bon appetit. I mean he'd told them Can't you see I'm having dinner with my girlfriend, you sons of . . . And me, ask me how I took all this. I put this piece of steak in my mouth, and I had to practically push it with my fork and take six drinks of water to get it down, I couldn't even swallow. I thought As soon as we leave this place, we're dead. They're going to gun us down. The place was decorated like a convent, right? And I could see myself hit, bullets all over my body, thrown against the door and rolling down the stairs drenched with blood, dead at Alexis' feet. Horny unicorns! There were flickering torches in wall brackets and everything, and I sat there waiting for some kind of explanation. . . . He was never going to let him in, but it beats me why. He never told me . . .

Another time, after that, he asked me out, when we were in Acapulco?, because he never let up . . . Come with me, I've got some things to do, he says, very brusquely, you know—decided. And he starts driving down all these dirt roads, just paths practically, right?, the scariest places in the universe. We went by about three hundred and ten trees, like this, trees and trees and more trees, through these places where there were no roads or anything, until finally we got where we were going. It was these buildings, but like sheds or shacks, you know?, wooden buildings, primitive and all slapped together, big, great big, and dark and gloomy. They opened the doors and we went in. I was practically fainting, right?, I mean I'm the world's biggest coward. I don't know why all these things happen to *me*, I'm such a 'fraidy cat. But of course that was the first time. The next few times I was more prepared, and there'd be these boats or little planes coming in, and they'd start unloading all these crates and boxes of stuff— smuggled in, you know?, contra, contraband?, cases of liquor, or machine-gun clips, boxes of machine guns and drugs, and he'd go

and check them and pay for them. I mean, of course back then, I
didn't know what was in the boxes, don't get me wrong. Anyway,
they loaded two of those big trailer-trucks, those big huge ones?,
with the stuff, and when I got back home I'd be green, white,
blue, every color you can think of. Because on the way back I'd
put on makeup, pink rouge, eye shadow, the whole works. I'd say
to myself He's going to notice in a minute and he'll die, because
he didn't like me to wear makeup . . . he didn't like me to wear
makeup. At. All. . . .

When he came to see me, when I first met him, I didn't dare go
out with him. I just didn't dare, I wouldn't have gone out with him
for all the money in the world. I mean, back then I was this little
squirt, I was this little schoolgirl and he was a man twenty-seven
years old, right? He was this *adult*. And also he was married,
right? But anyway, he kept coming to see me, for a long long
time, and I never went out with him. *Never.* Of course go out, I
mean there are other things you can do than exactly go out, right?
But it took me a long time to feel guilty. I was Handsome to the
Maximum's girlfriend, and then I started going out with Gabriel
Infante. And the times I finally did go out with Alexis back then
were incredible. They wiped me out. Once he went to an ice
hockey game with me and some of my fifteen and sixteen year old
girlfriends. Can you imagine what he must have felt like? He
went away very very let down, I'll tell you.

But he kept making these trips to Mexico City. He kept after
me. And on one of those trips I went out with him, and we went to
the Quid. But it was strange because all night long he looked like
he was in this awful, awful mood, mad at the world, or at me, I
didn't know, really bad. And after months and months, when I
finally started going out with him like all the time, he admitted
that he'd never hated me as much as that night. And you know
why? Because I had on these false eyelashes, and he hated them,
they made him sick, he thought they were repulsive, not to mention that every two minutes they came unstuck and I kept having
to go to the powder room to glue them back on. And to him, I
mean what fascinated him about me, what he liked best about me

was my hair, this streaked blond hair I had. I streaked it. But then this time when he came to see me my hair was black and pretty long, about here, and these ridiculous false eyelashes, and he thought I looked like a monster, a horror, I shocked him, and he was *so* shocked that he stopped seeing me for a long time. He didn't come back to see me.

So time passed, I don't know how long, and I was working in the Palacio de Hierro, and at the time it really felt like an iron palace, I'll tell you, because I was always thinking about him. He was a man I *liked*, if you know what I mean, and Handsome to the Maximum was always traveling, and none of my other dates made me feel so good, good *enough*, you know? And since I'd never dared to go out with him, you know like he was inside me *here*, and I carried him with me everywhere. It was like I was pregnant. I'd whisper to him all the time. Can you imagine? He'd go in and out of my mind all day, every day, like this needle embroidering his initials on the hem of my brain. I was frustrated, I'll tell you. I felt like I was trapped inside a pillowcase of suffering. My skin burned, and I felt sinful, like I was about to explode from this unspeakable desire. If he'd ever noticed . . . I kept thinking about what would've happened if I'd gone out with him and things like that, right? Insatiable . . .

One time the Jalisco Sisters came by work for me, and we walked down to the Zona Rosa. We were walking along talking, and all of a sudden we bumped right into Alexis. We were standing face to face with him, you know?, and when I saw him the only thing I could think of to say was You don't know how much I've wanted to see you. I didn't say Hello, I didn't say another word, all I said was You don't know how I've been dying to see you, with this longing, painful look on my face, I swear. Really? he says. That was the whole of our conversation, practically . . . Uh-huh, I said, passionately, Are you going to be here long? And he goes Yes, why don't you girls go wherever you're going, and we'll meet in that café on the corner in fifteen minutes. I said Sure, we'll see you there. And all three of us cheered up on the spot, I mean the idea of such an appetizing meeting, if you know what I mean. We were all so happy and smacking our lips and making all this racket. Like predators, I'm telling you. So the Jalisco Sisters went to the café with me, and then they left. . . .

So then Mauricio shows up, the singer and sports guy?, oh you know, the judo and karate champion for about ten years? More. I'd go out with Handsome to the Maximum during the week, and on Saturday and Sunday I'd go out with Mauricio. But he was using a lot of drugs, you know, and he'd turned into the evilest guy you've ever seen in your life. You can't imagine anybody meaner or with a worse temper, ever. He spit on the world, he beat up on everybody, half killed everybody, everybody. You have no idea. Listen, let me tell you, he had a Corvette, a little tiny thing, you know?, like this, and we'd get in, and he'd put this newspaper on my lap so the people in the cars going by, they were all higher, right?, so they couldn't see anything. Ay, he was . . . One day we went to see an apartment, I went with him to look at this apartment. When we get there, you know what happened? This drunk guy leans out from someplace, and he sort of does this with his glass, like toasting me, to your health, like that. I was all loaded down with packages and stuff, because somebody'd just tried to steal the car, and so the windows, I mean the doors had been forced, so you couldn't leave anything inside. So here I was, all loaded down, and I was going in like that because Mauricio was already inside, and we were supposed to meet there. It was, well, supposedly for when we got married, which we were never going to do I assure you, and which we never did either. I was carrying all this stuff, and there was this door open, and I saw these two men inside drinking, old guys, real well dressed and all. And so anyway one of them goes like this with his glass and goes Psst, psst, señorita, and he stands up and comes over toward me. Mauricio saw all this and he almost took him apart! He almost tore the guy in half. The guy falls down on his knees, the guy gets down on his knees in front of Mauricio, you know?, and he says Please, I beg you, please, that's enough, please. And Mauricio is hitting him and hitting him, in the face, too, and hard, I swear, really hard. Horrible, right? The man's face was already burst open, all open and smashed and bloody. I couldn't watch. I put my hands like this over my face, horrible, horrible, horrible. . . . So as soon as I see him, this one afternoon I'm telling you about, I'm such an idiot, I say Oh, you've got a new car, let me see it, and I fly outside to see this car, a Mercedes-Benz. Let me see it! . . .

Nobody ever reported him. It would've cost him his titles in judo and karate if he'd ever chopped anybody, don't tell me it wouldn't. But nobody dared to report him, and he was champion for eleven years. Or more . . . Think of all the people he must have beaten up. Just think of it. . . .

So there I was beside him in his new sportscar, and I saw Alexis go into the Kineret, but I couldn't warn him or anything. I watched Alexis order a beer, and I couldn't even send him a note or get a message to him or anything. All I could do was watch— and just every once in a while at that, you know?, out of the corner of my eye, and all twisted into knots from nervousness. I watched him finish his beer and start fidgeting. He was getting bored. But I was petrified, sitting in that car watching all my chances for a meeting longed for, suffered for, suffered for in the *extreme*, go down the drain. So to make a long story short, all of a sudden I realized Mauricio had said something. I'll take you home. Who knows how long he'd been saying that. So I said Okay, take me home, because I'd seen Alexis leave. I kept saying with all my heart Tomorrow, tomorrow I'll locate him through that blond guy, you know?, Frontoni. Remember, he had that store right by there? They were good friends. Or if not that, then I'll call Acapulco, but tomorrow I'll try to locate him . . . darn it, yes, tomorrow for sure. . . .

So the next day I get up at eight o'clock in the morning, and I start calling this blond guy's house. He never answered. By nine o'clock I was dressed, made up, and standing in the door of his store, except there was no store there, he'd sold it but I hadn't noticed, I didn't know about it. Um, so then later on I run into Tito Caruso, and I tell him my sad tale. Can you believe what happened to me, a guy I'd never gone out with, in the Kineret, a date, I was

going to, I was, on the dot, Mauricio, over there, the Jalisco
Sisters, and now that we've decided to go out, oh, I wish . . . I
wished so much, I'll tell you, that not two weeks before this I'd
written Sarita and Jacobo a letter to Acapulco asking them to invite
me down there, I really wanted to go, to rest a while, get some sun,
but what I really wanted was to grab apathetic Alexis', um, how to
put this delicately, genitals, and now I really could go out with
him, now I definitely could . . . I mean, if he was still interested,
right? Because after all the things that had happened maybe his
previously aroused, if you know what I mean, interest might have
gone down. And then look what happens—before Sarita can answer my letter I run into Alexis. It's that he had a lot of business in
Mexico City, right? What a wonderful coincidence! So then Tito
said Who is it? Interested, naturally, because he wasn't crazy
about Handsome to the Maximum. But I go No, no, you don't know
him, he's this guy that doesn't live here. . . . Not to mention I
didn't want to tell him, right? Because, well, Tito was worse than
seven hundred Mauricios. About then this, oh, it was Andrés
Gutiérrez, Andrés comes up, one of Big Jalisco's boyfriends—you
know him, right?—and he catches me standing on the corner, and
he says Hi, babe, didn't you go to work today? And I start in. Oh,
I'm so depressed, because and so on and so forth . . . And all of a
sudden I break into tears, and I told him what happened to me, and
I keep crying and crying and crying, crying like my heart was
breaking. So he says Tell me who it is, I'll find him for you. No, no,
I say, there's no way you can know this guy, he doesn't live in
Mexico City. That doesn't matter, tell me who he is, and I'll try to
find him for you, I'll find out where he's staying. Tito didn't understand what was going on, but he was trying to figure it all out, get in
on it, you know? What a desperate situation . . . But finally he
saw, I mean, three was a crowd, right?, so he made some flimsy
excuse or other and he left. So then I said Alexis Stamatis. I was so
embarrassed I couldn't look Andrés in the eye! How stupid! Andrés
says this, I'm so stupid, and he starts banging his forehead. Ay,
Andrés, I said, is it so terrible? It's that I stood him up! he says, I
was supposed to have breakfast with him and I forgot! I don't

believe you, Andrés. I swear to you! I swear. He's in the Hotel
Presidente. Word of honor, Andrés? Sweetheart, I swear, and so on
and so forth. So we ran to a telephone, with sudden, unexpected
lasciviousness, speaking for myself, all cheered up all of a sudden,
and unsuspected secretions, if you know what I mean. We called,
but he wasn't in. He'd left a message at the desk that if anybody
called he'd gone to Puebla. So I called again at seven o'clock that
night. I went to the Palacio de Hierro and called him when I was
getting off work, but he still hadn't come in.

I always took taxis. I mean I had a car and everything but I
didn't know how to drive. I'd had a car since I was fifteen, but
Dressed Like a Man or the Jalisco Sisters had to drive it for me
until I turned eighteen and learned how to drive. But then I was
afraid to learn, so I was stuck. Severo. That was my car's name.
It was one of those real serious, sober-looking Austins, right?, all
upholstered in black leather. But that day Mauricio came by to
pick me up and take me home. I told him I was sick. . . .

I called him again at eleven. Alexis, I said, I got lost yesterday, I couldn't talk to you, I had this problem and so on and so
forth. I want to see you, I told him. And he said Me too. He said
Get over here as fast as you can. When can I see you. I couldn't
go out so late, you know how *that* goes. When can I see you, as
soon as you can, can I come and get you now?, he keeps saying.
We'll go out dancing. I kept trying to figure out how to escape
from my house, so nervous I was biting my nails and everything.
Oh, the ups and downs I was going through. . . . I *can* escape,
I'll *never* escape, I *can* escape . . . You know . . . As soon as
you can, Alexis was moaning. I don't know, I was saying, I don't
know, you tell me what time we can see each other, and we'll see
each other, I've made up my mind. So finally he says I'll be
waiting for you tomorrow at six A.M. And I said Yes, *yes*.

Imagine, if he'd said Right now, I'd have been screwed. I mean
there was no way because it was already practically midnight, and
there would have been this not to be believed scene at my house.
No way they would've let me leave. So anyway, I got up at four-
thirty in the morning, and my mother says to me, Where are you

going at this hour? Where *would* I be going if it's Friday, I said,
I'm going to communion. At this hour? It's that I have to take a
bath and all first, there won't be time to come back home afterward. I remember exactly what I said. . . . My mother said How
can you go to communion if it's five o'clock in the morning. Well,
Mama, then *you* tell *me* where I'm going. Imagine . . . I've got to
go to communion at this hour, I say, because we've got to be at
work at eight at the store, we're having a meeting. She was in a
housedress and she smelled like Alka-Seltzer. So I'm leaving now
because if I don't, I won't have time. She looked like hell, and I
looked like the cat that swallowed the canary. So then anyway, I
left. I already had a taxi waiting for me. The sun hadn't even
come up yet, and the lava rock walls of Pedregal, the lightposts,
the benches, everything was neat and in order. So then I go off
supposedly to communion, at five-thirty in the morning.

When I got to his hotel room, I sort of tapped on the door. I
knocked on the door. . . . What a tacky way to meet. Now that I
remember it I could die. . . . He opens the door, all elegant in
his robe, practically glowing, mentholated, motionless, and you
know, transcendental . . . and he gives me a kiss, a kiss I swear
that lasted about a thousand years, incredible, I kid you not,
almost forever, long long long, this sweet burning kiss like life
itself, overflowing with juices, biting, chewing, airtight, soft—
and within it that magic tickling thing got more and more and
more concrete, desire, a desire that started pulling little tiny
strings in all the most vulnerable parts of my body. So that's how
it was, at last, thousands of kisses tailor-made for just you, the
perfect fit, like something you've been waiting for forever. Something you wish for and finally it comes. . . .

When he closed the door, I was already naked. And do you
know, the television was on, this one-eyed thing flickering and
flickering, and the test pattern was on. Afterward we talked about
a million things. A girlfriend, not *girl*friend you know, but a
friend that was a girl, came over about nine or so, and we all had
breakfast together right there, the three of us. Then there was I
think it was boxing or something, some kind of special they were

having on TV. So then, from that time on, I started going out with him a lot, a whole whole lot. I took trips to Acapulco every chance I got, five or six times a year. And he came to Mexico City every fifteen days or a month. He called me all the time. We spent the weekends locked up in his hotel room.

(*"For miles of silence we would glide through a caress that led to paradise; for hours and hours we would nest in a cloud, like two angels, and then suddenly, in a tailspin on a falling leaf, the forced landing of a spasm of love."*)

5

In the Palacio de Hierro all I made was peanuts

And to top it all off, Handsome to the Maximum wanted to make a comeback, can you imagine? He started to be so poor, I mean so so poor. I'll give you an example—he'd bought this car from Gabriel Infante, right? But since Gabriel liked me a lot but I wasn't speaking to him anymore, he had this grudge against me, like this worm always following me, just lying in wait. . . . So the first time he saw his chance to screw somebody that I cared about, which was a roundabout way of screwing me, right? he screwed Handsome to the Maximum. He screwed him by taking back the car because he'd missed a couple of payments, he was behind in the payments. I mean, can you imagine? Behind in his payments . . .

Before they took the car back he came to see me. We were on the way to his house, and on the way we bought these twenty-centavo breadrolls. We bought these twenty-centavo breadrolls, right? It was when we started to be poor, because the big idiot wanted to make a comeback. We'd buy these twenty-centavo breadrolls so he could take them to his mother, and she could stuff them with whatever was left over from lunch or dinner, you know, and that was what we had to eat. Tell me something—do you think that report, you know, by those detectives?, do you think that had anything to do with what I'm telling you now? I remember one time we put all the money we had together, and we had fifteen centavos, so he bought me some Jello for dessert. Jello! For dessert . . . I mean, we were poverty-stricken, we were in the worst poverty you can imagine. Then later we could only drink coffee, we didn't even have money for twenty-centavo breadrolls. How could I ever believe that a guy like that was a drug dealer, a pimp? So then they took his car back. But, oh, I forgot, even before they took his car, he'd walk to pick me up, to save gasoline. Picture this—I was working in the Palacio de Hierro on Durango, and he lived in Colonia Narvarte, which is what?, three kilometers away? So we'd walk back to his house and there, finally, get in the car so he could drive me home. Because he never drove me in a truck, right? I mean back then he had to scrape together ten or fifteen pesos to be able to drive me home, and then another ten or fifteen pesos to go back himself, so that meant scraping together thirty pesos, right? My house was way at the far end of Pedregal, can you imagine?

So anyway, we started living so poor, but romantically poor, right? We'd chip in all our money, and then all of a sudden he'd buy me a slip, right?, all of a sudden he'd buy me a pair of shoes—which wound up hanging in The Two Turtles, by the way—and all this so we could get married. Until finally he took a job as a shrimp importer or something, I mean, get that, the big drug pusher, the white slaver. Before I starved to death. Of course, later I found out he wasn't working, and he still doesn't have a job, right? He was one of those guys that brushed his teeth with some kind of special something so they'd be white and shiny. He said it was magic powder. And he brushed his teeth with warm water, boiled water, so he'd have teeth people would envy and be real healthy and all. He was the dandy to beat all dandies, a real Leading Man. . . .

One day we went to the Paseo, the movie theater? We didn't have any money, but we were madly in love, and we still drove a car at this time I'm talking about, so we were going to the Paseo. But I completely forgot that the offices upstairs from the Paseo box office are where my uncle has his office, right? The King of the Mountain, the Uncrowned Champion, the Power Behind the Throne, right? . . . So we get to the Paseo and Handsome to the Maximum went off to buy us a cupcake or something, and while he was buying whatever it was I stood and looked at the posters of the movies, and the stills and all. And I hear my uncle calling me. Come here, sweetheart. Because he'd seen me from his office, who knows how, and he'd come downstairs. We were standing under the marquee, and he says Run up to see Rebecca a minute, she's in the office, go up and tell her to come down, go on up. So I say Okay, I'm on my way. I couldn't very well tell him I was with Handsome to the Maximum, could I? I said Okay, I'm going. So I walk upstairs and Rebecca, who was his secretary, was nowhere to be seen. There was nobody in his office. I mean I was even surprised, because it was wide open.

So then listen to this. When I came back downstairs he says Better go back up, because I don't think you ought to see this, this fucking son of a bitch is going to get his, right here, I'm telling you, huh?, so you better go back upstairs. And I go *Huh?* Right now, he says, go on, right this minute. These men you see here?—and he points to these two guys from like the Secret Service, these big official bodyguard types that look like a cross between a baboon and a hippopotamus and are about as scary as the Tonton Macoute, have you ever passed one of these guys on the street or seen them with the President or anything? It's like a refrigerator with a gun, this deadly chill, right? When these guys catch him, he says—because he had all this pull in very high places so he had called in a hit squad from Central Casting, I kid you not—when these guys catch him he says, they're going to shoot him, so you'd better get upstairs, eh? So then I, do you think for a minute I'd go upstairs?, I go Then they're going to have to start by shooting me first, because I'm going to look for him. So I start looking for him, right?, and the two guys didn't try to stop me. I went in the bakery, but he wasn't there. Where'd he go? I said to myself. I went into that restaurant next door, then the bookstore, down the alley to the parking lot, into the drugstore at Sanborns, and then I started getting desperate, and anxious, desperately anxious. I mean the police finally got bored looking for him, my uncle even got bored. I started very calmly looking for him and then look at me, I'm yelling for him at the top of my lungs. And he's nowhere. I yelled Where are you, where are you, and no answer, Handsome to the Maximum was nowhere to be found. I looked for him in all those little restaurants up and down the Reforma, and he just wasn't there, and I'm beginning to feel really roughed up and hurt myself, now, and threatened too, helpless.

So then finally, I went into the bathroom at Sanborns to fix my face, and when I came out I looked over the restaurant, and I see him eating sour cream enchiladas. Can you believe it? Enchiladas suizas? In Sanborns? Since we got separated, he went into Sanborns and was eating, right? So anyway, I was scared out of my wits and I go Run, run, let's go, come on, get in the car, hurry up, let's go. Don't ask questions, I said, that's all I said, let's go, I'll explain later. So when we're in the car, when we're driving off in the car, I say What do you think happened? And then I told him. So he says to me, Why didn't you tell me that a minute ago? I'm going back, he says. And he heads back, imagine, to find my uncle. I was ready to die, from fear, right?, I mean imagine. Please, just keep going, I say. But he wouldn't listen to me, we headed back to find my uncle, but we couldn't find him by now, thank God, so then he took me home. Masturbating fire-breathers!

So I get to my house and there's my father. . . . What happened! You see, my uncle had already called him, so me, with my poor powers of persuasion, I mean how was I going to sweet-talk myself out of this one? I go Wait till I tell you what my crazy miserable uncle just did. You won't believe it. Tell me, my father says, what happened? Let me hear it, what happened to you. Nothing, I say, I was walking along with Tito Caruso, dressed such and such, I say, and my uncle mistook him for that guy Loco Valdiosera. He was looking out the window when we crossed the street, and I waved at him and everything. Do you think if I'd been with Loco Valdiosera I'd have said hello to my uncle? So then I guess my uncle ran in the office and got his gun, and then listen to what he did, he shot at Tito Caruso. Three times. Bang, bang, bang . . . I changed all the names, right?, to protect the innocent. So that made my father so mad that he called my uncle and told him never to meddle with my affairs again as long as he lived. My uncle trying to say But listen, that wasn't what happened, that's not true, right? But he couldn't get a word in edgewise. It was that scum Loco Valdiosera, I swear, he'd try to say, but my father believed me, okay? Because my father believed everything I told him. . . . I mean, he was my *father*, for goodness' sake . . .

My uncle was this politician, right? He was always mixed up in political stuff, and he was a congressman or a deputy or whatever you call them. Weird things like that—not to mention that he was one of those, how shall I put it?, very imaginative people. He had these fantasies. Like a paranoid. He was always thinking that somebody was following him and that everybody wanted to kill him. So he always walked around loaded down with rifles and machine guns and things. I kid you not. He had every kind of pistol in the world. He carried pistols in all his pockets. A really strange type, right? But he was real funny, real friendly and nice and all, but the way he treated me was terrible. Because he loved me so much. Until the day he died, the person he loved the most in his whole life had been me, I'm not kidding. Aside from his own kids, of course, because he depended on his kids a lot, he adored his kids, but aside from that, he always said the only family he'd ever had in his life was me.

But we were talking about the Palacio de Hierro. What I earned was a joke, I worked for peanuts in the first place, because every time anybody came in I recommended things we didn't sell. I'd say to the people, I, uh, listen, why don't you try Nieto? I was . . . For example, I'd say Where did I see some cut-crystal ashtrays? I was in the Exclusive Gifts department, right?, and they'd come in to buy ashtrays, and I'd say, I, uh, no, where I saw some heavenly, heavenly ashtrays, but truly divine, was in that little shop—what's its name? And I'd send them somewhere else, I'd recommend all these other boutiques . . . Because I was going through this thing, this phase where I had to be as, um, no, no, not up on things, no, not snooty, what's that word for when you're honest, I mean, like when you say what you think or when you tell just the truth, exactly. Screw something. Uh-huh, scrupulous, honest. That's when you're on commission, and you don't just try to get them to buy from you, right?, but buy what's right for them? Well, that was the first thing. Another thing was that I told everybody my troubles. I mean my tragedies. Because then another thing was, that I got this idea I wanted to commit suicide, or else I'd get sick, or I'd call in that I was sick when I spent the day with Alexis, like I told you. So I was about as good a saleswoman as a kick in the stomach, I never sold *any*thing. My pay was like eight hundred pesos, or when it was good maybe a thousand, twelve hundred with commissions, twelve hundred. So I'd buy things—I was going to marry Handsome to the Maximum, remember? So since we were supposedly getting married, I started buying stuff, all kinds of stuff. I bought so much stuff. . . .

It was always a kick with Handsome to the Maximum, so much, so much fun, because with him I went through things, I swear, that were schizophrenic. You know he was this real gigolo, right? But there was one thing—we always, always told the truth to each other, especially him, because he said he always *had* to tell the truth, it was like this obsession he had. So anyway, one day he leaves on a trip. Oh, I remember, he'd had this big fight with one of his best friends, with Tito, you know him, and he made me promise I wouldn't speak to him. Not one word. He wasn't such a great friend of mine, right?, but anyway he'd forbidden me to speak a word to him, absolutely positively forbidden it. So this one day Handsome to the Maximum had to go to Mérida. He told *me* he was working, or rather that he was getting in some truckloads of shrimp that were coming in frozen from somewhere, and supposedly his job was checking in the shipments at five o'clock in the morning, when they came in, right? And then he had to sell them to the distributors. It seemed like a perfectly normal job to me, but like I didn't quite believe him, because he was such a gigolo. But anyway he had to go to Mérida to settle accounts on the shipments or something. Anyway, he wasn't in Mexico City to settle accounts on the shipments, no, he wasn't in Mexico City. . . .

So then Tito Caruso came to see me. He said Listen, I want to talk to you because, well, um, he says, oh sweetheart, listen I want to be your friend, I really really do, so please let me talk to you, this is not my fault, and so on and so forth. Well, yeah, really, I don't have anything against you, it's because of Handsome that I can't talk to you. So he says Well but I've got this problem, he says, crossing his eyes, since it was on account of me that you started going out with Loco Valdiosera, I feel the moral obligation to tell you what's going on. He had this oracular tone, very deliberately theatrical, you know, trying to sound mysterious. Well? I said. Well, listen, Loco Valdiosera is in Mérida at this very moment, and he's with this girl—specifically he's in Cozumel and he's with . . . When he said that to me, at the second he was saying this to me the bell rang, and that meant I had to go eat, right? And it had hit me so hard that I just turned around and started walking, and so he started walking along behind me. Ay sweetheart, speak to me, what's wrong. I couldn't answer him, it was like I was hypnotized. What is it, sweetheart? I automatically went up the stairs, I mean those black electric things, the escalator, right? I walked into the cafeteria, and I still couldn't talk. And to make things worse he yelled all the way upstairs at me from downstairs, Her name is Leonor Cifuentes! Do you know her? She was a tramp to beat all tramps. He's with Leonor Cifuentes! he says. He was yelling, but those were the last words I could make out. . . .

So I walked on into the cafeteria and Ugh, I said to myself, I don't think I can eat. I felt awful, right? Just awful. I even felt guilty myself. So I went back downstairs and I went into Sanborns. The head waitress at Sanborns was a friend of mine, this incredibly nice woman, she was always so nice to me, one of those normal producers of children and normal collectors of good commonsense advice. Of course, I didn't pay much attention to the advice back then. So anyway, I went up to her and sat down, and she says What's the matter? You look so sad, what's wrong? So I go Oh, babe, I just found out about this big big problem I've got, and so on and so forth. So she says You don't say. Yes, I say. Somebody just told me this terrible terrible thing about Handsome to the Maximum. Oh, don't worry, she says, don't worry, it's nothing, don't . . . And at that . . . I mean look at how life can be, really. . . .

I was on my way out of Sanborns, and I decided to call this real close friend of Handsome to the Maximum's, this, well his best friend. I said Napo, listen, I've got to talk to you, *got* to, so come and get me please. I'll be there in two minutes, he says. And at that, I mean I was talking to him on the phone and who should appear but Tito Caruso again. Oh sweetheart, please, forgive me, and so on and so forth. I still hadn't started going out very seriously with Alexis, or else none of this would have happened. . . . I was talking to Tito when Napoleon got there, because he lived just about two blocks away. I said Get lost, Tito, run, don't let him see you because he'll tell Handsome to the Maximum you're the one who gave me the story, and I don't want him to know, so go hide. So then here comes Napoleon, right? Tito hides and Napoleon comes in, and he says What's up? You sounded terrible. I told him what had happened, and he says Well, I'll tell you, it's true. It's true, precious, I've never wanted to say anything to you about it, but yes, it's true, and you've got no business still thinking of marrying Valdiosera because you'll have a miserable life, you're better than that, don't be a fool. And listen to this. Then he says You deserve better. I think he wanted to add Like me, for example, but he just gave me his sermon, big brother, right?, and left. Once he told me not to be a fool, to stop going with Handsome to the Maximum, and certain things like that, once that happened, well, you'd think it had started raining and he'd left his convertible top down, he just vanished. So then I went back to my counter, because by now it was time to go back to work. I go in and my boss says Excuse me . . . excuse me for asking, she says, but why such a sad face? Look in the mirror, she says, you're so pale and drawn. And those bags under your eyes!, she says. So to make a long story short I left the boutique and went outside again and started walking. I had to bite my tongue not to howl. I was walking along like a tormented cadaver, living through this sensation like the whole world was laughing at my disgrace and misfortune. It had started to get cloudy. I remember it like yesterday . . .

I was walking past Sanborns, right?, and I turn and look inside, and who should I see in there but Handsome to the Maximum himself. I caught sight of him and you can imagine, I thought I'd seen, not the devil, the devil himself wasn't the half of it. So I storm in, furious, with smoke coming out my ears and nose and mouth all at once, completely out of control. I go inside. I storm in like a hurricane and I stop, barely containing my fury. Handsome to the Maximum was with some friends of his I didn't know. I stopped next to him and I said Come outside, very huffy and arrogant, right?, come outside, we've got to talk. Those were the first words I spoke to him. Hey, beautiful!, how are you, sweetheart, I was killing time till it was time to come by for you, and so on and so forth. Come on outside, we've got to talk, now! So at that he stuck his hand in his pocket like this, in his pocket, he pulled out some money like this, he didn't even look at how much he pulled out, and he left it on the table, and we went outside. Word of honor he left money on the table, and we just walked away. So then I said to him Will you please tell me who you were with and where you went. Oh baby, he says . . .

Listen, Handsome to the Maximum was one of those guys if you asked him what he did yesterday, if you didn't see him for example, right?, and you asked him, he'd go Why I was at home. And if you suspected something, and you said Really?, just for example, or especially like What did you do?, he'd get furious, all you had to do was halfway doubt his word, you know, and he'd explode, he'd start raving, he'd hit the ceiling. So but that day he said Oh baby, what's wrong, what are you talking about. Tell me who you went with and where you went! And then I added Just please tell me. Oh baby, why would you ask that, nobody, I didn't go anywhere with anybody, and then he started with the shrip shimpments I mean the shrimp shipments and Mérida and who knows who and so on and so forth. And then Did somebody tell you some wild story? Fake as a seven-peso bill, the man. So then I said Look, if you tell me you went to Mérida with somebody, or to Cozumel, or to Isla Mujeres, it's not going to matter to me, I don't care, but if you tell me it's not true, I'm going to have to say good-bye to you once and for all, because I'll never forgive you for telling me a lie, I'll never forgive you for that, so I'd rather you tell me who you went with, where you went and what you went for, I say, because I already know anyway, but I prefer to hear it from your own lips, so tell me. And can you believe it but he went crazy and started yelling at me right there on the sidewalk, right there on this sidewalk in front of Sanborns, like a wild man, completely bonkers. He . . . You remember before, where the parking lot is, used to be the Paseo de las Jacarandas? It was called the Paseo de las Jacarandas. For the trees I guess. Anyway, started screaming, screaming, SCREAMING. Handsome to the Maximum, not the Paseo de las Jacarandas. That's what I get for being such a stupid jerk, he says, for being such an asshole, for answering your stupid questions, I've been a jerk my whole life, I try to tell you, try to convince you of something, but that's okay, believe whatever you want to, whatever suits you, I don't care. I mean really telling me off, right? He did everything but pee on me, I'm telling you. He made me feel like a blob of green stuff. Those attacks, those explosions, you know?, of his always practically annihilated me. They took me right to the brink of destruction. But from there I told him, almost like nostalgically, you know?, Well, if what you want to do is say good-bye, no problem. Good-bye. With a capital G, right?

And I went back to my counter, dragged myself rather, to the um, to the, to my place. . . .

Three minutes later he calls me. I answer the phone and, oh, as I was coming in my big boss, the head saleswoman, the girls I worked with, everybody was waiting for me. It was below you to have stood that from the Green One. Everybody called him the Green One. Because get this he always came in in green suede shoes, green socks, everything green, but all different greens. So my bosses gave him the name. It's below a young lady like you to have stood for such vulgarity . . . Because you know they were right next door, and they had heard every single word Handsome to the Maximum had said to me. They heard everything but everything Handsome to the Maximum had said to me. Imagine! And they were so mad, so mad, but I hadn't noticed they were there. When I walked in they were all waiting for me, to give me a piece of their minds. Scolding me, right? And just then the telephone rings. I answer the phone, and it was Handsome to the Maximum, alias the Green One. And he says I want you to know that I'll never speak to you again as long as I live, and if you run into me on the street one day, you just pretend you don't see me because I'm not saying hello . . . *Bang*, he hangs up on me. He didn't even give me time to open my mouth, but then again, the telephone rings again and he says the same thing, except he doesn't hang up right away, he sits there listening to see if I answer him. And me, me, forget it, I was furious. I was like gunpowder, I was spitting fire, I was like an atom bomb, I was ready to blow up and take the Palacio de Hierro with me . . . Take all of Mexico City with me! Shit! . . .

Three minutes later the telephone rings again. They were still scolding me, but you know these were people that had known me since I was a little girl, the people I'm talking about, the head of the floor, all of them. So anyway, the telephone rings again. I mean, they weren't just giving me a piece of their minds, they were giving me all they had, trying to make me see the light, right? And in the middle of this heartfelt bawling-out I'm getting, the telephone rings again, and it was that bastard Handsome to the Maximum. You can imagine how I was beginning to wish for Alexis' presence about now. Perfumed farts! And he starts saying But you better remember, I'll never forgive you for this, do you hear, I want this perfectly clear, I'll never ever forgive you for this. So he treats me like a rag and then *chíngale!*, he hangs up on me again. By now I was like, oh, I was like Ready for Blood. That's what my grandmother always said. . . . My grandmother was this ancient little old lady, real proper and sort of palsied, right?, but she had this mean streak in her. I may smell ripe, she always said, but I'm not dead yet. So she always said, another thing she said was I'm ready for blood. So he calls me again, yet again, right?, and I said Listen. Just you listen for a minute, buster, I said, I've got a couple of things to say to you, so you just listen. It's *me* that's never going to speak to *you* again, you hear? You're common and vulgar and I never want to hear your name again as long as I live. Period. And I hung up.

So about fifteen minutes go by, right?, and he calls me again. Ay, sweetheart, please, forgive me, my love, please, I found out who told you that story, how could you believe him? Very clever, right? The first thing that came to my mind was that Napoleon had seen Tito, right? So then he says to me, How could you believe him, and the transformation was so radical, like from night to day, right?, that it sounded sincere to me. You know those people, all they want to do is keep us apart, break us up, darling, plus the fact that somebody that's capable of saying things like that . . . How could you have paid any attention. I found out who told you. And I feel terrible about it, really, I'm hurt, how could you believe it, please, forgive me, and so on and so forth. So then Miss Gullible here, me, Miss Foot in her Mouth for every year since 1955 to now, I say to him, Ay, baby, how was I supposed to think that Tito would tell me a lie. And he says All I was waiting for was for you to tell me his name! 'Bye, and *bang!*, he slams down the receiver. He hangs up on me *again!* I mean *please*. Oh, I forgot, he says he's going to kill him, he's going to murder him, and he hangs up. So there I was like a madwoman running all over Mexico City trying to find Tito. I went over to the Jalisco Sisters' house, and we jumped in Severo and took off looking for him, until we finally ran into him in that restaurant they put in where the Astoria was, you know? And I said Tito, Tito, Handsome to the Maximum's going to kill you, hide because he's ready to murder you, run, quick, hide. And I told him what had happened.

So anyway, to make a long story short, the next day I went to work again and guess what? Handsome to the Maximum and Tito both come in, I mean together. Handsome to the Maximum's got his arm around Tito's shoulders, can you believe it? And they're walking around looking in all the showcases, looking at all the little gifty things, right? Vases and ashtrays and little blown-glass swans and things, just strolling through, like buddy-buddy, right? They'd ask how much this cost and pick it up and turn it over and look underneath and from the side and all and turn it around like they were thinking of buying somebody an exquisite little ceramic bullfrog, right?, and they didn't even look at me. Buddy-buddy. Could we gift-wrap it, and how long would it take to send it to who knows where, and so on and so forth. I mean once I was two-timed, tamed, stepped on and tamped down real good, tied to the stake and burned, right?, they just passed by, pulled this dirty filthy stunt on me, strutted through and walked out. Grrr . . . Buddy-buddy.

("*May noise split your teeth like a dentist's drill, may spider's legs grow out of all your pores, may you only eat used playing cards, may lightposts kick you as you walk down the street, may an irresistible fanaticism cause you to prostrate yourself before garbage scows and all the dogs of all the inhabitants of the city take you for a fireplug, may you say Fried flounder when you try to say My love, may your hands try to strangle you at least once a day, and instead of throwing out your cigarette-butt, may it be you they toss into the spittoon, may your family amuse itself by deforming your skeleton so that mirrors, when they see you, commit suicide in revulsion, may your only diversion be sitting in dentists' waiting rooms, disguised as a crocodile, and may you fall so madly in love with an iron safe that you not be able even for one instant to stop licking its keyhole.*")

Confluence of cumulous memories and the throbbing light of everyday

A lot of times we'd eat at the Jalisco Sisters', you know, I like them a lot, a lot, well, but with reservations, right? Nothing in life is absolute, you know what I mean, like everything is both yes and no, black and white, lust and chastity, don't you agree? Including the Jalisco Sisters, of course. One of them is the biggest tramp I ever knew in my life. She's the wildest girl I ever saw, I mean the most immoral, but at the same time, I don't know, she has the most peculiar personality, because she has this incredible heart. I know, for example, that she'd like to settle down and have a house and kids, live a more or less normal life, but at the same time I know that no matter how much she'd like that, she can't, she couldn't, she just couldn't, because there are all these *demands* she has. Like on life, right? She likes money a

74

lot, and she likes to spend money a lot, she likes everything, you know, like that, a lot. So naturally, she's always had to have somebody around to help her out, economically speaking. She and her sister have, um, how do I put this, well, since they were little girls they've lived this very liberal life. I mean they outdo themselves, you know? But at the same time they got furious at Mercedes because she told us she walked around naked in front of her babies. They criticized her like crazy because they think that's the height of immorality, as they put it. How could she let her sons see her in the altogether. You see the contrast? Or the contradiction, whatever? Certain things scare them, like two little twin boys three months old seeing you naked, but them—oh, them, well, think the worst and you won't be far wrong. A very undefined morality, to put it mildly, right? But they're so nice and so friendly and all, like all true tramps, right?, and I've known them for years. Big Jalisco and Little Jalisco. I've already told you Little Jalisco reminds me of a match, right? She has these incredible flare-ups, all of a sudden.

We were going to eat, right? And Dressed Like a Man comes over with these racing, you know, driving gloves because that rash of hers even comes out on her hands. I met her, I'll tell you, I met her in the funniest way, at school, right?, but in the strangest way. . . . I think of her as my best friend, right? In spite of the fact that she's the only person that's ever been able to, or I mean tried to hurt me. It's like she's the person I love most, that's my best, my very closest friend, and yet she's the person who's tried to pull the worst double-crosses on me. . . . I think she's warped, somehow. . . .

So anyway, we started eating, and the Jalisco Sisters were talking about these terrible money problems they were having, because their problems are always money-related, like I told you, these money problems, there's not enough money in the world for their money problems. And about that time also, Dressed Like a Man had gotten in this—well, she'd started buying and selling jewelry, the really good stuff, I mean, not costume jewelry, and she said this lady had just stuck her for seven hundred and eighty thousand pesos, and she won't pay her, no way in the world. And *she* doesn't have anything to show, no paper, no document, no IOU, no voucher, no nothing. All she has is a check from this lady for two hundred and thirty-four thousand pesos marked Insufficient Funds. That's all. Because she sells you these jewels without a receipt or asking you for identification or anything. And I mean, she sells really really exquisite jewelry, but just a handshake, right?, just a word of honor . . . Even if she doesn't know you . . . Imagine. So she's ruined, right? The Jalisco Sisters and I were talking and talking, I don't know, about desserts and pies and drinks or even softdrinks and how bad all that stuff is for you and about recipes and chocolate and restaurants, all the things we liked, right? Dying laughing, trying to keep Dressed Like a Man from talking because she always got off onto her Problem, like that, capital P Problem, and we were up to here with the poor thing's Problem. So anyway, we started talking about our families, things that had happened to us, gossip, you know? Like you and I are doing at this very minute. . . .

There was this other time we were eating like that, exactly like that—the Jalisco Sisters, Dressed Like a Man and I. . . . Big Jalisco is thin but Little Jalisco, I'm telling you, she's, if you've ever seen her, she's skinny skinny skinny skinny—you've never seen anything like it. She has legs like this, ay . . . It was . . . Anyway, we were eating, right? There were four of us eating. And Little Jalisco starts telling about the outer loop or the peripheral or whatever it was they were building over by her sewing school. It was back when they were building the loop, oh, I know, it was that freeway?, and there were these ditches this big, I mean gigantic, where they were putting in the ramps and overpasses and underpasses, that loop-the-loop thing, the cloverleaf?, right?, these big round cement columns to hold up the highway and all, and she was walking along one night, right at the door of her sewing school, and this guy rides by on a bicycle, and *chhh!* he slaps her ass, and she swings around mad as a hornet. You asshole, you'll get yours, and so on and so forth. And the guy comes back! The guy comes back and *chhh!*, he slaps her again, somewhere else. It was pitch dark, right? And she says she was *furious*, ready to kill this guy, so she starts looking for rocks to throw at this guy, but it was too dark. So she starts running. And so then the guy gets off his bicycle and runs and catches her and starts wrestling with her, you know, struggling. He grabbed her and he started twisting her. He twisted her arms, her hands, her breasts, everything. So then to make a long story short, since she wouldn't let him have his way with her, if you know what I mean, he grabs her by the feet and picks her up and holds her upside down in the air. In the air! I mean, you can imagine how easy, as skinny as she was and with the skinny little legs she had . . . And to scare her I guess, he holds her headfirst over one of those holes, he sticks her into one of those great big huge holes for the loop, right? He stuck her head in the hole, this guy, and she kept saying Turn me loose, let me go, let me go, what are you doing to me. . . . I'll tell you, I exploded. Pfpfpfp, and I spray the soup, a whole mouthful of soup, I spit it all over her, like this—pfpfpfpf. It was vegetable. I couldn't control myself, I burst out laughing and *chíngale!*, every drop of the soup . . . She was drenched. I mean, imagine, What are you *doing* to me! . . . Picture her screaming that! Squirrel afterbirth! . . .

But mainly we'd talk about our families, right? Especially back then. I . . . For example, I was very close to my father, because my mother was totally . . . Let me see how to explain this . . . I wonder what the words are for my mother. . . . Well, one of those people you can never talk to because they're always attacking you. Always on your back about something. I have never, never, never, I mean to this day I have *never* received one single nice word, one word of encouragement from my mother. It's that she's so strange, so strange. . . .

Awhile back she was dying. Didn't you hear about this? She was dying from not being able to breathe? She was suffocating? No, you heard about that, didn't you? This burning, this flame that started at her toes and ran right through her up to her head? You didn't? Well, she was in bed, right? And she calls me. Oh, daughter, my daughter—like that, real weak, right? Forget it, like a bureaucrat's fart. I'm sick, she says, dragging the syllables out of herself, oozing them out. She's in anguish. Oh, what's happening to me, darling, I'm so sick, I'm so sick. Why? What's wrong with you? I don't know, I don't know, but it's this burning sensation that starts at the tip of my toes and rises, rises, rises, and I feel like I'm choking, here, touch me, feel how I'm perspiring. And she was perspiring, I mean she was *sweating.* . . . So then to cheer her up, right?, I say Oh Mama, don't be silly, it's nothing, what could you have . . . My feet are burning up, she screams, they're on fire. Just hold on a little, just hold on a little while, I'll go get my brother. So I go to my brother's room. Great big tears are rolling down my face. Mama's sick, I say, Mama's so so sick, I don't know what it is, she may be about to have a heart attack. So my brother stops me, and he says, he's half asleep, he says What's wrong with her, sitting up in his bed, what's wrong with her. She's sweating all over, she feels like her whole body's on fire, and she's burning up, and really, it's no joke, I mean she really really *is* sweating. Call the doctor, quick! he says. Gimme the telephone. Come on, dial! Well then gimme the telephone and I'll dial it. Go give her some water, something, right? And just about then we hear somebody laughing. Laughing out loud, like in hysterics. She's gone mad, I say. I mean, we thought something had happened to her, you can't imagine the howls and howls of laughter. So both of us run in to her—we're in our pajamas, right?—and we get there and she's rolling around on the floor. So Miss Mentally Defective here, I go Mama, Mama, what's wrong, what happened, I was scared to death, imagine how all this had scared me. My brother helped her up, but she just kept laughing. . . . So then, she says Wait. Wait, just wait a minute, let me . . . And she laughs some more. . . . She was in bed, what had happened was, she was in bed and she got terribly terribly hot, she was burning up, right? So she stuck one leg out to cool it off, to see if she could bring her fever down or whatever, and she sees that she'd gone to bed with her wool kneesocks, up to her knees, still on, she went to bed and forgot about those foot-warmer things, you know?, with the reindeer and all them, with these socks on. And she thought she was suffocating!

No, my mother is one of those people . . . Well anyway, I was telling the Jalisco Sisters and Dressed Like a Man about all this. No way I was going to talk about Alexis, right? That was too intimate, and anyway sometimes your family weighs you down more than your boyfriends, a lot more, right? Just to give you an idea about what I'm talking about, my mother was one of those people that all of a sudden says Ay, to think how much I love you. But she has never said I love you or come up and given me a kiss. Never ever ever, since I was a little girl, oh no. She's very stiff, very standoffish, you know, very strange. Of course, she's terrific in some things, real funny, you know? But affection, like, oh I don't know, kissing you or hugging you, or saying That looks so nice on you, no, never, never. . . . So then anyway, I was very attached to my father, and besides we were a lot alike, we got along perfectly. But my mother was one of those people that couldn't stand me to mix with a different kind of people, no way, I mean me to go out or run around with people she didn't know, that she didn't know their families, right?, forget it. I mean they had to be one hundred percent aristocrats because if they weren't, she just turned up her nose. Everybody that wasn't quite aristocratic enough for my mother, they weren't worthwhile, you know what I mean . . . No, no, no, she wouldn't let . . . no. And so of course, I couldn't stand that . . . You know what I mean? I couldn't stand those ideas. Because even if I grew up that way, in that way of thinking, I couldn't stand it. I never accepted it, even if I didn't know any other kinds of people. When I grew up, then, my mother and I started to have a lot of problems. Because I had these friends that she didn't think were the right sort, you know?, were good enough for me, or just girlfriends, or people she hadn't met before, and et cetera, right? So anyway, the problem kept getting bigger and bigger and bigger, and also because it turned into this like I dare you thing, a challenge?, between my mother and me. And that challenge, is that right?, got so powerful, so strong and powerful that it turned into hate, turned into such pure unadulterated hate that I couldn't stand to look at her because I thought she was so unfair and . . . unfair to the nth degree, I mean. And strange, right? I think I really hated her. . . .

She was a person I'd say, for example, Mama, listen I'm going to the movies, I'm leaving to go to the movies now. And she'd say All right, but be home by five. So I'd say But listen if I'm going to the movies at four, I mean it makes sense that I won't be back

before seven, six-thirty or seven, right? I want you here at five
o'clock!, she'd say. Mama, the movie won't be over . . . Then
leave in the middle, because I want you here at five o'clock. That
was the kind of person she was! Or then I'd say, for example,
Somebody invited me out to dance, and she wouldn't ask you who
or where or anything. She wouldn't say a word. She'd say . . .
The only thing she'd say was You're coming home late, huh? Like
a threat. Like saying You come home late and you'll see what's in
store for you. . . . But she wouldn't ask you any questions. I
mean it was unsettling, right?

So she kept getting harder and harder for me to take. Because
put yourself in my place—I never knew when I was going to
catch her in a good mood and when I was going to catch her in a
bad mood, when she was going to yell at me and when she was
going to look up with a smile on her face. She was one of a kind,
you know? A person I could never manage to get to know. So
anyway, to make a long story short, the moment came when she
finally said Where are you going. And I exploded. What do you
care! So she said As your mother, I have to know where you're
going. And so I go Listen, you're the last person on earth to know
what I do. . . . So she comes over to me, and I say Get away, I
hate you, I hate you. . . . I'd say things like Oh, what I'd give to
go to your funeral, I don't know what I'd give . . . Why don't you
die before I get back? I can't stand you! I hate you! Back then I
truly truly hated her. . . . Anything, any chance I got, I'd say
these terrible things to her, right? So of course, we fought all the
time, every few minutes we'd be at it again. . . .

One day we had this terrible argument. It was over . . . oh, it
was because I'd gone out with Mercedes and her husband because
they were celebrating their first anniversary. We'd gone to the
Diplomatico. They had ordered a daiquiri apiece, and I'd ordered
a lemonade. And they said Oh, just try this, here, try it, you
know . . . So I tried it, right? I took a little sip like this out of
Mercedes' glass and *sploosh!*, I spilled it all over me. . . . So
when I got home my mother was waiting up for me with her hand
raised like this. So I open the door . . . I open the door like this
and Chapultepecan prophylactics!, *chíngale!*, she slaps me. So I

say What's the matter with you! . . . She'd smelled it, right? Not
to mention my clothes were the biggest mess you ever saw. This
daiquiri had spilled all over me somehow, but I swear I hadn't
been drinking, no, no way, I had *not* been drinking, there's no
reason for me to lie about that now, right? So anyway she says
Ay, and to top everything off you come in drunk. And she slaps
me again. Whack. Where have you been? And I was so furious I
started screaming at her. Yes, I'm drunk, because I went and
slept with one of my clients! And I had to get drunk to work up
the nerve! So then you can *imagine*—she started really beating
me then. And the more she hit me, the more stuff I told her. He
paid me two hundred pesos, look here, and Yes I did, and I liked
it too, and Uh-huh, two hundred. Because deep inside I thought
if I could get her mad enough I might make her so mad that she'd
hit me so hard I'd die. And Wow, I thought, because all I wanted
to do was die. You have no idea. She made my life miserable! But
to make a long story short, my father heard us, my father was still
alive then, and he jumped out of bed and stopped the argument
and everything. . . . She made my life utterly miserable!

So then since it was only about nine o'clock at night, it was
early, right?, I call the Jalisco Sisters on the telephone, and I say
Come over here, please come over, I need to talk to you. . . . So
they come running over to my house as fast as they can, and the
stupid idiots knock on the door or something, I don't know, but
anyway, my mother catches them and she says What can I do?
My daughter hates me, what am I going to do? The two skinny
things just stand there like little birds. I want to tell her, *here,* in
front of you young ladies and in front of her father, that she needs
medical care, this is not normal. Where have you ever seen a
daughter who doesn't love the mother that bore her? And We have
a psychiatrist who, and so on and so forth. My mother goes I want
her to promise she'll see a psychiatrist now, right away, I want
her to promise me that in front of all of you. So then I say Okay,
right? My father was putting ice on my face, and Big Jalisco, the
one that was going out with two, or sometimes more, guys at the
same time, ran over to her house to get a steak. See this scar?
Well it's from then. It was a real history-making beating. . . . So

anyway, that was at the beginning of the week, I don't remember what day exactly, and on Thursday I got an appointment with the psychiatrist. The Jalisco Sisters and my mother, between the three of them, they took me. So I went, right?, and it was neat. He was the most expensive friend I ever had in my life, that's what he was to me, you know?, because it cost me an arm and a leg and part of another one, but he was the best thing that could ever have happened to me. . . .

For example, he'd ask me how far back I could remember my life, right?, and which things had made the greatest impression on me . . . And stuff like What's your relationship with your brother, from the time you can remember, and How has it been since then. What it was like with my mother at first, with my father, with everybody I could think of, with everybody in my life, right? This psychiatrist kept writing all this stuff down, and then at the next session he'd ask me questions about it. He'd ask me about what he saw in what was written down there, right? And then, it was strange, one day he said Tell me, why do you hate your brother? . . . But at the time he asked me that I adored my brother, right? So I said No no, I adore him, I love him very very much. But he said to me, Well but look, you can see here, at such and such a time you hated him, did you not? You can see that you hated him. . . . Oh, well, he did this to me and that to me . . . So then I started talking about that, because my brother was the biggest two-faced little pest, he'd wait till my mother went out one door and he'd beat me up with his belt; my mother would come back in and he'd start crying and say I'd hit him with the belt. He did terrible things to me, he was always punching me in the stomach . . . I mean, he did the normal things any kid does to his sister, right? And the first person that came in, I mean it could have been anybody, he'd start tattling on me, telling on me, right?, even if he'd made it up. We got along terrible, right? But that was just a stage, or a phase, whatever you call it, because later we became close, close friends. We dressed alike, we went out dancing every day, we'd always go to some cabaret together, because we loved to go out, right? Together. We went to night-clubs, together, we danced together, we went to parties together,

I mean we were very very attached to each other, right? But he was good for me because in the first place I was a little wild. I did all kinds of crazy things. And in the second place he thought I was, and I guess I think of myself that way too, well, that I was a good little girl, one of the best little girls in the world. And I needed that support, right?

All day my mother kept me practically in tears because she insulted me and picked on me all day long. She'd say terrible things to me. Um . . . I'd see people in cafés or at school or in those family kind of parties, and I'd sit down and talk to everybody. And then my mother would come along and say Today I finally discovered once and for all that you are bound for perdition, you did such-and-such a thing, and you're prostituting yourself in an apartment in Colonia Condesa and so on and so forth. She'd tell me all this stuff like that, to make your blood boil, right? So with him, finally, little by little, I got rid of the idea, you understand?, this idea I had like engraved on my skull that acting the way I did was evil. I mean like I was this bad person, right?, that I was lost, really and truly depraved but that I didn't realize it. . . . He was good for me because my mother changed, she changed a lot, like the one under psychoanalysis was her and not me. I mean I'm not going to tell you she was sweeter or anything, or more affectionate, no, but she changed a lot, she got calmer, a whole lot, a lot, what's a good word? *Normal*, more feeling, more human, uh-huh, more human, so I could understand her better.

Ay, those dinners . . . The soup was awful, we were talking about our mothers; the meat was delicious, about our friends. . . . Napoleon had a really nice apartment in Colonia Roma, a really really nice penthouse, with a pretty pool, and he started inviting us over. Tito and Handsome to the Maximum too, who lived, I mean both of them, but not together, right?, in Colonia del Valle. And Gabriel, who was renting a house with horses and everything out by Las Aguilas somewhere. But from the very beginning they all treated us, I mean us girls, right?, treated us like we were really special. What I mean by that is they respected us, to the extent that *nobody*, *ever*, *ever* tried to take advantage of us, if you know what I mean, *ever*, and they were . . . I mean they could have taken advantage of us easy enough, right?, because we were a bunch of pretty silly schoolgirls, you know. I even had a string of boyfriends from that group of guys. I had boyfriends that to this day, to this hour are the wildest kids in the world. And one of them, I'll tell you, he never kissed me, let alone, you know . . . Of course, there was a reason, they had women and gambling and things up to their ears . . . Even some pretty mysterious stuff . . . They were I don't know, they were as crazy as we were. . . .

I mean, like for example, they put little lights in the windows of all their apartments. They had a little red light and a little green light, little bitty, like Christmas tree lights, a little blob of red light and a little blob of green. There was a signal we had for the door—first two rings, then nothing, then two series of three rings. Then if it was okay to come in, they'd turn on the green light and open the door. But there were times when they were with some girl or doing something they didn't want us to see, and those times they'd turn on the little red bulb, right?, that they'd also turn on if we were inside and somebody else came, right? Sometimes these big-deal people, very important people, big shots would come, and we'd have to leave, and since there was just one door, they'd put these capes over our faces, or raincoats, right?, so they couldn't see who we were, and so we wouldn't get in trouble or something, you know?, as though I would get mixed up with somebody else. . . . There were also places in the apartments, or houses in some cases, right?, these places we couldn't go into. And that was very, like, troubling. It was just too romantic, too exciting, and of course too weird. I mean all that was missing was little humpbacked butlers, okay? Or dwarves . . .

But anyway, physically speaking they always showed us nothing but respect. Personally speaking. On the other hand they showed us no respect at all in terms of what they'd talk about in front of us, for example, because you'd even think their sole pleasure was in us hearing . . . For example, every day some girl supposedly committed suicide because of one of them. And sometimes it really happened, okay? I mean sometimes the suicide worked. But sometimes it was just attempted, right? I mean the word—*attempted*, right? Like the day I told you about Mauricio and this girl, the one that shot herself in the tire? The one that tried to shoot herself? But she shot herself so perfectly, I mean she'd figured it out, I think, so it hit her in the tire. The tire of her *car* . . . It went all the way through and came out the other side, you've no doubt heard of cases like that. Let's just say that she wanted to make a statement, okay? But other times it was serious. I even remember this one time when we went over, and Napoleon was screaming into the telephone, Please, don't be stupid, please please don't. . . . Because this other girl, I think, had a gun in her hand, to shoot herself with. I don't know whether she shot herself or not though. . . . Napoleon was one of the wildest people in all of Mexico City, and he had these four little French poodles with those tails like this, like a brush for washing out baby bottles?, little itty-bitty things, that were so sweet . . . And he was crazy about those dogs. . . .

Then there was Gabriel Infante too, right? He was always going to parties I didn't go to. He said they were fun. . . . And we weren't sure whether he liked Little Jalisco or me, but between yes and no and maybe and a couple of margaritas, one day he kisses me, and we started going out together, right? It was always the degenerates that caught my eye, you know? I mean like serious guys, guys with . . . How do I say this? Well, that are serious, right?, serious. . . . Maybe it's that I'm so easy-going and fun-loving and all, and I'm looking for the opposite, right? But I also looked for somebody . . . Not look for exactly, but like found, I identified better with serious people. Umm . . . I like deep people, people with something inside, where you have to figure them out, or they let you guess at them, where there's more and more, you know? I mean . . . superficial people irritate me. I can't stand superficial people, and I don't like people that are too good, like goody-goody types? I don't like all that good in people because it strikes me as being weakness. Or fake. And I don't like weak people no matter how you slice them, and men, well, I like them to be a little mean. Mean is the word. And not fake . . .

So anyway, I started going out with Gabriel, and we had this really stormy relationship, to put it mildly. Because he was a drug addict, incredibly addicted and . . . Well, with all kinds of problems, no? So anyway, when I started going out with him . . . He'd stopped studying odontology but he was earning a lot of money as a betting agent, like a bookie, right?, and a racedriver, and a stunt pilot, you know flying at exhibitions and fairs and stuff?, and since I've always been this Mother Superior, this Sister of Charity type, as soon as I found out about the school, about the odontology, I started trying to get him to finish, to get his degree, to graduate, to go into practice, on and on and on, pushing him to finish. So then this other guy, Napoleon, who was a little strange too, I'll tell you the truth, got to be my friend's boyfriend, got to be Little Jalisco's boyfriend. . . . So then while I was going out with this guy, I kept urging him on so much that he did his thesis. I typed it for him, with two fingers, right? The Biblical system of typing—you know, seek and ye shall find— because I did *not* know how to type, but I did three hundred pages for him, and when I gave it to him, instead of thanking me on his knees, he starts calling me all kinds of names because he had given it to me all scribbled and scratched, right?, and so there were times when I got so tired, of reading it and typing and all?, I got so tired that I'd jump from one page to the next or even to the *end* of the next one, because I'd forget I'd been at the beginning and I was dying to finish it, you know? I mean I made such a mess of that thesis, but I *did* it for him, no? I mean I tried. So to make a long story short, he graduated, he got his degree and everything. This guy that had never planned to practice wound up giving up racing for an office in Colonia Hipódromo. But I'd broken up with him a long time before that. Nothing out of the ordinary ever, ever happened except for this really incredible respect. This terrific respect, right?

So I was talking about all this with my girlfriends and with the doctor. First with the doctor and then with my girlfriends, actually—during those delicious dinners. . . . The psychiatrist was bald, and he had this wart on his neck, two black teeth, and hair like an adolescent bird's-nest. He'd say Well—trying to give the question a little weight by this little quiver in his nostrils like this—and when you were thirteen where were you studying? Just as an example. And I'd say Well, uh-huh, when I was thirteen I was at this school, and I did such and such and I said so and so and my friends liked me and my enemies spit at me. And he'd go on—And your mother? What did she do when you were thirteen? So *then* I'd remember my mother, okay? Because my friends were more important to me than my mother, right? It depended on the day. . . . But I'll tell you the truth, my mother had one of the most horrifying childhoods you can imagine. Because for example, my grandmother, when my mother was little, my grandmother broke into seventeen pieces, her whole body broke into seventeen pieces. And my mother had seven sisters, all younger than her, right?, and my grandfather was Italian, right? So then, who knows what for, they deport him. I've still got this picture of him on a horse, covered with dust and looking all filled with emotion in front of the cathedral at Zacatecas, beside this big gang of guys with huge sombreros and rifles and knives between their teeth. . . . But then, since my grandfather wasn't Mexican and he had to leave, there they were, with nothing, right? So my mother did laundry from the time she was ten years old to take care of her sisters, you know the story. But between hunger and epidemics and all that, poverty started killing one little sister every year, until the only one left was Emma; I'll tell you about her in a minute. And my grandfather had disappeared somewhere in Europe calling Mexico *la gran puta* and *chingando* Mexico's *madre* and generally hating it. We never heard another word from or about him . . . My dear widowed grandfather . . .

So then, when I thought over these things, you know, comparing cases as they say, what I had versus what she had had, well, I started to understand her, right? She couldn't understand me because she'd never lived through what I had lived through, or studied what I had studied, or gone to the places I had been to. So finally I saw her and the whole thing a little clearer, and we started getting along a little better, right? A little tiny bit better. At least she didn't butt into my affairs anymore, she didn't bug me so much about things, and above all she gave me a little more

room, a little more freedom, right? I mean it wasn't that she *gave*
me freedom, it was more like I took it. Not to mention that when I
started being this rebel, I started leaving home. I'd just run away,
but I ran away just to my uncle's house, I mean I want that part
clear. I never went too far. . . . I'd run away with my suitcases
and my pictures under my arm and everything, but I'd come back
in a couple of days because of my father, because my father, poor
man, he was the one that really suffered. He was such a good
man, so he was the one that really suffered.

My father, speaking of my father, you know he was killed at
the jai alai matches over some bets. He was wonderful, right?
Because when he died, when my father died, since I was always
the strong one in the family, the one that held everything together, the one with the strength to do things . . . Because my
brother is a wonderful *brother*, right? But my brother is one of
those people that aside from the bets he makes at the cockfights
doesn't really care much about things. He has, as he says, a
profession by default, employees by default, lovers by default.
Because he's a person that's just not responsible enough to really
run things. He's not the administrator type, you know? And he
couldn't care less about things either—nothing, nothing, nothing
matters to him. He doesn't have any money? Oh, gee, I don't
have any money. I mean, he's like Who cares?, right? He's like a
bohemian, is that the word?, and then when my father was killed,
how do I say this, how do I explain . . . He had puffed him all
up, right? My father made us think we were hot stuff, right?, the
crown of creation as he used to say, that there was nobody prettier
or smarter or stronger or cleverer than we were. I mean in the
whole world. So when my father died we were dumbstruck, right?
My brother hasn't gotten over it yet, no, I'm telling you the truth,
he hasn't gotten over the fact that my father isn't here anymore.

Don't ask how my mother took it. . . . My father was her whole
life, for the forty-five years they were married. My father made
her breakfast for her. My father even bought her underwear for
her . . . She never even knew what a telephone bill looked like,
or that such a place existed as where you went to pay things,
right? Nothing. A person that got married when she was fourteen

years old to this nice man that manipulated her, no, wait, that managed her her whole life. He managed everything, he took care of her, he treated her like his daughter her whole life, right? Very sweet and very touching, sure, okay, but like a china doll or something. So then when my father died, I was the logical choice, right?, logically I was going to be the one to more or less pick up the reins of the house. My unbelievable mother . . . This is a true story—we had the same cook for fifteen years, and my mother didn't even know what she looked like because she had never gone into the kitchen. She knows how to cook, I'll give her that, because she *can* cook, but she had never ever once walked into the kitchen. She didn't even know how to give a maid orders, because my father always did all that, right? So when they mugged my father and killed him, I had to do everything. Because my mother was incapable of doing anything, she had no strength to do anything.

So then I got married, but I took her with me, right? First we lived by ourselves for a year, but at the end of that year I changed my mind, and besides my husband didn't want her to live by herself in a big house so far from mine, or ours, because he felt sorry for her, right? She looked so defenseless, so defenseless and useless that we just couldn't leave her, right? So we took her in with us. And everything is fine, right? Of course, that's ignoring certain small details—let's just say that everything is ambiguously fine. For example, just a few minutes ago practically, just the other day. You remember the last time, when I was so bad and we saw each other? And I said Ay, I'm so, I can't tell you how, I'm so bad. . . . That was a terrible terrible terrible period for us. A very bad period for me. I was having these awful fights with her that seemed to go on forever—in fact I don't think some of them are over yet. Because my mother had gotten it into her head that I was in love with The Monk. I mean rea-goddam-lly! So all day long she kept harassing me. I was so in love—you know with that voice of hers—I called him, why did I call him, I went out, why did I go out, why did I fucking breathe, right?, why this, why that, why the other. . . . I was going out of my mind and it was really getting to me, but I couldn't say anything to my husband, of course, so I was really really bad, really in bad shape.

So I had a lot of fights, I mean one fight after another with her, right? But putting all that aside, I'd say we lived really really well and got along okay, right? She was always, well she started getting serious about mind control, studying mind control, she'd spend all day long letting herself be hypnotized and practicing different kinds of concentration or meditation or whatever it's called. Of course, that's actually the least important thing to her, right? Really she does a lot of public relations, she organizes dinners, goes to meetings, enters all the television sweepstakes and contests and stuff, makes pies, makes flowers out of this bread dough, flower arrangements, little figurine things out of papier-mâché. That's all she does, but she has a perfect life. She's old now, and I'll tell you the truth, she's very very strange. . . . One day I was with my husband in the bedroom and we heard Mama go into this fit of laughing. It must have been about six o'clock in the morning, so we ran in to see what was happening. So—you know what it was?—she was trying to put on her stocking and it wouldn't go on. In the dark she couldn't get her stocking on, and it turned out she was trying to pull on a glove, one of those long ones, those formal gloves?, up to your elbow, you know? She didn't realize it, so she stuck her foot in, and then she kept saying Why can't I get this on? She never realized what she was doing. . . . Or take the other day, for example. She'd gone to take a bath, and all of a sudden she screams and runs out of the tub, she was scared to death, because she felt like her feet had glue on them, she could hardly pick them up off the shower floor, they were so heavy. Her feet and legs had gotten so heavy, they felt like lead. She thought she had a case of exhaustion, of collapse from exhaustion. What it was, that she had put on these furry, real real furry house slippers, you know?, the pink ones?, she always wore these furry house slippers. And she had forgotten to take them off when she got in the shower! So I said Good Lord, you take a bath like that, you can't even see it's your house slippers? Sopping, sopping wet! . . . Can you imagine? She was standing there going Oh my God, why are my legs so heavy? . . .

I kid you not. My mother is hilarious. My mother is a real joke. . . .

I went to the psychiatrist for just one year because he was unbelievably expensive. Not that I cared so much about the money, my father was paying for it, so I mean I didn't care about the money, right? I went twice a week and all kinds of hilarious things happened. On the other hand I ate with the Jalisco Sisters every Saturday and sometimes on other days. For years and years we had dinner together every Saturday, and you know what? . . . They were the real psychoanalysts. I mean, they didn't realize it probably or anything, but they were real therapy for me. . . .

("Life—and I'm speaking from experience—is one long slide into stupidity.")

7

Some irregular conjugations

We used to, and especially if it was Sunday, we used to always go to Cuernavaca after our little get-togethers, after our Saturday dinners, to go to Cuernavaca to have a Bloody Mary. Imagine. We'd go have a Bloody Mary and then we'd drive back to Mexico City. Well, so this one time we had a wreck. We had this terrible wreck, and the guy Big Jalisco hit died—there was Big Jalisco and then me and then Little Jalisco. In the car? We had a wreck at what's the name of that place?, where the Arroyo Restaurant and all that is?, in Tlalpán—the *Arroyo*, you know, the place with the carnitas. We were coming back from Cuernavaca because we always used to go down there every Sunday to have a drink. We even had to chip in money for the gasoline because we sneaked off without anybody knowing. So anyway, one of those

times we were driving back about ninety miles an hour because
they were having the grand opening or something of this place
called the Zero Zone. It was this café, right? And we were supposed to meet Handsome to the Maximum and some of his buddies there, right? But I think he was probably the least important
one. Really, Handsome to the Maximum was the one that counted
the least then. Little Jalisco was supposed to meet Napoleon,
who's her husband now, or, well really, it's more like she's one of
his wives, right? Speaking of which, she was the first one of us to
get married. She saw him about fifteen times in her whole life,
fifteen times she sees this guy, and she marries him. Little Jalisco
married Napoleon. So ask me how it's all worked out for her,
right? Big Jalisco wanted to see Gabriel—I think, uh-huh, right,
she had already broken up with Tito, right, so she was coming to
see this guy, but we weren't sure whether he wanted to go out
with Little Jalisco or with me. She'd just broken up with Tito
Caruso. And as though all that weren't enough, I was starting to
go out with Mauricio—he hasn't been in the story much, has he?
Well, anyway, the important thing is that we had all said we'd
meet there, so we were driving about ninety miles an hour, like a
bat out of hell, to get there, right? And this drunk guy jumps out
in front of us. In the middle of the road! He wanted to bullfight
the car. So this toreador jumps out and coming along at the same
time was this Valiant, right? It was right on top of us, so we
couldn't dodge the guy, so we killed him. The car just ran into
him, we ran into him, I ran into him, Big Jalisco ran into
him. . . . He crashed into the windshield, his whole face, like
this, smashed into the windshield, and then he landed in a tree.
One side of the car ran up on the curb, and with this unearthly
racket we were driving along knocking down little trees, like this,
one after another, until we finally crashed into a big one. Nobody
said a word. I mean, can you imagine? We have this terrible
wreck and nobody says anything? Nobody said a word and then
the three of us sat up. Little Jalisco pushed the door open and the
three of us got out, right? And when we were out nobody still said
anything, the only one that said anything was me, and I screamed
Let's get out of here! Run! So we started running, but when I

finally dared to turn around and look, the only one running was me. I was running down the street all by myself, can you imagine, completely alone. So then I stopped, right? . . . I stopped when I saw that nobody was with me, nobody, absolutely nobody. I turned around, and I started to walk back to where the wreck had been, and the racket, the blood, the trees, us. The car was still there, and you could see people, but I couldn't figure out what was happening, you know what I mean? I went a little closer, like hypnotized, *drawn* to it, you know, and when I got closer I saw these people giving a beating so, I mean so terrible to the Jalisco Sisters that my knees got weak, and I felt like the whole world was caving in on my chest, right here. . . . Two guys, these two guys had Big Jalisco by the arms, and another guy was punching her in the stomach. They were pulling Little Jalisco by the hair, they were grabbing her hair and dragging her along. And kicking her. They were in big, big trouble, right? And in bad shape, the two of them. So then I thought to myself, I don't know karate, I don't know judo, what do I do, right? Do I just give up, or what do I do? So about then they start grabbing my girlfriends one by one, they grab them like this, by the hair, and they push them down to the ground, so they can see the guy close up, right? He looked like somebody had hung him up in the tree, but hung him by his feet, right? And he wasn't dead yet. . . . It was this twenty-year-old kid that was celebrating because he was going to the United States the next day to be a bracero. He had his cap on and everything, right? He was drunk out of his mind, completely, completely drunk. . . . So they'd push their heads down to his face, with his head down, right?, so they could get a good look at him. . . . He was muddy, and he had blood all over him—he was in bad, bad shape. It was an awful sight. . . . So anyway, I mean what could I do? The first thing that occurred to me was to go to the Zero Zone to get my friends . . . What else could I do?

So about then there came along this big huge old car, like they used to make?, this antique, sort of creeping along, real real slow, with a bunch of kids driving, honestly, like children, I mean little children, right? So I pulled the door open on the driver's side, and I jumped in, which gave them a horrible shock as you can imagine. I almost scared them to death, and they started saying, well first they said Ouch! when I got in, but then they start saying, start asking me, Ay, what *happened* to you, what's wrong, what's happening, why'd you get in, and we almost had a wreck ourselves. But by that time I'd taken the wheel so to speak . . . It was this '39 Buick, imagine, and I could barely drive Severo, that was about fifteen years newer . . . So I said, I'm taking this car to Insurgentes, so hold on. There's not enough gas! We'll never make it! But all they could get out of me was We're going to Insurgentes, how far to Insurgentes? I hijacked them, right? Like a hijacker . . . I wanted to go tell my friends, because no way I was going to call my parents or the Jalisco Sisters' family. I wanted to go tell my friends, and I was terrified we'd see a cop and the kids would start screaming or saying something. . . .

So anyway, I finally got to Insurgentes. . . . And as we were coming in to Insurgentes, I saw I was absolutely covered with blood. So then I remembered the Jalisco Sisters, right? Big Jalisco, I was sure I'd seen her getting out of the car—I could see her perfectly getting out—but Little Jalisco, who was on the passenger side, I couldn't remember her getting out, right? Had she gotten the door open or hadn't she? And the noise—I hadn't seen whether . . . Since the whole windshield was smashed and all the splinters of glass and all flew in on top of us, with the way the guy hit the windshield?, I hadn't seen whether something had happened to the littler one or not. So I was terrified when I got to Insurgentes, right? All of a sudden it hit me, I panicked, so I jumped out of the car and ran in the restaurant screaming We killed a man! We killed a man! So everybody jumps up and says What happened. I screamed We killed him. *We killed him!* That was all they could get me to say. . . . Everybody rushed around, they tried giving me some sugar, they gave me little pieces of bread, they patted my shoulder and said There, there . . . And I could feel the tears running down my cheeks. Gabriel Infante picked up a napkin and wiped the blood off me, he wiped off the sweat and blood. . . .

All of a sudden I looked over and I saw them slapping Little

Jalisco's cheeks. Napoleon was slapping her cheeks over at the other door of the Zero Zone. So I walked over there to see how she was, to see how she'd managed to get there. . . . Mauricio held my, he helped keep me up. I staggered over there, but I was so shocked and catatonic and she was so shocked and catatonic, both of us horrified, right?, that neither one of us was making any sense. All she would say was Bastards, bastards, we killed a stupid bastard! And back then, I'll tell you something, back then we didn't use words like that, none of the three of us ever used bad words, and there she was screaming Bastards, they carried my sister off with a gun! So then the guys slapped her so she'd answer them, snap out of it, you know, and tell them where they'd taken her sister. At gunpoint, no less! But all she would say is They carried off my sister. That's all they could get her to say, she was like a record stuck in one groove. They shook me too. Andrés and Tito were there and they kept saying But what *happened*. And I kept saying We killed a man! But *where* . . . We killed him! Anyway, to make a long story short, they couldn't get anything else out of either one of us.

So finally they put us into two cars. Little Jalisco in one and me in the other, and they took off. They made us get out of the cars a couple of blocks away and had us walk around a little bit, and when we'd calmed down a little, when they saw we had calmed down a little, they tried to get us to come to again, right? So then we were starting to make a little sense then, right?, and little by little we put together what had happened.

So then Tito rushes off. Tito goes to a telephone and he calls my parents. He went to call my father immediately because my father, well, my father knew a lot of people, right? So he called to tell him. We were over by the Sports Complex, at a public telephone over there, but my father was at the Eighth Precinct station with my brother, because my brother had just had a wreck and he'd totalled five cars, plus my father's made six. He'd gone to the police station half an hour ago, but not my mother, because my mother had heard about the wreck and running over the guy and everything, right? Because the other Jalisco Girl, I mean they carried her off with a pistol and all, but those people were so, well, so decent I guess you could say, that they took her to a police station instead of taking the law in their own hands. They took her to the police, and they could have lynched her or something, right? I mean they had every right to lynch her, didn't they?

So Big Jalisco had called her mother and father, and her father had gone to the police station to see her. Her mother, on the other hand, had called *my* mother and told her we were all at the police station. This all got a little confusing, right? So when Tito told her we were there with him, over by the Sports Complex and not at any police station, my mother said Why don't you just bring them home. . . . Little Jalisco had escaped the same way I had, or more or less the same way, anyway. She managed to break away from them all of a sudden, because after her experience, that experience with the guy on the bicycle?, she had gone and taken these self-defense classes, right?, so now there's no man that can shove her around anymore. . . . So I'm not real sure how exactly she got loose, but she broke away and she ran off, too, right? And then both of us went, but not together, right?, went to the Zero Zone, went our separate ways, but we both finally got there. . . . Of course, she'd been beaten almost to death. . . .

So Handsome to the Maximum . . . He'd taken charge of the little kids and their '39 Buick, and then later he stayed at the police station all night. . . . My father and Tito did all the paper-work and made all the arrangements and everything to get Big Jalisco out, and finally they got her out on bail. The man died three days later. He was all torn up inside, right? Everything, every little piece of him inside was broken and smashed, but thank goodness, all of us were safely protected, even me, and a little while later we were as they say free and clear. Or almost, because Big Jalisco started doing these very strange things, behaving very very weirdly, like bananas, practically fruit salad, you know?, and all I could figure out was that that was one of the side effects of that awful awful accident. . . .

Months later, take for example, we were both working in the Palacio de Hierro. So one day she says to me, Listen, I really don't feel like going out somewhere for lunch, on the street you know?, and it just so happens that a friend of mine, this old, old friend of mine, invited me to his house for lunch. So she says Will you come with me? So I said Why, if you want me to I'll go, of course. She goes It's this friend I've had for years and years, and I'd really like for you to meet him. . . . I mean it sounded perfectly normal to *me*, right? I thought This guy might actually want to meet me, so I said Okay, sure, all right. So we left and I went to lunch with her. It was at this apartment on the Paseo de la Reforma, really chic, and this guy had a butler that opened the door and everything. He was very very elegant, this man, I mean, very well-known, and very, *very* high-class. . . . All my life I'd heard about him, but he was one of those people I'd never come in contact with. For some reason, right? But I guess it was that the Jalisco Sisters had talked about him so much, and had described him so well, I mean down to the last detail, but anyway I felt like I knew him already. . . .

So anyway, we were sitting there eating, talking about Handsome to the Maximum because he was a friend of his, and he knew he'd been going out with me. And we were telling him he took better care of himself than a new baby. And that he was one of those people that were always making sure they looked perfect, that the part in their hair didn't get messed up or something. And this guy was laughing so hard . . . And he covers up, I was saying, he combs his hair back, or actually more like over here, so you won't see this scar he's got . . . And he's got these beautiful teeth, too, right?, that he brushes with this strange powder. We called it Mother Celestina's powder, who knows why, but that's what we called it. It makes them white, white, white. Not to mention brushing them with boiled water, still hot and everything, so they don't get soft. I mean does he love himself or not? Sparkling, sparkling white . . . And this guy was dying laughing. . . .

So we finished lunch, and all of a sudden Big Jalisco gets up and goes off like to the bathroom, right?, like she's going to the powder room. So he and I sat there talking about all kinds of stuff, one of those innocent, nothing conversations. So then I calculated, right?, I thought about it, and I said to myself She's taking an awful long time in there just to pee. She must be finished by now. . . . I mean she could have peed and brushed her teeth, washed her face, she must've messed up her hair and combed it again by now and put on new makeup and the whole thing, right? She could have started over completely by now. How embarrassing! Although she might have decided to do number two, too, right? Number two in a strange house! Who ever heard of such a thing! Me with my narrow mind, you can picture what I was thinking about her doing number two, me the little old nineteenth-century lady, Miss Priss, right? . . . But the guy that owned the apartment just kept chatting along, very calmly. . . . But deep inside I was so embarrassed, because I figured he was worried about the Jalisco Girl too, right? I mean he had to be, didn't he? And I was dying of shame that he might think she was in there cleaning the bathroom, like because she'd thrown up all over it or something, or something worse. . . . Luckily, he finally says What could be keeping our friend, eh? And then he goes Why don't you go see? So I said I think I will, now that you mention it, because she might have started feeling sick or something. So I went up these two or three steps because she had gone up these steps to the bathroom in the bedroom. I said Hey, what's up? Are you sick? I kind of tapped on the door . . . And she says No, no, I'm coming, I'll be right there. So then this guy comes up after I do, and I swear to God there was nothing abnormal or funny about this, or set up, nothing, he was just like this, calm, normal, very very elegant and suave, apparently completely at ease, not concerned about a thing. So he says Shall we turn on the television for a while? So I said Okay. So he turns on the television, and I sit down in a little chair and he lies back on the bed, real careful not to mess up the crease in his pants, right?

By this time it must have been forty-five minutes since Big Jalisco had gotten up from the table in the dining room, when all of a sudden she opens the door, and I turned around to say Who ever heard of such a thing, what were you doing in there . . . She opens the door and what do you think? She comes out without any clothes on, not a stitch, completely absolutely stark naked. I think she was some kind of sexual maniac . . . That kind of thing, I'd never even *heard* of such things, I mean I was already a big girl, I mean my father had just died, I was going out with Alexis and Mauricio at the same time, I wasn't a virgin or anything anymore, I was a member of the pack, a friend of these crazy friends of mine, right?, but me know about this kind of thing? No way. Forget it. . . . So there she is completely naked, with her breasts out like this, and her little triangle, right?, and her little narrow hips, and her nipples blue. Blue! Because she had put blue eye shadow or something on her nipples—and so then the first thing that came out of my mouth was You're crazy! And I grabbed a cushion off the chair and threw myself on the floor! So there I was, lying on the floor with this cushion over my face going Get dressed! Go get dressed, put your clothes on, right? And the guy says Oh, you're crazy, what are you doing! But he was serious, right? What are you doing? . . . So then I covered myself up, I mean my head, I didn't want to see anything, and I kept saying What's wrong with you, go put your clothes on! But what's gotten into you! . . . Then I don't know, I can't say what happened next because I rolled under the bed, and so I'm not sure whether I was there for ten minutes or a half hour or whether the bed creaked or not, really, because all this was just too much for me. I mean imagine, your lifelong friend, right? . . . I had this deep and terrible revulsion against her and against myself too. Or rather this was something coming from her that repulsed me, that made me completely lose control. I don't know if I was more embarrassed to look at her like that or at him.

So then I realize that I'm all the way under the bed, so I start crawling out. He was still dressed, but not quite as neatly dressed as he *had* been, if you know what I mean. I don't know, maybe his pants were unzipped or his shirt not so well tucked in. And she was lying there still naked, like she'd been making love, with this big sexually satisfied look on her face, and her blue-fingernailed hand patting her practically smiling vagina. . . . So when I sat up, she saw me and scooted over toward me, still dripping semen probably, it was probably drooling down her legs. And I went If you come any closer, I'll kill you, I'll kill you I swear it, I swear I'll kill you if you come one inch closer. And I remember that before I got to the door I fell down. So then, I had lost all my strength, so then on my hands and knees, I don't know, maybe it was the fright or the shock, but anyway on hands and knees I was crawling out and I kept screaming Don't come near me, I'll kill you, I swear I will. Until finally she says Come here, sweetheart, let me explain, come here—baby talking, right?—come back . . . I think she wanted to ask me why I didn't join them, don't you? But by then I'd gotten to the door, and I ran down the steps in one jump and ran out of the house. . . .

I think I was so inexperienced, I *guess* that was it, that I didn't dare just go away. . . . Then I thought What do I say to Alberto. He was my doctor, you remember the phenobarbitols? Where do I tell him she is, what story do I make up? . . . And what about her parents? Because they always came by our house to say hello, and Jalisco had told them we were going out to lunch together. . . . So there I stood outside waiting. I wasn't used to that sort of thing, and I was standing there nervous, tapping my foot like this and walking back and forth swinging my little handbag. . . . So when she came out you know what she did? She says Look how neat! He gave me a hundred pesos! Let's go buy a bikini. Why, with a hundred pesos . . . I mean, really! And then a little later you know what she said? She says We could start a little business. You know how? . . . Listen, I could go out with him and also with Alberto, and if you come and watch, because I think they like that, we'd get money out of them, and we could buy clothes with it and start a boutique. So then, like I told you, I thought to myself, This girl has a screw loose. Or two . . . I thought She's got brain cancer. . . .

We were walking along then, and all of a sudden she says We're going out with him tonight. With this guy, right? Oh, really?, I say. Uh-huh, we're going out with him. Galvanized vaginas! And listen to what an idiot I was. . . . Uh-huh, she went on, I just got off the phone with Alberto, and I told him we'd just run into this guy in the street, and he'd invited all three of us to go out with him, that he was your boyfriend . . . It's that Alberto can't stand him because he knows we used to see each other, right?, so I told him he'd invited all three of us up to his house for dinner, and Alberto said he'd come by for us about six, that we'd go out for dinner and then go to the movies. . . . And I never dared to tell her no. Can you believe that?

Fornicating fork-tailed fiends! So we did. The four of us went out for dinner. About this time I don't know if you remember, but I'd just gotten this false tooth put in, which by the way later came in by itself, although I was already a little old for such a thing by then. Uh-huh, this tooth was really famous. . . . You don't? When I was sixteen I had this tooth pulled because it was from my baby teeth, and when I already had this false eyetooth in, or a temporary one, you know, one day I said to my brother, Listen, do you think I've got an infection? Look at this little white thing. . . . And he says I think so, sis baby, because it's really white. . . . On my gum, right? So I said *Puta madre,* boy, that's all I needed. . . . What happened was that the real eyetooth had started coming in, the one before was my baby tooth, and it was crooked. Gabriel Infante had pulled it for me because I wanted a straight one, I wanted . . . Well, he said to me, I don't think the other one is going to come in, it's crossways in there, and we'd have to do an operation to get it to come in straight. So I said No, that's okay, let's put in a false one. . . . But it started coming in all by itself when it felt there wasn't this other tooth down there! Peppermint douches! So then we were having dinner, right?, and I took out my false tooth because it always fell out when I was eating anyway, I mean the new tooth had pushed it out of place, right?, so it wasn't in very tight and I could've swallowed it. Not to mention that Gabriel was still a little new at certain oral techniques, okay? So I'd take it out, like this, very discreetly, and wrap it up in my napkin. And then I'd talk like this, out of the corner of my mouth. Or in profile, right? So then, but every time I picked up the napkin to wipe my mouth with, *chíngale!*, the tooth would fly out and there I'd have to go to find my eyetooth. . . . You can't imagine the excuses I made so nobody would notice anything! It always happened, thousands of times when I was Mauricio's girlfriend. I had to laugh like this, and he never noticed I had a tooth coming in. Can you imagine! How could I tell anybody I was getting a new tooth growing in when I was nineteen years old! How embarrassing!

So anyway, to make a long story short, we went out to dinner and then we went to the movies. And this man, who's extremely rich and extremely famous, right?, puts his arm around me in the movies, and he says You're going to be my new sweetheart, and your friend is going to be the *puta* I go to bed with. His exact words! He watched the movie a little while longer and then back to the business at hand. He sisses, like this, real real quiet, Jalisco beside him and one seat away Alberto. You'll be my sweet virginal sweetheart, he said. . . . You're going to be my new sweetheart, he kept saying. . . .

For me it was this overwhelming, staggering experience, right? I mean I thought I'd brought all this on or something. The nakedness and the hundred pesos were just the high spots, right?, in an experience disgusting and frightening enough in and of itself. A hundred pesos! I mean I had to tell somebody about this, get it off my chest, unload it, free myself once and for all from those breasts staring at me with their two blue nearsighted eyes, stabbing at me with their sharp points, from that rapacious, sweaty, pornographic . . . Aaagh! So I mentioned it to a close friend of Alberto's. Of course, it took you can't imagine how much nerve for me to say anything, but I needed to tell somebody, really. So I called and made a date with him, we went to a café, and I said this and that and the other happened to me. . . . He was a really good friend of Alberto's and he'd even gone out with Big Jalisco, the older one, right?, once or twice. He was studying medicine. He planned to have a really fancy high-society kind of practice. . . . He shuddered so much he spilled beer over the edge of his glass, and he said to me, Alberto's really in love with her, he's really serious. If we tell him and try to turn him against her, all we do is get our *own* britches dirty, right? Can you imagine what it'll be like? And he always says she's not a one-man woman, but if we go tell him this now, we don't know how he'll react. Let's wait a while and see what happens. . . .

Wisdom or intuitive bullshit? What do you think? Well, what I thought was, that this was Andrés Gutiérrez talking, his closest friend, and he'd been involved in all kinds of adventures with him, in all kinds of projects I mean, he had a long history with

him. . . . What we *can* do, he went on, is cut her, you too, just
cold-shoulder her, so Alberto will see that we don't like her, we
don't approve of them going out together, we don't think she's
good for him. . . . Very sagaciously, like he wanted to be Tran-
quilizer Champion of the World, right?, like the guru of a new
international religion of triteness, and at the same time, how can I
put this?, very emotionally too, with a pang in his heart and a
lump in his throat as my menopausal grandmother used to
say. . . . Speaking into his glass of beer . . . Let's see if we can
make him feel pressured, if he'll give in that way. . . .

Andrés' ideas were so heartfelt, like hearing a vespers sermon,
you know?, that they spread like a balm of tranquillity over the
problem, like Nothing's really happened here, or It was all a
nightmare, a bad dream, don't be upset. And then this thick cur-
tain of silence fell, and nobody ever said another word about this,
nothing, not one single word . . . Or at least those were our
intentions. . . .

*("It is well-known, for example, that a rubdown with turpentine
after the bath immunizes us, in the majority of cases; for the only
thing that excites female vampires is the marine flavor of our blood,
that lingering reminiscence we carry of the time when we were
shark, or crab.")*

8

Natural copulatives

Handsome to the Maximum had gone out with Mercedes, or actually he was going out all the time with her. She was this friend of mine that had been my brother's girlfriend, remember? And she could tell by his face . . . Oh, it was awful. . . . Ask me whether he had a big J for Jerk written all over his face. You have no idea. . . . You want to know what she did? I'll tell you, she was a cutey, she was really smart, if playing your friends for fools was like playing golf, my handicap would be about ninety and she'd play scratch. . . . She . . . Anyway . . . But very pretty . . . My brother walked around in the clouds, from love, right? He was madly in love. And she made up this thing that so they could have a quiet, peaceful, warm, comfortable relationship and no-

105

body would come between them, they ought to get like engaged. Not really engaged, but like go steady, that kind of thing. But they weren't going to tell anybody. Nobody would know, right?, so it would be a secret and both of them would keep it their whole life long. So my brother said Okay. And so he'd go out every morning with Mercedes to take communion, at six o'clock in the morning. Six *A.M.* . . . Every day he'd take her to church, or to the park . . . I can't imagine anywhere else at that hour, it must have been true . . . So he was her boyfriend. . . . My brother was practically Mercedes' fiancé!

By the time we girls would get out of classes, get out of school, right?, we were ready to go crazy. I mean really, those afternoons, oh, we thought we were sooo worldly, and so wild, too, because we'd leave school and go over to the Zero Zone, which was very in then, or someplace like that. One day we went to Chapultepec, for example, with Gabriel and Handsome to the Maximum, to go rowing. . . . Or to Xochimilco, and we'd rent a boat and eat tortillas or something. . . . That's how we let our hair down, right? And Mercedes would go with anybody she wanted to, except I couldn't say anything because we always sneaked off and played hookey and stuff. . . . So I couldn't talk about any of this stuff at home, so there was no way my brother could find out about her, right? But I felt so sorry for him, and I wanted to protect him, I mean naturally I didn't want to see him hurt, so one day I had a heart-to-heart talk with him. Listen, I told him, you're being taken for a ride here, because Mercedes and I go out with all these guys, whoever we feel like, and she makes out with anybody she feels like, what's more. And you're her boyfriend to go to mass with, how wonderful, her church boyfriend, her communion boyfriend, you're her partner for all the communion services, right?, how sweet. . . . So anyway, to make a long story short, my brother called me a liar and told me never to stick my ass in any of his business again, it was all lies. So you can imagine, that was practically the end of our friendship as brother and sister. I'm not kidding, he was pissed off, he was furious. . . . He called me every name in the book. . . .

Well, so Mercedes started going out with Handsome to the Maximum, and me, with Mauricio, who besides singing had piles of money because he owned this light-fixture factory. I was still working in the Palacio de Hierro, right? And I had these two guys that were interested in me—Mauricio and Gabriel Infante—and they both ran around in that same group, right? But I could never make up my mind, so I'd make a date with one for one door and the other for the other door. So then when the time came for me to meet them, I'd say Well, I mean like if, for example, I was getting off work, whichever door I ran out, well, that's the guy I'd go out with, through the door and into whoever's car. Can you believe that? Until I decided on Gabriel and did his thesis with two fingers. . . . He was so wild . . . He graduated and went into practice and everything and he's still wild . . . His hair down to here, and streaked. I think he put lemon juice on it. And he still goes off to rallies and Grand Prix in Europe, and to car shows, and then of course he has his dentist's office. He works in huaraches, can you imagine, or in those canvas shoes like they wear in Acapulco?, espa, espadr, espadrilles?, and while he's waiting for the anesthesia to take effect, he goes out on the patio to get some sun, do a few sit-ups—and with no socks, he never wears socks. He's hilarious. . . .

Saturdays and Sundays, at the beginning, right?, Gabriel always made some excuse, for one reason or another he could never see me. He did this about five Saturdays and five Sundays in a row. . . . But it turned out it was because he was going off to the Jockey Club with all his buddies, all these guys, right? It was that this group had been together for years and years and years and he liked to go have his good time, bust a radiator at the track and do loop-the-loops in some hot rod so his buddies would fawn over him, be scared to death and then go ooh-aah over him, right? That's why he started not showing up on Saturday or Sunday, and about the fourth or fifth time this happened, I finally said Listen I don't think we should see each other on Saturday and Sunday. He immediately got suspicious, right? I mean it was only natural. Upset as hell. And so that was when he started wanting to see me on weekends *too*. But I had already by this time become real close to Mauricio, who for years, including I'm not sure but I think still is, who for years was a judo and karate champion, this real popular singer, and the owner of his own factory. Really a nice guy, happy all the time, very athletic, a singer, you know him. . . . So anyway, I was going out with him and with Gabriel Infante. But then Gabriel went to Europe on a trip, and when he came back all loaded down with trophies and cups and medals and stuff, I was going out with Mauricio once and for all. But when he came back he wanted, how shall I put this?, he wanted to formalize our relationship, right?, get married and all, but I didn't dare say anything to Mauricio, and I didn't dare stop seeing Gabriel without any explanation or anything, so, oh, it was a dreadful situation.

Because, I'll tell you some of the things that happened. . . . I don't know if you remember, but you've been to my house in Pedregal, right? There were two entrances, one through the garage where just as you went in, there was my father's study, right? And another one that went into a little hall that you walked into the entry and the living room, remember? And so at the same time you could go out through my father's study to the garage and on out to the street. I mean that makes sense, right? So anyway . . . Gabriel knew that this Mauricio existed. They were friends, but the kind of friends that first they'd made a bet to see which one went out with me, and then they'd stopped seeing each other for various reasons, so they almost never saw each other, or never. So listen to this, there I was talking to Mauricio one afternoon, in the study, and somebody knocks at the front door and my brother goes to answer it. There's a knock at the door, and my brother starts yelling Gabriel Infante, in person! So I could hear, right? How're things, man, and so on and so forth, first prize, Daytona, the pits. . . . So then he said Come on up to my room, I want to show you some magazines I got . . . Because my brother didn't know what to do with him, imagine . . . So he says Come on, I don't know whether my sister's home or not, we'll send one of the maids in a minute to go see. . . . I mean, of course he knew I was in the study. So I say Ay, Mauricio, run me to the drugstore, will you? And he goes What for? So I say Oh, I've got to buy some pills, run me over there, please, I need these pills. . . . And he says Pills for what? So I say I don't know, I don't know what for, but I need them, let's go, let's go. So we run out of the house. You're nuts, he says, and we run and jump in the car.

He was sort of on his way to a dinner party, so he was dressed to kill. Oh, and besides all this other mess, I was supposed to go to a party too, but not with either one of them, not with Gabriel or Mauricio either one. I was supposed to go with this guy that was kind of interested in me and Dressed Like a Man, this hilarious guy, a lawyer. He'd tell me all the time Oh, you're not stupid, you're very intelligent. So I'd go Why am I so intelligent? A Silk Tapestry, that's how you're intelligent, because look at it this way, we're having a conversation about culture, talking about famous painters, about literature, or classical music, and you, what do you do? Exactly what any intelligent person would do . . . Keep quiet, watch, because brainy people don't have to talk. . . . So I'd always say You're mistaken, I don't talk because I'm ignorant, I don't know anything about those things. How wonderful, Modesty personified! You are the incarnation of Modesty! So I'd say Listen—with a vulgarity or two thrown in, just to be convincing, right?—don't idealize me. Try to understand, I am what I am. . . .

So anyway, to make a long story short, there's Mauricio driving me to the drugstore supposedly to buy these pills. We get to the Insurgentes Pharmacy or whatever, and he gets out and says What's the name of the pills? I'll get them. . . . So I say Oh, any pills, any pills at all. Whatever you think. Biting my nails, right? I was chewing my fingernails to the quick. . . . So he says Sweetheart, what do you mean *any* pills? What are you sick with? So I say Well buy me some cherry coughdrops. . . . And at that instant I see Gabriel Infante go by down Insurgentes with his pipes wide open and sounding like a tank. . . . He'd turned into a real hot-rodder.

Oh, I forgot, on the way I'd said to Mauricio, And then drive me over to the Jalisco Sisters' and let me off there. So that's what we were going to do, but when I saw Gabriel go by, when I saw him driving down Insurgentes, I figured there was no point in that anymore, so I said Don't take me to the Jaliscos'. . . . Why not? So then I said Well I'll tell you, I changed my mind, I don't want to go there anymore because, um, I remembered something, I just remembered I've got to take them something. From home. Maybe you could just take me back home. . . . Sperm sandwiches! When we got home what was my surprise, I mean my terror, a cold sweating terror, to see . . . I'd gotten the cars confused, and it wasn't Gabriel that had driven by down Insurgentes. Gabriel was still at my house, there was his chrome-plated gargoyle-mufflered car. . . . His big hulk of a hot rod was sitting right in front of my house!

Ay, I say to Mauricio, don't come in, why put yourself out, let's just sit here and talk for a while, we'll sit here and talk for a while and then you can go on, right? And he says Oh, right, I've got to go, I don't want to be late for this dinner party. . . . No, don't worry, I've got a million things to do myself. So then he says Whose hot rod is *that?* Ever since we left your house it's been sitting there, but it wasn't there when I came. . . . Who knows, who knows whose car it is. . . . So then thank God, so then he says Well, I gotta go. . . . And he was just leaving when he goes like this, to give me a little hug, a little good-bye hug, right?, and a button pops off his dinner jacket. . . . I say I'll sew it on for you, don't get out, I'll run get a needle and thread, I'll sew it on right here, hold on a second. . . . But then I think If these two see each other, if these two catch me, if Mauricio realizes about Gabriel, then I'm screwed. . . . I mean I was really afraid some-body was going to get killed, you know?, not *me*, not that they were going to shoot me or anything, of course not, but that they might shoot each other. A crime of passion! A crime of jealousy and passion! Imagine, and all because of Miss Idiot here. . . .

So anyway, let me see, where was I? Oh, yeah, I got out of the car, and all of a sudden I say No, on second thought I guess you better come in, I'll sew it on for you inside. That's all I could do at this point. Gabriel might come out any second. And when I went inside, picture this scene—in the study, Little Jalisco with her feet, those skinny legs, right?, propped up on a table and her arms crossed like this. My brother was toying with a pencil on the desk, playing the idiot, and Gabriel with a pain in his heart . . . No, I mean a real pain in his heart. White, white, white—white as a ghost and his lips turquoise blue, I swear this is true, stretched out in a chair, waiting for me to come back because he'd smelled a rat somewhere. . . . And to top it all off my brother, Mister Sister of Mercy, right?, the asshole, had told him, had exposed me, had spilled the beans. . . . Well, okay, I'll tell you, man, the honest truth is that my sister's here. She left with Mauricio though, and who knows where they went. He told the truth because he'd never learned how to lie. So you can imagine the scene . . . When I came back, well . . . And every day I'd sworn I was going to stop seeing Mauricio, too. But I never did, right?

So anyway, I go in and what do you think happens? I go to get the needle and thread, and my brother is going like this, pss, pss, from the chair, moving his lips, trying to say every gross thing he could think of without making any sound, like this, like Marcel Marceau, right?, but just moving his lips. Every gross thing he could think of, everything. . . . Little Jalisco spun around and looked at me, and she was just about ready to punch me in the nose . . . Because the one everybody liked was Gabriel. Everybody *loved* Gabriel. So I came back with the needle and thread, right?, and I sat down between the two of them, between Gabriel and Mauricio. . . . They were talking about the car. Me in the middle. And I say to Gabriel, Hey. What did you do last Saturday? Because I never saw him on Saturday or Sunday if you remember. Nothing, I went out with the guys. Oh? Where? To a drag race and then to have a drink. Wow, how nice. Meet any pretty girls? Because he was already pissed off at me, right? Because I told him to find a girl to go out with on weekends and have a good time, right? So I said Didn't you find anybody? Un-

less he was too big a jerk to bear anyway, Mauricio had to realize
that I couldn't be going out with a guy I'd say something like that
to, right? So then I turn and say to Mauricio, Hey, Mauricio.
What ever happened with those perfume bottling plants you were
going to start? I mean stuff we'd discussed a million years ago and
for one reason or another never talked about again. So I was
throwing up this smokescreen, right?

So then Mauricio says Oh, I've gotta go, it's late. Okay, I say.
But then Gabriel Infante stands up too, with his bloodshot eyes
blazing. I mean, and Mauricio was a monster, this tall . . . He
stands up and he says Listen, man, uh . . . He says You name
the place where we can talk, you know, because I really want to
have a word with you. And I say Oh, um, what about? . . . He
says I need three hundred light fixtures for this hotel I'm going to
put in. Because Mauricio had this light fixture factory. So he says
I'm going to need about three hundred light fixtures, three hundred and ninety light fixtures I think it is, and I'd like to talk to
you. . . . So then Mauricio grabs his, um, he reaches for his, uh,
and he hands Gabriel a business card. I'll call you, man. Any-
time, I'll give you a good price, and so on and so forth. Okay.
Ciao. Ciao. . . . I said I'll be right there to let you out. And I
thought When I come back I'll tell Gabriel some story, I'll try to
smooth this over. . . . But Gabriel stands up again, and he says
I've got to get going too. . . . They could smell that rat, okay,
they both knew me. So I go Wait a minute, don't go just yet,
holding onto Gabriel, and 'Bye Mauricio, see you later, and my
brother and Little Jalisco are trying to push him out the
door. . . .

When they were gone I say to Gabriel Well, you caught me,
you found me out, you lifted your leg and sprayed your territory,
right?, so now, tell me, what are you going to do? . . . I think we
have to call it off, he starts. What we're going to do, I said, very
sure of myself, right?, almost authoritarian, is start stopping
seeing each other, I mean if that's what you want, once and for
all, or on the other hand, you can give me a chance to drop this
guy because I don't know how to do it, honestly, how to drop him

or anything else. How am I going to just say Adios from one day
to the next, That's it, so long, to hell with you. No, no, no, I can't
do it. . . . So then Gabriel is looking at me, and he says Oh, no,
sweetheart, I think this has to end once and for all, I mean this is
a problem, I really don't know what to do with you, you say one
thing and do another, so I think we better just break up. . . . So I
say Okay, fine, if you think that's best, who knows but . . . Oh,
he says before he leaves, I'll call you tomorrow, even if there's
nothing between us anymore, when we've both cooled down a
little . . . Okay, okay . . . Because I was dying for him to just
go, right? I mean The Monk was coming for Dressed Like a Man
and me any minute. And that would make three, which would
definitely have been the Mess to End All Messes. But then he
says No, I'll tell you, let's just get it over with now. Let's go
somewhere so we can talk. . . . And I say No, I can't, I really
can't. I'm supposed to go out to dinner with my parents. What are
you talking about, he says. You never went out to dinner with
your parents in your life. Yeah I know, but tonight we're going
out because they never ask me to do anything, and tonight they
asked me to go with them, so there's no way I'm going to tell them
I can't. So that's your final word—you're going to go out with
them? Yes I am, this time I'm going out with my parents. . . . So
Gabriel huffed out. Alone at last! Right?

I was throwing myself together and Tito Caruso calls. Listen,
darling, please, I'm going to ask you a big favor, please, I beg
you, don't treat Gabriel this way, you have no idea what it's done
to him, and so on and so forth. I mean back then we were such
silly *kids*. I mean this would never happen now, right? Of course
not, we were just kids and you know, at that age love breaks your
heart, you're always dizzy or fainting, or you feel like all the
oxygen in the world has been used up, and you can't breathe and
stuff like that, right? Ghastly. So Tito Caruso calls me. Don't do
these things, he's gone off the deep end, and you know he's not
supposed to drink, honestly, you don't know what he's like now,
you have no idea. . . . He was really upset with me, but my
glands, so to speak, were in no condition to listen to reason. I

know he's hard to understand, he says to me, but he's loaded himself up with cocaine and shut himself up in his bedroom, and he won't come out, and he's crying, it's not right, baby, it's not fair. It looked to me like he was trying to make *me* cry too. I felt miserable. Surprisingly enough he'd gotten to me. Oh, it was true, Gabriel had begged me to see him that night, begged me, and I'd told him I couldn't, I just couldn't. So I was really depressed for a while and I gave myself a lecture. I said I was the most perverse, contrary, selfish woman in all of Pedregal de San Antonio. . . .

Nevertheless . . . nevertheless, we went out with The Monk, and we went to this place called, I don't remember, one of those places with one hundred percent gays, oh, I know, the Safari, that was starting to get both kinds of homosexuals, and that that night it was especially oppressive, you know? We went in and we were bored in about two seconds. Bored out of our minds. The Monk, Dressed Like a Man, and me. Where had we ever gotten the idea we'd have fun there? The Monk was personal secretary to some minister and he was—well, before, he had studied in a cemetery, I mean a seminary, and he still sort of had that convent look, you know. Or conventional, anyway . . . So to make a long story short, by the second drink we said Let's have our own party, we're bored, why don't we go have a party with some different people, try to have some fun. The Monk kept saying It's horrible, I feel dirty. He'd look at me and whisper I feel filthy, I feel miserable, sweet Cheesecake . . . Even my words are indecent! All I feel for you are carnal emotions and it makes me shudder with impurity. . . .

That killed me!

So we went to The Two Turtles. We walk in, and the first person I catch sight of is Tito Caruso. When I see him, the second I see him, I run over to him and I say Oh Tito, I went to Gabriel's house and he wouldn't open the door. I've been all over Zona Rosa looking for him, through all the bars in the Zona trying to find him, where'd you leave him? At the last minute I told my parents some story so I could see Gabriel. And I've been everywhere, I say. I want him, Tito, I want to keep him. So he says

Really, baby? Yes, really, ask *her*. But Dressed Like a Man was nowhere to be seen. She'd popped into the bathroom to rub her cream or whatever in, because she was dying from the messes I kept getting into. . . . I can't take much more of this, she said, and she was crying What's going to come of this? What's going to happen? . . .

So Tito said good-bye to his little group, and he left and we could breathe a little easier once he was gone. But great flaming hellfire, what do you suppose he did? . . . Right. He went to get Gabriel, he told him I was there waiting for him, in The Two Turtles, and that I'd been all over looking for him, and so on and so forth. So then Gabriel comes in looking like death. As soon as I see him, right?, I pick up all my things, I grab my fur coat and my purse . . . This was when Dressed Like a Man and I walked around in fur coats, our mothers' of course. So we grab our mink coats and try to make a run for it. . . . But as we were trying to slip out, Gabriel says to me, he grabs my hand and he very slowly pronounces the word no. No, he says, wait, I'll drive you. So then The Monk, who didn't have a clue, and who besides that was a little leery of us, to put it mildly, since that episode with the maître d' and the restaurant, remember?, The Monk grabs me by the other hand, and he says No, if she came with me, I'll take her home. . . . Gabriel looked like a zombie, he was barely registering, you know?, very very slow, and his face . . . Well . . . He opened his mouth, like to stop us, he opened his mouth and he stared a second at the ceiling, he stared at me and then he stared at The Monk and then he closed it. He opened his mouth like this, and then he closed it. Like an asthmatic goldfish, right? So I go No, no, no, no, no, I'm not going with either one of you. But The Monk says to me very dignified, Please, Windmill Mine, I'll take you. . . . So then one of them starts pulling me from one side and the other one from the other side. Pulling me from both sides, Gabriel just clutching and The Monk pulling, and me not knowing what in the world to do, trying to hold onto my mother's mink with my chin. Until I'd had it. I let out a howl, I screamed Enough!, and both of them all of a sudden turn me loose and I walk out by myself. So I left in a fury. They turned me loose, and my girlfriend and I walk out, and The Monk runs out and catches up with us. He was dying to ask What's with this guy, huh, girls? But all he said was If you want me to, I'll take you both home. Uh-huh, The Monk took us home. . . . The Monk won the right to drive us . . . scared out of his wits. . . .

But what you don't know is that when we got to my house, he says Listen, before I came I was talking about you. And I go You don't say. Uh-huh, he says, with somebody that likes you so much, he admires you. . . . You have no idea what wonderful things this person said about you. This person says you're an incredible person, well, that you're so wonderful. That you're so much fun, so neat, and so on and so forth. Who said all this? I don't remember, I mean I don't recall the name. This young man who's champion of something or other, and sings, and knows judo, really nice, tall, good-looking, well-dressed. So I say Where did you see this guy? And he goes In the Zero Zone. I went by there before I came. I was a little early so I went by for a Coke, some little something, to see the guys, and I ran into this person. And when I said I was on my way to your place to go to a party, he said he knew you pretty well. . . . Gonococcal crocodiles! You get the picture, right?

By the time I got inside I was crying my eyes out, torrents of water running down my face and neck and into my ears. Oh, crying my heart out. . . . I called the Jalisco Sisters. What am I going to do? Oh, what? . . . At seven o'clock in the morning I called Mauricio. Seven A.M.! . . . What's wrong! Mauricio, I've got to talk to you. I thought he was going to make a big scene. And I had no idea what story I was going to make up to get myself out of this one. . . . I said What happened yesterday, how did it go? He yawns and says Why? What are you so worried about? Nothing, nothing at all. What did you do yesterday? So then I realized that none of it was true, he didn't know anything, that is to say The Monk had told me a lie. So before I'd hung up practically, I called The Monk. Tell me the truth! Good morning, Cheesecake, he says to me. He was just finishing breakfast and was about to go off to the secretariat or ministry or officialhood or whatever. Don't you remember what you told me last night? Uh-huh. So tell me, I say, tell me the truth—did you run into Mauricio or didn't you? But why do you worry so much about little things? . . . Yes or no! So he says again, Why do you worry so much? You just tell me if you really met him or not! No, pussycat, I didn't see him. What happened was, that somebody told me you were going out with him, and I wanted to find out whether it was true, so I played a little trick on you. . . .

Do you think that's one of the seven deadly sins?

("Under these conditions, I sincerely believe that the best thing to do is swallow a dynamite pill and very calmly light a cigarette.")

9

Two shows today, your favorite leading man

One day it was Dressed Like a Man's saint's day, or her birthday, I don't remember, something like that, right? And Mauricio called her to wish her happy whatever. Little Bandit—he called her that—Little Bandit, he says, what are you girls doing tonight? So she says Nothing, nothing, we don't have any special plans. Good, he says, because I'm taking you to the theater. He was singing in the Blanquita. I'm not sure, she says, and she said she'd talk to me to see if I could go. . . . So Mauricio himself calls me a few minutes later, and he goes Listen, can you come? Let's take Dressed Like a Man out for a celebration, okay? So I said Okay, sure, great idea. But I was Gabriel Infante's steady girlfriend then, I was still going out with Gabriel Infante.

So anyway, that was back when everybody was wearing these

tall tall hairdos, right?, beehives they were called, with black, pitch black hair, dyed black I mean. And I wore this makeup that made me look like a white geisha, you know?, with my face white and my eyes black and these big black eyelashes and black eyeliner and everything. Dressed Like a Man too, I'm telling you, the Dragon Lady had nothing on us. My eyes like this, right?, with the makeup to a point way out here, and my hair piled up to here. . . . But I was on kind of a short leash at home. Not my girlfriend, just me. My mother had me on such a short leash that I told her we were going to the theater with Dressed Like a Man's parents. Then I also had to make up this story to tell Gabriel Infante, to explain why I couldn't see him that night—I was busy working on his thesis and I had a lot of other stuff to do besides, so I couldn't see him, okay?

Dressed Like a Man came by to pick me up in a taxi. My mother, my father, my brother and I were sitting there watching TV. Well, Mom, I'm leaving, I say. So Dressed Like a Man comes in for me, *trembling*, because she really had no courage for this sort of thing at all, right? So she comes in. Okay, we're outside waiting for you, she says. And my mother pipes up Who did you come with, dear? With my parents, señora. Oh Mother, you knew we were going out with her parents. . . . So then my brother butts in Listen, did David come? Uh-huh, I tell him, David's out there too, David's going with us. He was his friend, right? My girlfriend's brother . . . So I say Why don't you come out and say hello? Dressed Like a Man turns white as a sheet because she's all by herself and in a taxi to boot, right? Why don't you go say hello?, I say, and my brother says No, no, but tell him we'll get together, ask him when we can see each other. My girlfriend was practically fainting, her knees were going clackety-clackety-clackety, like this. . . . Can you imagine what would have happened if my brother had come outside to say hello to David? She was ready to die. I wanted to make it believable, though, right? They knew I was going out with her parents, so I could come home whenever I got there. . . .

Well, let's go then. So we go to the theater, not a care in the world. Oh, don't ever do that to me again, she says, just think what would've happened. My girlfriend hadn't gotten over the scare yet. . . . So we went off to the Blanquita Theater, which for us was, well, forget it, right? We were almost there, and what happens but we have the worst lousy luck in the world. I turn around in the cab, we hadn't gotten there yet, and what to my surprise do I discover but a car right behind ours with Gabriel Infante and his very best friend, the wildest, meanest guy in the world, one of those guys that just loves a fight, you know? The two of them were always at daggers even with each other. They were really good friends, but all day long they were picking at each other and starting fights, and there they were right behind us. . . . For example, Gabriel Infante would say to this friend of his, Your hair's getting a little long there, isn't it? Because the guy's hair was falling out. They did all these things to each other, and there they were, right on our tail, waiting to turn the corner and stop in front of the Blanquita Theater. I can't tell you what I was going through. I said to Dressed Like a Man, What do we do? I don't know, we can go home if you want to. No, I said, no way, we'll try to hide so they don't see us. . . . They were going to the theater too. I mean he never went anywhere in his life, his whole life! . . . So we got out at the theater. We jumped out of the taxi as fast as we could. They still had to park, right? Mauricio told us he'd leave the tickets at the box office in my name, so we picked them up and went in, went straight to our seats, sat down, and then we tried to sort of keep our heads down like this. Tried to make ourselves invisible.

We were in the third row. So there we were, and all of a sudden Dressed Like a Man says to me, Ay . . . Ay, she says, don't look, don't look, but right behind us, *directly* behind us, three rows back, Gabriel and his friend are sitting. Gabriel Infante and Lindolf. Right there, she says, there they are right there. By now those two had clouded my night over pretty thoroughly, as you can imagine. . . . I didn't know whether to run or sit still. And Dressed Like a Man watching the empty stage with me, so all they could see was the back of our heads, although with those beehives that was enough to recognize us, right?

So out comes Mauricio, out comes Mauricio, the idiot, and he starts looking for us, right? And when he spots us, he says I'd like to dedicate my first number to a very special person. . . . I want to dedicate my very first song to her, and he picks up the microphone, and he says my name. And I say Oh, my mascara's running, what do I do . . . Because I started crying, I swear to God. And she said No, it's not running yet, don't worry, don't worry. Panicky, right?, because she was always the one with me when I got into these messes. I mean, imagine, all these things always happened to me when she was with me.

Back then there was this song, In love with you, da da da, Laura, and the singer would put in all these different names. Shaven pussies! So Mauricio comes out on the stage, and he starts singing In love with you, crazy for you, and then he sings my name. And all the names, every one of the names, all of these names that are supposed to be different—he changes them to my name. Instead of changing them all around? So at one of them, instead of my first name he says my *last* name. Try to picture it. By now I was hunched down in the seat, squashed into the seat, trying to turn myself into a piece of maroon velvet upholstery, right? I was trying to liquefy and drip onto the floor, anything to make this nightmare end. I turned around to look at Gabriel Infante, and Gabriel's face was writhing in hatred, his teeth were practically grinding into his brain. I mean I can't tell you . . . His face was all . . . I can't even describe it. What do we *do?* In a second, when the lights go out, Dressed Like a Man says to me, we'll make a run for it and ask where Mauricio's dressing room is and hide there. . . .

And the song is going on and on and on, right?, and then this kid starts running up and down the aisles paging me. Screaming my name, right? And I'm like this. I say Don't turn around, for God's sake don't turn around. So we didn't answer the page. We were sitting there absolutely expressionless, dead, dead serious, like this, very quiet and still and discreet, and very worried to say the least. And this lady sitting in front of us turns around and says Excuse me, aren't you the señoritas they're paging? And we say Uh-huh. Well, they've been paging you now for quite a while. Oh, we didn't hear, thank you. . . . In the Blanquita Theater, for heaven's sake . . . Mauricio had been standing right there in front of us, singing to us, pointing at us, so everybody knew who we were, and I felt about this big, I'm not kidding. . . . And then this lady says Well they're paging you. And then this screaming kid says practically at the top of his lungs that Señor Mauricio asks us to be sure not to leave our seats until the lights come on. When I heard that I wanted to die. I remember every excruciating second. . . . There was another act then. They turn on this bright bright spotlight. It was a tightrope act, where they always turn on the spotlight and the drums go brrrrr, right?, so they had this bright white spotlight on. And the usher yelling, so we had to stand up to get the message while the drumroll was going on. The usher was practically screaming our names, so we had to get up. So then I finally said Screw it, and I walked out while everybody else was still in their seats, when everybody could watch us leave. We walked out under those conditions, can you imagine?

As soon as Mauricio spotted us, he said Wait for me in the car, right over there, I'll be right there, it won't take me a second, I'll be right there, wait for me. And I swear to you that all the time I was going out with Mauricio, I never knew he smoked marijuana, I never noticed that about him. My father told me, okay? Certain reports had come into the district attorney's office, things like that, you know?, and it's true that Handsome to the Maximum, Napoleon, Tito, Andrés, all of them smoked, but I never believed it, okay? Word of honor. But you couldn't understand a word he was saying, we didn't understand a thing. . . . When he came back we didn't know what he was talking about, no idea. So then all of a sudden he says Why don't we go with him somewhere, some building, I don't know. . . . We waited in the car, and he got out for about ten minutes. I don't know who he went in to see. . . . Meanwhile, we played Sherlock Holmes, to see what we could discover, to see if we could find something. And we found this stuff like tobacco, some cigarettes, and we grabbed three of them. Dressed Like a Man and I both were scared to death, she starts scratching so hard I thought she was going to scrape all the skin off her shins. Stop scratching like that, I said, control your-

self. . . . I mean, all you could think about was the police, right?
So then . . . Lunch-hungry cunts! We were terrified. . . .

So then Dressed Like a Man, who's so impressionable, right?,
so emotional, when Mauricio came back she said Ay, Mauricio,
I'm so upset with you. . . . And Mauricio says Why, Little Bandit, what's wrong? So she says You didn't use to be this way,
Mauricio, what's happened to you, tell me. . . . And Mauricio,
just imagine how much attention he paid to that. He was on such
a high, he was flying so so high, and Dressed Like a Man wanting
to discuss her philosophy of life, right? . . . He was super
messed up, because he was always drinking, one after another,
always drinking and I think using drugs too, a real drug addict,
because his eyes would sort of stop focusing, right?, his eyes
would go like this. . . . So then he starts talking about all kinds
of stuff, unconnected, right?, completely inco, . . . What is it?
Incoherent, right. And nothing made any sense. He'd be talking
about one thing one minute, and then the next minute he'd be on
something else, I mean terrible, right? And Dressed Like a Man,
can you picture this?, she starts saying Ay, Maruicio, what is it,
what's happened to you, you were so strong, you were our pillar of
strength, you were our best friend, what's happened to your life,
why are you doing this? . . . To make a long story short, we were
suffering for him all the way to El Señorial, really deeply suffering, because I kid you not, you can't imagine how fucked up this
guy's head was. . . . But we were going to see this world famous,
universally famous show, from the Tropicana? That thing with
Fidel Castro had just happened, you know?, something to do with
Fidel, and all the shows on their way to Miami were coming
through here first. . . . There was practically an invasion of
Cubans. . . . So anyway, one of the shows came from the Tropicana with these practically naked women that you wouldn't, no,
I'm not kidding, you wouldn't have believed it, okay? All of them
tall and pretty, about six feet tall, with little itty-bitty tiny bikinis.
Like this . . . But they were incredible dancers, and they were
all really really beautiful. So the show was this supersuccessful
superproduction, no?, and El Señorial was the in place then. The

height of fashion, as they say. With good reason though, don't get me wrong. Oh, I forgot, we went to get some gasoline, and Mauricio, the guys at the service station were going crazy because very very very seriously, with the straightest face you've ever seen, Mauricio started talking about all this very strange stuff. He said things you never heard before, you know what I mean?

So we finally get to El Señorial, and who do we see but Handsome to the Maximum, Napoleon, Andrés, and this whole big mob of rowdies. Having fun, though, I must admit. So but Mauricio didn't want us to sit with them because he was jealous, very serious, very very strange, and completely out of it, so we sat by ourselves at another table, all the way across the room, like to over there, right? We were sitting there when all of a sudden Mauricio says Let's go dance, I think I'll dance with both of you, yep, first with one and then with both, I don't know, I promise I'll be a gentleman, a perfect gentleman, no, a little more of the Little Bandit, or is it the other way around?, or a little more wine or another little drink, or another drunk, another drunk!, another drunk? Well then, anybody'll do, I better dance a while with a no, listen, I'm telling you, don't let some guy ask you, and so on and so forth, right? . . . Okay, okay, I kept saying. So we were dancing. He and I. I don't need to tell you he could barely stand up, right? It was dreadful, dreadful, because after having seen him as the good, decent guy, an incredible person, wonderful, really, perfectly perfectly normal and all, suddenly he was like this, in this terrible terrible shape. We couldn't understand a word of what he was saying. Nothing. Zip.

I tried to find Dressed Like a Man in the darkness, but she had vanished, no, she was bent over the table, and then she sat up. I couldn't figure out what in the world was going on, whether she was crying or throwing up or what. So then I saw her do it again, and I said to myself I wonder what's happening, so I stopped dancing. Mauricio didn't notice a thing, he was still dancing in these circles around me. Dressed Like a Man's not there, I said. So he finally stopped dancing and we ran over, we left the dance floor and went to look. When we got there this very sad-looking man, real elegantly dressed, was lying on the floor, so we helped

him get up and straighten his clothes, brush himself off a little.
He kept saying You are divine, you are incredible, señorita. The
man hadn't taken his eyes off Dressed Like a Man since we got
there. So then Mauricio says to her, Well if you want to, you can
dance with *him*. He had on a dinner jacket and everything, right?
He's a gentleman, Mauricio was saying, he won't get you drunk
like that bunch of drunks over there, he said, pointing woozily at
Napoleon and his gang of Krazy Kocks. . . .

When we'd gotten up to dance, this man in the dinner jacket,
what had happened was that he had lifted his glass like this, like
he was toasting Dressed Like a Man and everything, right? So
when he saw that she was sitting there all alone now, he stood up
to ask her to dance. He didn't pay any attention to where our
table was, I mean he had to go up a step, so he wasn't watching
where he was going?, and when he tried to go over to Dressed
Like a Man, he tripped on the step and fell. And then lying there,
lying there on his back, he said Let's dance, beautiful. Just like
that, falling-down drunk, right?, and horizontal as a crocodile.
Want to dance, beautiful? He couldn't move. And he says You
are one great piece, señorita, he says. So at that Dressed Like a
Man starts laughing, and so that's why we saw her bending over
the table and straightening up again, like one of those things in
the back window of a car, right?, down and up again, dying
laughing. So now this man is swaying back and forth over the
table, saying If I hadn't met you, I'd have had to go back to
Aguascalientes, all the way back to Aguascalientes without doing
anything worth the time I've spent on this trip. Why? What do
you plan to do with *her?* I asked him. He took a slug out of
Mauricio's glassful of vodka, which he thought made everything
all right, and he even offered her an olive. If I hadn't met you,
the guy goes on, and you're so wonderful. . . . We were drinking
like fish.

So about then Napoleon and Andrés come over and sit down
with us, to the great chagrin of Mauricio, who takes Dressed Like
a Man off to dance. They'd just stolen a bus, I mean stolen a
busful of purses, and they'd gotten about fifty-seven hundred
pesos out of it, so they were out celebrating their exploits, as they

said. . . . Not that they needed money, okay?, because they really didn't. I imagine what it was was, that they needed a little high-voltage excitement, something a little dangerous. Proving something to themselves, right? I guess we all need that once in a while, don't you? So they boarded one of those Insurgentes-Bellas Artes buses at different stops. First Tito and Napoleon, then Handsome to the Maximum, and then a few blocks later Andrés and Alberto, in that order. It was this warm, quiet night and the bus was headed toward Ciudad Universitaria. It wasn't much later than quitting time for all the people working in offices and all, but it was already almost dark. What's that word? Just at something. Just at dusk. That's right, isn't it? Not *dust* . . . Just a little while ago, Napoleon was saying. See, it's the fifteenth. Payday, says Andrés. And health and good wishes for the birthday girl, says the guy in the dinner jacket, on his best behavior, trying to show his good manners, right? Whose birthday is it? Well, so when Dressed Like a Man came back to the table they practically knocked over her beehive. . . .

So I think it was a thirst for adventure, right?, the need for a change of pace, a little action, the need to even surprise themselves. . . . So anyway, a couple of them stood by the back door, you know, the exit, so when somebody pulled the cord and tried to squeeze out—Excuse me, excuse me, just let me, . . . right?—they'd barely stand aside, they'd all sort of crowd in so the person wouldn't feel the talented fingers at work—either from the left side so the other guy could exercise his dainty fingers on the right or vice versa, whichever, those silken fingers that removed their wallets, keys, calendars, whatever they could. I swear they could take off your panties without touching your garter belt. I kid you not. They were incredible. . . . But I don't think they did the thing with the buses very often . . . but when they did it, they did it right. . . . Generally, they had other kinds of business, we didn't know it back then, but things like loaded dice, marked cards, drugs and a little pimping. Napoleon said that one day he grabbed this lady's purse. Not on a dare or anything. He hadn't planned to do it, it just came over him, he said. He said she was a beauty, real sexy, she even smelled rich, and she was walking along swinging her hips like her mother was a snake. A snake and nine lizards. He said the smell inspired him, and the color of her dress . . . a smell like a bedroom with fresh sheets. . . . So he grabbed her purse. She had seventy pesos and a green card.

I've never been on a bus. Do you know that? Not once in my life, although Mercedes used to sit in the warm seats when she was twelve years old, when the boys from high school got up? When they got off with all their bookbags and packs and stuff, she'd sit down in the warm spot they left, and she said it was like being fondled. . . . Of course, that was when we were young, no? So anyway, the bus was full, jam-packed. Handsome to the Maximum was carrying a raincoat over his arm, and Tito would pass him the wallets and wrinkled bills. When Little Jalisco married Napoleon, she'd see him off every day by saying Hope you find lots of wallets. She'd say that to Napoleon, can you imagine? So Handsome to the Maximum would keep all the sweaty smelly booty—which they didn't need anyway—or not much, because sometimes they'd get into the worst binds over money, thirty lousy pesos, right? So all of a sudden this man in the back of the bus stuck his head out from behind his *Ultimas Noticias*, or whatever it was, and he caught them at it. Red-handed, right? They're stealing your wallet! Or some other saying that said the same thing, right? Everybody jumped and started looking around, so Tito pulled the cord and jumped out. Alberto was right behind him. They hadn't gotten to El Señorial yet. They wouldn't come in till later. . . . Right at the door, then, the guy this other man had warned grabbed for his wallet like he was clutching his heart, right?, and they said he wanted to jump off the bus after Tito and Alberto—the quote, pickpockets, unquote, right?—but even the bus driver tried to talk him out of it. So then he got a little scared and stayed on. Afraid to get off, right?, I mean he realized what might happen. So then the guy that had yelled stuck his head back into his newspaper. He yells Sir, they're picking your pocket, and he shocks the pants off them, it was so unexpected. Although Andrés says he's never had any fear of anything, he's never been afraid of anything in his life, fear's for virgins and midgets. . . . So then everybody said I'll drink to that. . . .

Now let me see, who introduced me to Napoleon? Gabriel. Gabriel introduced me to him, because he was his very very very closest friend, right? So then one day I was walking down the street with my uncle and my uncle, you know, he's the one I was telling you has always had these big political connections and all kinds of ties to Mafia types and gangsters and so on, right? So anyway, one day we were walking along Insurgentes, and we went by this jewelry store that Lindolf, the Apostle of Ferocity, had just put in. He'd just opened this jewelry store, right after he got out of jail. We were standing there talking when Napoleon walked by and my uncle saw him and walked over because he had to talk to him. . . . When we got in the car he says to me, So you know Napoleon Clotas? Where from? I don't know, I just know him, somebody introduced us to each other, a long time ago. . . . But how is it possible that you know him, how can you speak to him, what's your relationship with that man? Because I was pretty young, right? But anyway, I told him I'd met him at the café, I'd seen him with Tito Caruso and Gabriel Infante. And I went on to say he was always real nice with me, he liked me a lot. . . . Napoleon knew my uncle, they were like this with each other, close friends, right? So we went over and talked to him. My uncle was talking to him about something or other he had to talk to him about. . . . And later Napoleon and I became closer and closer. He was a real, real, I don't know . . . I mean, I never saw why people said he was such a bastard. I never saw that side of the guy, you know what I mean? I mean, because he was always more than a perfect gentleman . . . and single. . . .

But of course, he married Little Jalisco one day out of the blue. . . . They were the daughters of this big industrial magnet or whatever you call it, this guy that made millions selling old things, like used things I mean, like tires and scrap metal and things like that. He sold this stuff and made a fortune. But right away Little Jalisco started not getting along so well with Napoleon, because she was sterile and he wanted to have kids. And as though that weren't enough, she was way too jealous for him, I don't know, but anyway, they wound up pretty soon living together but each going his own way if you know what I mean. Free spirits. So he came in one day and Little Jalisco says Listen, I can buy these gorgeous emeralds. Napoleon told her not to buy them, that she wasn't old enough to wear a big matched set of emeralds, although he was making who knows how much money in this factory he'd just opened that made colonial furniture, right? But she kept on and kept on, she begged and pleaded with him to buy them for her, the necklace and earrings, and everything. So one day Napoleon comes home, and she says Oh darling, get dressed because we're giving a dinner party and it's black tie. And when he came downstairs . . . I mean, she sent a maid to tell him to come down because everything was ready, and he thought there'd be a houseful of people, right? This ritzy party . . . but when he came downstairs there she was all by herself, she'd had the dining room table set, and it was about twenty feet long, with candelabras and everything, and there was this dinner for two. And there she was with her necklace and earrings and rings and all these incredible emeralds, because she'd just gone out and bought them herself. She literally sparkled. So he got furious, of course. And since he wasn't ever going to be able to control her, in any aspect, right?, but especially with regard to money, he says Well, we'll just spend till the money runs out then. . . .

The Jalisco Sisters' parents died of cancer, did you know that? Two months apart. So they inherited like twenty million pesos, half and half, in checking accounts. So Napoleon started renting airplanes, and taking all his friends to like Africa and the Costa Azul, Las Vegas, Holland, and he paid their hotel and everything. He paid for everything. That was when they'd close cabarets. They'd go in and they'd close the place for them. One long private party . . . Until the money ran out, because what it was was, that he didn't want to get a divorce because then he'd have to give part of it to her, right? So they both started buying anything their hearts desired. Because it was a joint account, it was in both of their names, and they were married so it was community property. But of course, Napoleon spent the most. So then imagine a man like that stealing purses on buses. Inconceivable, right? But he used to go on those nocturnal jaunts too.

But I'm sorry, I was on the bus, wasn't I? On the man reading the newspaper, right? You know how I picture him? Sitting back at the back of the bus, like collapsed, and fat and sweaty, his forehead all shiny, two buttons popped off his shirt from where his belly bulges out all over the place, sort of breathing heavy over the girls in bikinis in the late edition of the *Extra*, right? So anyway, the bus starts emptying out little by little. At each stop all these people get off. Andrés says he was still trolling for a couple of purses more. So then when hardly anybody was still on the bus, the man with the newspaper felt two little pricks, one on each side, and Handsome to the Maximum says to him, This is our stop, or do you want to hold *this* for me? And he punches him with the point of a key, because they didn't carry knives, no way. They never used switchblades or anything like that. So the guy stands up and they pull the cord for the bell, Napoleon and Andrés are practically carrying him off the bus, and Handsome to the Maximum is behind them, protecting their rear, right? So they swing off the bus, which had slowed down, but they still had to run a few steps to keep their balance.

So then, they said, Handsome to the Maximum kicked him in the balls, and Napoleon pulled out a handful of filthy greasy gray hair, and they go This is so you'll learn to keep your mouth shut, so you'll stop walking around with your jaw loose and your tongue flapping. From now on you'll keep your mind on your newspaper, huh?, and *chíngale!*, they give this guy a lesson. So then he's on the sidewalk, and they said they kicked him, but their feet sort of sank into this mushy dark flesh of his. Just sunk in, right? Dressed Like a Man says Do you think his mother had said a prayer for him this morning?

You know I don't smoke or drink or anything. Well, I've noticed that when I've had a drink or two, and I go to the bathroom or some other place like that, closed in, you know, I get dizzy, I get so dizzy, it really hits me. I get some kind of claustrophobia or something. But we went into the bathroom in El Señorial. We stood up and went to the powder room. It was two feet by two feet.

And you know what we did? In the washroom we took out those cigarettes we'd found in Mauricio's car and we lit them. They smelled terrible, just awful. Dressed Like a Man took a few puffs off one and immediately the whole place was full of smoke. We couldn't even see ourselves in the mirror anymore. And then on top of that with that thing I get, I start saying to Dressed Like a Man, Get me out of here, I'm going to die, I'm going to faint and crack my skull open . . . Because I was already bumping into things, I'd already run into the door. So to make a long story short, she grabs me and pulls me out of the bathroom, right?, she rescues me from the bathroom, and we're both coughing like consumptives. Consumptives? You know, like we had pneumonia. Or I mean tuberculosis.

So anyway, the two of us are high as a kite and coughing like crazy, but each one of us coughing in a different style, right?, and we look at each other and all of a sudden there's this overflowing, riotous, wild happiness everywhere. Everything is *joy* all of a sudden. There's all these people and lots of noise and bright lights, and everybody's sort of blurry but I can tell that they're, everybody's dancing. People dancing all around us, dancing past us, right?, so finally we joined in and started dancing too. We joined the crowd. We loved to rumba, you knew that, right?, oh, we were fools for the rumba. And there were all these people, all these girls going by, I don't know, I swear, I couldn't tell you who they were, but Dressed Like a Man and I watched these people dancing, and all of a sudden we started dancing along with them, da da da dum, da da dum dum, dancing like crazy, and all of a sudden we hear Bravo! Bravo! Encore! Hurray, they're yelling, and at that we turn around and I'm seeing very strangely, right? But anyway, as I concentrate on looking at what's happening, I look all around and there's nothing, just all kinds of lights and reflections and things. But down there, down *there!*, there's Handsome to the Maximum and Napoleon and everybody waving wallets and clapping, applauding us, right?, throwing change purses and napkins and all kinds of stuff up to us. Can you believe that the dancers in the show danced through the tables to get up on the stage? And we didn't realize it was all part of the show, I mean with all the smoke in our eyes, we just caught the fever. The rumba fever, right? So imagine these big-busted half-naked, or almost completely naked, long-legged Cuban chorus girls beside these skinny idiots, which was us. We'd just danced up the ramp and nobody stopped us. We were right up there on the footlights, can you believe it? With the spotlight and every-thing on us. . . . When I looked up from dancing, I said to Dressed Like a Man, Mauricio's not here. So we got down off the stage, nervous because where was he, right? The guys were still applauding and even stamping their feet and jumping around. And we, as you can well imagine, were completely disoriented, out of it, completely dizzy in more ways than one. Mauricio was thrilled, he was crying and crying, he couldn't believe it, he was hugging us and crying and crying. He said Oh my love, oh sweet-heart, oh darling, you had your debut, you had your day-byoo, right?, you're in show business now, and so on and so forth, and he was crying he was laughing so hard. And he was so drunk. But at the time I didn't know what had happened. It never occurred to me, I mean *then*, I didn't realize we had been in the show, right? We were just dancing, as far as I was concerned. None of this Oh my God how embarrassing how could I have done such a thing oh what will people say nonsense. None of that. It was like, well, no big deal, you know?

So then, um, we left. We were walking through the parking lot and Mauricio says Well. Well, where would you like to go now? I was so out of it I couldn't even talk, honestly, so I shook my head, No, nowhere, nowhere. But Dressed Like a Man says Lis-ten Mauricio, I've got an idea, why don't we pay that bitch a visit that's bothering my friend here? Who?, Mauricio said. That old lady that goes to the Palacio de Hierro and pesters her, you know. . . . Because there was this lady, who later he married by the way . . . And it was true, all day she hung around bothering me, pestering me, every day, she came to the Palacio de Hierro just to pester me. So Mauricio says Okay, that sounds like a good idea to me. . . .

At the Palacio de Hierro even my bosses had noticed that this lady came in to bother me all the time, but they didn't know why.

So they put this policeman in to guard me whose name was Serafin, like the angels, right? Is that right? Well, it's close, right? To take care of me. But I changed his name and he's still my friend today. His name was Serafin, and he thought he was this real handsome he-man type, he thought he was Charles Atlas or somebody, right?, and I didn't think his name fit him, I didn't like it, so I called him Spartacus. Every time he came in he'd say Here, feel me, feel this, seventeen inches of rock-hard bicep. And I'd go Heavens, Spartacus! You're unbelievable. . . . What a gorilla! He'd come to my house in San Angel on Sunday sometimes to visit me, because he ran around with this other mastodon, a guy named Bloodhound, I'll tell you about him in a minute, and we were big buddies, right? . . . Now he's chief detective, or whatever you call it, in the Palacio de Hierro, how's that? And you know what he did one time? He ran into me one time, three or four days after The Monk liberated me, and so one day I was on my way to the Palacio de Hierro, and Spartacus sees me, and he sort of moans Ay, señorita, señorita, I'm so glad to see you. He hugs me and everything. It's so good to see you! But what happened to you? And I say Nothing, why? And so he says Why, you look so weak and pale. Haven't you noticed how tired your face looks? And in those days I still had a little life left in me, right? Or so I thought. So I say I don't know, Spartacus, what do you see? Ay señorita! He seemed to really be feeling sorry for me. Well, I say, you know I *have* been a little under the weather now that you mention it, I've had a little cold, but I didn't think I was that far gone. Ay, señorita, you look exhausted, exhausted. Come with me, he says, I've got a friend over here, there's a department over here that has some creams and things, they say they're the best money can buy . . . I'll take you over to see what they prescribe, excuse me I mean suggest. . . . So we went over to this counter, and they sold me about six hundred pesos' worth of goddamned cream. I still have them. But one of them did get rid of blackheads, I'll say that. You won't believe it but it got rid of my blackheads. . . . I was with my mother, we were over in the fabrics, and I didn't even have time to say I'll be right back.

Spartacus just swept me away because he said I looked completely wasted. Can you believe that?

So anyway, this lady would come in to bother me, and she'd complain and bitch and scream and threaten me. She swore that Mauricio was her husband, I mean, the dramas of daily life, right? And me, not a clue. On the other hand, it wasn't true that Mauricio was her husband, what happened was, that she wanted him to be and all, but he wasn't. And she was very attractive. She was nice looking. So then Dressed Like a Man says Why don't we go pay her a visit, huh?, so we go and we yell up at her. By this time we were all talking like drunks, right? . . . So we go and we yell up at her. By the way, she lived in Chapultepec Morales, over there by the Auditorium?, on that avenue, you know, the one with all the trees named after that poet, I mean the street, not the trees, what was his name? Anyway, you know where I'm talking about, right? So we go over there. By that time all I could do was move my head, shake my head No, no, no, because I was so tipsy I couldn't even pronounce the word noooo. So we get there and Mauricio gets out and starts yelling Hey! Hey! Bitch! It's me, Mauricio! . . . And since she didn't answer he pulled out the ashtray, out of the car mind you, and threw it at her window. Look out here, you bitch! The car was in the middle of the street with the lights on. It was a Corvette. Come out here, you bitch! he says. Lights started coming on in all these windows, right? People were sticking their heads out. Dressed Like a Man was going scrtch, scrtch, scrtch. . . .

When she came to the window sort of patting her hair and making signs with her hands like this, like What do you want, right?, I could picture her with her thighs all bloody from her torrential menstruation, and spitting out three or four aborted fetuses. And Mauricio's in the middle of the street going I came to tell you to leave my girlfrien' alone! Shut up! Shut that drunk up! a man's voice yelled. Come shut me up you son of a bmbrbm! And he staggered back to the car and picked up this jack handle, right? Hey bitch! Bitch! He could barely stand up, and he was waving this iron bar around like he was winding up to pitch it through her window. I came to tell you to leave my sweethear' alone! We're goin' ta get married, d'you hear! And so on and so forth. . . . So then Dressed Like a Man gets out of the car and slams the door and with this voice like you never heard, it sounded like a bottle of whisky with a megaphone, she starts yelling too. Yeah! Yeah! Leave 'er alone, you old bag! Whydyou haf to bover my frien'? I was still sitting in the car, going psss, psss, because I couldn't even whistle. And since they wouldn't listen to me, I just gave up and lay down on the steering wheel. So then the horn starts blowing like a foghorn. . . . So Mauricio finally finished his windup, and he pitched the jack handle at the shadow of his future, right?, and it crashed through this window with the lights on about two floors lower down . . . About that time you could hear sirens in the distance, right?, and coming closer by the second.

So we drove off, zigzagging down the street, grazing a parked car now and then. Dressed Like a Man decided to sleep at my house, because she couldn't very well go home in her condition. So Mauricio drove us to my house, and by now he was even more bent out of shape than when we'd left the theater. Are you happy?, he said, and he looked around to look at my exhausted, drunk, terrified face. Terrified because he wasn't looking where he was going, right? It was only by sheer miracle that we weren't all killed, I'll tell you. So we got home, *somehow* we got home, and I say to Dressed Like a Man, Okay now baby, not a peep, okay? Discretion, right? We don't want my parents to hear us, do we? We couldn't turn on any lights, right?, so I took her hand and guided her into my bedroom. Well by this time we were beginning to be ever so slightly clearer-headed, or *I* was, so I pulled out some pajamas, with the lights off, and we put them on. Everything still as a mouse. I wasn't so blind now, I'd gotten used to the dark, so I buttoned up my pajamas and felt my way to the bed, and finally I lay down. But Dressed Like a Man, since she was much much tipsier than I was, because she'd been seriously drinking, she drank a lot anyway and she'd drunk a lot even for her, she was really not in the best of shapes, to put it mildly . . . So she was headed for the bed, and by feeling around she thought she'd found the bed, right?, and so she says At last, I mean she *thinks* she's saying this to herself, right?, just sort of breathing it, but she's so drunk that she absolutely yells it. *At last! The bed, at last!* And *chíngale!*, she dives, and all of a sudden you hear this crash. *Ándale!* So I say What happened, what happened, and I start trying to find her in the bed, in this huge bed of mine, but nothing. She's not there. So I thought Well, when she dived in she must have gone all the way over. Over the bed, right? So I grope around on the other side of the bed, and she's not there either. So I'm whispering Where the hell are you?, scared to death because I sat up and peeked over, and she wasn't down at the foot of the bed either. So I thought The earth opened up and swallowed her, she vanished, the boogeyman came and ate her. How was I supposed to know, right? I mean look at it from my point of view—I hear this crash, this *At last!* and then this crash, and abracadabra she's gone, right? So there I am in the dark, drunk, on my hands and knees, crawling, feeling around all around the bed. And then I finally found her, lying on the floor on my side of the bed. I mean if she'd hit what she was shooting at, she'd have landed on top of *me*, the idiot. So there she lay. She looked like a frog stretched out to be dissected or something, or no I'll tell you, she looked like a flying squirrel frozen in flight, because when she dived like that, trying to dive into the bed, bang!, I mean she hadn't calculated too well, and *chíngale*, she hit the floor, and she just kept lying there like that, with her hands stretched out.

I couldn't pick her up, you know, no way, so I grabbed her by the hair. What happened? What happened! Get up, don't be silly . . . By the hair, right? But she goes Ay-yi-yi . . . A cry of pain. . . . So I say Goodness, why didn't you answer me? And she says Oh don't worry about me, I didn't think it was worth making a lot of fuss over, uh-uh, no noise okay?, but listen, I think I broke a little rib. . . . That's how quiet she was when we got home. . . . Why make a racket, I think I broke a rib. Ay, no. She was like the Woman of Steel, okay? And to make a long story short, she had bandages and a corset and I don't know what else

for who knows how long. And do you think she complained. . . .
She never said a word. No . . .

*("The no, the nonovulate no, the nonnate no, the non-noumenous
no, noo, the postmuck-cosmos of impure zero no's that non't, no they
non't, and nonce and for none they non't. No they non't. . . .")*

10

If I'm lying, may my teeth fall out!

One day I ran into Handsome to the Maximum, I just happened to run into him by the pool at the Hotel Presidente in Acapulco. I'd been wanting to give him my condolences about his mother for a long time, about the death of his mother, right?, which had been the biggest tragedy of his life, because he literally idolized her. They were so close, the two of them, Handsome to the Maximum and his mother. You know that guy on television Gordolfo Gelatino? Well, like that. She'd have given her life for Handsome to the Maximum, too, she adored him, simply adored him. So when I saw him, of course, I gave him my condolences on the tragic death of his mother, and he asked me out to dance at the Zorro.

He was dynamite, you have no idea how great he was. We'd stopped seeing each other for this enormous period of time, and

138

now we were going back to going out together again, and nothing had changed, it still made me see stars, you know what I mean? He was the biggest liar in the world, of course, he two-timed me with every girl that stood in front of him long enough for him to say Hey baby to, and I knew all about them, too, right?, but since I liked him, I thought he was fun and all, and at that time I was not *at all* in love with him, why I just thought Great, who cares?, right? I just like the guy. Of course, I pretended he had me walking The Street of Broken Hearts, he sort of expected that of me, because he was always fooling around, you know? I swear. I mean listen to the things he'd do to me. . . . He'd say Oh baby, listen, I've got to leave early, I've got to go home early tonight because a shipment of shrimp is coming in tomorrow. . . . Because he wasn't working, oh no, I mean he told me he was, that he met these big trucks full of frozen shrimp, who knows where, right?, and I was unbelievably gullible, I thought it was all true. So he'd leave me at my house like about eight o'clock at night because the next day a shipment of shrimp was coming in. So one day Andrés calls. Andrés Gutiérrez, right?, he calls my house, one Sunday, calls for Handsome to the Maximum, and so I say No, gosh, no, Andrés, he's not here because the shrimp truck came in, and there was some kind of mess with the packer. And he says What shrimp? So I say Why you know, the *shrimp*, those shrimp he meets. Oh no, baby, as far as I know, I mean I've never seen or heard of him meeting or going to meet any shipments of shrimp or anything else. . . . So then, of course, I call Tito. I dialed and Tito answered the phone. So I asked him if the story about the shrimp was true. By then I'd been going out with him for about a year and a half, right? Something like that. So he says Oh beautiful, as far as I know there are no shipments of shrimp. What shrimp? So now I knew. . . .

Or another thing—I'd go to his house and there would be these bobby pins. So I'd say Where'd this bobby pin come from? Oh, the maid must have dropped it. Although he had a houseboy, right? It must be the maid's, sweetheart, she must have dropped it. And then in the john, I swear to you, there were bobby pins all over the place, and women's stuff, right? He always said they were the laundry woman's. So anyway, to make a long story short, right?, one day Handsome to the Maximum, not one day, I mean every so often he'd say When are we getting married? And so we'd talk very seriously about our wedding and all, and the next day I'd say Are we going to look for an apartment? Apartment? he'd say. Yes, we talked about it yesterday. Yesterday? So I'd say Oh, this idiot. . . . He never made any sense, right? So finally, this one day he says Listen sweetheart, there's, I want you, uh, I want you to know that, uh, that I really like marijuana. I mean I smoke a lot of marijuana. So I want you to be the first to know, because if you're going to marry me, you've got to know about it, right? All the guys smoke it, all my friends smoke it, and I'm not going to stop because it really relaxes me, okay? So I need to know from the beginning whether you can accept that, because I hate to have to go out in the hall or somewhere to smoke it every time I'm with you. . . . This big speech, okay? He confessed he smoked marijuana in this very innocent voice, with a tremor and everything, okay?, his voice was shaking, but at the same time he had this very practiced-looking, mercilessly practiced-looking look in his eye. So since I hated the whole idea, I mean I darn sure wasn't going to start putting up with a person that never made any sense when he talked, although when he talked the most beautiful teeth in the world sparkled in his mouth, but I swear from one minute to the next he couldn't remember what he was talking about, he was *random*, you know?, and the same thing had been happening to me with Gabriel and Mauricio. They never remembered what they had been talking about yesterday! So anyway, I broke up with him. Or little by little, right?, and then later he always wanted to talk and stuff, so we became good friends. We got along just great, right? Afterward.

I think Gabriel initiated him. In drugs? Although he never never *ever* offered any to me, I never so much as heard the words, You want to try—? I even talked to my psychiatrist about all this. Because it was weird. I was in this very strange world, how can I explain it?, or actually in a lot of worlds, because after this I went out with other groups of friends, these Beautiful People guys, all these real aristocrats. And it was the same thing with them. Or worse . . . There was a flood of drugs that you can't even begin to imagine . . . And nobody ever got me started. . . .

For example, we were at this party, sitting around just like this, this nice party, right? And this bunch of people came in and somebody says You didn't bring any snow? Snow was cocaine, right? They'd come in and ask You didn't get any snow? They'd all ask each other, especially whether they had any pot. Pot was marijuana, right? And I'm going to tell you the truth. I never tried drugs, I mean I *could* never have tried them, because I'm the scarediest girl in the world, the biggest coward of all times about things like that, and just thinking about it, I mean, never, never. Never.

And listen, one time we were in this apartment in the Zona Rosa and the whole group was smoking, right? I was the only one who didn't smoke. There was this little red spotlight on and psychedelic posters all over the walls. Napoleon was like disc-jockeying. And all of a sudden I think, I'm high. I hadn't noticed, can you imagine?, but I'd been in that apartment so long, and there was so much smoke you couldn't see a thing. I can't tell you how panicked I got. . . . Every two minutes I'd get up and go look at myself in the mirror to see if I looked any different, and everybody would laugh. . . . Everybody was eating and laughing, and there I was in hell, I mean suffering the torments of the damned, right?, looking at myself to see if my face was changing, to see if I was turning into a degenerate before your very eyes. But never, no, nevereverever.

One day Dressed Like a Man went out. There was a period when she was living with me, remember? So anyway, like I said, she went out and she told me to come by for her at this party, to come pick her up at such and such a time. So I went over with The Monk, who drove me, and I went up by myself, and as I was going in Dressed Like a Man gives me this big shove and she pushes me into the kitchen. She says You're not leaving this room. The Monk had stayed in the car, and about five minutes went by. So finally, I came out and Dressed Like a Man was in the living room with a bunch of very well-known kids, I mean like bankers' sons and politicians' sons and top-drawer businessmen's sons, okay?, everybody very high-class, and they're all sitting around the coffee table and they're all, I mean every one of them, smoking pot. And they had, you know what they had? They had three little boxes of that candy they make in—what's the name of that city? Celaya? That like fudge stuff, that comes in those cute little crates made out of wood? Uh-huh, that stuff, Sweet Box, right, that everybody laughs when they see the signs. Dirty minds, right? Anyway, with the munchies, eating this candy. There was one of them with his eyes fixed on the Great Beyond, with his pupils glued, *glued*, but on nothing, like he was watching the ghost-girl of del Valle doing a striptease or something. And Dressed Like a Man dying laughing. She says she didn't try it, but I'm not so sure. . . . So we sat there a while talking, laughing and sort of making fun of them, listening to all this stuff they were saying. . . .

Dressed Like a Man was in real bad shape back then, she said she felt so alone. She'd just broken up with her boyfriend, and she resented me going out with Mauricio, right? . . . I'm the kind of person that when I like somebody, I'm not saying this about myself, lots of people have told me this too, what I do, if I like somebody I *make* people like that person, I practically *force* you to like that person I like, right? I push you together, I get you all involved until, well, you have no idea. Anyway, I make people like this person, whoever it is that I like. But then when I don't care about that person anymore, when that person doesn't matter so much to me anymore, well he just doesn't matter anymore, you know?

But Mauricio, at the beginning it was lots of fun, and it was simple. It was like I'd talk about him almost all day long. He was like My Hero, right? He was funny, he told jokes, he sang, he was Black Belt in karate, he knew judo, and he had his own factory, so he had all this money. He was pretty hard to believe, right? So since Dressed Like a Man was all alone, since she didn't have anybody at that moment, almost all day, I mean almost every day, she'd run around with us, right? Oh, and also because she'd almost been mugged two or three times besides. So we wouldn't, like around the time she'd get off work, we wouldn't have anything else to do, so we'd go by and pick her up. And from what she'd seen and heard for herself and from what I had made her feel, like I was explaining to you that I do, plus certain other things, well . . . so anyway, we'd go by and pick her up and stuff and spend all this time together. And as is only logical, right?, little by little she fell in love with Mauricio. She fell in love through my experiences. What's that word for that? Precariously or vicariously or something. She fell madly in love with him, and one day when we had gone out dancing, since we lived so far apart, I told Mauricio to let me off first, since I lived farther away, and then take her home so he'd have somebody to talk to on the way back, right? Because going back . . . So on the way to her house, you know what happened? Porcupine-skin diaphragms!

The next day was Sunday. Dressed Like a Man was super lazy, she always got up late, I mean really *really* late. So the next day at eight o'clock in the morning she comes over to my house and sits down. She says Listen, I have to talk to you. . . . I was in my robe, but I say Okay, pet, terrific, have a seat. . . . And I never, I mean how could I suspect what all this was about, right? So just then one of the Jalisco Sisters calls me. We were real good friends at that time, so she calls me on the phone. I say to her Boy, what a strange morning . . . The two laziest people I know, Mauricio and what's-her-name . . . Mauricio, two times he's called me on the phone already, and both times he's said Listen, sweetheart, do you really love me? Of course, Mauricio. But listen, really, do you love me a whole whole lot? Why yes, of course, Mauricio, I love you. And in a few minutes, I go on to the Jalisco Sister, I don't remember which one, a few minutes later Dressed Like a Man shows up, yes, right here, she's here this very minute. I don't know what's gotten into these two. So listen, I'll call you back. . . . No, really, I'll call you right back.

So I get off the phone, and Dressed Like a Man says to me, Listen, first I have to ask a favor of you. Sure, I said. Well, it's that when I tell you what I'm about to tell you, I want you to hit me, spit on me, pee on me, insult me—you can do anything you want to to me, you can say anything you want to before you turn me black and blue, I don't care, but whatever you do I want us to still be friends, okay? So then she tells me that on the way to her house she had told Mauricio to stop the car. But Mauricio said No, Little Bandit, because that was what he called her, right?, No, it's too late, we'll talk tomorrow because it's just too late tonight. So then she said Come on, Mauricio, I need to talk to you. Please. And Mauricio goes No, Little Bandit, not now. If you don't stop this car, I'm going to jump out! And she opens the door. So he stops the car, right?, but it really bugged him though, because if anything bugged him it was mistreating his car—I mean if it came down to a choice between his Corvette and me, well . . . And he'd had to slam on his brakes, so you can imagine how mad he was. He turned off the engine and she said . . . Oh, I forgot, he always told me that he liked her a lot, he adored her and all, but she wasn't his type, and she was even the kind of girl he wouldn't go to bed with if you paid him, he wouldn't even give her a little kiss, even as a favor, right?, the very thought of kissing her turned his stomach. So anyway, she said to him, she slid a little closer on the seat and unbuttoned his sportcoat, and she said to him, Listen, Mauricio, did you ever fall in love with your best friend's girlfriend, or like his wife? No, he says, uh-uh. . . . So then she says Well I have, and right now I'm head over heels in love with You. . . . And Mauricio says he got the shock of his life. He was indig, what's the word? Indignant? So he says This is incredible, I can't believe you're doing this, how can you say what you're saying, you're like a sister to us, how can you betray us both like this? . . . I'm going to take you to the nearest telephone and you can call her and tell her what you just told me . . . Right now. . . . But then she said Listen Mauricio, I don't care what happens later, but right now what I want is for you to kiss me. Just kiss me! That's all I ask . . . one kiss!

When Dressed Like a Man told me this part I broke up, I mean picture it, Mauricio having to kiss her when he loathed even the *idea* of kissing her, right? But I said Ay, I'm sorry, I'm not laughing because I'm not taking this seriously, it's that I always laugh when I get nervous, and this makes me nervous for Mauricio, poor thing. Of course, that was a lie, I was laughing at the situation, right?, because Mauricio is so solemn and serious, and I could just see him. . . . So then, she said, Mauricio grabbed the steering wheel and said very firmly, No, please don't ask that of me. . . . And I broke out laughing again. . . . So then she says Please, Mauricio. Kiss me. I beg you. . . . So then, to make a long story short, she said she finally told him she'd wait till we broke up, and then when I broke up with him she'd go out with him any way he wanted, right? However he wanted it to be. So when she was through, I said Listen, don't worry about this, now that you've told me, it's finished, okay? I forgive you. I'm not mad at you or anything, really. Quite the contrary, I admire you for having the courage to tell me about this like you did! And I pecked her cheek, and it was like kissing Mercedes, right? I told you she was identical to Mercedes?

So about noon Mauricio and I went out. And of course, Mauricio didn't know where to begin. . . . He worked himself up and he worked himself up and finally he started trying to say Listen sweetheart, what happened uh, I mean I want to tell you, uh. . . . Mauricio didn't know how to tell me, and I had to really control myself, right?, because I was ready to blurt out laughing. But he finally got it out. He said Darling, this and that and the other thing happened. I never told him that Dressed Like a Man had come over first and told me everything, but he said he never wanted the three of us to go out together again. Or run around together or anything. Two or three months later it still made him mad just to think about it. To think that she had done that to us. But what I found out a long time afterward, was that the two bastards, or I mean the bitch and the bastard, had gone to this motel in Cuernavaca and had spent the night together that night, they slept with each other, right?, and since she'd never gotten home, she came to my house, to talk to me and to get her parents to pick her up, so they would think she'd stayed over, can you imagine? The bitch came over to cover her ass. I guess that should have hurt me, but you know?, it didn't. I found out about this when I already had other things to think about, I had other interests by that time, right?, I was more mature, I had gotten a little distance on things, so to speak, other ideas about people, right? So I really don't think it hurt me. . . .

Later on I had another boyfriend that was this politician. He spoke four languages, and he was the private secretary to this minister. I mean not a preacher, right?, but this like cabinet minister? He'd come over, and Dressed Like a Man would shoot over to my house faster than an Aztec fart and start going What do you think of so-and-so's speech and What about this bill that what's-his-name introduced. . . . She knew everything in the world about politics. She knew who wrote whose speeches, who was in trouble, what the national debt was up to by now, everything. . . . She was this expert at political affairs, right? . . . And I've always been pretty calm, wouldn't you say? But there's a limit. . . .

One day the three of us went out one afternoon for a drive. Dressed Like a Man and The Monk were chattering along about politics. As usual. So I, very calmly I say Why don't we talk about something else? . . . Okay, just let me say this—Listen Pancho, so García, so the Secretary of Public Works, what do you think of what they're up to? I mean this bill . . . And so on and so forth, right? . . . And so finally I couldn't take anymore, so I said Listen—to The Monk, right?—listen, Pancho, would you do me a favor? Of course, sweetheart, what is it? . . . So I said Turn the car around and let's leave my friend here at her house. Both of them turned as white as Popocatapetl's peak, they blanched. And he says Oh, but what for? . . . Because I've had it with her, that's why! So just turn around and drop her off at her house, okay? . . . And he says I don't know what you're so upset about. . . . So then I said Listen I don't give a shit, so I don't know why you should give a shit about why I'm so upset, okay? So don't say another word, don't say another word or in about two seconds I'll have had it with you, too. . . . So we left her at her house, right? I mean we're still friends and all, but don't think it was over then, oh no. She kept throwing herself at this guy for a long time after that, uh-huh, at The Monk, the one that thought when he talked his words were indecent. He'd say These carnal thoughts I have of you are sent by the devil. . . . He killed me! He'd say No, no, my Little Nymphomaniac, we can't live on *that* alone, and You don't like poetry, I don't know what we'd do, you don't like art. . . . So I'd say You know, you're absolutely right, I don't know what we'd do. . . . And he'd say to me, like when we were in my Aunt Emma's bedroom—because we'd go to bed together over at my Aunt Emma's house, right? . . . You saw what happened the other day, we had the chance to talk about classical music and poems and everything, and what happened? When I said Do you know so-and-so's poetry, you said I give a you know what, . . . so imagine the future for us! . . . And it's true, I said I don't give a *chingada* about that stuff, stop talking to me about poetry—live it, be it, wrap yourself in it, speak it to me, choke on it for all I care, but *don't talk about it* . . .

He was hilarious. And Dressed Like a Man kept throwing herself at him, for I don't know how long. And later, when I broke up with him, she still kept throwing herself at him, but he really never paid any attention to her. When I was just about to get married, one day she came to see me with him, but I mean pretending they'd just run into each other and decided to drop by and see me, right? But I tell you, the only times anybody ever tried to do me dirt, were those times. It was her . . . And she was one of my best friends, Miss Dressed Exactly Like a Man herself. . . .

Life is a real *chingada*, isn't it?

(*"Until Rubén Darío there was no language cruder or smellier than Spanish."*)

11

Two renowned breasts posed on a sun-drenched bed

Listen, one day the Jalisco Sisters called me on the telephone. They were with Dressed Like a Man, and they were all going to go to Acapulco. Wow, how great, sounds wonderful and so on and so forth. So they go Why don't you come with us? Oh no, I don't think they'll let me. . . . But to make a long story short, I tell my parents about it, and they say, more or less, right?, they sort of say Yes, but without specifically saying Yes or You can go, okay? . . . So then my uncle shows up at my house about this time, that afternoon I think it was, because he was supposed to eat with us, so I say to him Guess what? The Jalisco Girls asked me to go to Acapulco with them, so I'm going to Acapulco. Who else? he says. Well, some other girlfriends of ours, I say, I'm not really sure, like Dressed Like a Man and maybe somebody else, somebody older, some cousin or something, and he says *Oh* no, no way, you can't go, no way we're letting you go like that, you're out of your mind, you going to Acapulco all by yourself, no way. . . . So my brother had gone to the movies. And my uncle says We'll see, wait for me, I'll be right back, uh, just wait here. . . . I was in tears. My heart was broken. Wait for me, he says, and my uncle went to the movie theater to get my brother. I was one big puddle of tears. You're not going, no way, and so on and so forth. . . . So anyway, he went to the Polanco Theater, because that's where my brother was. You have no idea, he knew every move we made. And he pulled my brother out of the movie, he went in and started yelling his name all over the theater until he found him, and he dragged him home, right? So they get home and my uncle says We'll all go to Acapulco, your brother and I will go with you, so pack your bags, I'll take you both, we'll all go. . . . Just great, right? All I needed, the two of them dragging me off to Acapulco. All I could do was cry. . . .

So anyway, he took us, and we get to the Hotel Presidente at two o'clock in the morning, after a series of messes and mix-ups like you wouldn't believe. And to top it all, he didn't take anything, no bags, nothing. . .not a change of socks. . . . He looked exhausted, he was a wreck, with his shoes untied, as usual, and everything. He got married that way, did you know that? He never tied his shoes. So with his shoes untied he goes off to Acapulco, a wrinkled sloppy mess, no underwear, nothing. Nothing. . . . So anyway, we get to Acapulco, and the first day I go down to the pool, right? I go down to the pool, and my uncle yells at me from the hotel, from up in his room out the window, right?, Come heeeeere! He wanted me to come back upstairs, right? So I went back upstairs, can you picture me, twelve floors up in my bathing suit, and he says You know who you were sitting next to? Did you even look? You see them? And you wanted to come by yourself! You see those two? Right next to Pepita the Poxy and Velma the Venus Flytrap. So I go And who are they? They're pretty. Oh, you don't know them? They own the two biggest

whorehouses in Mexico City, that's who they are. . . . Well, so I
say Shit, how am I supposed to know, God. Why should I know
they run these whorehouses, right? . . . Oh, so you don't know
them? he says. Well, since you don't know them, I'll introduce
you. . . . And we go downstairs and he introduces me. . . . So
you won't sit down by those two anymore, so you'll know who they
are, he says. . . . Two minutes later I sit down again, and my
uncle shows up, and he says Pss, come here a second. . . . Don't
you see who you're sitting next to now? No, I say. . . . Well,
she's so-and-so's mistress, the mistress of a friend of mine. . . .
No less, right? . . . I'm telling you, the evil-minded old fart was
driving me . . . I couldn't stand him. . . . So now he starts drinking. He doesn't drink, but he sat down to have a drink and say
hello to people. I kid you not, he's crazy, he knows more people
than anybody in the world. . . . He sends out four thousand
seven hundred Christmas cards, just to give you some idea. . . .

So I finally sat down with the Jalisco Sisters and Undressed
Like a Man, who whatever you say you have to admit has a nice
body. . . . But like a war orphan, I'm telling you, with all the
scars from The Heartbreak of Psoriasis or whatever it was, but a
very nice piece as men say, a real dish, although it pains me to
say so. And she was running around with Carlos Stamatis, who
was the Water Ski King of Acapulco, a really good-looking guy
that immediately started getting interested in me. So I would see
him sort of on the sly, right? Carlos and I would get this boat, and
we'd sneak off from my uncle, right? To the high seas. Back then
I was, no, really, I swear to God, I was the most virginal girl in
the world, you have no idea. Saintly wasn't the half of it. So I'd go
out with him, but scared to death, right? Hysterical. . . . So one
time there we are way out at sea, no land in sight, and the gas
runs out. So I thought uh-*huh*, right? Classic. Quite a joke, ha
ha, the gasoline runs out, right? . . . I thought, Carlos set this
up. But we did have all these dangerous, exciting adventures on
the high seas. . . . So anyway we get back to the dock the best
we can, the dock at the armina or the marina or whatever, and
they let us borrow a jeep, and we went back to the hotel. And

guess who was keeping my uncle entertained. You guessed it, Undressed Like a Man herself, Miss Nervousness, Miss Just Like Mercedes. She'd been drinking with him for about six hours, and the poor man was, well you can imagine. But that was okay for *him*. He was still watching to see who I was sitting next to, who I was talking to, who I so much as said hello to, right? I mean the day I went down to eat with all my friends, boys and girls both, right?, he came in and made me leave because Pepita the Poxy and Velma the Venus Flytrap were there. I couldn't believe it, there was lobster and everything, the table looked like a movie set, and my uncle comes in and makes me leave because these so-called ladies of the night were there. I mean, really . . .

That night my brother went out to go bowling, and since the Jalisco Sisters had finished off all the red wine at lunch, they were asleep in their room. So my uncle asked Undressed Like a Man and me if we wanted to play poker, so we started looking for one more player. And we ran into Carlos Stamatis. So we went up to the room, which was two floors. I mean it was a two-story room. It had the living room downstairs and two bedrooms upstairs with these wide, wide beautiful beds, king size, I think. I felt terrible, especially because Carlos had known my uncle for years and years, because when we started playing Carlos kept trying to make a pass at me, he'd put his hot little hand on mine and fondle my knees and all. . . . My uncle kept rattling on about fabulous business deals and horse races and things. . . . You'd love my uncle. No, I mean it. He's always had this great imagination. Plus he was drinking. So all of a sudden, he starts telling about how wonderful this horse was he'd bet on and won I don't know how much money, this horse that cost like a hundred and ninety thousand dollars—U.S. dollars, right?—some incredible amount of money. I was very uncomfortable to say the least, so when my uncle asked Dressed Like a Man, because we had gotten dressed by this time, to play poker, right?, when my uncle invited her upstairs to see some pictures of this famous racehorse, well I relaxed a little. I was as innocent as a little saint, you remember, but I had this feeling something bad was going to happen when I looked at Carlos' face. But he was a nice-looking guy, and he didn't talk much, so I sat there and talked, and he sat there looking at me with those great big black eyes of his. So anyway, to make a long story short, in about ten minutes, or not even ten minutes, he leaned over and kissed me. And then he tried to get a little fresh, so we sat there struggling for a while. Carlos, I said, I'm surprised at you! The way he ran his roving hands all over my body, you can't believe it, for example over my breasts, and I was saying Carlos, no, Carlos no. I didn't know that at that exact same moment upstairs something very similar was going on. . . . Yes, upstairs, in one of the rooms on the second floor of this room. . . .

My uncle, you see, all of a sudden my uncle planted a kiss right on my girlfriend's surprised lips, and then he started getting handy around the house if you get my meaning. So then, she told us, by the time she realized what was happening he had unzipped her pants. No, *her* pants. So she scratched and kicked, she tried to slap him. The feeling of his body, hard and soft, hard and soft at the same time, right?, and the tickling, his fingers pinching and poking, the moans, the panting and puffing, the way the bed started to creak, the way their bodies started to move, the way her hair escaped her bobby pins, the way her flesh surrendered to his hands, she told me all of that. So then my uncle opens a drawer in the dresser and took out his pistol, can you imagine? He waved it around in front of her face, and he said If you don't keep quiet, I'll shoot you. And he banged the gun down on the bed. I mean it didn't bang on the bed, but you know. . . . Like this. I'll shoot you if you don't keep your mouth shut! So there they were—the pistol, the dresser rocking and rolling, the pistol bobbing up and down on the bed, the unzipping pants, the gasping mouth. She says something snapped inside her, and from that moment on she didn't voice a sound, she didn't sigh or sob or moan or pant or anything. My uncle undressed her very slowly, very slowly, and all her buttons and hooks and snaps opened under his hard horny fingers. And he was thirty-six years older than she was, can you imagine? And he rolled her stockings down very very slowly, and

then her panties, and he deflowered her, bang!, without any sort
of preamble or subtlety or anything, with the pistol right there
next to her on the bed, bouncing along with the bed, shaking with
the bed's rhythm. She says my uncle was making more noise than
an overheated pressure cooker, and he was sweating, and his
body was hard and soft at the same time, blubbery was I think the
word she used, not soft, but she says she didn't feel anything, not
disgust or anything. . . . It's that . . .

My uncle was this mystery, this what's the word? Like a mystery or a riddle. Like enema . . . Enigma? . . . Back then he had
this fur and leather business. . . . Listen, my uncle was very un-
usual. He was this really nice guy, and he had the exclusive
rights to import all kinds of stuff, plus he had nineteen drug labo-
ratories. I mean like pharmaceutical drugs, don't get the wrong
idea. He even wound up owning a bank because he wanted to
break this monopoly all his friends had on the financial end of
things. But his construction companies got into big trouble,
right?, they were bleeding him dry, terrible, you know. So he
went bankrupt with a bang. When they killed him he was in
really really bad financial shape, really bad. Sometimes, though,
I'll tell you, there were days, and I saw this with my own eyes,
when he'd win a hundred thousand pesos, or even more, on one
horse. At the races, right? Four straight Tuesdays, every time, he
won more than a hundred thousand pesos on the same horse, and
one Thursday, to like crown this achievement, right?, he made
more than a quarter of a million pesos. But he lost an incredible
amount, too, right? That was at Santa Anita. . . . But later he lost
a whole fortune. I don't know how much money he lost. . . .

And another thing, his kids all have this brain thing, right?, I
mean they're incredibly brainy, intelligent, right?, with these
I.Q.'s about 200. Or higher. Strange, you know? Because out of
three, two of them are truly geniuses, incredibly intelligent. And
my uncle would tell them these fantasies, like the times he killed
people and how many times he was attacked or mugged or something. . . . You probably remember that my uncle was famous for
being one of the nicest men that ever lived in Mexico City, a

really really friendly, nice guy, you can't believe anybody could be so charming, right? He'd talk to you for hours and hours and tell you one legendary exploit after another. For hours. Things that had happened to him, you know?, but ninety-nine percent of the time they were lies. Except he was such a great storyteller you'd be fascinated, right? Then he changed, though, because when he got rich he wasn't that way anymore. He said so himself, he'd say No, before I sort of felt an obligation to make people like me, but now that I've got all this money I don't give a shit. You know what I mean? He changed tremendously. I mean he used to tell us, his kids for example, my uncle would be with us somewhere, or maybe over at my house, and since he'd tell us this stuff, these fairy tales of his, he'd keep us fascinated all day long, the kids would just eat it up. . . . He'd tell about the time he killed this guy, or he'd killed this other guy, and when the, the— what is it?—the Mafia had been after him, and he'd beaten up fourteen hired killers, ay, and all about getting mixed up with this other gangster, but I mean The King of the Gangsters, right?, a hired gun, this other real well-known guy. And he'd say things like . . . What was I telling?

Oh, right, about that one of his sons, the very apex of I.Q., and good at everything he did, this kid asked for a rifle for his birthday. So my uncle gave him this .22 rifle so he'd learn to shoot. . . . And he was really a good shot, too. He learned fast. So then one day they were playing and the boy aims the rifle at the girl, at his sister? And the girl gets scared. Naturally, right? Who wouldn't? So she puts up her hand like this and says No, Toñito, no, no, get away, but she made this quick movement like this, right?, like this, and the gun goes off. The boy's holding the gun and it just goes off, right? And the bullet shoots out straight at the little girl's neck, it hits her in the neck and it goes all the way through. All the way through her neck . . . like across diagonally. And the bullet sticks here. It lodges, right?, here. And not to mention that it was one of those expanding bullets, a dumdum I think they're called, so it lodges here, and when my uncle sees her, and when her mother sees her, forget it, they ran in and grabbed her and raced her to the hospital. . . . It was on the way that they noticed that the little girl still had the bullet in her, because they really hadn't even looked. I mean, they knew she was shot and all, and the bullet went in, but they hadn't looked closely to see whether it came out again, you know? Who'd think to do that? Anyway, to make a long story short, they took it out. . . . And life's incredible, isn't it? The bullet had gone all the way through her throat, all the way through, and diagonally, and nothing was broken. Or injured or whatever. Of course, that didn't keep her from being almost dead. It was serious all right, don't get me wrong, and she was between life and death for I don't know how long, weeks and weeks and weeks, but she got better, she pulled through. . . .

So then my uncle gathered up all his . . . because he had every caliber pistol there was, all sizes, right?, and all prices, all makes and models, old and new and antique and everything, and all kinds of machine guns and everything, all the latest stuff. Everything that came on the market he bought. But not after this, right? On the contrary. It was a big lesson for him, a real lesson . . . a terrible lesson. . . .

So anyway, my uncle was going out with Dressed Like a Man all the time now. He two-timed my aunt with real Mexican brio. *Olé!*, right? And my girlfriend got more and more shy and introverted and bitchy. She was in a bad mood all the time. I mean their relationship was the pits. So bad that one time she pushed him down the stairs, and my uncle rolled all the way down the stairs and broke a leg. Thirty something steps he fell down, right?, thirty or forty steps made out of volcanic rock in a house in San Angel. *Chíngale!*, and arms, legs, noise, head, hair, hands, feet, banging and crashing, here goes this blubberball with clothes wrapped around him every which way, and *surprised!* And then guess what she did. The telephone rings, right? They were in Dressed Like a Man's house at the time. They'd had this argument, and she pushed him down the stairs. So there was my uncle lying in agony on the floor with his arm and his leg broken, and he's moaning and whimpering, and the telephone rings right next to where he's sprawled on the floor in all directions. So she walks downstairs and picks it up. She answers the phone, and it's this friend of hers, and she starts having this conversation. With my uncle lying there practically in pieces. And him thirty-six or thirty-seven years older than she was. She says she even sat down on his wheezing carcass. That she sat down on him and sat there talking for more than six hours. My uncle had given her that lava-stone house as a gift, plus three rings she wore on three different fingers of her left hand. . . . It was the longest phone call in the history of the Mexican Telephone Company. She didn't ever want to hang up.

But I've got to tell you about Bloodhound. . . . Because basically all this was his fault, he got my uncle interested in guns and weapons and stuff, and it was him that made Handsome to the Maximum a champion marksman, I mean sportswise he was something, right? But I'll tell you he was a very very *very* strange man, this old man, tall and skinny, like a scarecrow. They called him Bloodhound and he was about this tall with straight gray hair. He'd been a gunman or maybe a bodyguard for like three presidents, I think he even went as far back as Venustiano Carranza. But anyway, he was something. . . . His aim was not to be believed. He was about this thin and a real expert at guns. Still is. You remember that problem with María Flores? Well, he was the expert witness. It was Bloodhound that had to examine the pistol and testify, because he knew everything in the world about that stuff, he's a specialist. And ooh, he was the kind of man that, well, that liked to kill, that's the only way to put it, he'd kill with no hesitation, like no scruples or morality or anything. And he was sexy as everything. . . .

So anyway, we were going out dancing. . . . Everybody had an Afro, and I was this little chick, right? We were all really young then. And my uncle liked, I mean if you know what I mean, he liked Dressed Like a Man and me.

So anyway, he liked us a lot, and on Sundays we'd have breakfast with him, early. Dressed Like a Man and I would have breakfast, and sometimes Spartacus would come, the guy from the

Palacio de Hierro? And Bloodhound would tell us all his adventures. He'd tell us things that happened to him. Incredible stuff, really. Like one time he was coming out of this place called The One Two Three Club or something, and he says all of a sudden these five guys stepped out. I mean he told it just like I'm telling you. He said So these five guys come after me and they start shooting. One of them hits me in one leg, and another guy gets me in the side. So I say Gosh, Bloodhound, how awful. What did you do. Oh, I forgot, he said, I fell to the ground, right? I fell. And *then* I said Gosh, Bloodhound, what did you do. . . . Nothing, he says, I killed them. But the funny part is that then an ambulance came, from the Red Cross? He couldn't believe it, he was moved to think that an ambulance had come to take him to the hospital. . . . But he had to hide, so he ran off, so they wouldn't take him to the Red Cross. . . . He had to run away. . . . And the really funny thing about him was that how he'd escaped from the ambulance was more important to him than how he had killed five Christian men, because all gunmen are Christians, did you know that? They wear crosses and little St. Christopher medals and everything, and they pray religiously every day and everything. . . . Really, they're really religious. . . .

Bloodhound said he could kill a man in I don't remember how many fractions of a second . . . fractions of a second. . . . He needed just this long, right?, to kill a man. That is, if they shot at him and missed, if they didn't kill him first, all he needed was, I don't know, milliseconds to do away with his enemy. . . . He told me I think it was eight hundredths of a second or something like that, eight hundredths of a second, *chíngale*. That was how long he took to kill somebody, that was all. . . .

He was really a good gunfighter, right? Incredible gunfighter. . . . And he took Handsome to the Maximum under his wing, like a mother hen, right?, and he trained him. He trained him really well too. . . . I had this medal at home that Handsome to the Maximum won once in a contest, and some kind of a diploma or a certificate or something from some other marksman contest where he shot and won a prize, the top prize, first prize.

He gave it to me sort of like a souvenir, right?, one of those kind of things. But I think before I got married, I think those were some of the things I threw out before I got married. . . . I kept them like eighty or ninety years, and then they weren't any more use to me, you know? . . . Those things that aren't any use to you anymore, so you throw them out, right? . . .

("Does the gnawing sound in your ceiling, your silence, bother you?")

12

A certain voraciousness had seized us

Sometimes we'd get together to talk about our problems. And when we sat down we'd start talking about all the stuff that had happened, changes in marriages, good orgasms, boyfriends abandoning their girlfriends and vice versa, women, husbands running off with The Other Woman, things like that. Take for example, one time Big Jalisco told how she'd made love to two guys at the same time, and to make it last, she'd performed some kind of mysterious things with her hands, who knows. She told such stories! Little Jalisco, one day while she was married to Napoleon, she got vaginitis or some kind of venereal disease of some kind supposedly off a toilet seat. And Dressed Like a Man had gone to Gabriel Infante's office, who you know is the grossest man in the universe, I mean the foulest mouth of the century. And she said

159

he said Come on in, skinny bitch. So she says Hold on, Gabriel, don't be so vulgar, and so on and so forth. All my patients have to accept it, baby, he says, take me for what I am, or else they can *chinga* their *madres*, right?, just *chinga* their fucking *madres*, don't come dump your shit on me. . . . And you stand there with your mouth open, because you can't believe that's how he treats people. . . .

I mean the other day, for example, I called him. . . . And he goes Wow, baby, you wouldn't believe how heavy things are. I mean I bopped down to Acapulco the other day, and they'll lay mary jane on you right on the street, can you dig that shit? They'll bodyblock each other to sell you the stuff. I'm not lying, two or three of these dudes will stop you and give you a free hit, right?, like in the ice cream store, cause some of them have better weed, I mean it's golder gold. They'll stop you and rap on you to sell you snow, baby, I mean the real stuff. . . . But I can't talk like him—he's hilarious, with all the latest words they use and everything, super with-it, a little too super with-it if you ask me, because you can't even understand him, right? . . . When he's finished telling me some story, I have to say Wow, Gabriel, I didn't understand a word of that. Not one goddamned word. So he calls me every *puta* and *hija de puta* and *chingada* and other name in the book because I don't dig him, right? I mean Dig it? So he goes I'll tell you the truth, baby, the shit is getting heavy in Mexico . . . Because he was telling me this story about drugs that you wouldn't believe, how he'd been living with these prostitutes from Canada, and about how they had this circus, and they were keeping him and all, the whole sordid story. And all of a sudden he says No, no, not yet, sweetie, you can't close your mouth, just hold it, stay like I left you. So I say Listen Gabriel, are you with somebody? And he says A patient, here, nobody. And you're telling me all this pot shit and how high you got, in front of a patient? So he says Not to worry, baby, she's a kid but she's very heavy, a very heavy chick, I mean, and she's twelve, so what's the big deal? And she's back there, I could hear her, going Tell her I know the score. . . . I swear to God. I know the score, and Tell her I'm hip. . . . So Gabriel says How old are you, baby?

And she says Twelve. . . . Hear that, cunt? I think around here you're the only straight arrow there is, the Old Fashioned Tight-Assed Cunt. I swear, this little girl was twelve years old, and she was sitting there getting braces or something going Tell her I'm hip, Gabriel, tell her I've got a little buzz on right now. So imagine. That's Gabriel Infante. . . .

But I was talking about Alexis, right? He'd been living for a long time with this famous movie star, this blond American really, really famous actress with yellow eyes. Her face was on all those boxes of soap, you remember? But one day they broke up, and it was a real blow to Alexis, because he was unbelievably in love with her. So then he had never gone out with a girl from Acapulco. In fact, he had never gone out with a Mexican girl, from Acapulco or Tampico or anywhere. So this one day he decides to get married, to make his parents happy and all that, and to see if he'd calm down a little bit, because he was so wild you wouldn't believe it. Around this time he told me a great story, but I've forgotten it. . . . He was in a reformatory or a prison or something, . . . I don't remember. I've completely forgotten it. But he told me all the stuff that happened to him, what he had . . . Shoot! I wish I could tell you. I've forgotten . . .

Once he went to this dance where all the high society of Acapulco were. Back then he was blackballed from almost all those places. They had closed all the doors to . . . Everybody thought he was wild in those days because of him running around with actresses and living off women and stuff. That was about it, though, that was why he was so supposedly wild. . . . So anyway, he was at one of those crème de la crème parties, standing beside the pool, watching the bullfight from the fence you might say, and he says to his brother, Carlos was his name, he says See that girl over there? And he pointed at this black-haired girl with a turned-up nose and eyebrows painted so they sort of slanted up and out, remember that style? . . . Anyway, Yes, said his brother. Well that's the girl I'm going to marry. . . . And to explain it and to like convince himself, he said She's pretty, she's got lots of dough, she'll do. . . . He says he thought it all out, in great detail . . . And she's a decent girl, he says, like to say the last word, and he asked her to dance, and in six months he married her. He married this girl, and so then they came to Mexico City for their honeymoon the same day as the wedding, because her parents had given them a house for a wedding present, right here, on the Paseo de la Reforma, so they spent their honeymoon in the house. . . .

Alexis spent his whole wedding night crying. He cried all night long, crying something horrible. He says he cried and cried and cried, and she kept saying Why are you crying? I'm such a prick, he said, I should never have married you, I never should have. . . . Because he found out that very night that he was going to be miserable, from the moment he first, well, possessed her, right? Or was he already miserable by the time he kissed the bride at the end of the big church wedding ceremony, while he was still in Acapulco? He didn't know it at that moment of how shall I put it? . . . When he woke up in a fit of depression and repressed anger, like a moral hangover, that's really what it was, a moral hangover. . . . Although later he always said that at the precise moment they said I do, he became the most miserable man in the world. . . . So all of a sudden there he was, I mean picture it, in their big house full of elegant furniture upholstered in navy blue velvet, with a woman he didn't love, who didn't attract him, who didn't even excite him, you know? And who on top of everything never for a second stopped looking at him with this questioning, soft look that made him shudder with . . . So finally he said Let's go out, okay?, let's go dancing. So as not to be faced with her nudity or some shocking scene of recriminations and an attempt at some impossible adjustment. So he says Why don't we go out. . . . So with the look of a man hanged already, after four burning hours of melodrama and anguished misunderstanding and reproaches, truly Mexican hours, you might call them, he says Listen I'll be right back, while you're getting dressed I'll just go for a walk, and I'll be right back. . . .

He says his self-possession came back to him when he sat down in one of the bars at the Continental Hilton. He ordered a half bottle of whisky and two glasses, hopefully, right? He spotted the ass of this American girl with strong suntanned legs. He says that Yankee girl's ass smiled at him, so he raised the two glasses and winked professionally and asked her to have a drink with him. She was staying in the hotel, and she had just gotten back from Tequesquitengo, if you can imagine. So they were sitting there talking and talking, and they finished the bottle. So then they went up to her room to see whether she'd been gypped on some crafts things she'd bought. And they were in that room for a week, what with semen and coming and going again. They didn't leave the room for anything, even once. But at the end of the seventh day was the twenty-seventh of July earthquake, you remember? The 1957 earthquake?, when the Angel of Independence fell over? . . . So he ran out, terrified, right?, thinking about the woman left by herself in that huge house, and he ran to see what was happening, to see whether she'd gone back to Acapulco or was still there or what. And he ran all the way, with tourists in pajamas or nightgowns out in the streets, and police cars with their sirens blasting and everything. The disaster seemed to stare him in the face from the red lights of the ambulances. . . . When he got there, from the outside it looked like the house was ready to collapse. When he went in, she was there with some friends of her parents' that had been staying with her, this old couple that were desperate to leave and find out what had happened to their own family. They lived in Mexico City, see? Anyway, she was terrified because she didn't know what had happened to him, she was surviving on tranquilizers. They'd been looking for him at all the Red Cross stations, Green Cross, at all the hospitals in the world, all the police stations, everywhere. . . .

So then he says that when they got to Acapulco, he had a talk with her. And she said he was crazy if he thought he was going to get a divorce, because she was a Catholic and she came from a good family. She was never, never, never going to give him a divorce. . . . So things started going from bad to worse, terrible every minute, right?, until the day came they made that classical decision. . . . She was never going to give him a divorce, he was never going to make love to her. Or no, I'm not sure, I don't remember exactly, I think it was that he didn't love her. So they

each started living their own life, right? You go your way and I'll
go mine, right? But she wanted to have children, so she worked
out some way to get pregnant without Alexis finding out who the
father was. Can you imagine? And she had two children. . . .
When I first met them they just had one, and who'd ever suspect
that Alexis, Mr. Who Gives a Shit, wasn't the father. Anyway, so
he said. And as for him, he chose to be a bachelor the rest of his
life, live exactly the way he wanted to. . . .

In 1957 I was in Europe. That was the year I went to Paris with
Gabriel Infante, and then we went to Spain. From there he went
on to Greece, because he was on a tour with the Drivers of
Death. . . . I was going to stay four months, and then we were
supposed to meet in Venice and get married. I mean those were
his plans, not mine, okay? He was going to talk to his parents in
Greece. They were coming back from Japan and were supposed to
meet him there. He planned to tell them we were getting married,
and he wanted us to go back to Mexico married and everything. It
was like this sudden passion, very exciting, right?, very romantic
and all, but I was only nineteen years old, I was going to be
nineteen on my next birthday, so I thought I was a little green for
matrimony. So anyway, when I got to Venice and all, I didn't go
to the hotel I had reservations at, I went to this other one. And
later I found out that he never even went to look for me, because
he met this very sweet, innocent little Italian girl in Monte Carlo
and left the stunt driving tour and everything. Fallopian drain-
pipes! Oh, I forgot—in Paris he had this sensational apartment.
It was this little tiny place with this neon sign in the window, the
name of a hotel. It was a hotel room. He had a sink and everything right there, a door that opened into practically a closet with
a toilet that looked like a dragon. And with a hose, with this little
hose they had, he ran water from the sink to the toilet. And to
take a bath you had to put a little board across the top of the toilet
and stand on it and hose yourself down while keeping your balance. The water went into the toilet, right? Hilarious. . . . So
anyway, when I got back to Mexico, Gabriel called me from
Belgium. He said Listen, you're a person I love very much, and
I'm used to you, to the way you are, right?, and I really really

don't want to lose you, but I've got this problem. I've got this
problem because I just met an incredible girl, a young, innocent,
sweet girl, I mean a girl that would be a problem for me to try, I
mean for me to live with, but I want to get married, and I'm not
sure whether I want to marry you or marry her, so while I'm
making up my mind I'm going to stay in Europe for a while, okay?
But I'll write you. . . . So I tell him, Listen, don't worry about
writing, because I never want to see or hear from you again. . . .
Okay? We were crazy as hell. And you can guess whether he was
in Europe two weeks later or at my house in Pedregal de San
Angel. . . .

Once all of us, I mean all of my friends and I, were having
dinner together. There was Handsome to the Maximum, Gabriel,
Andrés, Napoleon, two or three of Tito Caruso's friends, you remember. And Alexis. We were having *carne asada* and salad at
La Cabaña, in the Zona Rosa?, you know that place, eating and
drinking wine and all. Alexis and I. The tablecloths were yellow
and the meat was juicy, and this guy comes over and sits down
with us. And all of a sudden Alexis turns around. Like this. And
he says Excuse me, son, but I didn't hear any of us here invite
you to have a seat, and I in particular don't want you to sit down,
so why don't you do me a favor and get up and get lost before I
lose my temper. . . . That's the way he was. I mean that's the
way he was! Of course, he only did that kind of stuff to other
people, you know? He was perfectly normal with *me*, nice, calm,
really great, sensational every way you looked at him. . . . I
didn't really know who he was. . . . Because everybody talked
about how, everybody was scared of him. . . . But with me he
was just incredible. . . .

We'd already been together for years, years and years and
years. And everybody knew he'd been going out with me for a
long time. So we were sitting there eating, and Handsome to the
Maximum asked us all over to his office for drinks. So my
girlfriend Dressed Like a Man comes over, and the first thing she
says to Handsome to the Maximum was, Has anybody ever told
you you have the most beautiful eyes in the world? And then she
said, like immediately, right?, barely giving him time to breathe,

I think that's the way Baby Jesus's eyes must have been. . . . Imagine Handsome to the Maximum listening to this! Everybody cracked up. They must have laughed about that for three weeks. Imagine! But everybody thought she was terrific so we all went to Handsome to the Maximum's office for a drink. . . .

I walked Dressed Like a Man to her car, because she was supposed to go meet my uncle. So when I got to the office everybody was already there. It was this really luxurious, really fancy book joint, which was made up to look like an import-export office, but it was really a place all these bets came in to and where they did something like confidential public relations work. Or something like that. So anyway, I tiptoe in, I tiptoe in real quiet, because I wanted to go to the bathroom, and I didn't want anybody to necessarily notice, right? So I tiptoe in real quiet, they were all in the other room, and I slip into the bathroom and close the door. You could hear every word they said. They were talking and talking and talking. . . . So anyway, I heard somebody tell Alexis not to be a jerk, like why?, if he'd been with me for years. Don't be an idiot, Napoleon was saying, I'd love to be able to stick with one person that I really got along with. Handsome to the Maximum blurted out that he had wanted to marry me for a long time. Andrés said something too, . . . like, What's more she's great-looking, and so on and so forth. I was trembling, not knowing where all those tender words were leading, right? So then somebody says So what are you kicking her out for, then, man, if everything else is going to shit? I heard Alexis sigh and admit that he didn't know, he just didn't know. . . . So why don't you marry her?, Andrés insisted. . . . So then I come out of the bathroom, tiptoeing again, right? . . . I left the door ajar a little, so it wouldn't make any noise?, and I straightened my skirt and sort of puffed up my breasts, like this, right?, under my sweater. And I walked in. And as I walked in, I mean this wave of welcome washed over me, I think I was shaking. . . . Alexis was like proud of all the nice things they had been saying, and he came over and was so sweet to me. . . . He was always very sweet to me, I'll have to say that for him, but this time he was unusually, abnormally sweet and loving with me. . . . So anyway, he put his arm around me and smiles and all, and we sat there and talked for a while, right?

As the boys started leaving, Napoleon says to Alexis, So we'll come by for you two, okay?, you're going to like it, you're going to love it. Handsome to the Maximum had to make some phone calls, and then he was supposed to come by the hotel too. So we all said good-bye. . . . What happened was that I would tell them at my house that I was going to Cuernavaca with Dressed Like a Man, and I'd go with Alexis and we'd shut ourselves up in the hotel. I think it must have been That Old Black Magic putting its spell on me, I mean I didn't care about anything. I'd be with him, and we'd go out and walk through the Zona Rosa, we'd have dinner in the Zona Rosa, we'd have breakfast in the Zona Rosa. All day long I'd see all these friends of my mother's or of my father's, and I couldn't have given a *chingada*, right?, I mean I didn't care whether they saw me or not, whether they *all* saw me. I don't know if it was irresponsibility or what . . . I can't figure out what it was. To this day I don't know if it was rebellion or irresponsibility or love. I don't know . . . I'd do anything on a dare. . . .

So we were in the hotel, and I said Where are we going? They're coming by for us, Alexis started. He was grinning and happy and as carefree as a bird all at the same time. They're coming by to pick us up because I said I wanted to try LSD. And he grinned at me mischievously, and he says They said they'd find some and give me . . . When I heard the word LSD, the second I heard that, I said, I swear, I said Tell me it isn't true. Okay, it isn't true, he says, like he'd just told this hilarious joke. So then who knows why, but I started to cry. You're not getting into that, Alexis! This can't be! To make a long story short, I tried to convince him for about ninety hours not to go. Oh please, Alexis, please don't go! He finally grabbed me by the arms and looked me straight in the eye and said Now listen. If you don't want to go, don't go, but I really want to try it. . . . He must have been about thirty-six, or no, about thirty-five, about thirty-four years old. He says I'm going, I'm going and that's it, because I want to try this. So I tore myself away from him and threw him this devious look, trying to torture him, and I said Well I'm not going. . . . But he kept getting dressed, right? So I gathered up all my stuff, I was banging things around, and with all the viciousness I could muster, right?, muster?, I said, I'm leaving. So go, go, no sweat, take off. The man was happy, right? . . . You really don't care whether I leave or not? I said. I really don't care, he sneers, like the perfect master of the situation. Like to punish me, right? You really don't care? By this time he was shaving, and the way he shaved was the funniest thing you ever saw, by the way. . . . He always shaved with one foot up on the sink. He put it all the way up on top of the sink. I mean strange as hell, right? And he leaned on his knee and shaved. So anyway, I said Okay, then, adios, good-bye, take a good look because this is the last time you'll ever see me, you'll never see me again as long as you live. . . . All of this with these infantile sobs and dying moans, right?, these tragic, desperate, incredibly earnest dramatics. Do you think he so much as turned around to look at me? I won't come looking for you, don't worry, he growled. So I left, and I punched the elevator button, like this, right?, insulted and pissed off and crying like a water faucet. For me love was like this recipe—a little bit of the hunger of the senses so to speak, a lot of real emotion, and a pinch of a need for the world to see that somebody belonged to me. And that I belonged to somebody else too, you know what I mean? Although sometimes it was more like a battle between real emotions and the vulgar impostures of the romantic leads in some eighth-rate soap opera. Of course, I didn't dare let myself think like that back then, right? So anyway, the elevator boy came up and he said You're going, señorita? They'd known me for years, because Alexis always stayed in the Hotel Presidente. So they'd known me practically forever, the employees on every shift. Yes, I'm leaving, I said, but I didn't get in the elevator. That adolescent, bourgeois, I-won't-go of mine, all my stupid foot-stamping . . . Those snide, nasty remarks of his, the way they always got in the way of our love, that arrogance . . . So there I stood, or really wavered, right?, if that's the right word, and finally I said No, I don't think I'm leaving just yet, no, thank you. I told him I'd ring for him later, and I went back. . . .

Alexis . . . Basically all these situations were my fault. Not
giving in was probably the way to have handled things, I should
have been as stubborn and ferocious as all these other people
were. So but I rang the bell, because all the rooms had doorbells,
I ring like this, hard. I punch the doorbell, and I hear him come
twee twee twee, and he opens the door whistling. And when he
opened the door, I said What are you whistling about, asshole.
And he says Because I'm happy, because I'm about to have a new
experience and I'm happy. And that hit me right in the gut, I
realized what I had to do. A new role for me, right? So I said Do
you know why I came back? By now my voice was all choked up
and broken, right? . . . And he says No. Why *did* you come
back? So you'd say you're sorry, because I can't go like this, I
can't go like this, you have to apologize to me. And he starts
laughing. He laughed so hard I thought he was going to break
something, I swear, his whole body shook. So I said What are you
laughing about? Well, it's one of two things he said, either I
laugh or I tell you to go to hell, so which would you rather?
Choose, he said, because with you, I either laugh or I tell you to
get the fuck home. So I gathered up my last shreds of bedraggled
dignity, right?, and I say For the last time, Alexis, apologize.
Please, because I don't want to go away like this, if you don't say
you're sorry, I'm going to have to leave, and I don't want to do
that, I really don't want to, so please apologize. . . . So then he
saw how desperate I was, he saw that I was sincere about this, so
we started talking. I listened to him, I didn't look at him, I could
hear that snotty, affected self-assuredness of his. So we started
over again with that same idiotic dialogue, I mean two idiots talking, right?, and it got super late. So finally, we rationally decided
that he was going and I was not. So then Napoleon and Handsome
to the Maximum came up and said What's wrong, aren't you
ready? And he said, Napoleon said, Listen, what's with that
face? . . . Because my whole face was swollen from all the crying, right? So Alexis says Have you ever heard such a thing, this
crazy chick doesn't want to let me go. . . . Oh, no? And did you
tell her to stuff it? Handsome to the Maximum said, but laughing,
right?, because he was always incredibly sweet to me. So then

Alexis says No, but I'm telling you she doesn't want me to go, these youngsters today aren't like they used to be. Well, if you're so scared, Handsome to the Maximum says, we'll just go have a drink, you don't have to take a little trip yourself, do you? And by this time I was in such a mess, and so terrified . . . Napoleon whispered in Alexis' ear, You can get the acid and take it home with you if you want to. . . .

So to make a long story short, we all went. Alexis swore on all the saints he wasn't going to try the LSD. Lysergic something something acid. Whatever . . . I had washed my face about seventeen times with cold water, of course . . . Everything was like those movies, with flashing colored lights and everything. Alexis swore by the sacred prepuce of Our Lord and by Our Lady of Sweet Clitoris that he wasn't going to drop acid, and in fact, the only thing he did was help them finish off a lid of marijuana. Which was nothing for them, right? I mean, . . . So I tried. . . . I took about three slow puffs off a little cigarette Napoleon handed to me, and I held in the smoke, ugh, the smoke. But then what happened was that I immediately started laughing, like this ha-ho-hogh-hogh-hogh, because I was choking, I wanted to get rid of that smoke, because all of a sudden I had this terrible attack of nerves. Fear! Like a kid, right?, like in those anti-drug crusade movies. . . . Swear to me this'll go away, really, swear this'll go away, I kept saying. And you know what I did while they were drinking? I'd go to the bathroom and look in the mirror to see when my face was going to start undergoing transformations, I swear to you, and of course, they were laughing, hilarious, perfectly normal, and there I was in front of the mirror waiting for my face to change, waiting to start looking like a drug addict or a degenerate or something. . . . And I cried, too. I started crying again, I think I told you about the first time. Not because the cigarette had started taking effect, one stinking marijuana cigarette, right?, it wasn't that at all, it was from sheer terror, from being idiot enough to be there, from shame. So then Alexis saw that I really *had* made an effort, that I'd really tried hard, right?, but that this was like a mortal leap for me, like taking a little spin on the flying trapeze or something . . . Without a net. . . . Not something I'd done just because, you know, just to see what it felt like or something, not at all, but something a lot lot worse, completely beyond my world, my nineteenth-century Mother Superior Sister of Virginity world of ideas, beyond the call of duty of my love or my need for him. . . .

But on the way back he apologized about a million times, and he scolded me, he yelled at me for being so hysterical. He called it a voluble temperament or something. Volatile, right. . . . Baby, you behaved like a real idiot, like a complete jerk, I'm not kidding, I can't believe how you acted. I don't know why I go out with you when there are so many women around. They even offer to pay me, he said. So where's the watch? . . . Because he said I owed him a watch for going out with me. . . . Are you saving up for that watch you're giving me? he says. . . . So we went back. To make a long story short, *that* time he didn't try LSD. . . .

But Handsome to the Maximum did. I don't remember if it lasted thirty-six hours or forty-eight, but that night he went out and stood in front of the Angel, and he stood there for hours and hours and hours. . . . And he didn't know whether the most sensational part of it had been the lights on the cars, glowing like jewels or mandarin oranges, or the slow ripping of sunrise, or the column getting bigger and bigger and bigger, swelling and rising like some proud erection, as he said, or the birds thundering in the palm trees on Florencia Street, or the boiling windows of the Hotel María Isabel, or the great ideas of the traffic lights. The traffic signals. The great . . . Can you imagine?

("*Ay, my monkeyest mine, / My tiny great-grand life, / I walk you / like this / by the tail-o / I toddle and totter / tumble and claw you / and then lick, oh I lick your little halo. . . .*")

13

The ghost-girl of del Valle

My mother's sister's got this lover, right?, this Nazi lover. I mean
a real, dyed-in-the-wool Nazi, he was with Hitler and everything,
one of the ones that persecuted and castrated and hassled and
killed Jews. Listen, I mean he *still* hates them. He says he still
dreams about the two-thousand-year Reich, how about that?, and
his name is Kurt, and he's this Lithuanian. . . . Once he explained to us that for years and years, but I don't know whether
this is true or not because I've never heard this from anybody but
him, but for years and years Hitler gave the Jews all kinds of
chances to get out of Germany, did you ever hear that?, that he'd
given them five years to leave Germany? . . . These Jewish
friends of ours say that's just not true. . . . And he says he told

172

them, "On such-and-such a day, at such-and-such an hour, the persecution is going to start." . . . But see, the Jews would have to emigrate without a thing, the way God sent them into the world, right?, with just what they had on their backs. So naturally, nobody wanted to leave and leave their fortunes, right? So that might even be true, do you think?

Kurt says that in school, from the very first day, they taught you to hate the Jews, really awful, I mean demented, evil stuff. He says that from the day he had the power of reason, they started telling him the Jews ran the world, they were this inf, this, what's the word?, inferior race. And they were going to ruin everything, and take over everything, and that's why they were accumulating so much wealth, that everything was controlled by the Jews. So he says that they always always told him this stuff, like it was a class, all the time, something you learn in class, and you're never never supposed to forget it, they taught him that. Is the word dogma? So anyway, for five years they kept telling them that on this one day they were going to kill them, and the day came and nobody had believed it. There was just a minority that believed it, right? So at twelve o'clock at night they started rounding up the Jews. Kurt says that the plan was that they were going to put them all together in different concentration camps, and then little by little they'd liquidate them. And since they were this inferior race, they knew they weren't going to, I mean they couldn't rebel or anything, you know?

So anyway, all these Hitler troops start rounding up the Jews. Nobody even knew whether they were going to kill them or not, they just took them off to jails or concentration camps, and at some given moment they *would* start killing them in the concentration camps, but the Jews just let themselves be carried off without anybody knowing what they were going to do with them. I mean, they'd always been persecuted, locked up, hassled, and all, so they thought that they'd be left alone in the ghettos, is that how you say that?, in the ghettos. Dressed Like a Man's mother says that they thought they'd be isolated, you know, cut off and poor and all that, but that nobody would *bother* them or any-

thing. . . . Not even the Germans knew what they were going to
do—Kurt says *he* didn't even know, so how were the Jews supposed to know? They made them turn over their wives and parents, their little children and all their belongings. Listen to this—
Dressed Like a Man's mother told us that they'd say Who do you
love most? And if they answered My husband, they'd take off
their mother, or their father. And if they answered My mother,
thinking maybe she was already old or there are lots of women or
something, then they'd take their husband or their children away
from them. It was terrible, right? And then they kept *on* screwing
them, in all kinds of ways, because in a while they'd be back for
the survivors and take them off to the concentration camps too.
That's what happened to her. . . .

So anyway, Kurt and my Aunt Emma showed up one afternoon
smelling to high heaven of Palmolive soap. They started off saying
Listen, we've got this problem. . . . This was during the time lots
and lots of people were coming to the house with condolences and
all and to tell us how sorry they were about my father dying. The
rosaries and all that were finished, but our friends kept coming to
visit us, so naturally I thought Kurt and Emma . . . Because I'll
tell you, otherwise I wouldn't've opened the door. . . . Bisexual
anteaters! . . . If I'd ever suspected what they had come for, I
wouldn't've let them in the house. . . . So they came in and said
Listen, we've got this problem, they said, but you, now be frank,
be honest with us, tell us the truth because you can tell us the
truth, and they went on like that, and finally they said Tell us the
truth if you mind if we spend the weekend at your house. . . .
And you know, they've got all kinds of money, they've got their
own house and everything, right? Can you believe this? . . .
We've got this problem and we don't know how to tell you what it
is, you're going to think we're crazy. . . .

So anyway, it turns out that they'd seen a girl in the
house. . . . I mean like you'd see a ghost, an apparition, you
know? . . . They were at home and Emma, who's lying in bed,
says Kurt, honey, a girl just walked by. . . . Because all of a
sudden she saw this girl go by. . . . So she says to Kurt, A girl

just walked by, I mean *just* walked by, a second ago, like she was
going into the bathroom. So Kurt grunts Oh Emma, you're having
a dream. . . . She just went in the bathroom, Kurt, I swear it!
Really? Yes, I swear to you. . . . Señorita! he yelled, where are
you going? But there was no answer. . . . They were both real
quiet, they like held their breath and listened, and then they
heard the toilet flush. Who's there? Kurt bellowed, and he gets
up, walks into the bathroom, turns on the light in the hall, and he
doesn't see a thing. So he goes back into the bedroom. When did
you see her? he said. He had his back to the door, and he was
walking toward the bed, not in a great mood as you can imagine,
and he was muttering Emma, you're crazy. . . . Look! she yells,
and Kurt spins around, and he swears he saw this smoke-colored
nightgown floating along. She just walked by again! Emma was
crying. She just went in the sewing room! So she started yelling
Come out of there or I'm going to call the police! Come out of
there right this minute! She got out of bed too and stayed right
behind Kurt, who was creeping along, real slow, trying not to
make any noise, all bent over, like he was dragging one of those
ovens from the crematorium he intended to throw the girl or whatever it was into. So then they turned on the sewing room light,
and they didn't see anybody. . . . Emma started crying
again . . . Oh, Kurt, I swear, I swear a girl came in here, I swear
to you. . . . She was blond, and she was all dressed in white,
and, I swear, a blond all in white, and I saw her go in the sewing
room. I'm not crazy. Kurt, believe me please, because I know you
think I'm crazy. So then they went back to the bedroom, Kurt
trying to calm her down and whispering all kinds of soft velvety
stuff to her and promising her he wouldn't turn off the hall light or
close the door. . . . Well, they got back in bed, and Emma had
just about gotten over her crying fit, when same song second
verse, here goes the same figure by in front of them again, down
the hall, real slow, slipping along with quiet peaceful elegance,
almost transparent and obviously real, maybe some kind of joker
or a crazy lady or something, but definitely a beautiful teenaged
girl. . . . So now Kurt is convinced, there's no doubt in his mind

anymore, so he shouts at her, Excuse me, señorita, could you
go away please. . . . Nothing. I mean *nothing*. He tried to get up
but he couldn't. Señorita! So then they started arguing about
whether they really had seen her or not. . . . But they heard the
bathroom door lock—the key-thing turned twice around like it
does—and at that Emma grabbed what she could, whoosh!, just
like that, she grabbed what she could get her hands on, just
snatched up like her underwear and an overcoat . . . just whatever she could, you know?, and they ran out of the house and got
a hotel room to stay in that night.

The next day they went back to the house. They were eating
and Emma froze, catatonic, I mean *petrified*. She couldn't move.
She was eating, and the ghost-girl just sort of went by in front of
her like that, opened the closet door, put on a raincoat and rain-
hat, can you imagine, a *rain*hat, and stood in front of the mirror
and adjusted it on her head, standing there looking at herself in
the mirror and fixing herself and kind of fluffing up her blond
hair. Kurt says he'd just put a spoonful of soup in his mouth and
he saw Emma like that, frozen, so he passed his hand in front of
her eyes like this, you know, to wake her up. When she didn't
react, he waved his hand like this again down in front of her
eyes. . . . The ghost-girl, anyway, the ghost-girl opened the
closet door she'd just got through closing, like it was the front
door of the house or something, or the door down at Sanborns by
the Angel on Reforma, and she waltzed through it just as unconcerned as you please and closed it behind herself. Kurt by this
time was shaking my aunt. . . . So Emma described the scene to
him, practically scared to death, and even like she couldn't believe it herself, and they both stood up and said to the closet, Is
anyone there? And since there was no answer, they jerked the
door open and started pulling out jackets, overcoats, scarves,
mufflers, you name it, all the stuff in the closet. If you're here,
I'll fucking kill you, Kurt says, and they're pulling all this stuff
out of the closet. . . .

Another night Emma says, this other night she says that she
felt this cold. They were asleep, and it was about three o'clock in

the morning. . . . Ever since that first time they'd seen, I mean like the ghost had *appeared*, you know, they'd slept with a night-light and the hall light left on. So anyway, Emma got cold and she started groping around, but she couldn't find the covers. Kurt, she says, and she had to open her eyes because she was half or mostly asleep, and she couldn't figure out where the covers had gone, you know?, like they'd fallen off the bed. So get this, when she opens her eyes she sees the girl, transparent and sort of wispy like cigarette smoke, blond, with this nightgown or something that looked like a white nightgown on. . . . She was pulling the covers off her and standing there laughing. . . . Emma started shrieking like a banshee and shaking Kurt like crazy. She rattled his teeth practically, trying to wake him up, you know? . . . Now by this time they had hired some old ladies that were famous, I mean famous as hell, for their prayers. People said their prayers were strong, they really worked, like indulgences or something, you know?, and they hired them to say the rosary in the house every day. . . . They were getting ready to sprinkle holy water in all the corners and bless the house and everything, but Kurt put his Lithuanian foot down to that. . . .

So here they descend on me and say couldn't I help them, couldn't they stay just a few days while they looked for an apartment and sold the house. So I said Sure Emma, of course, except our money situation is the worst. . . . I mean, my father had won thirty-five thousand pesos at jai alai, and he'd gotten mugged as he was leaving, and they'd gotten him in a full nelson and killed him. Strangled him, right? So he died without you know, a last will and testament—I think the word's intessomething. So I told them, If you guys can help us out a little with the household expenses, terrific, you know?, just for your own food and stuff, because we don't even have enough for ourselves. My brother still doesn't have a job, and there are days we eat scrambled eggs and stuff like that, so there's not a single peso left over for you, you know? . . . Ay, how can you even think! Kurt said. That's what we were going to ask you to let us do, help out with the household expenses. . . . Oh, sweetheart, pipes up Emma, how could you even mention such a thing, that's the only way we'd think of staying in your house, if you'd let us buy all the food and everything for everybody, I mean for all of us, I mean for your mother and your brother and you. . . .

Infected gallbladders! Listen, they stayed for three months, I mean three months of torture, of *torture*, because the man never once left the house, never, I mean never never never. All day it was talk talk talk talk talk. You couldn't do anything, and what's more, as though that wasn't enough, all day he was saying stuff against the Jews. . . . One of those people with a one-track mind that repeats the same thing over and over and over again. . . . So listen to what happened—they stayed for three months and at the end of three months, they left. It bugged the hell out of us, too, because she drank sixteen cups of coffee a day, and he drank fifty-four, I mean we counted them, fifty-four. . . . Every twenty minutes he was asking you for another cup of coffee. And don't think he was the type to get up and get it himself, oh no, he'd grab one of the servants, my servants, or he'd say to me, Would you make me some coffee? So all day long my poor servants had to fart around in the kitchen making him coffee. And all of a sudden they leave. . . . You ever see them again? Us neither. . . . They never came by, they never said Thank you, kiss my foot, nothing . . . And my mother, of course, every day with that voice of hers she uses when she prays, of course, that praying voice of hers, they saw they had a golden goose, or I mean at least a goose, like every other mother, she was just oozing sweetness, they come in, settle down, take it easy, don't have to pay the maids, don't have to pay for anything. . . . But what happened was, get this, they were in the house three months, and they ran off all the maids we had because they couldn't stand the pair of them, so they left, and after three months, not even a thank you, you know? . . .

But one day I asked Emma for the keys to her house, her house in Colonia del Valle with the ghost-girl and everything. I'd told The Monk about it, and we were really excited about going out there, I mean like champing at the bit, you know?, so I made this deal with the Jalisco Sisters, and they said, this was the story, okay?, they said they were going to stay with me to see if we could see the ghost-girl. . . . The Monk was supposedly coming by their house for me when he got off work at the Ministry, right?

It was this two-story house, modern, full of these big potted palms and vases and religious pictures like *The Last Supper* and the *Souls in Purgatory*. Why are they all chained up if they can't go anywhere anyway? I asked The Monk, because see there were all these women in this forest of fire and flames like licking at them everywhere. . . . That's not a *photograph*, says The Monk, making that face he makes like a Ministry secretary, it's a painting, and the painter imagined the souls in purgatory that way. It's not that that's really the way it is. . . . Right next to the front door there was a closet full of overcoats, like I told you already, so I said to The Monk, Look, here's where the ghost-girl went. . . . The bedrooms were upstairs. Just one of them was for sleeping in, though. They'd put in a sewing room in one of them, and in the other one they had a bunch of chairs sitting in front of this giant television set. . . . Then we opened a closet, and what do you think it had in it? Pictures of wrestlers and boxers all over the place—from Mouse Macías and Birdy Moreno to Rubén Olivares and El Santo. . . .

Did I tell you about Emma? Well, listen, whenever there was an important fight or wrestling match or something in Los Angeles, she'd be off like a shot off a shovel for Los Angeles. No kidding—during this time I'm telling you about, Butterfingers Nápoles had had a fight, and she left Kurt in my house and went to the fight and sat in the front row. She was a fan, I mean a *fanatic*, I'm telling you, and she had every boxer and wrestler in the world stuck up there with thumbtacks. And sixty years old! She knew all their weights, all their measurements—you know, "the tape"—she knew who'd fought who, who went for the eyes, all that, right? She knew all the wrestling holds and all the technicalities. Why, she knew the names of the referees! . . . And— oh, I told you how Catholic she was, didn't I? Well, then, so get this. . . . She'd sit down to watch the tube, she'd turn on the tube, and she'd pick up her beads. . . . She'd say like five rosaries, honest, or three rosaries a day. And then she had this book, *this* thick, all dog-eared and falling apart, the pages falling out, with lots of stuff about prayers and things like that, you know? Well, she has to sit down and start praying at five o'clock in the afternoon so at eleven o'clock when she's falling asleep in the chair, I mean while she's watching Mannix and Perry Mason or some singer—or like Los Mariachis, you know, that kind of stuff—while she's watching this stuff, she's praying, you know, all the time, so when they say Good evening, at eleven o'clock at night on the television, she says Amen. . . . I'm not kidding! . . . Amen! . . . She prays while she watches TV, no? And when she'd watch the fights on TV at my house, she'd pick up her beads and start in—Hail Mary, *full of grace*, The Lord is with Thee! Holy Mary MOTHER OF GOD! Hit 'im you sonofabitch, kill 'im, kill 'im! What're you waiting for?! HIT 'IM, KILL 'IM, KILL 'IM! Our Father who art in heaven, *Hallowed be Thy name!* You fucking bastard! *Chíngale!* You let 'im hit you again! Pansy sonofabitch, hit 'im, HIT 'IM IN THE BALLS, KILL 'IM! That's how she said her rosary, right? And when the rosary was finished, the boxing match on TV would be over too. . . . But I'm telling you, that's not the half of it. It was incredible, because while she said her rosary, she'd be crying all the time. Oh, and she prayed to the Moon, la Luna, you know? . . . Emma, when the moon came out, prayed. With twenty-centavo pieces, right? She'd take these twenty-centavo pieces all wrapped up tight in little tiny pieces of paper and hold them in her hand and pray. I tell you, she'd be riding along in the car, just riding along, talking to you, real happy and everything, all wrapped up in whatever it was she'd be telling you and all, and all of a sudden she'd see the moon, take out her twenty-centavo piece, wrap it up in a little piece of paper, and start crying. And she'd cry, and she'd cry, and she'd cry. . . . I mean the minute she said Hail Mary, the minute she said Hail, the minute she said Hai, the minute she said Heh, the minute she said H, these big tears would already be rolling down her cheeks. . . . I don't know why. There was so much inspiration when she prayed that she cried. . . .

But anyway we were in her house, right? Can you imagine that

The Monk had never in his life really kissed me? . . . I mean, sure, I kissed him, right?, but for the inspiration to come from his side, no, never. Not once! It scared him so much, he was so scared I'd find out he didn't know how to kiss or something, I don't know, that he never even shook my hand. . . . So of course, I thought he was never going to function, if you know what I mean, and I was just consumed by curiosity, you know to find out, because I also thought he might be gay or something, so I fixed it so we'd have to spend the night together, and get rid of the last doubt, in the ghost-girl's house. The thing is, he was always too servile and wimpy, in spite of working with like the Prime Minister, too much of a jerk, not to put too fine a point on it, and like, like strange, you know? Like he had this complex or something, right? He always acted so scared and mousy, you know, like he was terrified or something. Of what, I don't know. I thought Maybe this guy's got a sexual thing or something and thinks going out with me will solve it for him. Besides, I never gave much thought to LOVE with The Monk. I never believed in that. It all happened so fast I never thought about it, I didn't have time to think about anything. . . .

He was always on this literary kick. He'd call me his wood nymph or his silken tapestry or his whirlwind or his cheesecake, or his little bug or his water. He'd sit there looking at me with those camel's eyes or cow's eyes or whatever you call them of his, and forget it, I was ready for the ghost-girl to show up, or die, or something. . . . I didn't know how I was going to keep from laughing if he ever really made a pass at me, attacked me for real, or if he tried to undress me or started to take off his own clothes. I swear, I didn't think I could control myself. So anyway, we drank some coffee and turned on the radio—we had it figured out that ghosts didn't like noise—and tried to postpone the hormonal moment, if you know what I mean, talking about Kurt and Emma, saying how pretty their Ampeer-style furniture was and smacking our lips over some little Italian cookies we'd bought ourselves on the way over. . . .

Let's see, I told you they'd been staying with us for two

months, right? Okay, so you know what they'd bought us not long before? Four *chamorros*—four pork shanks, I mean they weren't even good enough to buy one apiece. Did you ever try to eat one? Yuck. They bought four bony pork shanks. And every day I was going out and buying Kurt ham for dinner. . . . Because I didn't tell you he didn't eat just anything. He'd eat Campbell's soup, preferably split pea, and broiled steak or roast beef, right?, only the best for old Kurt. So this one day Emma goes out to this auction with her girlfriends from the sewing school, and Kurt stayed at home. By that time we couldn't stand him anymore. . . . It was one Sunday night, and when Emma came back, she came into my bedroom. I can't stand that Nazi anymore! I mean really angry as hell, right? I was in bed. . . . I mean *puleez*, she went on, Olivares is fighting in San Antonio next week, and we've already got the tickets and everything, and now the big stupid Nazi doesn't feel like going. But I don't care! I'm leaving and I'm leaving right now, *right now!* Castrated kangaroos! So, she leaves. You think she cared if she was leaving Kurt there on our hands? But just like that, as happy as she could be, forget it. . . .

So the guy stayed a couple of more weeks in my house. And the worst part of it is, that Emma wouldn't have anything to do with him anymore, if you know what I mean, she said she didn't have time to see him, you know, and she was selling the house and all, lock, stock, and ghost-girl. So Kurt goes crazy. He spends twenty-four hours a day telling us Emma's life story. He was so pissed off that he started telling us what he thought about Emma, I mean *everything*. And us sitting there listening to it, my mother, my brother, and me, listening to it, listening to him, you know, but on top of everything he was so slow, so simple, I mean this guy was so *boring*, we couldn't stand him anymore, we couldn't bear to be around him anymore. But we didn't have a lot of choice, you know. . . . Do you have any idea what it is to see a person twenty-four hours a day, sitting there in your house, in your *living* room? . . . And twenty-four hours a day, not moving? This guy didn't move, I mean he *never* moved. Or picked up a newspaper, or a magazine, nothing, never. The only thing he ever did was sit there and smoke and smoke and smoke, staring at the walls, off in a cloud somewhere, and drink coffee and coffee and more coffee, all the time. All you had to do was walk by, though, or stick your head in the room—and you could've been *any*body, it was all the same to Kurt—and he'd start bad-mouthing Emma again, or sometimes he'd start talking about the war, right? Because he'd been in Russia besides, in, what do you call it?, Siberia? So he'd talk about how they'd deported the Jews, how they'd crucified them and castrated them and stuck their sex in their mouths, about how there'd been millions of them that had never made it to the ghettos, and about the famous night of the Provocation, Crystal Naught or something like that, and what they did to them in Ponar, and I mean Ponar was like death, right? I mean, everything he told was like war stories, gory stuff and traumas and things. Fifteen days of that . . .

So finally, one day, and we were fed up to here with this guy, one day they threw Dressed Like a Man out of her house—oh, now I remember, it was this cold rainy morning, really cold and rainy. Because she owed three months' rent. . . . They called in the lawyers and threw her out, her and her brother and her mother, all of them, and guess what?—That's right!—All three of them are Jewish, I mean the Star of David in the middle of their faces, and Kurt here in my house. . . . So this maid of Dressed Like a Man's comes in, because they'd cut off our telephone, so we didn't have a telephone, so she comes in and says Señorita, they said to tell you that they'll be right over here with their things. And me with Kurt . . . During this time I'm telling you about there was this first cousin of my father's here too, because he'd come from Mazatlán for the funeral, and he'd stayed over to supervise some repairs we were having done to the roof. So sure enough, they swooped into the house, just picture this—Dressed Like a Man, her pimply brother, and her pushover mother. And that was like the last straw for my brother, right?, forget it, my brother's freaking out, he can't believe the whole thing. You better lay down the law from the beginning! he keeps saying. And

my mother's practically in tears—Tell them we simply can't re-
ceive them!—you know how my mother talks. . . . Well, so anyway, Dressed Like a Man came in with her mother sick, her
brother all pimply and droopy, Celerina, her maid, right?, as
dark-skinned as ever, and all their furniture and stuff. It took us
all night to get all the stuff packed in the garage and down the
halls, right? And all this time Kurt sitting there in his chair with
this cigar and this blankety-blank coffee. . . . So my mother has
no idea in the world what to do, right? Dressed like a Man says
Tomorrow we'll find a hotel, but can we leave the furniture here
with you, just for a few days? But her mother was sick sick sick, I
mean physically, so we said Let's put your mother to bed, we'll
wait for her fever to go away, don't worry. . . . You know how
long her mother took bed rest? Guess. . . . Four years. Four
years! And some-odd days. . . . We were sleeping on the *floor*.
My brother slept in his bedroom with David, Kurt in the armchair
in the living room, my uncle in the maids' room because we didn't
have any maids anymore, Dressed Like a Man with me, Celerina
on top of my father's desk, and the two older women in a separate
room. So finally, when disaster struck, Kurt left.

We never saw him again, but a year later we found out that
Emma was mad at us because we'd told Kurt she was sixty. Well
I mean, she was pretty old and all, but she was beautiful, a really
really good-looking woman. And she's had plastic surgery and all
besides. So he was going to be fifty-six or so his next birthday.
He's a lot younger than she is. And he *asked* me. . . . Well, I
say, my mother's sixty-five, and she's not supposed to be much
older than Emma, although she doesn't look her age, they look
about the same age. So my mother was listening to all this, and
she chimes in and says She's sixty. . . . And Kurt never came
back, never ever, I mean he never even came back to say thank
you or anything. All he'd done was talk about her, about how she
was frigid, she was a woman that was sexually tired or worn out or
something like that, that she didn't move, if you know what I
mean, and he said he didn't know how she could've had so many
lovers, because she'd been married eleven times and every time

the marriage broke up because her husband found out she had a lover. . . . I mean, Emma had a life of her own, you know. . . . And so he says he can't imagine, with all the experience she'd had, how she could be so naive and foolish. Because when it came to sex, she was supernaive and innocent, right? . . . Well, so anyway, everything Kurt told us about Emma went in one ear and out the other, because we never said a word, we just sat there and listened to him, like this. . . . So Kurt left and told her, can you imagine?, that *we* had said that she was frigid, that she'd had all these lovers, that she was sixty years old. . . . So then my mother found out, I don't know how, and she called them up on the telephone and said Don't ever come back to my house again, how could you, how could you treat us like this after we've sacrificed so much to have you here! . . . My mother said terrible things to them. . . .

Well, of course when I was in their house with The Monk, none of this had happened. We were talking about the fifty-something cups of coffee a day Kurt drank and some *very strange* letters The Monk was leaving for me all over the place. Until finally the conversation kind of petered out like your salary at the end of the month. . . . It was about two o'clock in the morning, so we turned off the radio. We had to sleep, too, right? So we went upstairs to the bedrooms, and I went into the bathroom and came out absolutely swallowed up in this nightgown, like a tent, you should've seen me, of Emma's. And boy, you couldn't believe The Monk's face when he sees me in that nightgown. Clean mind, clean body, he leers at me, and he shoves this piece of paper at me and disappears into the bathroom. I was a little scared, right? Because I'd never met a guy like The Monk. And besides I wanted to pep him up, you know?, do it like with Alexis or Handsome to the Maximum, like with the people I was used to dealing with, but I always came up short, if you know what I mean, I always flunked the test. Because it was that The Monk is one hundred percent serious and one hundred and ten percent proper. So I was like terrified, terrified. On the one hand I was boiling over with curiosity to see the ghost-girl, and on the other, well, like I had all these *questions* I wanted answers to. And excited, you know, turned on, like sexually. And this little piece of paper in my hand, all scribbled over with ulterior motives. . . .

Sometimes I dream and I come. Many times I dream of you. Other times it's just me myself—my hands, my mind, and me. But it's not so complete, let us say, that way. Not so much for lack of a vagina, not so much because one cannot live without vaginas, nor for lack of the conversations, intimacy, tenderness, communication, but rather for lack of lips. One can't kiss all alone. There is no way to replace the smooth, soft, warm, moist sensation of tongues, mouths, lips. There is even less way to replace the sensation of a light kiss as soft as a whisper, like that kiss the other day, which I still feel. . . . It is not the same to feel one's own skin as to feel the velvety, silky skin of another person. And really, why act like children? There is also no substitute for a moist, soft, tight vagina.

I could hear the water running in the sink and then, instead of coming out all radiant and smelling like Colgate, The Monk starts banging on the door. At first I couldn't figure out what was going on. But he kept banging harder and harder, really violent, you know?, so I got up out of bed. Why did you lock the door? See, he had locked the door. Me? So I immediately thought This guy is screwing around, he's trying to make me think it's the ghost, so I picked up on the joke, right? When really all I wanted to do was wipe out my irritation with reading his letter. Did you read it? he asked me. What? The piece of paper. Yes, but I didn't understand a thing, and I handed it back to him. He took it and folded it three times. You're a very very intelligent girl, he said. . . .

Well, to make a long story short, ten minutes later we were naked. But The Monk didn't dare touch me. He'd come close and then jump back. My skin scared him, or the situation, I don't know, and he was shivering, like he had a fever. And then all of a sudden, a chair fell over in the dining room, and we froze, both of us. The ghost woman, he cracked. A cat, I said, my Aunt Emma has a cat. Or at least I hoped, fervently I tell you, that she had a cat. We were like hypnotized, and then I took his face in my hands, like saying Come on, enough nonsense, let's talk about serious stuff now. . . . An intelligent man, I thought, very sensitive, young, naive, inexperienced. I kept telling myself that, but by that time with about as much sincerity and affection as you'd have for a fish. . . . But all of a sudden The Monk turned into a sexual octopus, and he started fondling me and caressing me all over. I couldn't believe it—a sensual, sexual mass, a little primitive and terribly terribly passionate, fierce, greedy, and wild. . . . At that point we didn't know that the ghost-girl was between us, that she was lying there soft and light and almost transparent beside us, or I mean between us, and that some of those arms that were like repetitions of The Monk's, or a tongue, or that weight, or maybe that distance between The Monk and me, manifested, is that the word?, manifested her. It all made her real, but *scary* real, you know? So finally, The Monk could never find a good position, or stay in it, he couldn't manage to get comfortable, he kept bumping into the ghost-girl's legs, they got in his way, or maybe into mine, and he couldn't settle down. He kept slipping out, so I held him, a little impatient as you can imagine. I tried to get it in for him, you know how it is, and *chíngale!*, he came, and came, and came. . . . And at four o'clock in the morning, the same story. The ghost-girl was an acrobat or something, I don't know, because she always raped him before I could. . . . Then another ejaculation, you know, and another failure, not a kiss or anything. . . . I said to myself, This guy's going to die on me right here, and I thought of these friends of the Jalisco Sisters?, these guys that just like to watch, you know?, and they even pay just to watch? Was The Monk one of those guys? But he didn't masturbate or anything, no, he didn't even touch himself, he didn't even touch *me!* . . . That's why we blamed the ghost-girl, right? And half-an-hour later, same story. The Monk must've been full of semen. . . . Then I began to like mother him, very very tenderly. So then we deduced, you know, figured out that it was the ghost-girl, so we went to sleep . . . sound asleep. . . .

So anyway, that's what happened, and that's all that happened.

So then, listen, it was six o'clock in the afternoon, and he got up to open the curtains, and I saw his white little fanny and I started giggling. I mean, I got tickled, all nervous, from seeing his fanny. I got this nervous laughter. . . . But listen, before, when I woke up and saw him so close up, I said What a divine nose he has. I was just knocked out by that nose. So when he opened his eyes, I saw the color of his eyes for the first time in my life. I'd never seen his eyes, I mean, I swear, I'd never seen his eyes because I'd never seen *him* so close up. So of course, I'd never been able to see the color of his eyes. So when he opened his eyes, he says Are you watching me? And I said What a divine nose you have, and What a beautiful color your eyes are. And he started laughing, can you imagine, and when he started laughing I saw his teeth for the first time too. . . . What pretty teeth, I whispered. The better to eat you with, he says. . . .

I never talked to him the way I'm talking to you, you know what I mean? I mean, when I talked to him, I always looked down because I was ashamed by how much he'd read, or because I got this nervous laughter, or maybe just because he bored me, like when politicians start talking shop. So anyway, he got up and opened the curtains. Ay, the sun was fiery red, a red so beautiful, so beautiful, that I forgot I was hungry and thirsty. . . . The bedroom got red, red, red. The bed, the ceiling, the furniture, everything turned red. And he stood there, looking at me, real serious, like a bullfighter. And he walked over and started pulling down the covers, uncovering me, little by little pulling down the red red sheets. And you could see his shadow on the wall, right? A black silhouette on the reddish-orange wall, because the sun was red, red, red. . . . The Monk saw himself, too, on the wall I mean, and in real life, too, and he swelled up with pride, and sperm too, sort of shivering, like he couldn't believe it, almost blazing, and of course red, like the blessed souls in purgatory. . . .

And days later, when we were arguing in the Memorial Park and Garden, there was another red red sun on the graves and headstones, and I remembered that silhouette, that shocking, proud silhouette, because I only went to bed with him that one time, that's all, and I got pregnant. . . . Not to be believed, right? We did it one little time and I got pregnant. Or I mean we made love, you know, not we did it. . . . Well, at least I thought I was pregnant. Let me tell you about that. . . .

("When the sun sets the city ablaze, one must have the soul of a Nero!")

14

On sentimental tendencies or transitions

Gelded giraffes! Dressed Like a Man's mother, I know her real well, she even lived with us once. . . . I'm not sure why I'm telling you this. . . . My girlfriend would come in, for example, and she'd say How do you feel, Mama? And her mother doesn't answer her, she just keeps watching television. So she yells Hey! How are you! And she doesn't answer her. Mama, I'm talking to you. . . . I heard you, she says, and she keeps watching the television. . . . The kind of lady you don't think is even real, you can't believe she's normal, you know? . . . I mean I'm no psychologist, but I think she ought to be walled up somewhere, she ought to be in a home for the mentally unbalanced, I swear to you. . . . She was in a concentration camp, she's got this number tattooed on her arm and everything. She's not so old by the way. . . . They killed her whole family, even this twin sister she had, all her other brothers and sisters, her aunts and uncles, her cousins, the whole family. Like one of those stories you hear and you go Gosh, like you just read about in books. . . . Like for example, she had to be the lover of this woman that worked there who at the same time was the lover of this Nazi guy, this petty bureaucrat she said, and they tried to hide her in a pile of corpses they were supposed to take out of the camp on a wagon, under some kind of cover, right?, but some soldiers were there, or they were too close or something, and she couldn't escape, so there she was, naked and filthy, all covered with dead bodies, and they buried her alive in a huge hole, and she finally got out at night with the help of this passionate lover of hers. *Female* lover, right? . . . I mean like from the horror movies, awful stories. . . . And Dressed Like a Man is her only daughter, so I think she must have grown up hearing these thousands of war stories. Her mother lets her do anything she feels like, and she even meets one of her boyfriends, and she says You'll never be true to him, don't be a fool. . . . She doesn't want her daughter to tie herself down to just one man. . . . There's not one single man in the world that's worth that! she says. So she throws these boyfriends at her, she lets her have all the boyfriends she wants, she *pushes* her, I kid you not, to go out with all these guys at the same time. Like six, okay? It messes up her ego, you can imagine. It like confuses her so much that the poor thing keeps getting all these skin diseases like psoriasis and some kind of licking something, lichen, I don't know, from being so insecure, right? Because her mother—she tells her No, you have to have many, many boy-friends, you can't give yourself to only one. And at home we all thought that was so she wouldn't get married, so she'd be depen-dent on her mother longer, so she wouldn't leave her. . . .

I mean Dressed Like a Man, when she lived at my house, she'd come in and get into my bed, she'd take off her clothes and lie down. And her mother would bring in a tray with about a hundred things on it, she'd make her all different kinds of food so the señorita could eat whatever her little heart desired. . . . She'd put all these dishes in a row, and Dressed Like a Man would choose,

like one from Row A and two from Row B, practically like in a
Chinese restaurant, right?, because she was really really spoiled,
right?, by her mother. And my theory about this is that she hasn't
really grown up because all that stuff is like bowing to a little girl's
every whim, don't you think? She's still not a woman, she still
hasn't been able to find herself, and *she* blames the pistol and my
uncle, but *I* think it's her mother, her mother tattooed with a
number on her arm, right? So now Dressed Like a Man has feathers
for brains, I mean she'll only go out with rich kids and all that,
right? *Really* rich kids. She always wants to go to go-go places, and
it's like martyrdom, she goes through a whole martyr routine because Bloodhound won't let her go. . . . Because Bloodhound goes
absolutely everywhere with her.

Take, for example, one time I got home from modeling, and they
were just serving dinner. David was Dressed Like a Man's first
cousin, but he'd lived with her for years and years, and he was
really close to my mother too. . . . So there we all were, minus
Celerina, and our two mothers were shuffling back and forth with
the silverware and napkins and stuff, the bread and the coffee pot
and all that, right? When my brother saw how surprised I was, he
said Celerina's in the sanatorium. So then Dressed Like a Man
explained it all like to me, but really to everybody else too. . . .
What happened, she says, was that day before yesterday she told
me she was pregnant. Señorita, I'm going to have a baby. Ay Cele,
how'd that happen? I guess I was careless, señorita. . . . So what
are you going to do now, right?, that was the next question, they
didn't ask her when it was due, right?, or anything. Like ignore it
and it'll go away or something. So then before the sun was up the
next morning she starts hearing whimpers. She says she got up,
and Celerina was crying Oh señorita, it hurts. . . . She was in
pain. . . . Where, Cele? . . . My stomach hurts, señorita, it hurts
very much. . . . You think a little anise tea will help? No,
señorita, it hurts very very much. Well, what do you think it is? I
don't know, señorita, but I think I'm going to die. . . . She was
rolling around and twisting from the pain, right? So Dressed Like a
Man didn't know what to do, so she woke up David and my brother,
and they decided to take her to the hospital and think about it

there. They took off like a rocket, right?, and they finally persuaded the hospital to look at her, after all these problems with cards and forms and money, you know how they are, right? . . . So I had spent the night that night with Alexis, in the Hotel Presidente?, and all day I'd been in this fashion show at the Palacio de Hierro. So anyway, to make a long story short, they'd barely touched her stomach, and Celerina started to howl like a soul in purgatory. Dressed Like a Man grabbed her cream and started rubbing it into one whole arm, like this, like a crazy woman. And about then this nun comes out, and so she stops rubbing and she says Excuse me mother, I mean sister, what's wrong with her? She's having her baby, the nun said angelically. And she had never worn maternity clothes or anything, I mean nobody in the whole house had noticed a thing, and Dressed Like a Man says when Celerina told her about it she thought she was like a month or like two months along, right? How was *she* supposed to know? . . .

So then she says to the nun Well, uh, mother, give her a sedative, for heaven's sake, *please,* or something for the pain. Oh no, she says, no sedatives, these girls must learn what it means to be a mother, they must know the sacrifice and pain of being a mother. . . . Mother my ass! You give her a sedative and give it to her now!, I demand it, because I'm the person that brought her here! . . . But the nun says I'm afraid we can't give her anything. . . . So my girlfriend goes And I say you'll do it and do it NOW! Well, about then, no, wait, so then Dressed Like a Man and this nun had a huge fight. But about then the doctor comes out, the doctor that had delivered Dressed Like a Man, in fact, and he says Hi, darling, come with me a second, come here just a second. So she says she almost fainted of fright at that, because she didn't know what the doctor was going to tell her. . . . So guess what . . . He says Help me here, okay?, because there aren't any nurses right now, and I need you to help me with the delivery . . . okay? And Dressed Like a Man says that the rash started popping out, even on her eyes, she says that she was ready to die. Because on top of all the problems the poor thing had of her own, right?, having her help deliver a baby, I mean . . . So she says she went in and they put gloves on her, and she started helping, although she felt like she was about to faint, that she was in a state, you know?, and every square inch of her body itched. So just then a nurse or a nun, or a nun-nurse, whatever, came in and she was out of there like a shot. She says she'd never thanked God so fervently in her life, so she ran out and started running to the car, because the boys were waiting for her in the car, and they drove her home in twenty-four hundredths of a second. Or less. I don't want to know if it was a boy or a girl, she said, or *what* it was. Forget it. In fact, added her mother, I think Celerina is going to give the baby up, there in the hospital, because there's a home for foundlings. Pass that fish, said David.

Celerina is practically Dressed Like a Man's big sister, right?, she's been with her forever. She respects her so much, and she adores her, absolutely adores her. But when they moved into my house, she said that she was quitting. So Dressed Like a Man says But Celerina why would you leave? Because I corrected you in front of the boys? If that's why you want to leave, that's kind of silly, don't you think? I mean you leaving for a little thing like that, really Celerina, I've been too good to you for you to, I've given you too much for you to leave over a silly thing like me correcting you in somebody else's house, for you to want to leave. . . . Well I'll tell you, señorita, Celerina starts, you know I don't like to be corrected in front of people, but that was just the straw that broke the camel's back. . . . I want to leave because I can't stand to work for you anymore, period. Because in all the years I've worked for you, you've never been willing to see that I'm just a common woman, a vulgar, common woman, a low-class woman, you want to treat me like a lady, you're even afraid of me, of what I'll think. You see I'm a little mad or a little upset, and you get all nervous and scared and you don't know what to do, you can't do enough to please me. . . . You say Oh Celerina dear, please do me a favor, my pretty pet, oh my love, please, would you do me a favor and bring me . . . Well, señorita, I can't work for you anymore. I like people to yell at me, I want to feel like I work for somebody strong, somebody that will boss me, not somebody that's afraid of me. . . . You see, sometimes I get cross and nasty, and I even yell sometimes, and you just stand there with your mouth open, you don't dare do anything. . . . And I'm sick of it! So I'm leaving, because I can't work like this anymore. . . . I'm going to find a house where they'll yell at me, where they'll treat me like what I am, because that's what I like. . . . With balls! With spunk! Shit on this!

Okay? And the funniest thing about it is that Dressed Like a Man was telling us this story over sips of hot chocolate with tears in her eyes. I was cracking up when I told you, right? Not Dressed Like a Man. She'd tell you the story like she was the cold wind of suffering personified. It was a big trauma for her, I'm telling you. She was so disheartened, poor thing, so sad. . . .

So anyway, her mother all of a sudden pushes the sugar bowl to one side and drops a piece of blue paper in front of me. I found this in your bedroom, dear, and if you wouldn't mind terribly I'd like you to read this to us aloud because neither I nor your blessed saintly mother . . . David choked on his fish. Well, I don't understand a thing, she said, not a word. . . . It was a letter from The Monk, fortunately one of the first ones. My brother looked disgusted. Where do you find these guys?, he says. I tried to think for a second as I scanned the lines, still chewing, right?, and half waiting for somebody to break the strange silence. What, do you collect them or what?, my brother said.

  . . . There was a word, two words, weighing heavily on me, and it does no good to tell myself that words have no weight, "that the word is not the thing." (Though there is that anecdote which relates that one afternoon Korzybski was standing beneath a tree speaking with his students, when someone ran past shouting, "Run, a tiger is coming!" His students began to flee too, but Korzybski stood firm under the tree, exclaiming, "Wait, don't run, remember that the word is not the thing!" and the tiger came and ate him!) "Te quiero," I wrote, in one of my first letters. Well, and what of it?, I have asked myself a thousand times. What does that mean? It is only a word—in English one unblushingly writes, in any letter whatsoever to any person whatsoever, "Love" or "Affectionately." Et alors, qu'est-ce que ça veut dire, "te quiero?" With love, affectionately, je t'aime, te quiero—are they not all the

same? Yet it has weighed on me like a stone, a weight which has virtually crushed me. But I have now learned to unburden myself of it, I am becoming free. Une parôle ne signifie être engagé, n'est-ce pas? Not that I retract what I said, but that it is not a question of a tiger or of eating anyone up. . . .

After that letter, and lots of letters like it, my relationship with The Monk was going to be a very short one, as you can imagine, and nothing worth talking about would ever have happened if I hadn't gotten pregnant. . . . I mean one single time in my entire life I go to bed with him, and I wind up pregnant. I couldn't sleep, we tortured ourselves over it, we argued and talked about it all day long, we turned it around and looked at it from every angle you can imagine. I got hysterical, of course, and the poor man was scared to death. I vomited up everything I ate. And we'd go over to the San Angel Cemetery. We had some scenes there, well . . . but the upshot of it all was, that I wasn't pregnant at all, right? But of course, I didn't know it at the time, I thought I was pregnant, and this doctor even told me I was pregnant, *very* pregnant he said, and I needed an abortion. But I mean how sad, you know?, because I never told him the truth, and I've been trying to decide whether I'll tell him someday. . . .

Because we'd go over to the Memorial Park or the Garden of Eternal Rest or whatever they call it, to discuss things, right? Because I lived right nearby, so we'd go over there because it was private, quiet, still as the grave, in fact, you might say. . . . We'd meet at Path 8, Plot 5, and we'd sit and get our problems off our chests, right?, with all these marble angels and crosses and boring inscriptions all around us. I mean they were *monotonous,* right? So anyway, we didn't know what to do, so we'd sit there and like keep watch that nobody crawled out of their tomb. . . .

About that time was when his boss, the Minister, right?, like the *Cabinet* Minister, I told you, would have dinner at our house once a month. So The Monk told him everything and the Minister said he was going to give us like a scholarship, right?, some kind of money or . . . a *grant,* right, to Paris or London or anywhere we wanted to go, but I don't know, I really didn't like the idea. . . . I'd actually started sort of to like the guy, you know?, even his camel face, he was great, but we were so different. . . . To start with, he'd gone to school in this seminary, and he was the most intellectual kind of man in the world, and I was the most—how to put it?, the most flighty, right?, the most scatterbrained girl, I mean if I sat down to read *Little Lulu* once every ten days, it was too much for me, I'd wind up in bed with a fever. No, really, I was the most superficial thing in the world. And he was just the opposite, right? I can promise you I was the first girl he'd ever gone out with. . . . Really, it's absolutely true. . . . And I had to have this tragedy, okay? . . . He cried and cried. He really suffered terribly. . . . He'd say things like, You're going to ruin my life, you're going to destroy my political future, my intellectual future, my career, everything I had planned for my life, and it's all going to be finished because of a silly pregnancy. . . . So to make a long story short, we decided I'd get an abortion, right? I'd already taken these pills, you know, and I'd had shots and everything, but I hadn't had my period in two months. . . . After the Big Scene, right? After even the Minister and everybody else in the world had found out, had stuck his nose in, over this stupidity of mine. . . . So I couldn't very well just tell everybody it was a false alarm, you know? . . . So everybody thought I'd gotten an abortion. That I was really pregnant, right?

The way it all came about was, that there was, this one day when these guys asked me out to dinner, I went and I ran into the Jalisco Sisters. We were in the Bellinghausen Restaurant, in the Zona Rosa?, and they had all decided they were going to play this practical joke on me, and pair me up with The Monk, The Friar from Guadalajara, The Archbishop of Camels himself. But Pancho—which was his real name, have I told you that?—Pancho had stood them up, he didn't come to dinner because he was studying something or other, he spent his whole life studying. So all my boyfriends, I mean friends that were boys, right?, paired up with all my girlfriends and odd man out was me. So they decided to go play cards or something over at Andrés' house. . . . So they said We'll go by and pick up a friend of ours so you won't feel left out, and I said Okay. I didn't suspect a thing, right?, because you know The Monk gave me gangrene of the liver, right? Every week calling or sending me letters and stuff . . .

So we drive by for him, and these guys call him from down on the corner and tell him to come downstairs because they're here to bring back some books he's let them borrow. . . . I mean that was the only way to get him out of his house. . . . So then he saw me, and stand back!, he was like Dracula faced with a crucifix, he went white white white, and then his lips turned back and he hissed, and you could see his fangs and everything. I was furious too, but these guys finally made us all laugh, so in a little while we were taking it like this big joke, right? Like it was supposed to be. . . . So anyway, we were all supposed to meet at Andrés' house and they fixed things so I went with The Monk, in his car. So he went back upstairs to get this rabbit-skin jacket he had, a great coat, I'm telling you, and all these lollipops. . . . Here, he said, I brought you some lollipops. He lived in Tecamachalco, and we were meeting over in Prado Churubusco, all the way over there, right?, so you can imagine how long it took, how much time we had to talk, and all the stuff we talked about. I mean as fast as I always talk, right? . . . So anyway, to make a long story short, we'd talked and talked and talked and by the time we got to the party. . . . By the time we got out of the car we were engaged. Well, not engaged, but we were boyfriend and girlfriend. . . . No, I swear to you. We got out holding hands and everything. . . .

It's that he had said all these incredible things, such incredible things about *me*. And some weird vibrations, too, of course, like *we love to end love*, right? He'd absolutely enveloped me in words, and we'd laughed about that little adventure in the restaurant, remember? And then he started Love is only a word, an invention of the twelfth century. And he described my sentimental education, as he called it, he said it was the name of some book, my sentimental education, okay?, as the result of gooey romantic movies and too much television and vulgar popular music, like Oh baby, oh baby, why'd you leave me so sad and blue, right? . . . And while he was talking, it was like he was undressing me with his words, like he was running his words over my breasts, you know, and licking my nipples, and all of a sudden I realized I was wet, wet from the words, right? I thought about all the countless times he'd called me on the phone and I'd treated him like dirt, and always telling me some new piece of gossip about Tarcisio the maître d' or some new craziness like going out with me gave him the sense of going on a journey not only around my body but around my life, and how new and strange and novel it was, with my girlfriends, my friends, my world, everything that pertained to me. *Pertained,* can you stand it? More than an erotic adventure, he'd say, in me he was seeking—I mean the way he talked made me want to scream and laugh all at the same time, you know?—he was seeking a door to knowledge, to a society, to a way of life. I was strange and unknown, like the future, and inexplicable, like dreams. . . .

And the things he asked me to do! He was always wanting to go out with me, and I'd stand him up or make up millions of excuses. So a little bit because of all that and another little bit because his nose in triplicate, an original and two copies, right?, made me laugh, I kissed him. Because he'd said I don't remember what color my skin was, or my eyes, and I couldn't take it anymore, so I kissed him. I had to teach him how to kiss, because like I told you he was so shy. And timid. Magazines, friends, movies, none of them had really taught him the ropes, if you get my meaning. . . . And so what started out as this impulse, right?, grew into something too big to describe it all to you. . . . None of my girlfriends could believe it. . . . But The Monk was so sweet and tender, tender as a little lamb, and he knew everything, he read all the time, except since he was secretary to the Minister, he worked till all hours of the night and even on weekends, so we really didn't get too many chances to see each other. . . . And when we did, I mean, when we were together the time just flew, all we did was talk, and petting was with verbs, right?, or adjectives. Or adverbs. I'd be a liar if I told you that he taught me everything I know, right?, but he taught me a lot. . . . I owe a lot of it to him. . . .

Then came the part about the pregnancy. I wanted to go to Paris or New York to have an abortion, but The Monk couldn't get

away, so we found this clinic in Colonia Roma. Little Jalisco went
with me, trilling and chirping and happy that it wasn't her with
the, uh, problem, right? And I think that the doctor just looked at
me and could tell, I'm sure I wasn't pregnant, I swear to God, I'm
sure of it, I'm absolutely sure there was no fetus or anything, I
think it was some kind of nervous spasm or something. Anemia or
something. . . . So anyway, we get to this depressing gloomy
place . . . You know, or can guess, anyway, how those places
are . . . And without having had anything to eat, on top of
it. . . . I mean, it didn't have cobwebs and creaky doors, right?,
but gloomy. I think that was where they'd done the operation on
Leonor Cifuentes' nose, the plastic surgery, right?, and the cell
transplants or whatever. Silicone, maybe, I don't know. Anyway . . .

Anyway, they gave me this hospital gown, right?, and I put it
on, and they gave me a shot. And so then the doctor comes in,
and he touches my stomach. I'm going to auscultate, he says. I
made him write that down for me later. I'm going to auscultate, he
says, and he thumps me so hard I thought I was going to jump off
the table. I was expecting to see scissors and spatulas or whatever
you call those things, and forceps, like all these instruments of
torture, right? I was also expecting to pass out, because I thought
the shot they'd given me was some kind of anesthesia. Wouldn't
you? But instead of any of that, the doctor sort of patted me and
said Go have breakfast. Pardon? I said. So he pulled off his rubber glove, you know how they sound, right?, *shllp!*, and he says
You can go, I said. Quick, hop up, go. . . . So I left, right? I
leaned on Little Jalisco on the way out. How do you feel? Wonderful, I said . . . just great . . . a little hungry. . . . I mean, I
didn't feel *any*thing. Nothing, nothing at all, it was like I'd gone
in for a soda or something. I mean I was still a little nervous,
because you have to feel *some*thing at a time like that, right?
Take Big Jalisco—she's had four abortions, and she says you
always, she says that after the abortion you get these horrible
horrible cramps and nausea, and you feel like throwing up. So
that's why I say it was nothing, I mean the doctor laughed at me.
Dog's balls! And he still had the nerve to tell me I probably ought

not to have sex for forty days. Forty days! Can you imagine? Especially after what he did to me, shit . . . And it was barely eight
o'clock in the morning. . . .

About nine The Monk was coming by for us. *He's* the one that
looked terrible. He was in torment, tears and everything, a tragedy. . . . From the worry? So we were there waiting for him, and
I thought It's not fair for The Monk to get here and me just great
after all that's happened and all I've supposedly been through. Oh
no. I can't do that. So Little Jalisco says So what do we do? So we
planned that when The Monk got there, I was going to pretend to
be practically fainting from the pain and suffering. . . . So we
were looking through these magazines because there was a shop
downstairs from the clinic?, and we were waiting for him down
there. All of a sudden we got the nervous giggles because they
were supposed to do a D and C on me and all the doctor did was
play with my clitoris. . . . I mean that wasn't normal, right? So
we were standing there going through the magazines and all, and
we saw The Monk coming, with these big dark sunglasses, *this*
big, coming to get me all dressed in black. . . . Mr. Solemnity,
Mr. Tragedy, Mr. Face to Fit the Situation . . . Scorpion's foreskins!

So I quick leaned up against the wall, weak from pain, clutching my stomach, with a face the best actresses of the silent screen
would have envied. Can you imagine the giggles we had? We
couldn't look at each other for fear we'd crack up. . . . Little
Jalisco looked so worried, and when she helped me to straighten
up, she was almost crying. So The Monk gets out of his car and
tries to hold me up and help me walk, you know. His sunglasses
fell off his noses, and he almost stepped on them. The sunglasses, not the noses. So he picked them up, cleaned them with
a little paper hanky, he wiped them off, and he put them on
again. On his museum-quality nose. His nose was famous, bril-
liant, a work of art, long, long, almost indescribable. The Mona
Lisa of Noses. The Mont Blanc actually was more like it. And
like Mona Lisa, enig something, enigmatic, I can never remember
that word. . . . So they carried me . . . I leaned on the two of
them, like this, and The Monk's nose was practically resting on

the foothills of my breasts. . . . That was another of his expressions, right? . . . It took about fifteen minutes to get to the car, this very moving scene, my fake misery, the triple nose, Little Jalisco's handbag slipping down her arm, the reflection of my agonizing face in The Monk's sunglasses, my moans, and the car closer and closer. . . . Like a movie, right? . . . When we got there, Little Jalisco opened the door, and I go like this, leaning on the car and staring at the ground with this dramatic inability to lift my feet . . . And The Monk, that asshole, he trips and slams the door, and *chíngale!*, he breaks my fingers. Every one of them! My hand was like this, on the doorframe, right?, and he trips and falls and hits the door and it slams and *chíngale!*, there go my fingers. He broke every single one of my fingers. . . . So then I cried for real. . . . Then I was really in pain. You can't imagine the pain. The tears just gushed out, and I was screaming . . . real tears. . . .

Now Miss Honestly Agonizing gets carried to have some chicken soup. No, no, you have to eat. Eat, they say. Because I felt terrible, but from getting my fingers crushed, mostly. In fact, *just* from getting my fingers crushed. . . . They'd taken an X ray and put a cast on, put on this board, this split or splint or whatever you call it, and bandaged up my hand like this . . . and all in the same clinic. . . . The Monk had to feed me. Little Jalisco took out a pen and wrote Why should your arm want anything hanging on the end of it anyway? on the cast, and The Monk put Give 'em to the cats, let 'em have some fun. . . . So then I got bags under my eyes for real. . . . From the crying?

Honestly, I have to admit that in love, really in love, I must have really truly been in love only about two or three times. I mean to really love a person, depend on him, miss him, go crazy if he doesn't call you, want to have him beside you night and day, glued to the bed, all gooey and tender—two or three times I've felt that way, although I wouldn't dare call that Real Love. But The Monk was such a puppy, sort of, and he made me feel tender and loving because he was so serious and so passionate, but at the same time he bored me, you know? Always teaching me new words . . . I'll tell you some, like enigmatic like I told you, and migraine and epithelium and defenestrate and aardvark and, well, lots of words. . . . Always dragging in his books or these other people's ideas, trying to read me things out loud or talking about the latest adventures of Tarcisio the Waiter. . . . It put me to sleep, right? I'd start snoring. . . .

This Tarcisio, now that you mention him, he was always in the newspapers back then because these guys asked him to take them out to Colonia Industrial one night, and he said No, he said that he was going off his shift. He wouldn't take them. So they tried to hijack his taxi, they started throwing rocks at his taxi, and they broke the back window. So this maître d' taxi driver Tarcisio made one U-turn and then another one, so he was behind the guys, right?, on I don't remember the avenue, and he followed them, can you believe this?, he trailed them in his taxi, real slow and quiet, with the headlights off. And when he had them in range, right?, when they were like right *there*, because they were drinking and carrying on practically in the middle of the street, singing and stumbling along, you know drunks. . . . So when he had them where he wanted them, he stepped on the gas and ran one down, he knocked him flying through the air that is, because another one dodged him, I don't know how, and another one was too far away to hit. But anyway, one of them was really brutally banged up, his legs were crushed and he landed on the back of a bench, I mean like hanging over the back of the seat, right? So anyway, this guy's skull was fractured, and he's in a coma, or he was, and everybody's trying to catch Captain Tarcisio as the newspapers now called him, because somebody had gotten the license plate number, and the cab company had given them a picture of him. A photograph, right? So now he was this fugitive from justice, right? Wanted Dead or Alive. . . .

But that night . . . Dressed Like a Man's mother was spreading butter on this roll, and she kept saying, very threateningly, but politely, right?, I'd just like for you to read it aloud, really, or don't you want to? I tried to look so uninterested I was about to fall asleep, right?, and I kept eating my cheese sandwich. . . . David and my brother whispering . . . The idiots wouldn't help me! Dressed Like a Man just looked at me, like she wasn't curious or anything. . . . My mother waved her hand through where a fly had just passed by and got up, completely unconcerned. So I cleared my throat with this little cough, right?, *ahem*, and I took two sips of chamomile tea and I started reading. . . .

. . . *There was a word, two words, weighing heavily on me, and it does no good to tell myself that words have no weight* . . .

And I interrupt myself, I look up, and I say Wouldn't it have been better to put There *were* some words, two words . . . ?

I mean think of it, me correcting The Monk's grammar. How about that?

("Everything was love—love! Nothing existed save love. And love was everywhere. Nothing could be talked of but love. Poached love, plain-vanilla love, love to the bearer on demand, love on the easy monthly payment plan. Love analyzable, love analyzed. Overseas love. Love on horseback. Papier-mâché love, love au lait. . . . With an ounce of prevention, a package of preventatives, cut short by short circuits, fouled by red tape. Love with a big M, a capital M, love dripping with meringue, pollinated with white flowers. . . . Spermatozoic love, Esperantoic love. Disinfected love, unguented love. . . . Love with all its accessories, love with refills; with its uncrossed paths, its undotted i's, with its stoppages of the heart and of telephone service. Love that inflames the hearts of hartebeests and firefighters. Love that touches the loins of lions, makes frogs croak in petit mort, lures the lurking green-eyed monster from its lair, and makes rabbits rabid. Love which feasts on ravishment and radishes, lust and lettuce.")

15

Let your body make a pact with another

When I was pregnant, uh-huh, back when The Monk would tell me I was as delicious as fresh-made bread, or a fountain of pleasure, or bedchamber music . . . Anyway, while I *thought* I was pregnant, there was this period when my brother and I weren't close anymore at all. He was on his wavelength, and I was on mine, right? So we sort of drifted apart. . . .

He was constantly going to Acapulco. Every eight or ten days he was in Acapulco. He went in this private plane with the Minister, The Monk's boss? He always took him and flew him back. . . . Leonor Cifuentes would go with them, she was this woman, this, how can I tell you?, she was sort of whorish. I mean red velvet shoes with a chain that hung from here to here, this chain with lots of those little coins hanging on it, right?, which back then I thought was to die, right? Strange, strange. This weird woman. The more you were around her the more you noticed, you know?, you saw her for what she was. She had all these clothes from somewhere like in Los Angeles or Hollywood or someplace called Frederick's, I don't know if you've heard of it, probably not, but they sold things like these T-shirts with the breasts cut out and crotchless panties and teddies that showed your whole ass, things like that, you never heard of this place? Well that's the kind of stuff she wore. The *only* kind of thing she wore. A really strange woman, weird, but she'd managed to dazzle the Minister, The Monk's boss, right?

So one day they invited me to go to Acapulco too. I mean the Minister was this old friend of the family, right? But he always came to our house with his wife, this painted-up outrageously alcoholic ex-opera singer, that spent practically her whole life in a sanatorium. When they were there he'd always, I don't know, it was like he tried to imitate her aristocratic mannerisms, because he was this really not so high-class person, in fact he was sort of, wait a minute, The Monk told me, like a riveter, but that's not it, arrivsomething, like he'd just arrived, right?, so he'd even talk the way she talked, with her little hands folded over forward on her little withered arms, like a kangaroo or a trained dog or something. And he laughed entirely too charmingly when he was with his underlings, but he'd just barely laugh, like it was hard for him to do, when he was by himself, like a big effort. So anyway, he was this old friend of my family, and a cabinet minister and The Monk's boss to boot. Once when my father went bankrupt in some business, he poured in I don't know how much money and saved the day. He seemed perfectly respectable, right? He came to my house once a month to eat, and one day, after my father died, he shows up with Leonor Cifuentes. They'd just put his wife in another sanatorium, so my mother didn't make a face or anything. . . . I spent all my time by the pool, I've spent practically my whole life lying in the sun, so I had this great tan. So they come out to say hello. . . . They come out into the yard with their drinks, trying to be charming, right? Hey! Hi!, blah blah blah . . . So I said hello and everything. . . . Later on, Leonor was laughing over some double-intending, is that right?, double-intending nonsense my brother had been saying, she was a little tipsy, right?, and you'd have thought the dining room was a brothel. My mother was trying to not look too lost, but the stiffness of her back and the way her head kept turning back and forth certainly looked to me like the patronizing supervision of Polly the Poxy or the habits of Velma the Venus Flytrap. They started telling these jokes, right?, these certain kind of jokes, and Leonor would act them out, no doubt even more vulgarly than necessary, to the great delight of the Minister. So they repeated their invitation about a dozen times until my mother finally said Yes, exactly the way the Secretary of State accepts a presidential order, if you know what I mean, and the only reason even then was that I'd be going with my brother. . . . So they leave and it's Adios, adios, be sure to come . . . both of them *very* concerned about my going, right? . . . So to make a long story short, they took us to Acapulco. . . .

One room for me and one for my brother—perfect. We changed clothes, and they say Let's have dinner, are you ready yet? So we went to this place on the beach, how shall I put it?, dark, um, and small, and, um, private. Pretty impressive, right?, if not altogether reassuring. Leonor said it looked like a museum because there were all these dried, or stuffed, I don't remember, all these dried fish hanging everywhere. So you know what the first thing the Minister does is? He says Let's dance, no less, with the same sort of gallantry you would have said Señorita, may I have the pleasure of this dance with you? That was his equivalent, right? My brother like ignored him. And Leonor says Oh yes, please, get up and dance, it's the first time he's ever danced with anybody but me. So I looked over to see if it was all right with my brother, saying to myself Wow, terrific, hey, no kidding. . . . Never in his life, Leonor was going on, how wonderful, you must have made a marvelous impression on him, how nice and so on and so forth. So I was smiling like from ear to ear, and I got up to dance. . . . And we're not out on the fucking dance floor yet, we haven't even started dancing, and the guy's pasted to me. I mean you have no idea. . . . He held me so tight, so tight, and he started saying all this stuff in my ear. You are lovely, dear, for example, let me look in your eyes, I have never seen a body such as yours in my life, what I want is to love you, my sole devotion will be to make love to you, I love you more than even my own mother, your image is engraved in my heart, I love you and I will always love you, I'm mad for you, if you aren't in love. . . . He said he wanted to know it now, that I, well I don't know . . . who knows. . . . I just wanted to run, start screaming, cry, I didn't know what to do, really, I mean it, it was a terrible terrible shock for me. . . . So I said I think I'll sit down now, Minister. Imagine! I thought I was pregnant with The Monk's baby, The Monk was his employee, and he had been a friend of my family for years. Not to mention that he was about forty years older than me. So he says No, don't go, I won't let you, I controlled myself when you were a girl, but suddenly you're a woman, with a woman's smell, with a woman's problems, and the discovery dizzies me, atrophies my senses and my reason, unbalances my very being, and drowns my heart. I'll never let you go! I know this is what your father would have wanted. I offer you my heart, my memories even before you were born, my political power, my wealth. You are the woman I've been waiting for from the first moment I touched your body. Let your skin melt into mine. Don't you feel the attraction between us? And I am no longer myself, my old, worn body is now young and vibrant once more. . . . I mean that's got to be lies, right?, or maybe he was drunk? I didn't know whether this was some kind of a put-on or what, right?, a joke or what. . . . Horrible. . . .

So we get back to the table, and I wasn't saying a word because I didn't know whether my brother had noticed anything or not. I mean we'd been supposedly dancing for a *long, long* time, I don't know how long. So I got back to the table completely mixed up, almost dizzy. And I saw the Minister sort of hiding behind a co- conut shell with some drink with a parasol in it, he and my brother had their heads together, and the Minister is making these motions with his hands like a magician about to perform a magic trick for about the two-hundredth time, you know what I mean? And Leonor's saying to me Oh my dear, you don't know, you're going to be my guardian angel, you're going to save my I don't know what, and so on and so forth. I mean, she . . . she was practically kissing my feet. Like I'd say, we'd be upstairs in the room, and I'd say I think I'll go downstairs for a while, I think I'll go down to the beach, and she'd give me this divine hat she had bought in Paris, because she traveled like you wouldn't believe. . . . Not that she was all that well-dressed, but she had a few really great things. Especially things for the beach, really out of sight things. So she'd let me borrow this hat, this low-cut T-shirt with a bag to match, shoes, everything. Because I hadn't worn anything but a bikini since the first day. . . . She treated me like a queen, I kid you not. Like she'd say Listen, go with The Monster, just like you are. She called him The Monster, now I'm beginning to remember this. . . . Go with The Monster because he wants to go take something somewhere and I feel sort of lazy. . . . Go with him, right? I shouldn't have told her about the dance floor. . . . Within three days she had decided to make a true-life *puta* out of me, or if not that then one of those courtesans.

The whole trip was a nightmare, a horror. I mean he kept attacking me so much the first day that the next morning I put these paper pincurls in my hair, I rolled my hair up with the rollers made out of toilet paper with flowers all over it, and I left the room like that, so he'd see me looking as depressing, as repulsive, as possible. I wanted to horrify him, to disgust him, repulse him, you know? I think he's perfect for you, Leonor said, he's elegant, handsome, rich, intelligent, powerful, ambitious, tender, and old. . . . That is, as though all that weren't enough, he's old so you have almost nothing to lose. . . . But he was an animal, really an animal. . . . We'd be going downstairs in the elevator, in the elevator mind you, and he'd try something *inside* the elevator. We'd be inside, he'd stop the elevator, and he'd be all over me. . . . I mean who knows what he did to the elevator. It was this condominium, we were staying in this condominium? And me terrified of elevators anyway, right? And he stops the elevator, just stops it, between floors! I don't know what had gotten into him. . . . My brother and Leonor would be downstairs waiting for us, and it would take us sometimes forty-five minutes to come seven floors downstairs in this brand-new elevator. Can you believe that? And besides the terror and all, he'd get me so wrinkled or try to take my bikini off, I mean horrible. But it was that Leonor was my only supposed friend, I mean I couldn't breathe a word to anybody else, but I saw that he had gotten Leonor to prepare me or set me up or something. And this Minister was super important in Mexico City, right?, and he was helping my mother out financially, and a lot of times he had gotten us out of these really awful binds. Anyway, who was I going to tell? Who was I supposed to accuse him to? What was I going to gain by telling his wife, for instance?

One day he borrowed our house for some meeting . . . Pornographic iguanas! I bet we took a thousand trips. That kind of trips . . . But sometimes I went with Dressed Like a Man, to vary things a little, right? And I'll tell you, I don't know but what he might have tried something with her, too, I don't know. . . . But I think he must have, although she never said anything to me about it. It's that she didn't think he was so awful. She actually liked that skin of his all wrinkled and hanging off him like crepe from the years and years he'd spent in the shadowy world of high finance, and his shiny little pencil moustache and his thousands of gray hairs. . . . Leonor, at the same time as all this was going on, Leonor was still his lover, his mistress, right? *And* she was crazy about my brother, she had this mad crush on my brother. . . . But not my brother for her, not the other way around. He even got this ring with three diamonds in it from her that was so awful that he gave it to my mother to take the stones out and have them remounted to give it to me. So anyway, Dressed Like a Man and I started going together, and the Minister was dying of jealousy. Dressed Like a Man would keep him entertained, and I'd go to the beach, and when I got back I'd tell them all about who I'd seen and who I'd gone swimming with, and he would be so jealous he'd practically go out of his mind, he'd whine and snivel and writhe and everything. With everybody else he was forceful, right?, and bad-tempered, he'd act terrible, he'd order people around like slaves, but they'd hardly have turned their back, they'd leave us alone, and he'd start moaning and whimpering, grr, and mixing in a few tears to make it look convincing. . . . Before you is a desperate man, he'd say. I live in a hostile city, I sleep in an unpleasant, cold and empty bed. I've lost my self-confidence, my house is full of things that are only awaiting you. I never thought I'd be the prisoner of such real and terrible anguish. I live only for you now, I depend on you. What does it cost you to love me? Think instead of the experience you can gain. Et cetera, et cetera, et cetera . . .

But I was saying that he borrowed our house for this meeting or something once, I don't remember exactly what it was, some secret conspiracy or alliance or something. So there was this party, and they sealed all these packs or pacts or whatever. When people started leaving, my mother went off to bed. There were just a few of us left. But it was already late, and so all of a sudden I said Well I'm going upstairs, and I left everybody down there, downstairs. In fact it was my brother's responsibility, right?, he was the one that was going into politics. So I went upstairs to bed. . . .

I was just putting on my nightgown when the Minister came into my room. First there was my parents' bedroom, then you went down the hall and there was my room, and then my brother's room. So I was there in my room, and the Minister walks in. Just walks in! You can imagine how I jumped! I was terrified. Next door was my mother asleep, and downstairs in the living room there were about a dozen bigshots and personalities, right?, and my brother and some hookers. Shit! He tries to get my gown off, and he's saying We will sanctify this bed, you'll see, offer your body up to me, I can't wait any longer. . . . You must. . . . And I was scareder than I'd ever been in my life! So you know what I did? I ran into the bathroom, and I kept pushing and kicking the door and shoving at it until I locked myself in. What an idiotic thing to do, right? I turned on the shower and got in, pajamas and all, because I didn't want to hear what he was saying. I covered my head with my arms, and I kept saying I can't hear you, I can't hear you—madness, right?—but he kept talking, there on the other side of the door, telling me about how he needed me and trying to explain why he'd attacked me, lunged at me like an

animal, and describing all the so-called Adult Pleasures of Love,
the advantages that experience can give, and I don't know what
all else. Because I refused to listen, plus I didn't want to hear
when my brother came upstairs and beat him to shit. . . . But do
you think he cared whether my mother and brother heard
him? . . . He was banging on the door and yelling Open the door,
you can't do this to me, you must hear what I have to say . . .
right?, and me going, over and over again, incessantly, I can't
hear you, I can't hear you, feeling the water pouring down my
face and body, like anointing me, cutting me off from the Minister
and his catastrophic desires. I was traumatized, I'll tell you. Till
finally I all of a sudden turned off the shower. I yelled You're
going to regret this, but still not opening the door, right?, I swear
you're going to be sorry, because I'm tired of this! You've pushed
me, you've driven me crazy, I look like a crazy woman in here
standing in the shower, you've made me act like a crazy woman.
Because what I'd just done, I'm telling you, what I was planning
to do, and the way I was reacting, I mean, it was like mental
illness. . . . You've made me a mental case! I didn't have to lock
myself up in the bathroom or turn on the shower or get wet or
anything! So I started screaming for my brother to come upstairs
and for all the people to stay, and trying to wake up my mother,
to try to scare the guy off, you know? . . . Numb, I was absolutely numb, standing there in the shower deranged, absolutely
mentally deranged and hounded almost to death. . . .

Now he's not a Minister anymore, he's living in the United
States. He's a representative from Mexico to some international
organism or something. Oh. Organization. My brother saw him in
Washington not long ago, and he says he goes out walking all by
himself every afternoon, dressed up like for some big event or
other, like reconnoitering the land for some hoity-toity big-shot
parade, right?, or a procession or something. Can you imagine?
Since he always had to be just so for whatever happened, perfectly correct and attired as he put it, you know?, perfectly
proper, for whatever happened, he spruced himself up from the
waist up for daytime and for nighttime from the waist down. . . .
All those mixed-up and unreal passions from his past, those

fierce, absurd passions, and all the dilemmas of the thousands of impossible situations in the Ministry have turned him into one of those super-charged, turbo-propelled bureaucrats, those guys that make every minute count for five. . . . He's turned into a boiling cauldron, a wild bull in the roar of the crowd at the Plaza Mexico. . . .

I could have eaten his balls in a soufflé. . . . For days I hated him, I seethed with hatred for him, and I was constantly bathed in sweat for fear he'd call or show up. . . . But one afternoon The Monk asked me to some meeting where the President was going to be. I could tell the President! Okay?! He and my father had gone to school together, and at one point my father had even been his boss in some public relations firm. That's why we were always treated so well. I mean my uncle practically made a living off that cloudy schooldays past. . . . And he liked me, he really loved me. . . . He loved me most after this one time, one September fifteenth at the Palacio Nacional when I asked him why he didn't yell Viva la Virgen de Guadalupe! like this priest named Hidalgo did, so he could put every Mexican in the world in his pocket. . . . When the President usually smiled, his smile was just sort of on his lips, right?, no further. . . . But that night he actually laughed, so of course, all the members of the cabinet were tickled pink, and the senators and everybody, including their rosy-faced cherubic smiling wives. . . . It was terrible to see them like that, all so vertical and straight and shiny and neat for the grand occasion, but it would have been worse, no doubt about it, to take one of them's clothes off or see one of them take his clothes off before getting horizontal, you know what I mean? And suffocating. God, on top of you, you know?

Dressed Like a Man went with us. . . . So we got there, and I ran over to say hello to the President, give him a little kiss, right?, wish him good luck and all. Butter him up a little. He'd been really sweet to me even before my father died, but he was even more so now, because he knew how alone and dependent I was, and how badly off, like financially, right? . . . Just to make sure, I talked to him about my father's last days, some business deals my brother was in, and some of the craziness my uncle was

up to, I think I told you some of that, right? And then I told him
the story of this guy, this friend of Napoleon's, that landed at
some hotel in the city in a helicopter and picked up two French
chorus girls and took off straight up in the sky and came back the
next day, just under the wire for the show. . . . He loved my
scandalized shocked face and all those funny words I use sometimes, right?, they made him laugh harder than anybody. But
then we kept being interrupted. Everybody wanted to monopolize
him at once. . . . Dressed Like a Man knew all about everything,
so she asked me how it had come out. . . . I told him, I said, and
he said But how can, how in the world. . . . Well, señor, I repeated, I really don't know what to do, I have this terrible problem. And so on and so forth, right?, this public servant making a
nuisance of himself, he won't leave me alone and I don't know
what to do. And he said, but not in that official voice, you know,
he dropped that, he stopped talking like he was giving a speech,
and he stared at the shiny surface of a sinuously carved and curv-
ing desk made out of this incredibly rich-looking red wood . . .
Listen, let's do something, try to work it out yourself, and if you
can't, or if you see there's no solution, call me, and I'll see if I
can step in for you. . . . Dressed Like a Man looked at me with
the smuggest, knowingest, that's the way to go about things look
on her face you ever saw. So The Monk comes up beside us about
then and offers us some hors-d'oeuvres. . . . I started humming
Who's sorry now . . .

So soon after that there was this dinner in Los Piños, and we
were invited because the Minister was going. I had filled in the
First Lady by now, partly to be able to get out of having to go pass
out toys in those working-class neighborhoods, you know, that she
wanted me to go with her to. Oh, I'm just not up to cheer, blah
blah blah. So . . . so I went to this dinner with The Monk. I mean
almost all of us knew. . . . If you stopped and looked at The
Monster, you could see that he was just a fifth-rate Machiavellian
along in years and way over his head in his Position, I mean he
had very distinguished wrinkles in his face, right?, but at the
same time everybody talked about his binges and his self-
indulgence to put it in a nice way, his excesses, you know, and

the really low-class way he guffawed and fawned on people and flattered them, right? Without meaning a word of it. So we were sitting there at dinner and the Fist Lady says to him, And tell me, Señor Minister, aside from liking young girls in bikinis, what else do you like? . . . And a little later she says I know you like little girls—trying to get a rise out of him, right?—because it shows on your face. . . . And later on she says You can tell from twenty yards away that you like little girls and tight embraces. I'm not far off, am I, Señor Minister? I can just see you down in Acapulco, I bet you really let your hair down, you must really pull out all the stops, she said, little drops of saliva in the corners of her mouth, like an eagle pouncing on a rodent, right?, her eyes gleaming and her claws ready. . . . So the Minister looked appropriately cornered, he must have known something was up, don't you imagine?, the cat was out of the bag. He mumbled something, but his heart wasn't in it.

About that time, or a little before, we'd gone to Miami—Leonor, my brother, the Minister, and I, in his plane. Into his private plane and off the four of us go. Japanese condoms, Kleenex, wads of cotton flying through the air, up above the clouds. So we get to Miami, right?, and that night we were planning to go to a striptease show. How great, oh terrific, right?, on and on and on. And supposedly I was the most excited one about it because I'd never seen a striptease, right? In my life. So I was supposedly all keen on going. . . . We'd been out shopping all day, with our minis on, very a la mode, right?, up and down every street in Miami. So then he says You girls put yourselves together, it's late. . . . Every two minutes they were calling my brother's and my rooms. . . .

By the way, when my brother and I went downstairs to breakfast . . . From the very first day, I said You do the talking because I don't know how, you order because I get embarrassed. . . . Okay, relax, he says, don't worry. So he goes Miss, miss, pliss . . . eggzz . . . And he made this sign, like this, right?, with his fingers like *twinkling* in the air, my *brother* fluttering his fingers at the waitress, can you imagine?, and the waitress goes *Guat*? Tu eggzz, tu eggzz, pliss. . . . And so then he says Can you believe that waitress? I tell her tu eggzz and go like this, and she can't figure out I want them fried. . . . Because he drew the little ruffle, the white, right?, in the air with his fingers, can you believe what an idiot? . . . I always have a wonderful time, to *die*, with my brother. I mean picture us ordering breakfast with two words of English. Really! . . .

So, Are you ready? Uh-huh, we're ready. Good, they say, come to our room, right? We'll be right there, we say. One final touch-up, and we go over to their room. Gosh, they call us to hurry up, and he's still in his shirtsleeves. You're not dressed yet? Shit! That's the way we talked to each other. Not like acting tough or on a dare or anything, though, I just talked like that, like it was nothing, my face like not showing anything, right? Well, it looked like the adventure was coming to its climax. Imagine, I couldn't very well say I wasn't going to go. If I did say so, my brother would start in on me, Ay, how you act, how can you be that way, come on, you can't stay behind, come with us, you know how much they like you, and so on and so forth, they've been begging me to let you go. . . . So no way, right?, I was stuck, I was going and that was that, because I didn't want them to notice any friction or for there to be any misunderstanding or anything because I didn't want to go. . . . So then guess what happened next. . . . Leonor finished putting on her makeup, and she says to my reflection in her hand mirror, like she was laughing at some joke she'd missed, Can you believe it? she says, like a rehearsal for some high-school play, The Monster doesn't want to go. . . . And she turns around and drops this hint like, Oh, sweetheart, you're so sweet—I really want to go out, won't you stay with him? It was like none of her gestures were kosher, I'm telling you, the whole thing smelled fishy to me. . . . A little surreal if you know what I mean. . . . With the Minister, so he won't be all by himself. . . . I might expect anything, any time, a net, handcuffs, chains, shiny naked dwarves plastered with Vaseline. . . . And tomorrow, Leonor went on, you can go, if he keeps this up, then I'll stay with him. So I go Why don't we all go and just let him stay, if he wants to stay? But why have an argument, sweetheart?, she says. All of this in front of him and in front of my brother. . . . So then I say, I was very alert and all but my head was spinning, I thought I'd lose my mind, I say Oh, but I really really really want to go, *really*. . . . So my brother says Well, then we'll put it off, we'll all go tomorrow, no problem, not to worry. . . . But then Leonor starts talking real fast, gasping like she needed air or we were choking her by not going along with her suggestions. Oh no, no, no, no, *I* want to go tonight, *I* want to go now, really. . . . And she turns to my brother and says How can you be this way, how can you back out like that? She's trying desperately to make this work, right?, practically getting down on her knees and begging my brother, but she's incapable of faking anything, so you can see her completely deformed trying to do what she thought she had to do, to do her complete duty.

So I had to stay. Phosphorescent hemorrhoids! You know, in his room. When they left, I said Okay, they trapped me again. And I turned to him, and I said With all respect, if anything happens, if anything should come up, for example, if, heaven forbid, somebody should come in to mug you or rob you or something, or if you faint or get the vapors or something, call me—I'll be in my room, I'll be there, and I'll run right over and save you. Or if you get bored, you can call me and we'll talk on the phone, we'll talk all you want to. . . . It was hate, right?, pure hatred, not fear. Not fear. . . . Do you think it will be this way our whole life? he starts in. Yes, yes I really do, I say. . . . Him on one side of the bed, stalking me, and me on the other. Yes, it will always be this way with you, so I'm going to my room. *Hasta mañana.* . . . No, stay here for a while, let's watch TV, I swear I won't even look at you, I just want to be able to have your odor here with me, to know that you're here, I'm not going to touch you, I swear, look at me. . . . The television was on. . . . Let's just talk for a while, and so on and so forth. But he talked and talked and all of a sudden he trapped me, like this, he threw the bedspread over me. I couldn't move! You know, the way they do with lions and tigers. . . . I was screaming, kicking, spitting, frothing at the mouth, trapped, pinned, all tangled up in these covers, and he took off my bra. . . . You son of a bitch, you bastard, *chinga tu madre*, you know, and he was panting and breathing hard, with passion, right?, and wheezing. . . .

But I gathered all my strength, and all of a sudden I said Hold on, wait a second. . . . Everything froze. . . . He'd ripped off my panties and all my clothes, my stockings, everything. . . . If you're going to keep molesting me, then it's on your head! . . . He didn't understand what was happening, but he turned me loose, he let me get up. . . . You listen to me! He turned me loose, and I had the marks of his fingers all over my arms, and scratches all over my body. . . . I sat down and I said Do you know Loco Valdiosera? And he goes Sure, he's a friend of mine, we live on the same street, and he's done some jobs for me sometimes, and blah blah blah. I snapped on my bra. Why? he says. By this time his eyes were halfway bugging out of his head, they were about this big. Where do you know him from? he says. I go out with him. What? he said. Uh-huh, I got out with him, with Loco Valdiosera, he's my boyfriend. But he's . . . ! Yes, yes he is, and I'm going to tell you something. . . . He looked at me like a cornered animal. . . . If you keep bugging me, I'm going to tell him. I've had it up to *here* with you!

I'm not sure he believed me at first, or thought I was making it all up, or what. But we started talking, and little by little he saw that I was dead serious, I wasn't lying. Not to mention that Handsome to the Maximum was involved in some really, really heavy stuff back then, and the Minister knew about it, as luck would have it, all this intimate stuff, right? So finally, he realized that it was true, that I was really going out with him, so he didn't bother me again for the whole rest of the trip, he didn't even speak to me. We had this terrific talk till late that night, it must have been five o'clock in the morning, until they came back and all. By that time we'd been talking for a long time, right? It was all just talk by then. At least on that trip he never tried to molest me again. Maybe . . . I think . . . maybe that was even the last time he ever touched me, you know I think it was, because that was the last trip I ever took with them. After that trip I never went anywhere with them again. . . . I'll tell you—you know when that was? How long ago that was? When Kennedy was killed. We were

in Miami then. . . . The day he was killed, we got to Miami in
the morning, and everybody was smiling and happy, everybody,
even the maids, supposedly because the Republicans were better
or something, I don't know. I mean they said they were sorry
about Kennedy the man, but it was better for the government. . . .

Anyway, but the Minister kept calling me every day, and I
invariably hung up on him. I never talked to him. He sent me
convertibles, flowers, all kinds of presents, and all they managed
to do was worry my mother. You don't know how hard it was for
me to send all this stuff back to him! I'd barely hear his voice on
the telephone and I'd hang up. Until this one day, you know
when?, the first day I worked as a model at the Palacio de Hierro,
the day I broke up once and for all with The Monk. Anyway, one
of my maids came in and told me I had a call from the Ministry of
whatever. So I go to the telephone and say Hi, but you could have
told from the way I said it that I'd already lost the taste for waltzes
and poetry and abstract art and all that that went with The Monk's
niceness. But it was his boss, Señor Minister, the efficient, dedicated public servant, the VIP Secretary of State or whatever. I
recognized him, but I said Hold on just one second, okay? He
must have been surprised because like I told you I always
slammed the receiver down in his ear. . . . I said Hold on, just
one second, please. I ran upstairs to the other telephone and
whispered to them to hang up downstairs. I mean I called them,
but whispering, right? What's up? I said. Nothing, he says, but
first, thank you for not hanging up. . . . You're welcome. . . .
Because listen, I want to ask you to please give me another
chance, I know I've acted impetuously and that maybe I've been a
little rough, that I was wrong, but put that down to my insecurity,
to my passion for you, I can't control it, but now I want to make
you see that I want to make everything right again. . . . If I've
let you down in any way, tell me, if there's anything in the world
you need, however impossible it might be, tell me and let me
try. . . . To make a long story short, I gave him plenty of rope,
right? You're listening to a desperate man, he went on, an insom-
niac who dedicates his sleeplessness to you, and is grateful to you

for it because it allows me to think of you. I'm shaking, damn it! My knees get weak when I talk to you, can you believe that? Your hatred is like a millstone around my neck. . . . And you don't care, you don't feel a thing, because you don't see me. When can I see you? Can we go to the beach one of these days?

His moans were exciting me like never before, but I decided to stop him. . . . Well, I just want you to know that everything you've just said has been recorded, and not just on my tape recorder, on the Ministry of Public Administration's too, because my telephone happens to be tapped. . . . I could feel my fangs getting sharper by the second. . . . I don't know whether you remember all those things the President's wife said to you that day we had dinner in Los Pinos. She and the President know all about what's happened, and they know I'm sick and tired of it, so you better get worried, you better get a few more wrinkles, you better knit your eyebrows and purse your lips, and *squirm*, because that's the way it is . . . We're going to gift-wrap this little duet and send it to the President, and you're going to squirm, you son of a bitch, you son of a *chingada* bitch, waiting to see what he does to you when he hears the tape, okay?, we'll see if you can see once and for all that you make me sick, I can't stand you, I hate you to your last little love-word. . . . So you'll finally see . . . Oh, by the way, I'll send you a copy too. Didn't you think it was strange that I asked you to hold on a second? You, the Mack the Knife of financial circles? You, the guy who knows every trick in the book? You, the big wheeler-dealer? You, who doesn't miss a trick?

The Minister stammered a second, then there was this confused, heavy silence, until he came up with the most grotesque solution you'd ever believe. What a kick, har har har, you know that's the way we always play around with each other, right, sweetheart? How's the family? Meanwhile, I was fuming. . . . Well, I'll tell you, if this has all been a joke, I'm fucking sick and tired of it, you *chingado*, because it's been seven months now, or nine, or ten months. . . . And since these little jokes of yours go over like a lead balloon with me, you can just forget about them from now on, let's see whether this won't stop you. . . . Oh no, little girl, you're incapable of ruining me like this. . . . and then about fifteen more of those wheedling expressions, it was enough to make a wolf's mouth water. . . .

I'll bet, I said to him, I'll bet you'll keep your mouth shut long enough to listen to these tapes. And while you're listening, I want you to take a good look around your office and think about how you got there and all those personal papers you're going to have to find a real safe place for now, which I'm telling you not because I think you're an idiot but because I think you're a little short-sighted sometimes. . . . So then he started up again, Oh no, forgive me, I'm sorry, please, you know this has all been a joke.

My mother came upstairs about then. Pancho's here, aren't you coming down to eat? So I went downstairs, and he could see I was upset, so I told him I'd had a fight with the Jalisco Sisters. He says Oh Cheesecake, good lord, what do you want to have all these fights for, you're too good-hearted for that. I bet you've never had an argument in your life. You've never had a problem with a soul. . . . So I said Yes I have, Pancho, I've got problems and they're big ones. . . . So he says Oh Ladybug, you're the best thing since sliced bread, I swear to you. Forget it, I've never known anyone as good as you are. . . . So we finished eating, and he asked me to go for a ride in his car. . . .

He watched my reflection against the windshield, with my face as bilious as a bull with indigestion. . . . So as not to have to think, I told him to drive as fast as he could. You think I'm Santa Teresa or somebody! Well it's not so! I'm a common ordinary person, and I've got serious problems just like anybody else, but you don't want to see me for what I am! . . . Oh Ladybug, what problems can *you* have?, nobody would ever dare pick a fight with you. . . . So I said You're wrong, I don't necessarily pick fights with people, but people pick fights with me. For example, I said, right now I've got this terrible problem. . . . Your boss, Mr. Minister . . . And I spilled the beans. But this can't go any further! You can't tell a soul! And what do you think he did? He burst out crying! He lay across the steering wheel, and he said I'm a fool, you're not the girl for me, I deserve this for being such a fool. What a moron! What an idiot! And on top of all this, I added, he's even blackmailing me by saying he's going to fire you if I . . . How could I have been so close to you and never have realized, . . . he said. I've never learned anything, he said, *I'm the immature one.* . . . And he cried and cried and beat his head on the steering wheel. How can this happen? I've studied so hard. . . . And that's true, too, he and Alberto are the two best-educated people I know. You don't know Alberto? So he says How could this have happened to you? How could you have gotten yourself into this? . . . It was really him that wanted to break up. . . . You don't need me, he said, you need somebody else, somebody that can take care of you, somebody more clear-sighted, somebody more lucid, not a blind idiot like me. . . . So we broke up. I mean, we'd broken up before, lots of times, but we still went out once in a while, but this was the end. . . .

And I really did give the tape to the President, and he listened to the whole thing, and not very long after that the Minister stopped bothering me, and the First Lady gave me a trip to Europe, and when I came back, there was my very own gas station waiting for me, can you imagine?

("That is where this love, this great gratitude I feel for life, this constant desire to lick it and suck it, this urge to prostrate myself before everything in the universe comes from. . . .")

16

Oh I beg you, I beg you, ay I beg you . . . I beg you for compassion . . .

Because really one of these days I'm just going to sit down and prop my feet up, I mean listen, my uncle's wife brought me about five magazines one day, and I still haven't even opened them, I'm not kidding, I still haven't looked at them. She brought me a *Cosmopolitan*, en español, right?, about two weeks ago she brought it over and it's still sitting there. Every day she comes over and says Have you read the *Cosmo* yet? And the phone rings or Tito Caruso comes by . . . My mother screams or the maid trips over her own feet in the kitchen . . . I'm completely, how can I explain this?, I'm utterly and completely absorbed in my house. Honestly. If it's not the Jalisco Sisters, it's Dressed Like a Man or The Monk, not one bit less hysterical or screwed up than the others, either, I'll have you know. . . . Plus, I'm such a perfectionist that I pick up my sweaters and I look at all the seams to see whether a thread is about to break, and if there's the least little thing, there I go, ch ch ch ch ch. . . . I should show you the things, I should show you the pile of things I darned up last night. . . . I mean I'm not the greatest seamstress in the world, okay?, but I hate it when this part here comes undone, or when a thread breaks, or when it puckers down here, right?, like it does sometimes? I'll be talking on the telephone and going over my clothes and straightening them. I mean my drawers and everything, right?, so things are more or less neat. My mother swears our house has been cursed, and it's a torture just to live in it. She burns shrimp shells in an incense burner till the bedrooms and halls and everything, the whole house is full of smoke, or she brings in a priest to sprinkle holy water on all the walls. Mercedes comes in with the latest gossip about Florencia and these other new girlfriends of hers. The phone rings. Gabriel Infante is worried sick because his urine has been bloody for days. The telephone . . . Andrés is thinking about growing a moustache like the hands of a clock pointing to twenty minutes till five. The telephone again! Handsome to the Maximum is about to marry two women at the same time, and he wants to know whether I want a merry widow covered with little hearts. And that's the way my day goes, it just flies, I mean it gets completely away from me, like a sports car with what do you call those things? Turbochargers? You know what I mean?

("But tell me— / if you can— / what are you doing / sitting there / surrounded by fictitious beings / made of letters / accents / consonants / vowels / instead of flesh and blood?")

17

A *danzón* dedicated to Europe and the countries that comprise it

Listen, the first time somebody told me there was going to be a spiritual retreat, that this bunch of girls was going to Rome to spend some time with Opus Dei, I said That's for me, because since it was this super *super* religious thing, right?, it was my chance to get them to let me out of the house. So I went, but I skipped the retreat. . . . All the girls there had been pushed into going, I was the only one there that *wanted* to be there, that had gone of my own accord, right? So I could get out of the house and get to know Europe. The other girls were all like Florencia Reyes, who's that TV announcer now?, and people like that. So to make a long story short, they got us out of bed at six o'clock in the morning, and by seven we had to be at the first little talk. Can you believe Florencia came down with eyeshadow with all dif-

ferent colored glitter on her eyelids? And then at eight o'clock at
night, when you were ready to drop from all the stuff you'd done
all day, she'd start putting rollers in her hair so she could have
these spit-curls right here, right? . . . So we got to be good
friends, and we'd sneak off to breathe some of that air like you
see on the postcards, and we hardly ever went back to Opus Dei
or any of the other stuff. . . .

The second time I went to Europe, Florencia Reyes called me
up, and she says Aren't you just burning with desire to go back?
Of course, longing, *yearning* to go. Well I'll tell you, Sacred
Heart is having its something or other anniversary, and there's
going to be a what do you call it, a convention or something in
Brussels, and all of us ex-students are going. An alumnae reunion
I think is what she said, I don't know. Imagine. . . . And then
she added Let's go. . . . So in two days I'd renewed my passport,
gotten my shots and everything. I paid for the flight with a card
. . . sometimes life brings you unhoped-for happiness . . . so we
went. . . . Since all our friends were unbelievably repressed at
home, they really let their hair down there. Even on the plane
over, all anybody talked about was those plays on words?, like in
windows I think is what you call them, something like that—
pricks and tickles and kept women . . . Courtesans. You couldn't
believe it. There were times I'd go to my room and say Florencia,
I'm here, because for instance, I'd have gone to visit some other
girls in the hotel?, and she wouldn't open the door. I'd wander
around from room to room till six o'clock in the morning. Shit!
Let me in. Oh please, try to understand, just wait a few minutes
more. Just a little bitty while longer. . . . I swear to God. I spent
the whole trip in the hall.

All these incredible things happened to us. For example, we
got to Paris, and one of the girls, Lupita Aguilar, who had just
gotten there, I mean just that second, when she got off the bus
that had brought us in from the airport, she told the doorman she
had this terrible toothache, what could she do. So they sent her to
a dentist, right?, and she went, and when she came back she
couldn't even talk because her whole gum and cheek was swollen
up like this. But wait a minute . . . She gets back to the hotel,

and she shuts herself up in her room. They take dinner up to her, and she says to the bellboy, Just a minute, but in sign language, right?, making signs, because she couldn't talk, so she taps her lips with fingers and tries to say she'd had a tooth pulled and this is where it hurt, and she shows him her cheek. So the bellboy puts down the tray like a hot potato and grabs her and starts passionately kissing her. He thought she was telling him to kiss her right here, on the cheek. And Lupita couldn't even scream. The guy was in heaven because he thought those grunts and moans were from pleasure, right? . . . So they're rolling around on the bed, and they both start giggling, until she gave in from giggling so much. I mean just imagine. . . .

I went out shopping one day, and when I came back I was looking for some girls to show the things I'd bought to, right? I knocked on their door and said Hey girls, can I come in? And do you know what they were doing? . . . The two of them sitting on one bed and four or five bellboys on the other. They screwed the bellboys and waiters in every single hotel! Lupita Aguilar and Monica Dávalos Hurtado, a couple of incredibly snooty girls, right? Real bluebloods. . . . And they'd come to our room and say Listen, Florencia, um, aren't you going out with us. Listen, don't be . . . I swear, I swear . . . Some guys asked us out. . . . And she'd go Oh come on, really, I was taking a shower, because we took a shower early, you know, to get to bed. . . . Oh come on, don't be that way, come with us, don't be so. . . . So Florencia, supposedly such a martyr, right?, had to go out with them, so she'd throw something on and they'd leave. . . . I had dried myself off, and then I was getting dressed, like this, right?, and Florencia knocked on the door, and I said What's wrong, did you forget your keys? Ooh, you don't know what happened! *Chinga sus madres!*, you know what we were going to do? You know who we were going out with? Do you *know* who? The waiters from lunch! . . . But that's not even the best part. The best part is, that as soon as the waiters see them, they grab 'em like this, *rrruff!*, Hollywood-style, right?, and push 'em up against the wall and start kissing them! . . .

We always had the worst trouble getting them to bring us

breakfast. I mean since these other girls were going out with the
waiters, and they'd get in arguments or they'd slam the door, if
you know what I mean, at the last minute, they refused to serve
us. . . . Every day it was the same thing—they wouldn't bring us
any breakfast. They would never serve us! I was terrified to go out
with the waiters or the bellboys, but what could you do if you
went in and they treated you like dirt? . . . I mean if it's Tuesday, it must be Belgium, right? Who could you go out with? So
anyway, we finally got to the Casino at Monte Carlo. I'd bought
this horrible wig in Spain, one of those Cleopatra wigs, right?,
that everybody was wearing back then? And I'd put it on. . . .
We get to the Casino, which was this huge room with lots and lots
of people, not at all elegant, nothing elegant about it at all,
right?, and we're bored out of our minds in about two minutes. I
mean I don't gamble and neither does Florencia. So finally Lupita
comes in and says You know there's a room where everybody has
to wear a tuxedo, and the bets are umph, you have to bet a fortune, why don't we go? And she leaves. . . . I mean, to see absolute idiots come in and bet a stack of what do you call them like
this . . . So we went in and stood there. In this ritzy room, right?

Pruned-off pricks! In front of this roulette wheel, surrounded
by a jungle of potted palms and other exotic plants, in the midst
of the smoke and the noise of what is it?, checkers?, chips?,
chips and bets, I saw this incredibly incredibly handsome man. I
stood there fascinated, I mean I literally couldn't take my eyes off
him, catatonic. Listen, I said to Florencia, that guy over there,
am I dreaming or is he to die . . . And she says No, no, he's
incredible, let's go stand over there in front of him, come on, let's
see if we can get him to talk to us. So we made our way over
there. . . . One of his long manicured hands strayed up to caress
his heart from time to time. . . . His body had the glow of a life
of sports, under his tuxedo you could imagine rippling, almost
electrical muscles, like the muscles of a secret agent or an international jewel thief. The odor of his body evoked the sea, a
leather dice cup, a tavern filled with orangutangs, or a cock
licked in the darkness. . . . Such auras meetings take on in your
memory, don't they! At that moment, that night, I would never

get over it if I didn't throw myself at his feet and embrace them. . . .

But what were we going to do to meet him? He was smoking, one cigarette after another, and in the air the smoke drew vignettes of a romantic, adventurous past. . . . So finally, I say to Florencia Get me a cigarette. . . . I wanted to get him to light it for me, and when I said thank you in Spanish, en español, right?, he'd ask me where I was from, and the ice would magically be broken . . . or so I planned. . . . So Florencia went off and she came back with a package of cigarettes. I put one in my mouth and started pretending to look everywhere for my matches, right?, all nerves, almost desperate, a nicotine fit or something, more and more frantic. So this guy looks at me with no expression whatsoever, but Lupita, that idiot, who was in front of me and hadn't caught on, ran up and lit my cigarette. To make a long story short, I must have smoked a hundred and twenty-four cigarettes in that one stinking night. And this man never, never, NEVER lit one damned cigarette for me. He never even *looked* at me. I kept wondering if he was Swiss, French, German, English. . . . So finally, I decided to try something else, I decided to change roulette tables, and when I walked from one table to the other . . . Syphilitic serpents! The guy slinks along behind me like a hunter stalking his prey. . . .

About this time . . . You know in Nice you see all these old old ladies, about a thousand years old, as wrinkled as an old Kleenex, with all this rouge and wearing hats, right?, on the arm of boys with faces like a Nestle's Crunch, right?, with these chocolate-inspired pimples just sort of oozing out, like volcanoes just barely beginning to bulge up, like the crunchy things, what in the world are those things all over just under the surface of a candy bar? Have you ever been to Nice? These boys all made up, right?, you'd swear they were women. . . . I've seen more queers in Nice in an hour than any place else the whole rest of my life. And boys about fifteen years old with old women about a hundred and fifty. So about this time, all of a sudden one of those old old ladies comes up, jewelry everywhere, diamonds and emeralds and everything, and a gold cobra winding all around her arm, all the

way up, with about four hundred precious stones on about four
hundred rings that weighed so much she could barely move her
fingers. And out of her mouth, on this face that looked like it had
been plowed, comes this little creaky voice that says *Giovanni,
vieni.* . . . So then I knew he was Italian. . . .

So he stepped back a little and talked to her. Then he suddenly
came over to me. He smelled like crisp new bills. I realized it
was his look that had turned the old lady's face to parchment,
because it almost made me have an orgasm. Will you wait for me
five minutes?, he said in Italian, and I didn't know whether he
was saying my mother should be *chingada,* but I said Yes anyway, but I swear I didn't understand a word. A heat wave had
started spreading from somewhere just below my navel. Will you
wait for me five minutes? It was like the words hit me somewhere
right in the pelvic region. . . . So then Giovanni walked away,
that was his name, and, um, he walked away, and all my
girlfriends came over and said Okay, you ready to go? What do
you mean, go? So one of the girls who had latched onto this incredibly wealthy English guy, really handsome, she says Listen, I
need you to do me a favor, don't you want to come to Nice with
us. We were in Monte Carlo, right? Won't you come to Nice with
me? If you'll wait, I said, okay, sure, perfect, I told her, sure, but
don't bother me right now. . . . My heart and breathing were
going like a locomotive out of control. So then I noticed that
Florencia and Lupita were talking. But I felt so strange, like
somebody had taken all the tigers out of the jungle all of a sudden. . . . I was fearless. . . . Don't do it, they were saying, you
can't risk it, you know how Italians are, don't take the chance,
what if he's a sex fiend and you don't know it. . . . So I said I
don't know, maybe you're right, why am I so turned on by him,
it's not natural. . . . We better go, Monica kept saying.

So we were on our way out, and we bump into Giovanni on his
way in. At the door, right? He smelled like some secret beast in
Zihuatanejo. He asked me where I was going, and I said to Nice,
but it wasn't easy to say because my blood pressure was like an
espresso machine about to explode, him in Italian and me in
Spanish. So then he says No, we were going to have coffee. My

girlfriends disappeared like somebody had waved a magic wand, and we ordered two cappucinos standing there, just like that. He smelled like melon with cream, and his words were like the strong thin threads of a spiderweb I never ever wanted to escape from. . . . He wanted to know where I was going tomorrow, and day after tomorrow, and the day after that. . . . I told him Rome. He said he lived in Rome, and he gave me this card that I practically turned into a butterfly. I was shaking like a leaf! I was so nervous I couldn't even stammer out how to get in touch with me, not even my telephone number. He smiled and shushed me with a finger across my lips, put some coins down on the counter, and walked away. He waved good-bye from a distance like some intriguing young David Niven playing the most charming jewel thief and seducer in the Western world. . . . Mink miscarriages! If he had kissed me, I swear I would have died on the spot. . . .

Two days later we got to our hotel room in Rome, and we were lying on the beds, and Florencia says Ay, there's just no doubt about it. What? The Italians are unique in all the world, she says. What other hotel has had flowers waiting for us? Oh, that's right! I hadn't noticed. . . . So I say Here, hand me a rose to see how it smells. So she goes over and she says Oh look, there's a card! Oh, let's see. . . . It was from Giovanni. The flowers were from Giovanni! Can you believe it! Instead of smelling the rose I smelled the card. It smelled like a harlequin's mask, a sailor's fly, wet tobacco . . . I remember the smell perfectly, but I can't remember what the card said. It was like home-delivery insemination. . . . Burlap balls! There were thirty of us. Fifteen of us were staying in this one hotel, and fifteen in another one, to keep the noise down, right? We all traveled together, from one place to another I mean, but we didn't all take the same tours at the same time or anything, we went at different times, so we wouldn't be so conspicuously Mexican, right? . . . So Giovanni was staying over where the other girls were staying, and they had given him our whole itinerary, where we were going, when, what we were supposed to do and everything. . . . So he sent me these flowers, and I got up my courage to call him and thank him, but rats, he wasn't there. His mother answered the telephone. You can imag-

ine the message I left him. You'd die laughing if you heard her
tell him. . . . So then later Giovanni called me, and he asked me
if I could go out and have coffee with him. I said Sure, and before
I went out I took off all my rings, just in case, right?, my necklace, my watch, and I sprayed perfume under my arms and
around my, um, my pelvis, right? My girlfriends came downstairs
and took down every detail, license plates, color of the car, the
model and everything. They were scared to death, you know? I
wasn't wearing any stockings or underwear, and you could have
blown my dress off with a feather fan. . . . So I left with him, my
mind made up to be a lost woman, as though I'd bet my body at
baccarat. And me that doesn't know how to play baccarat. . . .

He drove his car as fast as the law allowed. I saw caryatids fly
by like you'd see iguanas fly by on the road to Taxco. I was
talking and talking, and he would turn and look at me and make
little faces at me, half supercilious and half amused. He kept
looking at me like he was asking himself whether I was wearing
underwear or not and making fatherly, pleasant faces because I
was chattering away, and he didn't understand a word, he didn't
understand a word I was saying. . . . So we went to this really
terrific place, this place named Piatsa dei Muses or something
like that, I'm not sure I'm pronouncing that right, do you know
Italian? Me neither, but anyway this café where they had a view
like Cecil B. de Mille. You could see every inch of Rome from up
there. . . . I was telling him about Mexico, because you know, I
step out of the country and I'm Little Miss Patriotism, right? . . .
His legs sheathed in smooth white corduroy spread as though he
were getting ready to put his genitals on display. And these moc-
casins he was wearing, I don't know, they looked like they were
made out of smoke, they combined the weight of diving shoes
with the lightness of a fencer's. I was chattering like I was trying
to stave off a catastrophe. . . . If he had touched me, in
fact. . . . Touched! If he had brought his hand close to my body,
that hand that from time to time crept up and touched his chest
near his heart, I would have screamed in fear and taken off running to St. Peter's Basilica. . . . My stomach felt hollow, terribly
terribly hollow. . . . And should I mention that my vagina too was

clamoring for something, in its own language of pulsation and secretion? That my whole life was aroused by this meeting? . . .

Where was I? Oh, yes, we were talking and we decided to go back. He asked me if I'd like to take another little trip like the one I was on now. I said I'd love to, it would be wonderful. So then he said In October would you like to do it again? Why October? So he said Because in October I could marry you. He thought about his words before he talked, so when he talked it was very very slow, very carefully, like he was taking a Russian exam or something. So I go Wow, this guy is bonkers, imagine, sheets and orange blossoms, what do you mean get married? He repeated it. Because in October I could marry you. In October? Yes, yes, I am serious, in fact I am right now proposing marriage to you. . . . I thought he was pouring on a little too much sauce before he ate me. . . . My breasts swelled under my dress. . . . But how can you propose to me, I mean we can barely even understand each other, it's hard just to talk to each other, and you don't know me, you don't know who I am or what I'm like, what I want out of life, where I'm coming from . . . He stopped me. He said I know perfectly that I will marry you because until I am married with you, I can not be happy. . . . When he said With you, like that, so cute, I had a spasm all over. I thought I was going to faint. Gagarin was going in circles around the moon, and my brain was whirling along with him every step of the way. I thought about his body then, but he seemed so remote from any desire. He smelled like oriental spices and Aztec incense. Oh, I forgot, he said something that I'll never forget. He said he was very stubborn, very *very* stubborn, and that whatever he wanted he sooner or later got, even if it took forever. . . . So he dropped me off at the hotel, to the considerable frustration of my body as you can well imagine. . . . That smell of his . . .

The next day Giovanni had to go to Torino because his grandfather was dying. I stayed in Rome for a couple of days, and then we went to Florence, and then we went up north to a whole bunch of places. And in every one of those places, in every hotel I stayed at, even if it was just for three hours, there was a basket of roses. Since he had our itinerary, he sent roses everywhere, and then he started calling me on the telephone. Oh, and he wrote me, too. Letters that smelled like thoroughbred horses and reminded you of divers in Tequesquitengo and the spray at the bottom of the cliffs. . . . He promised European skies, soft fogs, rows of chestnut trees, embraces, a last name, and even, I think, two but maybe three titles. You know, noble titles? . . . I had every waiter in the world translating his letters for me. . . . They were always Italian or Spanish. . . . I mean the waiters. So I started writing him letters too, but real simple, I mean superficial letters, but he was writing me letters as blue as the tide, as echoing as the surf, as repetitive as the waves, as romantic as a pirate, and as cool as a sailorsuit. But I couldn't *think* that way, with those kinds of words. . . . I'd shiver and press his letters to my naked body, or I'd even masturbate, thinking about the way he smelled, the way he looked. . . . He looked like dynamite. . . .

By Brussels I thought I was sure I'd marry him. . . . You know, one of those things that just come over you, and you even talk about them with just a drop of sadness, because it means the end of adolescent silliness and stuff, right?, of crazy hopes and sentimental hungers, if you know what I mean. . . . So I told Florencia, I swear I'm going to marry this man, I don't know why, sometimes I think I won't but most of the time I think about the way he smells, and it comes over me—I'm going to marry him, because I don't know, it's like he's really in deep, you know? But then—don't you think it was a little strange for him to be so far gone over a love that didn't make any sense? Don't you think it was *absurd*, this love for somebody he'd never even touched? I also thought a lot about Alexis and The Monk and Handsome to the Maximum, and about Mauricio and Gabriel Infante. They were like the pictures on a deck of cards, or like a Tarot deck, you know?, that you don't use anymore. . . . No, excuse me, that's what I thought about later, three or four years later, three or four disappointments later. I always compared Giovanni with all of them. . . .

Every time I went back to Europe, I was intoxicated by him all over again. It's silly to say it like that, isn't it? I was just hanging on the edge of desire, you might say, it was in the astringent taste

of the drinks, the eyes of a lot of men. Remember when Gabriel
Infante wanted to marry me? He took me to races and things with
him, and we sort of un-met each other in Venice, remember?
Well, all those same cities were just brimming over with sensuality now, and in all the hotel rooms, wherever I went, I swear,
roses were in bloom, there were ardent letters, and my breathing
got heavy. . . .

When I went back to Mexico I went to see this fortune-teller,
but she couldn't tell me anything. I was dying of curiosity. How
was this impasse finally going to be broken? Giovanni seemed
more like a sadistic Japanese cutting off a tenth of an inch of a
defenseless centipede's leg every day than like an Italian. So finally, my mother set up this appointment with this woman. They
were going to do a purge, no, some kind of white cleaning or
white magic cleaning or something, I don't remember, anyway
they were going to do a spell on me, right? Why didn't he touch
me if I was literally melting to touch him? Can you tell me? . . .
Why? Why? Anyway, the invocations or whatever you call them
were in this terrible hovel, all falling down, with dirt floors and
dozens of dogs that ran out barking and spreading fleas all over
when you came up. It smelled like wet ashes inside the hut. They
had all these scabby, emaciated chickens stepping around everywhere, and there were these unbelievable posters of San Martín
Caballero and San Martín de Porres and Our Lady of San Juan de
los Lagos all over the walls. . . . There was this little tiny brown-
skinned witch like a prune, and she wasn't wearing any shoes.
She was smoking this very strange-smelling tobacco, with marijuana I'm pretty sure, in a pipe, and she kept waving this broom,
upside down, you know?, in front of us. . . . I mean we were
curious and a little standoffish at the same time, you can imagine.
So she makes up this bundle of all different weeds and herbs and
things, with magpie feathers and pigeon wings, who knows, and
she starts sort of passing it over you and praying, and she prays
and shakes these herbs and things all over your body. On top of
your clothes, right? First she made like circles with it, I mean
more or less, and then she sort of brushed these herbs from the
top of your head down to your feet, and then she made these other

motions like this, sort of oval I guess, and then she made signs like this and then shook it all over you again. . . . And when she finished cleansing you, that's the word, I forgot it before, when she finished with these herbs and things, she made this rinse, this mouthwash?, out of holy water and spewed this holy water rinse all over your face and your head and your back, I mean all over, you've heard about this sort of thing, right? . . . One time my mother practically caught pneumonia, I kid you not, from the way this woman sprayed her, she got soaked with this holy water. So anyway then she took this egg, I mean a real egg and put it in the middle of the herbs, and she starts passing it all over you again, and supposedly that picks up all the bad spirits and humors and stuff, right? Then she breaks the egg, and you can see how clean you are. It's unbelievable. Out of this egg come spiders and lizards and dirt and scorpions and frogs and all kinds of other horrible monsters, I swear. . . . Although nothing ever came out for me. . . . But one day I went with the Big Jalisco, and I swear to God, to *God*, the old woman put an egg in the middle of all these herbs and feathers and stuff, she went like this, and raised it up over Big Jalisco's head, to start her passes with it, right?, and I swear, the egg broke. . . . And we'd taken our own eggs with us, so there was no way she could have fixed it up, you know, or tricked us or anything. So she took another egg and the same thing happened. . . . Fourteen eggs. Fourteen eggs! Every time she put one over her head, *chíngale!*, it broke. . . . Oooee, said the witch, you have the *mal de ojo*, you have many evil eyes, much bitterness in your heart. . . . And it was true, she was the most jinxed of all of us. Back then she was in pretty bad shape, hysterical. . . . Well, but you know it's impossible, you can't just take an egg like this and squeeze it and break it, right? And this poor little old woman would just pick up the eggs, and she picked them up more and more carefully, I'll tell you, and lay them in their little bed of herbs and feathers and stuff, like this, very gently, and raise it all up over Big Jalisco's head and *chíngale!*, they'd break. Every time. . . . She tried and tried to cleanse her. . . . She made Giovanni and me a ball of cleansing stuff so our marriage would be good, and so on and so forth. . . .

But all I wanted to know was whether I was going to marry Giovanni or not. I even went to this card reader in Paris, can you imagine?, this really good fortune-teller. Dressed Like a Man and I went. . . . No kidding. . . . Somebody had told us about her, I didn't know her. So she starts telling Dressed Like a Man that she was such and such and so and so, and that her boyfriend was older than she was, and he had this pain, something bothering him in his shoulder. . . . And that very day, who knows how many thousands of miles away, they were giving my uncle an emergency shot, these shots that when Dressed Like a Man talked to him that night he said he'd almost fainted from the pain. I mean wow, right?, and she told her her whole life story, and even that she was going to marry this guy on horseback in a suit of lights. You know . . . like a bullfighter? A suit of lights? So . . . anyway, she didn't know anything about her, not her name, nothing, and she told her her life backward and forward, I mean she was incredible. . . . So when I went in . . . You went in and she didn't ask you your name or anything, right? I'd go in and the same thing happened with all of them. They'd say I can't tell you anything, and they'd get up from the table. Nobody could read me. . . . Nobody could ever read my cards. Never. . . . They all told me the same thing, they had a headache, that there was this gray smoke from the candle, they couldn't see anything. . . . They said I was all closed up tight, I wouldn't let them in, not even take a peek. . . . Never, right? And I was like obsessed, I kept going and going and going, and nobody could ever tell me anything. . . . Nobody ever told me anything. . . .

You know something? One day I was in the Palacio de Hierro. . . . I had on this black dress, and I ran into Felisa Broder. She says Listen. Can I tell you something? Sure, I said, of course. . . . If you want to avoid some very bad luck, don't ever put that dress on again. And then she said There's something I want to warn you about . . . I practically jumped to put my hand over her mouth. Don't say it! . . . Because do you know that she's predicted every disaster that's happened at her house, like to her family! So now she's this santo. Santo's what you're called when you're like a black belt at predicting stuff, right? So anyway, she calls up my mother on the telephone, and she says Your daughter doesn't want me to tell her something very important, for her own safety, for the health of her and her nearest and dearest . . . But my mother is so superstitious that she says to her, Well if she says not to, there must be some reason, she must be right. . . . You know when this was? Big Jalisco had called me and asked me if I wanted to be a model. I said Sure. She had this fashion show that day at the Palacio de Hierro, so she says What we'll do is, you go and see if you'd like to do that, and then I'll introduce you around, I'll introduce you to these people; this woman who's the coordinator is going to be there today, and I'll see what I can do. . . . So I put on that black dress I told you about and fixed myself up a little, right? I was sitting in the audience, nervous to see the show, you know?, and the Big Jalisco comes up to me, and she goes like this, pss. Pss, wait right here and she goes back behind. So then this woman comes up to me and says Come along. . . . Big Jalisco had told her to look for a girl in a black dress, get the picture? . . . So she says You're so-and-so's friend? Un-huh, I said. Can you come with me a second? Sure, I said, of course. All the models were there, all dressed, loaded with jewelry, I mean really decked out, right? And she says We'd like to see if these clothes fit you, these clothes from a model that called in sick, to see if you can fill in for her. . . . And I'd never even *seen* a fashion show in my life. . . . Not even once, just the little pieces in the newsreels and stuff, okay?, although I had some idea of course, a vague idea, a *very* vague idea as you'll see in a minute, but I knew that the very word *model* made a lot of my friends' tails wag a little. . . . So anyway, I changed clothes, all excited, and these clothes fit perfectly, better than if they'd been made especially for me. It was this super important fashion show, so I said to these girls, I'll watch how you do it, I'll watch, and then I'll imitate you. . . . I kept feverishly trying to figure out how to do that, how to hide behind something and watch how they walked and stuff. . . . But the model that hadn't showed up was supposed to open the show. Not to mention that she was the most famous one and had the best clothes to wear. It was Barbara Morris, just so you know. . . . So this lady says to me, You'll save us, you'll see, just walk fast and as straight as you can. Keep your back straight. And the Jalisco Girl and her friends made me downplay my breasts, right?, and walk fast. . . . So anyway, they explained all this stuff to me, and I went out, a little nervous as you might expect, right?

All these big shots and executives from the Palacio de Hierro were there. And a lot of salesgirls had gotten permission to see this fashion show. So I walked out waving to them, hey, hey, and winking and smiling at everybody. Felisa Broder was out there in the crowd of women friends of Little Jalisco's. And guess who I saw out there? Ezequiel Arjona, that potbellied guy that married Dressed Like a Man? When I got back, imagine. They were all waiting for me, ready to read me the riot act. They're jumping up and down and waving their hands around like this, and squawking You can't do that, that's the last time you'll ever do a thing like that, a model never turns to look at people or smiles or waves or anything! . . . So I went out for a second run, and I was even a little scared this time, but everything was very professional, and what was even better, the clothes looked wonderful on me. . . . So that was, I think, a Tuesday, and on Friday there was this fashion show in Cuernavaca. Barbara couldn't make that one either, so they got rid of her because she was always standing them up and making them look bad, right?, so they put me in in her place.

When I got home I said to my mother Can you believe it, I'm going to start working as a model. . . . You can imagine—she hit the ceiling. A model! That's the one thing you hadn't thought of! Of course you, all you want to do is walk down the street all day anyway, be out all day, but I'll tell you, I'm warning you, you better never in your life come to tell me you're leaving Mexico City, that's all I need, and so on and so forth. . . . No, Mama, first, I've got to take this job because we need the money, right?, and second, if I have to leave Mexico City, I'll take you with me, so don't worry. . . . And the first show we had, which was in Cuernavaca, she had to let me go, because I mean we had to live. . . . It was the first one, so I said to her Listen, we leave tomorrow morning at seven for Cuernavaca, and we'll come back at noon. . . . So she says *Chinga tu madre,* I'll be damned if I'm going to get up at that hour, you can go to hell, and anyway you know what you can do and what you can't do, so do whatever you fucking please, don't get *me* mixed up in it, no *chingada* daughter of mine . . . et cetera.

I was traveling all the time. I spent two years traveling, I mean I got to be a professional at it. . . . But I went back to Europe five or six more times, and all except one time I saw Giovanni. I mean a boy in every port, right? Because in Mexico City I was still going out with Alexis, I was about to marry Gabriel, and Mauricio too, by the way, and I'd even fallen in love with The Monk. . . .

Giovanni could only see me at these very strange hours because he was a labor-union leader. He'd come by for me at eight o'clock in the morning, unannounced. And he'd sit in the living room and wait for me, to come out? . . . About nine o'clock I'd come out in a sweater this big, down to here, with my pajama collar sticking out. Because Alexis had given me this robe made out of spider webs or flies' wings or something, you know, those absolutely transparent ones. . . . Imagine, I never wear anything but flannel pajamas, what in the world was I going to do with a negligée. . . . I still have it. I don't think I've ever worn it. . . . So I'd just throw on a sweater and a skirt, with my nightgown or pajamas underneath, and go out with my hair like this, just like I'd gotten out of bed, go out for breakfast. So I saw him there in the living room in a cloud of smoke like a London laboring-man, smelling like cheese, with a satyr's hooves, right?, very conspicuous and heavy—like an enormous rock. . . . And I fainted. . . .

When the President gave me that trip as a present so I could rest up from my problems, I met Dino. He always went out with Florencia whenever we went to Europe, but this one time he came to the airport to pick me up, and we went out together for a couple of months. One of those guys that, instead of saying Hello, starts unbuttoning your blouse? . . . So it was very mysterious, within two or three days of my getting there, I started getting these threatening phone calls. Like We're going to kill you, right? . . . Giovanni had been going out with this woman that was divorced, but when he met me he stopped seeing her. So somehow she found out my name, in his address book or something, and she copied my telephone number. Back then I gave Opus Dei's number when I was in Europe. So whoever answered, she'd say Are you the Mexican? They'd say Yes, and she'd start threatening them—Get out of Italy or you'll be sorry. . . . Until finally, she realized that it was all different girls. So then she'd start calling Opus Dei and asking what my name was, where I was, what I was doing. But I didn't live there all the time, right? I'd just go there when I was in Rome. So I got scared, but I got really scared when they said You have five days to live . . . or Now you only have four . . . And so on. . . . And about then Giovanni disappeared. At his house they thought he was with me, and at the factory too, and I think so did this divorced woman, but I suspected he was spending time with some bald wrinkled vagina in Monte Carlo.

Meanwhile, so anyway meanwhile, Dino was full of life, racy, fun, he knew Spanish, and he didn't have any hang-ups. His smile practically made the sunshine look dim. It threw shadows for a hundred yards around, I kid you not. But I couldn't stop thinking about Giovanni. *You* figure it out. His lover, this divorcée, kept bugging me day after day, at all hours. I'd pick up the telephone, and heavy breathing, the phone would ring, and You die, or another time nothing but silence, and so on . . . all night long, every fucking night. And at the same time Giovanni knew I was back in Italy, so he was running around trying to find me. He was better looking than even Handsome to the Maximum, more virile than Mauricio, and shier than The Monk. . . . Screw her! . . . I told him, Listen, they're bugging me night and day, they call and say It's hot in Rome, you should find somewhere cooler. We'd talk in the street or at the door of the house, and I know we were watched by these gangster types. . . . They said I had five days to live, and this is the fifth. . . . Well, he says, I promise you they will never bother you again. . . . I couldn't take my eyes off him, I couldn't bear to keep talking about these stupid things, and all of a sudden I got this feeling I had made a

mistake. It just came over me. So I fell on my knees to get away
from his eyes, staring at me. So I wouldn't have to look at him, so
he'd forgive me for replacing him with Dino. . . . I closed my
eyes, and when I opened them, he had just absolutely vanished.
Jealous? I could barely get up. Something about the shadows,
something about the smells at that hour, reminded me of the first
time I'd ever seen him. In the casino at Monte Carlo, right? So I
moved, I went to another house. At midnight, can you believe it?
I mean they'd tell her I wasn't there, but those mobsters of that
stupid bitch's kept saying Yes she is, you talk to her, you tell her
we know she's there, we saw her go in, you talk to her, or would
you like us to go in and look for her ourselves? They knew every
move I made, what I did, where I went, everything. So Dino came
to get me at midnight, and we went to this other apartment. At
that hour, I don't know who was on the rooftops, those flat roofs?,
but you could hear moaning. . . .

So several weeks went by. Dressed Like a Man came to Europe
with this girlfriend of hers, and Dino didn't have any money to
take us out, I mean he barely had enough just for the two of us,
you know? So we were all like this, all sad and depressed because we were wasting those beautiful Rome sunsets, all locked
up like that, and Giovanni calls. He was constantly calling, but
they had told him I'd gone back to Mexico. He'd call to get my
address, and they'd always tell him they didn't have it, they
didn't know. So then he called back to offer them money to get
them to give it to him. . . . Every time the phone rang my vagina
quivered. I heard his name, and my heartbeat and respiration
took off like the Death Drivers. So finally, I just answered the
telephone myself, my sixth sense told me it was him. He was a
little hurt, but I figured he was the only person that could take us
out for rides and to see places and to dinner. . . .

Tito says he caught me by my empty stomach. . . .

So anyway, we all went out with him, and I explained everything to Dino and all. We went to dozens of places. But the third
time we went out, he took us home with him to meet his family.
This huge mansion, or a castle, really. There were chairs and
suits of armor all the way around the sala, as he called it, all up

against the walls, and sitting in these chairs were all his aunts
and uncles, cousins, brothers and sisters, grandparents, nieces
and nephews, all these people. It was like one of my fashion
shows. . . . But listen to what happened. . . . One of Giovanni's
cousins brought his girlfriend too, to introduce her to the family?,
this really pretty girl, Elsa. . . . It looked like a convention of the
Society to Improve the Genetic Pool, I swear. . . . The women all
had these long feathers that came down over their faces and these
big dresses made out of heavy brocade and stuff with trains so
long they could have had all the curtains in the Bellas Artes
auditorium remade out of them. . . . So anyway, Giovanni's
grandmother, this little old lady with all these diamonds?, the one
I had seen in the casino at Monte Carlo, remember?, she says to
Elsa, You really don't understand Italian? And this girl says,
she's waving her hands around like an Olympic swimming champion, you know the Italians. . . . She says Why shouldn't I understand Italian, I'm Italian aren't I? . . .

When we left, I said Giovanni, you're taking it for granted that
I'm going to marry you. Yes, he says, a yes as big and quiet and
solemn as Saint Peter's. Well, listen, I'm not . . . I had my
doubts, right? Dressed Like a Man and her friend kept saying
He's perfect, he's gorgeous, he's rich, and nobody knows him in
Mexico. . . . That last part I didn't understand. What? I said.
Well, just imagine being married to Gabriel Infante or Pancho.
The Monk! Pleeease! So the next day we went to this private
detective agency, and we had them investigate Giovanni. You
know—drugs, women, a prison record, social behavior, real estate, cash, that kind of thing. . . . We got such unbelievable reports back! I mean such incredible, unbelievable reports that I
started having second thoughts.

Maybe he's the one for me, I said to myself. Yes or No? That
was when I really started to think about it seriously. Of course I
talked to Dino. Listen, what do you think?, what do you say to
this? We were in this park, sitting in the warm delicate sun shin-
ing on the trimmed hedges and antique statues. . . . Well, think
about it, says Dino, especially if he makes your head feel so
cloudy, think about it. I'd ask you to marry me, but what would

we live on? You're not a rich girl, and I don't have a fortune or even a job or anything. . . . And I don't want to work. . . .

I called Mexico City, and they told me Big Jalisco was in Amsterdam doing a story on fashions for this Mexican magazine and also that Alberto and The Monk had gone with her, so why didn't we meet. . . . Dressed Like a Man and her friend couldn't, though, they were on their way to Verona. (*"They were celebrating Mary's adultery with the holy dove!"*) So I called Giovanni, and I said I had to go back. . . . It's incredible how nervous I got, talking to him. . . .

They invited us to this dinner at their house, with candles and crunchy crustaceans. He looked worried about the future, and he was making these really funny motions, like a comic, a cheap comic, practically like Under the Big Top. . . . Whenever I was going to see him, I didn't wear stockings or underwear, so I could breathe, you know?, because I perspired like one of those chained women in the Flames of Purgatory. . . . So we were at his house and his grandmother says to me, Oh, now I see why Giovanni wants to marry you. . . . She was a little tipsy. . . . You are a very open, extraverted, charming, beautiful girl. . . . She was trying to light this enormous cigar, and the lighter kept trembling in her hand. Her jewelry clanked. . . . Like good tourists we asked and asked, but we could never find out a thing about his private life. They didn't give us the slightest glimpse, not even one little memory. Just these very polite little smiles of appreciation or, I don't know, acknowledgment. Giovanni raised his glass and gave a toast to Mexico and its beautiful girls. . . . The terror that it was all going to vanish made me drink a little more than I should have. Giovanni sitting in the kitchen of my apartment. Giovanni playing with his roulette chips. Giovanni driving. My body itself was so obsessed, I think, because it was as though Giovanni had turned into this huge magnetic creature. I never stopped thinking about him, I never stopped wanting him, as though there were nobody else in the whole world. Giovanni promised to come to Mexico as soon as we invited him. . . . I was dizzy from all the wine, and the smell of mollusks floating through this elegant dining room brought on a kind of swoon that dragged me toward him. (*"My nipples were on fire to think of his rough chest, like felt. . . ."*) Had they put something in my wine? I dizzily remembered Spanish fly and some fantasies I'd have about these aphrodisiacs we tried to concoct in The Two Turtles. The Two Turtles! Giovanni would come to Mexico as soon as I asked him. Shit . . . when we were saying good-bye, I put my lips up and he kissed me on the cheek. Sputum-spitting gynecologists!

So I went straight to Holland, to start my farewell to the single life and try to decide whether I was going to get married or not, watching the clouds from the window of the plane. . . .

("Whip up a new maidenhead every five minutes. . . .")

18

The carnival of fundamental relationships

It never rains but it pours, right? We were going to Cozumel, there were two days to go, and my brother comes in. I was peeling one potato, and my mother was peeling another one, I mean we were peeling potatoes, and my brother comes in and he says Pss, sweetheart, and Miss Homemaker here, I walk over with the potato in one hand and the peeler in the other. He grabs my arm and pulls me down the hall into the bathroom, and he whispers I've got hemorrhoids. What! But don't tell Mother, you know how she gets, whatever you do don't tell her, you know her—They come out, I can just hear her, she'll say They come out because you're a drunk, because you drink too much, that's *it* for you, you stay up all night. . . . You know how our dear mother is, so . . .

And don't tell my aunt, either, he says, because she'll be bugging me about it from morning to night. And you know, I can't stand this stuff I'm putting on them, no kidding. . . . So I went to get some cream I had, and I gave it to him. Don't look. . . . For once he didn't have a cent. . . .

The next day I went to the Hotel Camino Real for a modeling job, and when I came back, the maid was wailing and crying. Ay señorita she says, they just took your brother to the doctor, he was burning up with fever. . . . That night I think, uh-huh, that same night I was supposed to go to Cozumel, I had this really important fashion show. And my mother had had to carry off my brother, burning up with fever, screaming and shrieking and everything. So I had to quick get on the telephone and find somebody to cover for me at Cozumel. Come on, love, don't be mean, on the telephone, right?, I'll come down tomorrow, it's just a week, don't be so snotty about it . . . my maid firmly and decidedly hysterical in the background. . . .

So to make a long story short, I went to the doctor's office, and my brother was sort of sprawled in an armchair, because he couldn't even sit up straight. They'd looked him over and decided they had to do an emergency operation. You can imagine my mother—Naturally, naturally! He's a drunk, how could he *not* have hemorrhoids, that plus who knows what else. The doctor said We have to operate tomorrow, but don't worry, all he's got is a rectal abscess. . . . He might as well have said cancer of the uterus! Oh doctor, come off it, tell me the truth, what does he have, doctor. . . . By this time my brother wasn't even talking, he was a sleepy, peaceful Mr. Nice Guy. My mother goes What do you think? Me? I think they should operate. So do I, she says. So we told the doctor. All right, then, check him into the clinic tomorrow morning early, and I'll operate tomorrow afternoon. . . . Castrated kangaroos! I had to go to Cozumel that night. And you won't believe this, but my mother sat there scolding my brother for having hemorrhoids, treating him like dirt. Unbelievable. I called every day to see how he was. How's my brother? Well, he's out of the operation, he's all right. And then, Ay, sweetheart, you can't imagine what's happened, we'll tell you later. . . .

They'd taken him out of the recovery room back to his own room when he was still out from the anesthesia, and my brother had to pee, but he was still out, right?, so he got up and kind of staggered around like a bear in the circus, just operated on, and he was grabbing onto things to steady himself. So when he got to the bathroom he fainted, and he grabbed the intravenous stand he'd dragged along with him, and he fell and knocked the whole thing over and smashed the bottle and everything, the stand and all, and they found him in a pool of pee and blood and broken glass. About that time my mother came into the room, and Florencia behind her, because they'd gone down to the cafeteria to eat but my mother, all of a sudden my mother says They must have brought my son out by now, I've got to go see him. . . . But he wasn't in the bed, and the way the sheets and pillows and all were all messed up scared them. So they started looking for him, and they opened the bathroom door and there my brother was, with his little pee-pee hanging out, his ass all bloody, almost naked and lying there in a pool of broken glass, like this, glass all over the place and the intravenous tube out. My mother started screaming My son is dead, get a doctor, get a doctor! So this hullabaloo starts and the ooo-ooo-oooing of all these howls. From the ladies? At that, Tito comes in and Florencia jumps on him and tells him to find me, quick, my brother had died. Mercedes came in too—Oh my God, what's wrong with him! My brother lying there unconscious. . . . Florencia was shrieking Señorita, señorita, get a doctor, a *doctor!* As though everybody wasn't already coming apart at the seams, here comes Little Jalisco. Oh my God, oh my God, he's going to get an air bubble through the needle, an air bubble. . . . So the party is getting even better, right?, and a doctor from one of the other rooms sticks his head out. What's wrong here? And all the women go Ay, doctor!, you couldn't hear yourself think, right? Ay, doctor! He's in the bathroom! He's got blood all over him! He's covered with blood! So he crosses the hall. They didn't even let him walk, they were pulling and feeling him and practically carrying him across, they were hanging on to his frock or smock or whatever you call it. Ay doctor, he's already dead, he's dead, they were screaming. Quiet! You're all hysterical! My mother kept running her fingers across my brother's head and screaming. So the doctor starts picking pieces of glass out of my brother's skin. Doctor, doctor, please, you understand, this is my son, we want to know what's happened, please, I'm sorry to bother you, and she's patting him and touching him and petting him, the doctor, right?, to treat him nice so he'd stay there and fix up my brother. . . . Florencia was moaning Ay doctor, how can we be calm when he's dead. And Little Jalisco kept yelling at full volume, Pull the needle out, pull the needle out, he'll get an air bubble and die. Until finally the doctor exploded. Shut up! That's it! I can't stand this, *you* take care of him! And did he care—he pulled out the needle and threw it at my brother, like this, bam!, *chíngale!*, he throws it and it bounces off my brother's chest, and he stalks out of the room furious. Hysterical!, the doctor is screaming, crazy women! So you can just see my mother by now. Idiot, she's saying, stupid asshole doctor, moron, *chingado* quack sawbones asshole. . . .

So nobody came to take care of him now, and all the sick people from all the rooms down the hall were hanging on their doors to see the dead man, right? Like this, hanging onto the doorframes, white as sheets, their hair all like this, these people holding up bandages coming loose all over them, and now and then putting in their own contribution to the confusion. Get a doctor, quick! So at that Mercedes, who by this time was, I can't tell you, she takes off downstairs like a Roman candle and starts yelling for the chief doctor and the administrator and everybody else she could think of. She sees this nun and she says Mother, there's a patient on the floor, and not one of those asshole doctors or prissy nurses will come help get him up. So at that very moment in comes Mauricio, he was just coming in, right? They'd all eaten together in the cafeteria. So my mother goes Look at your lifelong friend lying there, nobody will help get him up, look at him with the tubes and everything. So he goes over to pick him up. And then she goes on, Ay Mauricio, what do you think happened, this stinking doctor came in and when he saw him covered with blood. . . . Mercedes says that the only place they weren't afraid to pick my brother up by was his prick, she says he had blood all over him, so they just grabbed him by his prick and carried him to the bed. Did you really see me naked? he said. This is later, right?, when we were having breakfast one time. Uh-huh, in your birthday suit, you should've seen yourself. Well, you have to remember I was sick, my brother says. . . .

So anyway, to make a long story short, Mauricio picked him up and between him and Tito Caruso . . . Because the doctors never came, or the nurses or the aides or anybody else either. My mother was hysterical of course, crying and crying, and at that the other doctor, from across the hall?, comes out. My mother sees him and she screams Look, Mauricio, that's him, that's the idiot that tried to kill my son. . . . So Mauricio drops my brother, thank God on the bed, and he runs and grabs the doctor and starts punching him, *chíngale!*, and when they saw that, the other patients up and down the hall start dropping like flies. Fainting dead away! And *chíngale* again. They just sort of melted down. *Chíngale!* And the doctor is whimpering and saying I'm not even from this hospital. Well this is for sticking your nose in where it doesn't belong then! And *chíngale* again. At this Andrés and Napoleon show up. Mercedes was saying to Mauricio, No baby, stop it, please, stop, and since he doesn't pay any attention to her, can you believe, she dropped to her knees and clutched him around the legs, like this? Imploring him, right? Please baby, stop, don't hit him anymore, I beg you. So then Andrés grabs Mauricio from the back, he held his arms, and at that the doctor goes, real quick he goes bambambam, and he starts punching Mauricio, who they had, right?, they had his arms and legs pinned. My mother still crying . . . Polygamous macaws!

When I got back from Cozumel, they told me to wait at the house, because they were ready to bring my brother home from the hospital. That afternoon all his friends were coming by, and Florencia and Tito were going to bring over a projector and their pornographic movies. At that the telephone rings. I thought it might be from the hospital, they needed more money or something like that, so the telephone rings, and it was Bloodhound, I don't know exactly how he told me, but he was in Tijuana and my uncle had been killed. He'd been machine-gunned. . . . The two of them, my uncle and Bloodhound I mean, they were driving along and they'd been ambushed. Bloodhound managed to jump out of the car and roll into a ditch. They thought he was dead. . . . My uncle had been killed, can you imagine? I collapsed into a chair. The dress! I was wearing the black dress Felisa Broder told me never to put on unless I wanted something terrible to happen. . . . I tore it off, I ripped it off me. I felt like I myself was doomed to some noisy senseless death like my father and uncle. . . . A highway patrol car had stopped next to the car which was all full of machine-gun holes. The police sniffed around here and there, took notes, and then they took out the bloody corpse. Bloodhound couldn't do anything. They put the body into the patrol car and drove away. We only found out later that they were going to stretch the body out across the highway right after a curve, my uncle was so tall, I mean the body was so long, right?, and calmly wait for some unsuspecting car to come along. The squeal of tires didn't take long, either. This Maverick, the driver of this Maverick was taken by surprise, I mean, of course, who wouldn't be, right?, and he didn't have time to dodge the body in the road, so he almost lost control of the car. . . . The patrol car drove up to him and pulled him over. This very polite, very dark-skinned policeman got out and says Good afternoon. Good afternoon, says the driver, his mind racing to try to figure out what had happened. You just ran over a man says the policeman. . . . My uncle!

I'd just finished getting dressed when Andrés arrived. You look tired, he said. Well, I just got back. I was so stunned, and I felt so emotionally inept. I had the feeling I was going to fall apart inside at any moment. So then Little Jalisco, Napoleon, and Mercedes came in with my mother and brother. Carnival time, can you believe it?, and I was completely incapacitated. I don't know

what to do, I said to Little Jalisco. . . . She thought I didn't want
to watch the porno movies with my brother there. So she laughs
and says Holy shit, the things you worry about. . . . She was
fluttering like a turkey. So I went up to Andrés. Something's
wrong, he says. Einstein, right? I don't want to watch those
movies with my brother. . . . Really? I didn't even know how to
start. I felt like my mood weighed about a thousand tons, I was so
shocked and numbed by the news. My mother started passing out
little plates full of olives all over the place, peanuts, potato chips,
and all kinds of nuts and stuff. She had her mouth full when she
told everybody good-bye, to have a good time. I'm glad you're
here, she told me, I'm going to go visit your godparents, I'll call
you after a while to come pick me up. . . . I want to talk to you, I
said. Later, honey, I'm late, later we'll talk all you want to. . . .
Her vulgarity stabbed my heart. It was indecent. . . . I've got
something really important to tell you, I said again. I mean I
didn't want to blackmail her, I didn't want to give her the biggest
shock of her life, but the news was too awful for me all by myself.
After while, sweetheart, later, I need a little rest from the hospital, come pick me up in a little while, and we'll talk as long as
you want to. . . . About then Florencia burst in in a dress that
looked like a nightshirt with Tito right after her with the movies.
Little Jalisco told my brother not to make any dirty cracks. Mercedes seconded her. The first dirty remark you make, I'm leaving.
Because you know how funny he is, right? I mean they were right.
He's always saying these terrible things, hilarious, he'll say anything to anybody, so imagine, this was going to be a circus. And
inside me the pain kept getting worse and worse, like some kind
of sickening pregnancy. I felt like I was pregnant with an iguana.
Chinga my own *madre*, says my brother from his bed, stop has-
sling me, God damn it, I won't open my trap, so leave me alone.
Napoleon set up the projector, and we all sat down around the
bed. What do you guys want to drink? Andrés asked, and the
genital games were on. . . .

The first remark was from my fucking brother. Naturally. Florencia and Mercedes almost peed they were laughing so hard, and

me there with my secret. Their laughing started making me so
mad, so mad I thought I was being possessed. So finally, I said
Okay, it makes me feel awful that my brother would have so little
consideration for me, so if you won't think it's bad manners, I
think I'll just leave. . . . So everybody starts going Oh screw you,
stop being such a prude, you stupid bitch, and they all turned
around and stared at me. I thought I was about to throw some
horrible fit or have an epileptic attack or something, so I ran into
the kitchen to cry. . . . I came back with a tray full of little
sandwiches, and to get in the room I had to jump over my uncle's
run-over body. . . . One . . . Two . . . Three . . . Four times.
So the police could get bribes out of that many more drivers. . . .
I walked across in front of the screen—whistles, stomps, hoots,
you have no idea. I didn't recognize myself. And my brother gives
a series of Shits, so long and so grand, right?, that you'd have
thought they were prancing horses with ribbons and bows on their
manes and tails, the most beautiful horseshits in the world, with
big cleft hooves and incredible pulling power. . . . Little Jalisco,
Florencia, and Mercedes were going Ooo how gross, look how big
it is, ooo I can't watch, Oh Jesus shit, *chingada madre*, o-o-o-o-o,
right? And my brother like a madman in one long goddamn, look
at that goddamn, look at that goddamn, look at that, I mean I
never saw him run out of steam or burning froth, like a runaway
locomotive. . . . I knew I was about to be pulled under by some
black monster from the depths, so I decided to grab onto whatever
I could. . . . Lecherous lemurs! I could barely get the nuts into
my mouth, I'd grabbed such a handful. . . .

My uncle's corpse was creeping after me. It was all mutilated
and muddy. Mercedes kept saying Don't laugh so loud, idiot.
Florencia saw how down and out I looked, so she thought I was
really and truly upset about the movies. So finally, she said to
Tito, Okay, that's enough, she really doesn't feel right about this.
Really? So Tito . . . I mean it was like going to see *Quo Vadis*
and leaving in the middle, you know what I mean? So, but Tito
says Okay, okay, I'll put them away, I'll show them another time,
but I'll put them away now. . . . Andrés stood up, but Napoleon

pulled him back down in his seat again. My brother starts saying
What bastards, how can you be so cruel to a sick man, shit. Tito
started putting the movies and stuff away, and it was like he was
stuffing all the paraphernalia into my uncle's corpse with all the
people sitting there watching . . . embalming it with pornogra-
phy. . . . And my brother going What happened, buddies, let's
see some more. . . . No, some other time. . . . Like they had
smelled the smell of death. And I'm telling you, it was like it was
there, and the iguana wriggling around in my insides, so I ran to
the bathroom and shut myself up. I was so depressed, so terribly
terribly depressed, and shaking and scared. It was almost as
though my uncle's dying body was going to start scratching at the
door at any moment. The mirror gave me back a look so utterly
impotent and scared to distraction. . . .

Downstairs they were talking about my brother in the hospital.
Alberto and Big Jalisco had come in. They said my brother had
made a nurse and my mother leave. No, son, you're still dizzy. I
don't care, get out of here! So they put the commode or whatever
you call it, the bedpan, right?, in bed with him, and he went to
sleep, with my mother and the nurse standing behind the door so
he could pee in peace. And bang, he falls on his head and winds
up under the bed, which is about this high off the ground, right?
One of those hospital beds you have to have a ladder to climb
into? Unbelievable. And that morning my mother had been talking to some administrative-type nun, and all of a sudden she
turns around and she sees this nurse. Señorita, she says, what are
you doing here? Why señora, I came to get . . . Don't tell me, go
back to the sick boy, right now, shoo, don't leave him alone. You
can imagine what will happen if he dies here on you. . . .

Alberto and Big Jalisco started talking about The Monk then,
about his unbelievable carryings-on in Copenhagen. Did I tell you
about all that? Because he wouldn't go in anyplace, he refused.
For example, he refused to go into one single porno shop. He'd
stand there in the street while Alberto, Big Jalisco and I went in
to look at the magazines and buy fancy condoms. He pretended
he wasn't with us. As a matter of fact, he pretended he didn't

even know us. . . . Embarrassed, can you imagine that? One time we were at this show. It was in this big room and they were showing pornographic films. There were a lot of Mexicans in the audience, so you can just imagine, Viva Mexico and Ándale and Ay chihuahua, the whole routine, right? . . . We were like you wouldn't believe. . . . They were speaking Spanish, and we were speaking Chinese so nobody would know we were Mexican too. Oh, I forgot, and Mexican women, too, those really dark-skinned types, like secretaries, right?, with their knees like this, real squeezed together, ill at ease as hell, like they had on a cactus chastity belt. . . . There was no place to sit down so we sat on this thing like a bench, or a divan, right? Look at this, says The Monk, it's still a little wet where I'm sitting. It was this un-believably gross place, and filthy, you know, and we were sitting back in the darkest part. . . . Beside us there were these three drunk Danish guys, yelling all kinds of stuff and laughing and belching. The movies there—can you believe every two minutes The Monk would say What are we doing here, in God's name? . . . I said Pancho, for heaven's sake, try to enjoy your-self, like we really needed to see that stuff, right? So then The Monk starts going I'm going to vomit, I swear, I swear to you I'm about to throw up. . . . The Mexican girls were sweating by this time, they were about to faint, they didn't know what to do, and can you believe some of them threw themselves back and just stared at the ceiling? The Monk whimpering I'm going to throw up, let's go for pity's sake. So Big Jalisco finally says Don't be such a jerk. Alberto, too, he says Come on Pancho, don't be an idiot. . . .

So anyway, finally my mother called, and I said I'd come pick her up. How was I going to break the news to her? My father's brother had been machine-gunned to death. . . . I came out of the bathroom with my green face and my mouth open, gasping for air. . . . I could hear Bloodhound's voice while I was looking for the car keys. I'd open a drawer, and there was my uncle's body with his shoes untied, gory, and his muscles all contracted like a gorilla. His body was splattered all into itself. His eyes were open, and it was like they were staring in disbelief at his side ripped open by the bullets. A whole line of disgusting holes like chimpanzees' anuses, and out of them this flood of blood that kept dripping onto the car door, the dashboard, the steering wheel, my brother's bed, the carpeting. That poor wrecked body, face up, had finally been dragged out of the highway and set up on the toilet in the bathroom. I slammed the door. . . . How to break the news? It was hard for me to accept the fact, but basically I liked to keep news like that to myself. My father's brother had been machine-gunned to death. . . . My mother was going to go to pieces, she'd be destroyed, she'd go numb. I decided to just tell her, like that, I figured the information would give me my one chance to see her horrified and frightened. . . .

Because my mother is strange. She's never like in this world, you know?, she never, never notices anything, nothing seems to faze her. . . . I was sure she'd say it was his own fault, he was a thief, always jumping into things. . . . She's in her own world, right? News like that, such terrible, shocking news might wake her up. . . . That at least is what I thought. . . . And do you think she was shocked? I mean, she goes to group hypnosis and she never knows if they hypnotized her or not. . . . For example, one day she was leaving her mind-control class, and one of her friends says Listen, do you mind if my nephew takes you home, because I'm a little rushed. . . . Don't be silly says my mother, I don't mind at all. They were like five or six blocks from home at the time, right? . . . So this lady's nephew says I'm sorry, señora, I don't live around here, so you tell me how to go, and I'll be happy to take you. So my mother says You know where Ciudad Universitaria is? Well, she goes on, just go straight, and I'll tell you where to turn in just a second. . . . We'll be turning down a street with trees on it, and then we just go straight. . . . So my mother starts directing him, right?, Left here, take a right again here, and a right here. All of a sudden the guy says Señora, are you sure we're not lost? Because I think we are, because there are the boats, this must be Xochimilco. . . . When my mother heard the word Xochimilco, you can't believe it. . . . Are we at

Xochimilco? Sí, señora. . . . Oh no, young man, this is terrible, I
don't live here, take me to San Antonio, I live in Pedregal. . . .
But señora, I don't know. . . . Well, then, San Jose Insurgentes,
Guadalupe Inn. . . . But señora, I don't know where any of that
is, I live in Torreón Coahuila, this is the first time I've ever been
in Mexico City. . . . And do you know that my mother had forgotten her address, her telephone number, everything. I mean completely forgotten, she didn't have the slightest idea, not the
remotest idea. So then what happens . . . She says . . . So, oh,
that's right, they keep going around in circles and driving all over
the city, and my mother can't find our house. And what's worse,
she didn't have the nerve to tell the guy that she'd forgotten the
name of her street. She was lost in this labyrinthine city, this
maze of streets full of cars and blinking traffic lights. She didn't
recognize a single corner. The trees and streetlights looked to
her, I don't know, as faceless as the *very few* pedestrians she saw,
because it was getting to be like eleven or twelve o'clock at night
by now. The guy driving kept getting more and more nervous, and
my mother felt absolutely sure that she was suffocating, no two
ways about it. She felt like she was in prison, in a dungeon of this
castle, right?, in terrible pain and desperation because suddenly
she didn't know who she was. The terror of being *nobody*,
right? No address or telephone number or street. Vincent Price,
right? . . . And to make things eerier, the city was full of dead-
end streets and little alleys. They just kept getting in deeper and
deeper, like a fly in a spider web. . . . If we all forgot about her,
if nobody went to Missing Persons or whatever, she'd discover the
uselessness of her existence, she would just drop out of the world,
and the world would forget about her, she'd die in this car that
never stopped, that just kept driving down unknown street after
street after street, even if the gasoline ran out. . . . Forever. . . .
Die? Did I say die? All of a sudden she starts crying like a baby
and says Oh young man, can I ask you a favor? Sí, señora. . . .
So she says Take me to some television station so my children
will see me and come pick me up, take me to some television
station, any of them. . . . Because she gave up, she felt like she

was about to be dragged off into an insane asylum . . . poor thing. . . . She had about a hundred times more wrinkles by now. . . . Please, just one favor, just drop me off at a TV station so my children can claim me. . . . Ask any policeman. . . .

When my aunt heard the news, right?, about her machine-gunned to death husband, twisted and splattered and run over by cars, she turned beet red from trying to control the shock. She's had a nervous condition for nine years. Her nerves have been terrible ever since her daughter almost died from being shot by her little brother, her son, right?, I think I told you about that. When we gave her the news, we tried to cushion it by telling her all these positive things, these sweet things about death, like you do, you know?, and all we managed to do was set in motion a really frightful, frightful smash-up, unhinge her for the rest of her life. . . . She turned so red . . . I can't even describe it. . . .

You couldn't even recognize the body, and Bloodhound swore he'd kill the policemen without a second thought. It wasn't exactly a rational decision, but he wasn't confused or crazy with grief either, and he wasn't being the Veracruz macho either, it was just that another piece of butchery or two were needed before the whole thing could be fully and completely closed, right? One or two more deaths were needed, and one fine morning he shows up and tosses two badges on the breakfast table. One of them was a second lieutenant's. . . . The case was closed. . . .

A widow overnight, my aunt suddenly had nothing to live for anymore. Her children offered very few interesting possibilities, I'll tell you. All the exciting unknown attractions of the future had been nailed into that gray coffin as big as a Lincoln Continental, where the horrible remnants, is that the word?, no, remains of my uncle were lying. . . . Aside from a few memories everything started to curdle. . . . She'd walk around the city like a zombie, going into shops and stores and teenage hangouts, until finally this one day she went into the Palacio de Hierro. . . . I don't need to tell you, she never had a peso in her pocketbook, never never ever. And ever since my uncle's murder, she's felt like she's useless, like she's not any good for anything, that nobody cares about her, and so she rounds out her crying fits and frenzied dancing and desperate moans with walking around like this, shlp shlp shlp, you know, like one of those tired pregnant women that's walked from Atotonilco to Our Lady of Guadalupe. She made this vow, this religious vow, right?, and she can't carry any money, not even a five-centavo piece with a hole in it. And it goes without saying that she's not about to do manual labor. No cleaning, no working in her house, right? So, so as not to go crazy, she winds up being useless. So she comes over to see us every day. She loves my brother, she really loves him. So one day, she realizes she's stolen this pair of socks and nobody's caught her. And us, you can imagine, we're delighted, right?, because she's stolen this pair of socks that cost eighty some-odd pesos, and they fit my brother. So she finally did something useful, okay? So she sees she can still do something worthwhile, bring a little happiness to somebody, you know, do something for another person, give surprises, *communicate*. I'll tell you, from that day on Robin Hood was a piker! She stole everything in the world, everything you can think of, everything. But only from the Palacio de Hierro. And everything she shoplifts is for me. . . . Every time my mother came in and saw something new, she'd say From your Aunt? So my mother has me tell her, Listen, why don't we do something, why don't you shoplift expensive stuff, and we'll buy it from you at a discount. So she feels useful and fulfilled and all that and we come out okay, too. . . . Because my uncle's estate will go a long way. . . .

Well, anyway, to make a long story short, she brought us one of those robes like they're wearing now, you know that kind with a belt in front and the back bare? I was *not* going to wear it because it was imitation, I mean it was nylon and I don't wear imitation stuff. I may not have much money, but I've got my principles. . . . It's either Pucci or forget it. . . . And this robe did look like Emilio Pucci, but it was imitation. . . . So I went and exchanged it for some shoes. Oh, I forgot, I gave her three hundred pesos. How nice, she says, and everybody came out ahead on the deal, right? So now she's really happy, or pretty happy, it's changed her life. . . . Since she's started shoplifting she's happy, everybody can see it, my brother and my mother and everybody. And she does something for another person. She comes over, and she says to me, Did those socks fit your brother? No, but I'll exchange them this afternoon. So every day you can see me in the Palacio de Hierro exchanging things. . . . Ay señorita, this coat was a birthday present, but it doesn't fit. . . . And all the old ladies in the Palacio de Hierro know me. The funniest thing is, that a close friend of mine works in the lingerie department, the corsets and bras and all, I've known her since back with Handsome to the Maximum. . . . We worked together in Exclusive Gifts, this little tiny girl with dark hair, you remember who I mean? . . . And now my aunt goes by to see her all the time, she goes by supposedly to say hello, and by the time she's said hi, she's walking out with five bras, five panties, five girdles. Degenerate devils! *Me* she brings girdles, that I've never worn a girdle in my life. Of course, except for when I was modeling and they made us wear one, that's the only time, and as soon as I could I took it off. Sometimes I'd take it off anyway. . . . So she brings me these girdles! She brings me bras size 38-D, and I'm a 30-A. So imagine . . . They're like this. . . . So I go Ay sweetheart, my mother bought me these bras, but they don't fit. . . .

But getting back to my uncle . . . Imagine, riding along in a yellow Falcon, Bloodhound sitting there beside him, talking. Smile-wrinkles in his cheeks from laughing so much, he was a man that was always laughing, his whole face made jokes for years and years and years. . . . And he's laughing again, like the hiccups, right?, and Bloodhound too, about some messy deal they'd pulled off by a stroke of genius. . . . The Falcon is running like a Swiss watch, but there's something funny up there in the highway, an old horse, and they have to slow down, right? And all of a sudden this cracking spiderweb in the windshield, pieces of glass in his face, perfectly aimed shots in his side, dry splinter-pricks in his left arm, loud hot shots in his thighs. . . . His whole body collapses, like under a hatchet. . . . He never even knew that Bloodhound had managed to open the door and jump out. . . . Then the silence. . . . The motor had died, but the car was still rolling along in a straight line; his shrunken body was slumped over the steering wheel. . . . In silence. . . . That satyr's head of his was destroyed with such terrible force that it was a miracle that his teeth, they were knocked out like they were a dentist's display, it was a miracle that even his teeth were saved. . . . His knees buckled and convulsed and then flew open like in a gynecologists's stirrups. . . . His skin looked like it exploded in all directions, from obscene orifices. . . . Out of one of them, next to the little gold religious medallion, blood was still bubbling in a little red trickle when the police arrived. . . .

("A death car? A horse and a car. Beyond silence, under the asphalt, above the smokestacks, in the air, in my veins, making the night, the anguish, the walls, shudder with its hollow hoofbeats, the rhythm of death. A horse and a car.")

19

Conjugal conjugations

Mercedes had twins, and do you know, she never breast-fed them? She said that she tried, but it gave her this creepy sensation, she didn't like it, it made her feel strange. . . . She felt sorry for the babies, she said The poor things, it probably repulsed them too, you know? I don't know, she didn't like the way it felt, the way they sucked, the way they swallowed, the way they licked her. . . . Her own babies! It felt horrible, right? Besides the fact that I don't think she had any milk. . . . She didn't want to feel like a good little Mexican mother, or like Our Beloved Mother, or like any kind of mother, period. . . . That's why she refused to feed her babies. . . . And her breasts got like this, they got to be this big, and she got these sudden depressions all the time. . . . I don't think she even tried to breast-feed them, because like I say, the first time she tried it she hated it. No way, she didn't like it, nope. Or maybe she couldn't. Or didn't know how. . . .

We were talking about all this once, and Josefina, Mauricio's wife?, the one that came to the Palacio de Hierro all the time and yelled at me? You remember? She starts going No, no, how can a mother, because what makes a mother a mother is getting up in the middle of the night with her children. . . . Because she'd found out that Mercedes and Dressed Like a Man had nursemaids or nannies or whatever they were being called at the time, they didn't have to mess with their kids at night. I said it was enough to have your whole day screwed up taking care of babies, why screw up your whole night too, washing your nipples every three hours, right? But Josefina kept bugging everybody, saying a mother's not a mother unless she gives her babies her breast. And when you can't? says Little Jalisco. You always can, always, she says. But when it's just impossible? insists Dressed Like a Man. For example, I *can't*, says Mercedes. Where there's a will there's a way, says Josefina, because being a mother is a very responsible position, before God, and before men. . . .

Mauricio finally married her. When he wasn't on some drug or other, you know, he was a terrific guy, so at first everything was sweetness and light. But the problems started when he hears this wife of his tell the maid, We'll have chilaquiles and roast beef with salsa verde. And Mauricio comes unglued. He starts screaming. Never give orders in front of me, or anything to do with running the house because I can't stand it! I hate hearing you tell her what to cook! I never want to hear you say Pick up some frijoles, or Why don't you start frying those red snapper filets, or Be sure to buy sugar . . . ! He didn't want to hear anything about how the house was run, but he wanted to come home and find these exquisite meals waiting for him, okay? He thought, he wanted to live, I don't know, it wasn't real, the house was supposed to run itself by magic. No voices getting these wonderful dinners together. . . . He'd forbidden his wife to have buttons or needles or spools of thread lying around the house because he said it was humiliating for women to sew on buttons or mend things, so Josefina couldn't sew in front of him, although of course she didn't have time either, because as soon as he came in, she started having the fights of her life, he ranted and raved like a madman and beat her and everything. . . . Forget it! So this girl starts crying and telling us about how he's always cursing and throwing fits and breaking things. . . . Well, says Florencia, throw him out, run him out of the house. Kick him out, shrieks Little Jalisco. No, girls, God only knows I stand for it against my will, God and you girls, but I have to take it. . . . So they say But why the hell do you have to stand for such things, Josefina, throw him out, call your father and tell him to come throw him out, or we'll talk to some friends of your father's if you want us to. . . . I mean he won't be surprised, right?, it'll come as no great shock to him that you and Mauricio are having troubles, right? He knows he's your husband, he knows you're married, so what are you afraid of? . . . Call him, tell him. . . . No, don't worry about me, I have to resign myself to this, to resign myself. . . . This is laughable, right? . . . So Dressed Like a Man for her part, you won't believe this, but she married Ezequiel Arjona, a Mexican *charro*, on horseback and everything, dressed in tight pants with silver studs and clanking spurs and the whole show. . . . The bad thing is, that like any self-respecting mariachi, he chases skirts. Dressed Like a Man has caught him plenty of times, don't think she doesn't know, but he's a good boy generally speaking. I mean he has his little national shortcomings, right? He gets drunk, he chases women, he forgets to come home once in a while, and then he stands under her window and serenades her. I think this first baby will help them a lot. It'll be hard getting used to, but they've already started. . . . You knew she had a miscarriage at six months, right? They couldn't save it. After that it took her a long time to get pregnant again, and then she finally had a baby, a little baby. . . . But meanwhile, I mean after the miscarriage and while she was pregnant again, she got this thing, I don't know, she went sort of crazy, and she ran off with my uncle, married and pregnant and all, and she stayed with him until they machine-gunned him in Tijuana, really strange, huh? Then she had her baby, and three days after it was born, the baby got per-

itonitis, and they had to open it up the whole length of the canal
. . . or anyway the whole length of it. . . . And then a month
later who knows how, there had to be another operation exactly
the same way, just as serious, they had to do it, even if they
didn't know if the baby was going to pull through it or not. . . .
So I mean it's been hard, really hard making that marriage work.
It hasn't been easy. . . .

Another little sandwich? What will you have to drink? We were
at Andrés' house, and his wife talked with her mouth full. Her
name's Sandra, do you remember her? I knew her in high school,
and she was one of those girls that said she'd never sleep with a
boy because she wouldn't give him her treasure. . . . That's what
she called it—her treasure. . . . She said she was never going to
bed with anybody, ever. Never never never. She was brainwashed. She got this idea, she had this idea stuck in her brain, or
so to speak brain, and it just popped out of her every once in a
while. Her treasure! Not to mention she was completely unedu-
cated, un, I don't know, uncultured. Common. She dressed real
well, and she talks like this, very sophisticated, right?, very
proper and all, but the way she thinks is common. For example,
she's always making a scene, like they'll be somewhere, and
she'll see Andrés turn and look at somebody and *chíngale!* . . .
She screams and starts throwing stuff and everything. She throws
furniture. . . . She reads his mail, she looks in his address
book, she listens in on his telephone conversations, she trails him
places, can you imagine? Andrés will say I'm leaving, honey, I'll
be back about six, and he'll come in from his office at seven and
have to dodge things flying at him to get in the house. Pictures,
chairs, lamps, the toilet bowl, everything. She threw the stove at
him once. . . . They've already completely destroyed the house
two or three times, and they just knocked down a whole wall,
bang, just because Andrés comes in ten or fifteen minutes late.
And I'm not exaggerating, I'm not joking. And Sandra is the most
important thing in the world and parts of Europe to Andrés, I
swear to you. . . . His fat wife like an Aztec fertility goddess with
her hands over her pelvis like this all the time . . . long sharp
fingernails. Like this cute little piggy, right?, she lives her life

between the beauty shop and her mother's house. She runs through the traffic to get across Chapultepec Avenue, through the exhaust and the fumes of roaring cars to buy herself two little slices of pizza. . . . Four pounds more and her hips won't fit any chair ever made. . . .

She says to me, Ay, I don't think you ought to encourage Tito to go to your house so much. . . . And she tells Florencia too, just sort of offhandedly mentions it, okay?, she says Listen, your girlfriend, I mean a lot of people aren't very nice, your girlfriend, I know, does it because she's such a good-hearted person and she's so pretty and everybody loves her and all, but the world is full of shits, right?, and Tito will be the first one to misunderstand her, so if I were you. . . . I mean what it is, is, that Tito, whenever he has a fight with Florencia, Tito comes over for a visit and we write this fervent poetry. Like for example, If I seem sad and screwed to you, Well life's petty little shafts may have scratched me, But the day I take off for good, There's not a fucking eagle that'll catch me. . . . He drinks whisky with beer chasers and scratches his ass, talks about sex and tells jokes. He even acts them out sometimes. . . . And when he says the word *orgasm*, tears come to his eyes. . . . We write on the covers of two Daniel Santos records. . . . If I seem sad and screwed, Tito whispers, And you think I'm crazy because of you, he scribbles down, all nervous, Well, go fuck yourself, on a sudden inspiration, It's only because I was born to sing the blues. . . .

But the pièce de résistance of that particular get-together, I mean the most delectable morsel of gossip of them all, was Handsome to the Maximum's getting married. He killed a man, and he was in jail for, I don't know, and then all of a sudden he married two women. And they both knew about it! Little Jalisco would tell this whole story, from the very beginning, sprinkling in this pigeonlike purring and cooing and some mad magpie's squawks and caws. . . . You know there are certain people I've just erased, because so many things have happened to me, and I've been through so much so fast, problems I never dreamed I'd have, like I've been so busy thinking and worrying about so many things that I've just forgotten certain people completely. Lindolf, for example. As soon as Little Jalisco mentioned him, I remembered he'd wanted to marry me for a long time. A *long* time. I remembered this one day he was showing me his guns, this whole armory he had, one of those things where you don't remember whether he proposed or not, and over there was a sofa bed. Want to make love with me? I don't remember any of this too well. And I'd never thought of it again, in spite of the fact that I've seen him a lot, every once in a while I run into him. I mean, back then he was really chasing me, but I honestly can't remember the details.

Imagine, Handsome to the Maximum in the La Torre Baths. They're these Turkish baths, right?, with steam and all, and he was there because he used to go take Turkish baths there all the time. I say used to because this was years and years and years ago. . . . So anyway, this one time Lindolf comes in and says Listen, come with me because I've got this great offer for you, come on, the deal of a lifetime, I need to show you somebody. . . . You'd see Lindolf and immediately have the feeling he was, he was, I don't know, mutilated or something, but you didn't know where, was all. You'd look at his ears, his fingers, you'd wait for him to get up and walk to see if that was it, I mean you couldn't like *prove* anything, but there was something about him that made the word *amputation* come to your mind. I kid you not. Strange, huh? So they left this one place and went into another steam room. Lindolf says See? Don't stare, but take a good look at him. . . . It was this big brown guy with a moustache like Cantinflas, really impressive-looking but almost shapeless, this round puffing guy. . . . So he says to Handsome to the Maximum, Here's a hundred and fifty thousand down. Double that if you pull it off, and he gives him a big wink and hands him a little bagful of gold, like in the Middle Ages, I'm not kidding. Keep it for me, snarls Handsome to the Maximum, and he suavely pushes the bag away. . . . I mean, I'm not sure exactly what was said, right? But anyway . . . So anyway, he went to his locker and got his pistol, that much everybody says. And he hefts it like this, you know, and twirled it around, thought for a second about the consequences, or probably thought about the money, and he went into the steam room, still naked, incredibly beautiful, wrapped in

a towel that said LA TORRE BATHS. He walks up to this fat
man lying there on a concrete slab, and he shoots him three times
in the chest and head without uttering a word. . . . The pistol was
slippery from the steam, and it wasn't as shiny as he always liked
it to be. He went up to less than three feet away and shot one,
two, three times. The fat man tried to stop one of the bullets with
his soft mellifluous hand, open like this, like Halt, and that's the
way he stayed, like somebody had snapped his picture all of a
sudden. Motionless and surprised. Is it mellifluous? That doesn't
sound right to me. . . . Anyway, the shots echoed like in a bank
vault, so of course, dozens of men ran in. They charged in out of
the fog wrapping towels and sheets around themselves, some of
them with their little thing just like, like sprouting out of a little
nest of hair. . . . Of course, he didn't try to run away, so all the
Turkish bathers grabbed him immediately. . . . By that night he
was in jail already, and I mean, of course, in some newpapers
too, but he said he was showing the pistol to this guy, and it had
gone off three times, I mean since it was an automatic, he hadn't
been able, he couldn't you know, an accident, a really truly accident. . . . Lindolf paid some incredible amount of bail, but
Handsome to the Maximum still had to spend, I don't know, ten
or eleven months in jail. And he says they got him out to, well,
that he got out every night and went home for dinner or to the
Zero Zone with his buddies and everything. So then in jail he met
this forger that's one of the biggest forgers or counterfeiters or
whatever you call them in the world. In jail, right? . . . He's, I
think, Greek. So anyway, he says one day this man, one day
they're just sort of talking and this man says You're married. And
he says No, I'm not married. So this guy says Why don't you get
married. . . . And he says What for? And this Greek guy says
Well, it's very important to get married and have children, and he
gives him such a lecture on life, about what children mean and
what a real home is, and the longer he went on, the more Handsome to the Maximum thought this guy really had something
there, he ought to get married. . . . So then he . . . There were
these two girls he liked a lot, if you know what I mean. One was
Chiquis Monteforte, and the other one is Gabriela something-or-

other, who's the daughter of this really really rich general. No, there were *three* of them, three of them, but I don't remember who the other one was. So anyway he, I mean Handsome to the Maximum, right?, when they came to visit him, because all three of them were always going to visit him, continually, he asked all three of them, right?, I mean one at a time he asked them if they wanted to marry him. Although he was in jail, right? So the three of them were supposed to work it out, you get it? So two of them came in one day, and they said . . . First one of them comes in, Chiquis Monteforte comes in, a little dazed . . . No, wait a minute, I'm not sure which one got there first, Chiquis or the other one, but anyway, she says Yes, I want to marry you, because also I'm pregnant, so I'll marry you. . . . So I mean Handsome to the Maximum says Great, perfect. And he was going to tell the other two he was getting married, when the second one, whichever it was, the second one came in and said with class, but fake class, right?, I'm pregnant. You know how I picture this? Smoking with a cigarette holder. I didn't want to tell you, but I've discovered that I am pregnant. . . . So Handsome to the Maximum has a talk with both of them, and he said that he'd be happy to marry them both, but the ones that had to think about it were them, because he, and he said this so sincerely and decidedly, he had to hold himself responsible to both of them, hold himself responsible to Chiquis and hold himself responsible to what's-her-name, because he couldn't let them down, right? So both of them agreed to marry him. So since then each one of them has her own house worth exactly the same and in exactly the same style as the other one. He has exactly the same children with one as with the other. Twelve children, six with one and half a dozen with the other, and I think that until the last or next to last, they matched up exactly—boy boy, girl girl, boy boy, exactly, and they're all the same ages and even have the same names and everything. And do you know Handsome to the Maximum has told them lots of times, Listen if you want to get a divorce . . . In case one of them doesn't love him anymore, right? Because he sees other girls at the same time too, right? Not for nothing is he Handsome to the Maximum. And neither one of them wants a divorce, that's the last thing in the world, because they absolutely adore him. . . . I mean that's pretty incredible, isn't it?

Of course, at the time we didn't know how everything was going to turn out, and we never even suspected that Little Jalisco was going to get so fat she'd wind up in a mental hospital. Because the fatter she got the more nervous she got, and she kept getting more and more nervous until finally she had a kind of a nervous breakdown, right? Back then she might say Hey, how in the world *are* you! or call you on the phone happy as a lark, a little like Leticia Leteo, you remember her? Well, a lot like Leticia. . . . I mean she would either gush all over you, or she wouldn't speak, she'd cut you dead. The last time we went out anywhere together, one or two weeks before the last straw with her sister, I'll tell you about that in a minute, do you think she so much as said Hello or Good-bye? Nothing! I never heard the bitch open her fucking mouth. . . . When we got back home I got out of the car . . . Buck-naked bullfighters! So about then, Napoleon called and he talked and talked trying to defend her, you know, trying to put her bad manners and all out of my mind with stupid sense-less antidotes, I mean anecdotes. He talked and talked and talked. . . . Was she already crazy? She loved putting on these ugly faces, not speaking, shit. . . . I don't want to tell you how many times I told her to go screw herself. . . .

Or the married life of my Aunt Emma . . . In all our little get-togethers we *had* to talk about her. It's that she . . . imagine, she perfumed her underwear with green pears! She'd call me on the telephone all the time, before the ghost, you know. . . . She'd call me and say, Oh darling, can you imagine, Kurt told me he was sick and tired of making love in front of my candy corkscrew. So of course, I said Ay, Aunt Emma, what candy corkscrew are you talking about? So she says My Jesus, my Christ, my crucifix, I can't take it anymore, he called it a fucking candy corkscrew. I must have laughed for two hours, and when I calmed down. . . . Imagine . . . he called it a candy corkscrew! . . . Because the crucifix my aunt has *does* look sort of like a braid or one of those candy twists, you know, like a candy cane but twisted? . . . Ay, I laughed so hard, and then I said And what did you say to

him? . . . Oh, I had my say, all right. . . . Candy corkscrew? I
don't think you are capable of appreciating how beautiful my crucifix is, Kurt, this crucifix is completely carved by hand. . . . See
the veins? Can't you see the pain and suffering in his face? Don't
you see how all his tendons are knotted up? I mean imagine,
calling my crucifix, from the who knows what century, a taffy
corkscrew. . . . She couldn't believe Kurt had called it a taffy
corkscrew. . . . Imagine, her house was very calm and peaceful,
full of religious pictures and sayings like, Return to this house my
friend, here you will find peace and who knows what else, God
will illumine your path so that you, I mean nothing but stuff like
that, okay? Everything very religious and Kurt an atheist from the
word go, I mean a dyed in the wool atheist. . . . The only crosses
he ever made in his life had nothing to do with prayers, boy, he
crucified Jews on the doors of their houses. . . . He castrated
them and put their members and their testicles in their mouths,
he'd put them in their mouths like a pool ball in the side pocket
and leave them like that, nailed up on the doors, crucified. . . .
You know how I'd paint Kurt? A man dragging a crematorium
oven, like this, right?, pulling it through the streets of del Valle,
exhausted by the unbelievable labor his fate had given him, almost bent double, like this, pulling this crematorium oven and
throwing in all the Jews he sees, all of them, every single
one. . . .

So Sandra started pouring more coffee, and Florencia was just
about to start in on another story when I saw Dressed Like a Man
go like this, she sort of said Come on with her finger, right? We
had gone in her car. So I said We've got to go because it's already
midnight, we've got to go. Oh shit, said Josefina, you've been a
pain in the ass all night, stop bugging her, why are you such a
pain in the ass with her, stop bugging her. . . . And when she
says Stop bugging her, she goes like this, stop being such a pain
in the ass, and she sort of punches me like this, with her fingertips. So when she goes like this, something came over me, it was
like an instinct, I'll tell you, I kicked her so hard in the shin, I
kicked the shit out of her. And I said Never ever touch me again.
You better never even *think* of touching me again as long as you

live! Don't stick your nose in my life, I told her, it's easy to give
people advice, and I'll listen to you if I feel like it, but don't stick
your nose in where you're not invited. . . . Sandra suddenly
didn't know what to do with this little bowl of olives she was
holding. Don't step across this line, I went on. So then Mercedes
said that she had to leave too, so we left together. . . . Do you
know that Napoleon called my brother the next day worried sick
that I was pissed off? Listen, tell your sister to please not be
mad. . . . Like they feel like I can do whatever I feel like to
them. They don't just feel like it, they know it. They know that as
long as I'm on their side everything's okay, but the day I get
really pissed off at one of them, I'll make do-do out of them. And
they're right, too, they're absolutely right. I mean I don't understand it myself. I'm not sure whether I'm good or evil, whether
I'm a sweet generous person or a cynic, if I'm a Sister of Mercy,
charitable and all, or a gossipy old maid. For example, Little
Jalisco comes over and says It's that you're such a bitch, you've
got some good things, you love people, but you're a bitch. . . .
She's always had that impression of me, she always had that image. And so I'd tell her Why am I such a bitch, tell me why, and
she didn't dare, nobody dared give me reasons, nobody, I mean
it. Nobody had the nerve or something. . . .

I've known people that sweet-talk me, that tell me all the things I
am, because I need somebody to tell me, You're so sweet, you're so
pretty, you're a selfish bitch, you try to seem all noble and goody-
goody, and what you are deep down is, you're way off. It's that I
can be super fun, super conversationalist, super everything, but
when I try to act another way, when I like try to be more serious or
something, nobody recognizes me, nobody understands me. Like
the day I broke up with Alexis, for example. I said What do you
want, what is it you want from me. You want me to be Little Lulu,
Miss Goody Two-Shoes, a Maria Elena Mexicana, one of those
Patricias or Olgas you sleep with every eight days? A woman for a
couple of hours once a week? Well, forget it, I'm not interested.
You don't interest me because I want something I mean much
much solider, something deeper than that. Because getting is easy,
there's no doubt about that. You propose to me and I'll accept. But

I want you to get involved when I can't sleep, when I have time on my hands, get involved in my problems, my suffering, my misery, the things that kill me, that turn me into a wet rag, that scare me and repress me, I mean with my day in and day out conflicts, right?, things besides my vagina and my orgasms. . . . So he got furious. . . . I mean *keeping* is the hard part, I said. . . . When I talked to him seriously and said serious things to him, when I took on this different face and different body language, okay?, a different speed you might say, he got pissed off, he didn't like me like that. He huffed and puffed and yelled and got madder and madder. *Chinga tu madre,* you don't understand me! . . . It's not that I don't understand you, Alexis, I said, it's that you're so superficial and such a jerk, you have so few emotions, there's so little inside you, that you don't have anything to give. . . . That's why somebody terrifies you that offers you affection, understanding, that offers you her life story, her memories, anything. *You* don't understand that, you can't understand it. . . .

I remember all my Leading Men, all my dreamboats to paradise, and I say How funny, right? What did we see in each other? It was like we didn't even speak the same language, you know? Generally speaking, they had a completely different idea of life from mine and I loved them because of that, I think. Every time I went out with Alexis, The Monk would get so furious he could have died. Gabriel would get mad because I saw Mauricio. Why do you see so much of him? he'd say. . . . And Handsome to the Maximum—what keeps you so long in Gabriel's office? They were all dying of jealousy. . . .

I was the first woman The Monk ever had a relationship with, or relations with, I don't know. . . . He was like out to lunch, you know, like lost, really weird, right? Afterward he went out with Leticia Leteo for a long time, I think he was even pretty much in love with Leticia. And she told me he really didn't communicate with her, she couldn't get on his wavelength, he was like insensitive or numb or something. Then I went to Europe, and when I came back I started going out with him again. He was different then. . . . And when he thought we were like really together, I stopped seeing him because I was going to get married. Circumcised rhinoceroses! Even when I was married, but in just the civil part, the civil ceremony, right?, he came and got me and took me out of my house one morning at six o'clock in the morning. . . . I was already married, at least by a civil ceremony! I'm coming to that in a minute . . . Ay. . . .

Anyway, in spite of all that, I think I'll get bored one day, you know what I mean? And I think of myself as perfectly happy, don't get me wrong. My husband is super handsome and very understanding, and I can dress any way I please. I've got all kinds of stupid comforts and stuff, because I don't ask for trips to Europe, I mean not anymore anyway, I've already been to Europe thirteen times, it's not that I've gotten bored with it, it's that it hasn't been the greatest thing in my life for a long time now. I ask for things a little simpler than going to the moon, right? I don't know who to thank for my economic peace, I mean let's suppose I earn ten thousand pesos a month. That's what I spend on myself, on my house, my husband, on telling him, Listen, I'm going to buy you a pair of shoes, I bought you such and such. So why? Why aren't I happy? Why not?

I told The Monk about a million times, I'm not a stable person. . . . I begged him over and over again, Listen, have a little change in your life, get mad even if you don't feel like getting mad, yell at me sometimes, that even if he never got mad, to act like he was mad sometimes, because the moment comes, the moment comes when I get pissed off that nobody ever gets mad at me. I've even thought that if I told my husband I had a lover, he wouldn't yell at me. He'd try to understand, he'd put his arms around me. Can you imagine? I don't know how to describe him to you. I never talk to him about personal stuff, for example, or lovers or anything. I never have, never never ever. Whenever the subject has come up, it's just sort of taken for granted that we both understand. Like The Monk, for example. He's never asked me, Did you go to bed with him? And I've never told him we'd go to my Aunt Emma's house to sleep together. Never. I mean he *knows*, okay?, he knows who I slept with, but we've never talked about it, like talked. The only person we ever argued about because of the effect he had on me was Alexis. You can't, nobody

can just erase so many years from your life. He was my lover for
so long that it's only logical that he'd appear at certain moments
in my life. He's always showing up, just sort of slipping in. Besides, I adored him, I practically idolized him. I adored him with
my whole heart, is that the expression? But. I mean the day he
said Let's get married, I said No. Why, I said, you must have a
little sunstroke, I mean you must be completely off your rocker.
And it was almost impossible for him to understand what I was
trying to tell him. I just saw him the other day, four years after
that get-together at Sandra's house, four or five years later. I just
saw him in Europe, on the Costa Azul. I saw him every day, just
like that, we'd turn the corner and run into each other and all.
And every time he'd see me, he'd go It's like you didn't exist, it's
like you were in another place in time, because that's the only
way I can see you. . . . I mean, I love you and you'll always be
the most important person in my life. . . . You know he's completely gone on the Up! with Mexico thing now, right?, they even
put him in jail for it, for some drug thing, in the United States, he
was in jail there for a long time. But they finally got him out. So I
say Well Alexis, what are you doing now? He said I've got enough
money to never have to work again. With this bunch of lesbians
and gay guys always hanging around him, him always super well-
dressed, incredibly handsome. So he says It's true you're different
from me? So I go Uh-huh. You're not like I am? It's a whole other
world! We identified with each other before, I don't know, we
were discovering sex, he had this exciting, adventurous kind of
spirit, I mean he had a home, and we liked the idea of him
getting a divorce some day. What for, right? We liked the idea of
sneaking around, to tell the truth. The day he proposed to me, I
told him to go to hell. So now he's getting into this stuff as happy
as can be, in front of everybody. Toward the end he was using all
this cocaine, I mean all the time. I don't even want to know
anymore. . . . I'll tell you seriously, I don't want to know anything about it. . . .

Why did I start talking about Alexis? Oh, I remember, because I
always told Dressed Like a Man, I always said to her I get
tired. . . . I started off great with people. . . . I started off terrific

with people, everything went like a charm. I was Miss Best Friend, Miss World's Greatest Lover. Everybody would say You're just so great, marry me, they'd always wind up saying Marry me, but I always said No, I don't think you're the one for me, you're just not important enough for me to marry you. I remember, ever since I was a little girl I'd say things like that. For example, listen to this, I remember every word, we were driving along one day, Handsome to the Maximum and me, I mean I . . . Oh, I remember, and he said Why don't you ever get mad, why don't you ever scream at me. . . . And I said Oh, look, here's an earring on the floor, where should I put it. I didn't do it to bug him or spite him or anything, I don't know if you see what I'm getting at. . . . I don't think people have ever understood me, ever. Or for example, I'd go over, and I'd find this strange brooch in his bathroom, and I'd say Here, I found this brooch in the bathroom. Because I didn't want any explanations, I didn't care, I was happy as a lark, but on the other hand, there'd come a moment when I'd say Listen, I don't want to see you anymore. Oh sweetheart, what's wrong, why, what's the matter? . . . Nothing, it's just that I'm not interested in you anymore, you turn me off, I don't tremble when I see you, I don't get butterflies when you put your arms around me, and when we make love, it's like, I don't know, I don't feel anything. No, darling, you're mixed up, I think it's that, and so on and so forth. So I go What's more, I think I'll just get out right here, and I'd open the car door while he was still driving full speed. . . . It's always the same. I'll be just like this, talking, with my Leading Men as I call them, word of honor, I'll be just like this and all of a sudden I'll go I'm leaving, bye-bye. What's wrong with you? I'm bored. . . . That's horrible, isn't it? I'm bored, I don't want to be here anymore, so stop the world I want to get off, I'm through, that's the last straw. . . . Let's take The Monk for example, The Monk again. He'd come over and be as tender as a clam and all. All of a sudden . . . he'd be kissing me, and all of a sudden I'd say Stop, stop kissing me, that's enough kissing, I don't want you to kiss me anymore. And he'd go Why? And all I could say would be, Because. But why? Just because, because I can't take any more kisses. One more kiss is like the end for me, fatal, one more pass made at me is fatal, too much of anything, just this much more than I can take, and that's it, buster, I could die, I can't stand it. And I can't tell a lie. Ever since I was a little girl, when my mother would sing me like Hush-a-by-baby, I'd say Stop, that's enough, I know it by heart already, I don't want to hear anymore. . . .

Not long ago my mother gave me a watch that had belonged to my father with diamonds all over it. And I was telling my brother, This is like for some big shot, or a hick from the sticks or somebody, or somebody like one of those politicians strutting around in the senate. I don't like it, I told him, and about then Andrés Gutiérrez comes in, and my brother says You want to buy a watch that used to belong to my father? And he shows it to him, right? Wow, it's beautiful, what a terrific watch and so on, that watch has got style, and he buys it from us. The smile froze on my face. What's wrong, baby? And I go Nothing, nothing. Uh-huh, something's wrong, what is it? Nothing. But they can see in my face that something's bothering me. I mean I think I'm just the same, I think I'm this great actress at concealing my emotions. But Andrés says to me, No, no, baby, tell me what's wrong, I mean is something wrong with the watch or is this a joke or what. No, man, are you kidding, the watch is perfect. But I was suffering because I was watching his meta, meta what is it?, metamorsomething, watching him change from a young doctor to a powerful senator or ambassador or something, an out-of-date big shot, a big-bellied border-town pimp. I'm not kidding, I can't lie.

So that's why, I mean I always rub people the wrong way, you know what I mean? . . . I think I make other girls mad, envious, jealous, even my best friends. Dressed Like a Man for example . . . Not once in her life, never, has she said to me, I mean I'm always saying to her Wow, you look great, or Why don't you change this just a little bit?, you look great with your hair like that, leave it like you wore it yesterday. . . . And she gets unbelievably pissed off at me. . . . I mean, I tell her in all honesty, straight from the heart, because I like to see her pretty, attractive, and I know she feels good when people turn and look at her in restaurants and stuff, but she doesn't see that. You know?, I think she thinks I think I'm hot stuff because I'm a model and all, and that I look at her and go Yuck. I don't know *what* people think about me, I make all these guesses, but I know I'm kidding myself. They're like afraid of me, okay? I don't know, I really don't know. . . . But every time I go to some get-together with women I leave furious at myself. It's not Josefina's fault, or Sandra's, or Florencia's or Little Jalisco's. It's me. What terrible years, what a miserable time in my life. . . .

("Cover your face / and cry . . . / don't hold it in. / Vomit. / Sure! / Vomit / at that macabre paranoid stupidity, / vomit all over this dizzying stentorian cretinism / and this senile orgy of prostatic egoism— / stringy clots of disgust, / half-chewed impotence, / rancid juices of satiety, / hunks of bitter hope . . . / hours punctuated by whinnies of suffering.")

20

Every two hundred forty-seven men

Tito Caruso shows up this morning, and I'm leaving Florencia the apartment, he begins. . . . Because he got married, we had a party at my house and everything, I think I told you, and a couple of years go by, and he's getting divorced. . . . I'm going to leave her the furniture and everything, because I'm going to really break my ass this time, he goes on, this time I'm going to get serious, I'm dedicated, he sounded like a prophet, right?, now I'm going to work like a nig, I mean a slave, really get down to work and get ahead in life. . . .

Tito really is a hard-working guy. I mean, leaving aside his lies, the awful face he makes when he can't sleep, the off-color jokes he tells, the occasional little betrayal and turning over new leaves, and his madness for the rumba, what's left is that Tito is a hard worker. And Florencia, this wife of his, who's pregnant with their second child, he just left her. A beautiful girl, this singer, with legs, my God, you can't believe your eyes, and this sad-eyed look that drives men mad, and this beautiful hair down to here, I'm not kidding, gorgeous. And Tito comes over every day and drives us crazy telling us how any day now he's going to get to work. What's more, he says, I'm going to go live at the factory . . . My brother's factory, right? Perforated sheet metal. . . . But at the same time he hasn't been separated eight days, and every night he comes over to tell about these orgies, every one bigger than the last one. . . . Yesterday he came over all prepared, for example, he had had preventive washings and everything because this one now was going to be ho-o-ot, as he said. He just came from washing his underwear because they were all piled up dirty in some corner, I can't tell you, my brother and I thought we'd die laughing, I swear. . . . He's called Florencia exactly one time since he moved out, one time. And she told him he could come back under one condition, he had to prove he had been to Taxco. I mean, you can understand how it would be pretty tough to prove you'd been in Taxco, especially if you'd never even seen a Kodak snapshot of the place. It's that he spent one weekend with this chick, and he said he'd gone to Taxco on business. . . . And they have one son. They're strange, aren't they? That kind of real egotistical, selfish people, completely self-centered, that practically live their whole lives gazing into their own navels. Tito's the classic live-for-yourself boy. You don't know whether he's a pimp or a kept man, a jewel thief or a fairy godfather, but he's always dressed to the hilt, I'll say that, with these lace shirts and tight pants, I mean dressed fit to kill. Besides the fact that he comes from this family that's beyond help. All the males in that family are nymphomaniacs, or whatever you call men that are nymphomaniacs, it's like all day long they've got to be in and out, in and out. All day, every day. . . . That's the only thing in life they really worry about, like it'll run out some day or something, okay?, so at the drop of a hat, any old pretext at all, they call up some woman and bingo, *chíngale*, problem solved. I mean that's the way they deal with their problems, you know that kind of person? And they're all like that, his whole family. I kid you not, it's the only thing in the world they care about. . . .

So anyway, every day Tito comes over to tell me all about his problems and his sufferings and his ups and his downs, everything that happens to him. So one day he comes over, and he says I can't believe tomorrow makes two years I've been with what's-her-name, time really flies, doesn't it? With this lover he's got, right? And the next day it's, Screw her, I see a woman, I spend a couple of days with her, and I never see her again as long as I live, screw her and screw them all. . . . I'm not going to have anything to do with a woman that keeps me on too short a leash, no, no way, women, I'll tell you, women when they get you like that are disposable, you take one and then screw her, I mean you get rid of her. I swear. And then two days later he comes over, and It's my second anniversary, and where he's going to take her to celebrate and then bang, like take this morning, he tells me all his love stories, night after night, everything he does, and then all of a sudden he says Oh, that lousy cunt Florencia, she's a bitch, it's all her fault. And you say Well but look, Tito, if she follows you and catches you with some other woman, and if you know she saw you, she saw you with her own two eyes, and then on top of it all you went and you told her about all the lovers under your britches like water under a bridge, I mean. . . . Lousy bitch, whose side are you on! And he gets mad, I swear he gets pissed off at *me!* Now I get it, bitch, you play along, listening to me and all, but you've never been on my side. . . . But Tito, aren't I your crying towel? Aren't I the one you come and tell your troubles to? How can you say to me now that I'm exaggerating, and I don't know what I'm talking about? . . . When I mention something he's told me about two minutes earlier, he says I'm dumping on him. I swear to God, he comes and tells me stuff, and two minutes later he says I'm lying. Just this morning I was thinking I'm going to tell him, I'm going to tell him off. . . . I mean, with all the problems I've got and he comes and tells me his. At first you don't care but then you get nervous, you're loaded down with all this stuff, you feel absolutely saddled with problems, and if you stop and think about it, they're not even *your* problems, they're everybody else's, oh some of them are yours, sure, a few of them, but then the rest? They belong to all your friends all around you. Isn't that true?

Oh, I remember something. You know a couple of years ago, a few days before Tito got married, we were in this car, are you interested in hearing this? We'd been out dancing at The Two Turtles, and when we left we divided up, and Florencia, Tito himself, my brother, and I got into Tito's car. Little Jalisco, this guy about this tall, like a body-builder or something, then David and Dressed Like a Man all got in another one. They were in this Volvo they had, a yellow Volvo, one of those little bitty ones, we all left together, all at the same time. And we took off. Then all of a sudden we noticed they weren't behind us. We were on the Insurgentes bridge by now. We saw they weren't following us, the Volvo wasn't back there, so Tito wanted to be the big macho, he wanted to show off, I don't know, so he made this U-turn on Insurgentes and ran a red light, the one right at the bridge. Trying to backtrack and find them? So when he ran the stop sign, *chíngale!*, a cop pulls in behind us. He was right on our tail. A patrol car, okay? So we started to really roll, and along about Bajío or, I don't know, one of those streets, Tito turns right. We were going about eighty or ninety miles an hour, no, I swear, and Tito turns the wheel like this, and when we turn, right onto Bajío I'm pretty sure it was, we turn and the car goes into a spin, it starts skidding and everything, and we run under, I mean like into, *chíngale!*, right through and practically out the back door of this shoe store. Onanistic orangutans! Into the back room of a shoe store, for crying out loud!

I had just gotten back from the United States, and I'd brought back this dress that my mother thought was the last word in elegance. It was a horror, actually, but elegant, too, I guess, because this famous designer had made it and an aunt of mine that lives up there had given it to me. Anyway, it had this straight straight tight skirt, like a Marilyn Monroe dress, right?, with this gauze or, I don't know, crepe flower that grew out of its backside, a horror, and so I was wearing this coat of my mother's that looked great on me, shoes like this, this high, and everything. So anyway, to make a long story short, Florencia and my brother pulled me out the window. Tito's nose was bleeding. He was going to say something, but we took off running. . . .

So about now the cops get there and jump out of their car and start chasing us. We had about a half-a-block headstart on them. My brother and me running like crazy down one side of the street, and all of a sudden Florencia disappears and then Tito, too. So all of a sudden, the ones that were cornered were my brother and me. Or I. And this one policeman was coming this way, and another one that way, so then I thought What do I do, right?, so I got this idea, but I didn't have time to tell my brother. So anyway, when this first policeman comes up I grab him, I *embraced* him, actually, I grabbed him around the neck, and I go Oh please, oh please let us go, we didn't do anything. . . . I was really laying it on thick, right?, doing this routine like you can't believe, and looking for a chance to pretend I was fainting or something like that. Oh please, oh please . . . And my brother was propriety personified. Darling, turn the man's neck loose. Turn him loose! You idiot, if you don't let him go, I'm going to get angry. Let him go, dammit! And I'm like this, hugging him, because I was trying to seduce him I guess, I don't even know. . . . So this other policeman says No, señorita, don't worry, nothing's going to happen to you. We saw what happened, we know the boy that got away was the one that was driving. We followed him for blocks, right?, so don't worry, we'll go to the station, and you'll tell us the young man's name, and you can go home. . . . So then . . . Nothing, the dress that, like I say, was practically skintight had ripped practically all the way up to my hips, but since I had on a coat, you couldn't see, and my brother says Here, sweetheart, take five pesos, that was all he had in his pockets, and he says And you go on home. . . . So I say You must be crazy, my dress ripped, my makeup smeared, because it was running down my whole face by now, and I'm supposed to stand out there on Insurgentes and flag down a taxi? . . . They'd take me anywhere I wanted to go for a peso! I really think, if you don't mind, asshole, I should go to the police station too. My brother says You're not going to any police station. And all this time the cops were really being terrific. No, really young man, you two don't have a thing to worry about, we'll just get the name and that'll be it. So we were batting back and forth, and at that, another policeman comes up with Tito, handcuffed and all. This is the one that was doing the driving he says, so my brother sort of calms down a little, and the policemen take us to the eighth precinct. When we got there my brother panicked, he was terrified I was going to go into the police station, so he runs in front of the police, grabs the door by both sides of the frame, his arms like this, right?, and he starts yelling Not my sister, not my sister! Please! She doesn't go in there, my sister doesn't go in there! So I say Hey, no, wait, and I sort of wink at him. I'd talked to the policeman, right?, and he had sworn on his Mexican Mother's Heart that nothing was going to happen to us. So I say I talked to the man, it's okay. . . .

So we go in, and they keep saying to the jerk Tito that he has to sign this statement. . . . Because the cops were dictating it, like The young man was driving at excessive speed, and they're writing all this down, and all of a sudden, he says Not me, I wasn't driving. So who was? I don't know. You can imagine, my brother and I just looked at him, and finally I said You don't know? So the cops go Look, young man, this señorita is here because of you, so just make a statement, okay, so your friends can go home. This young man is worried about his sister. But Tito says Well, but I wasn't driving! So tell me, who was? This buddy of mine that we were in The Two Turtles, and he said he'd drive, so I said Okay. . . . Can you believe how stupid! . . . So while we're standing there watching the grass grow you might say, they go We'll do the test. What? The drunk test. What! Alcohol in your blood. So my conscience was clear, right?, because you know I never drink even one drink, so I went very calmly, thinking I'll do what I have to do because I haven't drunk a drop. . . . So I march up and do what people that aren't drunk do, right? They stand me with my hands out like this, with my head back and my eyes closed, and I mean, naturally, you get a little dizzy, naturally, right?, but feeling dizzy and with this skintight dress and everything, forget it, I still took off as straight as a dart.

Dizzy and everything, right? Oh, and he asked me, before that he
asked me if I'd been drinking, and I told him I hadn't drunk a
drop. . . .

So when they made up the reports, the agent from headquarters
says Señorita, I think you are not always completely truthful, eh?
Why? I said. . . . Don't tell me that you didn't sneak off to the
kitchen and have a nip or two. . . . I was, I couldn't . . . No,
absolutely not. So he says Well, the doctor's report . . . And do
you know what he'd put down? *Slight intoxication.* So my brother
starts yelling Slight intoxication! She didn't have a drop! So I go
Tell me why he put that, if I haven't had a thing to drink. . . . So
then he said, how did he put it? Well, he says, one infallible way
of proving intoxication is the voice. What? The tone of voice. So I
said I swear to you, I swear, this is my voice, this is the way I
talk, come to my house at five o'clock in the afternoon if you want
to, or ten o'clock in the morning, come whenever you feel like it,
and you'll see—this is the way I talk, this is my voice, just like
this. . . .

Meanwhile, beautiful Florencia was walking along Insurgentes
to the tune of wolf whistles and unmentionable offers. It turns out
that when the cops were catching up, to keep the cops from
catching her, she lay down as narrow as she could in the shadow
of a tree trunk. Can you believe that? I mean we all passed right
beside her and nobody saw her. So when everybody left, and she
knew she was safe, she got up and ran for blocks and blocks and
blocks, I mean I don't know how far it was, to San Angel I think,
although she was never going to walk all the way to San Angel.
And at the same time David, Dressed Like a Man, and Little
Jalisco got tired of waiting for us at home, so they started back-
tracking to see if they could find us. But they ran into Florencia,
somewhere around Altavista, can you imagine? And she told them
what had happened. They took them to jail because, and so on
and so forth. . . . We finally got out at five o'clock in the morning, freezing to death, and there they were outside the police
station waiting for us. So we all got in the car and left. But imagine how mad we were, because this idiot Tito had us there like

jerks for hours, because he wasn't man enough to shoulder his own responsibility. . . .

So then, sort of to apologize, right?, he promised to pay for this big party, which by the way was going to be his bye-bye bachelorhood party. We chose my house because it was the biggest, and we started inviting dozens and hundreds of friends of ours. Lobo and Melón and Feyote were going to play for it. Alberto was still going out with Big Jalisco with exasperating faithfulness. All our friends came, even The Monk, who had just finished his Ph.D. in law. Tito was Pleased as Punch, and we'd already completely forgotten about the little incident. . . .

I was just getting ready when Big Jalisco comes in and comes upstairs to my bathroom, she comes in and says Look what I brought you. It was clippings and pictures of a show we'd just done. Look what I brought you, she says, and she shows me these fashion shots. . . . Oh, how nice! We looked pretty good. . . . And we were talking. How terrific! You looked stunning here, look! And pleats and flounces, you know. . . . Until she says I've got to go, Alberto's downstairs waiting for me. All right. Okay. Okay. . . . So then I go downstairs, and I can feel a certain tension at the bar. Where's Florencia? So The Monk calls me over and says Listen darling, I need to talk to you. Okay, shoot . . . I was trying to say hello to all the guests, right?, smiling and showing off my neckline, but it was like everybody was on the other side of a big pane of glass, sort of vague, deliberately distracted. The Monk was saying There's been a misunderstanding here, you know, and I think you and I should try to clear it up. I want you and I to talk . . . What could I do? I said Okay. . . . And he's talking real low, very mysteriously, Well, it's that Big Jalisco told Alberto that you'd borne false witness against her, and she wants you to clear up the situation. . . . Borne false witness? What does *that* mean? You know, lied. Borne false witness! I started raising my voice. *What!* About *what?!* I mean who could remember. So he says Come with me, we'll talk to her, and he took my hand. . . . The Monk was like their best friend, but he was better educated and older, I mean they were all really well educated and great people and all, but he was *better* educated. I put all of them up on a pedestal because of their education. . . . So we go up to her. . . .

Alberto looked sick. With shame and embarrassment, you know what I mean? Since he would never dare have any kind of confrontation with me, I mean this was a terrible scene for him. So then she . . . I swear to God, listen, sometimes you wake up and realize there's evil in the world, that some people have black hearts, that some people are bitter, and they want to make the world taste bitter to suit them, right?, and that there's no way you can understand those people, you never *will* be able to, you don't know what makes them tick. . . . At least I don't, is that possible? Because I mean me personally, I'm talking about what's inside me, a lot of things have happened to me, a lot of things have hurt me, and I could never become cruel or mean, I mean hold a grudge against somebody for years and years, no matter who it was, a close friend or anything. . . . I've never dared to even *think* about really hurting somebody. . . .

So anyway she says to me . . . like she's about to pronounce the most disgusting words in the world, right? Like this, she goes, this is Big Jalisco, my friend for fifteen years, more, my neighbor, practically my sister, she says Why did you make that up about me, I mean all of a sudden, without ever so much as mentioning this before, I want you to tell Alberto why you said I went out to eat with you and went to bed with this guy and you watched me, that in front of you . . . I mean, it was a sentence of guilty in the first degree, the way she talked, this burning accusation, I was tried and convicted and hanged already, and all these faces standing around, my friends' faces, my guests' faces for heaven's sake, and they were all glaring at me. . . . And she went on, How can you dare say such a thing, because I know all the people you told and who's going around spreading the story all over now. . . . I was beaten beforehand, because the truth is, I had told Andrés, but I couldn't believe Andrés had told anybody, ever. . . . Andrés was worse than me, because Alberto was his best friend, they'd been friends since elementary school, and now they even had their offices together. Dipsomaniac dolphins! That whore's shady past wasn't going to ruin *me!* What happened was that she wanted me to give her a clean bill of health, you know what I mean? She was going to get married, and for all she knew, or maybe for all she feared, I might decide to tell St. Alberto. . . . But I just stood there, like I might have been going to turn on my heel and leave her standing there with the words still in her mouth, whether they damned her or me. . . .

She could've been Hitler's private whore!

So I said Please, I mean really, how can you say these things to my face. . . . And she says in this voice I had never heard before in my life, Do you realize you're bearing false witness against me to my face? . . . But think about what you're saying, I told her. . . . What do you want me to think about! And with a Guadalajara accent to boot. That's why I think I hate anybody from Guadalajara, they all do the same thing to me, they all rub me the wrong way. I mean the whole race makes me mad, they're all gossipy, snoopy, snide, troublemaking. . . . So she said Go ahead, tell him. . . . And I spit out You better think about this, I'll give you one more chance, I'll give you a chance to pull yourself together. . . . My brother and Tito by this time were just standing there, pale and not saying a word. . . . Pull yourself together and think what you're saying. . . . I mean, there may be this rumor, but you ought to tell Alberto that I'm not the one that spread it, somebody else maybe, but tell Alberto that I would never never ever dare do that. . . . But she says No, you're going to tell him the truth, because in fact, I do think you're capable, and besides we know it's you that keeps spreading this rumor, you, you. . . . But I kept saying Think about it, think about it good. I said that to her over and over again. . . .

I had this ring this big. It's that it's the only thing I've ever liked like that. I've never worn earrings or necklaces or bracelets or anything, but I was wearing this pearl ring with a pearl in it this big, huge, and this ring gave me three wishes. I'd rub it a little and concentrate real hard and go Make this guy kiss me, and in half an hour a big wet passionate kiss, and then I'd give it another little rub and think Make him ask me out tomorrow, and in fifteen minutes the guy would say Can you? Then I'd rub the ring again and ask for three more wishes. . . . And we'd start over again the next day, always the same thing, I mean with different wishes, of course, and at the end I'd always wish for three more wishes. . . . So that night, in my house, with angry threatening faces all around . . .

After I'd said Pull yourself together about eleven times, and she refused to back down, I went bang! and slapped her with the back of my hand, all the way across her face, from here to here, *chíngale!* . . . Instead of asking the ring to make her shut up, I raked the ring across her face from here to here. And I yelled Okay! Get out of this house this instant! Because listen Alberto, the only person I told was Andrés Gutiérrez, and you know you heard it from Andrés, right? So since that's the way things are, I'll tell you—it's all true, every word of it, so let's see you get out of this now. She got you in this, right?, so let's see you get out. You wanted this, right? Well you got it. I can prove it's true, so we'll just see, I gave her the chance to back down, but she's such a stupid bitch, because I'd never have said a word, I mean I kept the secret for three years, right?, but she's a miserable prostitute, she slept with a guy in front of me for a hundred lousy pesos. . . . How's *that?* A hundred pesos. . . . She went to bed with a man, and you know why I would have kept quiet about it—for you, because you're worth it, Alberto. . . . So in less than three seconds I want you out of this house! . . .

Of course, it didn't take them three seconds. . . .

The Monk congratulated me. I knew you were brave. . . . And I had just broken up with him. We were both drained when we broke up, you know? Because he was this intellectual. You know why we broke up? Because he was so religious, and he kept saying it was terrible, these carnal emotions he had for me were a torment for him. He was heavenly, just heavenly. . . . He'd call me and say I can't see you tomorrow, but you can do something for me. And I'd say What, Pancho? I want you not to say a word all day, do everything you have to do but be absolutely silent, you'll see, you'll be surprised to see what you liberate in yourself just from doing that, it'll be good for you. Or one sunny afternoon he calls and says Go out to the pool, look up at the sky, close your eyes, and count to three, do that two hundred and forty times, and he said that was some kind of an experience. He was crazy, crazy. . . .

So anyway they left, right? I mean they left. And my brother says Why did you just stand there. Me? Why didn't you ever tell me about this. And Tito says Why did you stand there and take that. You're a jerk says my brother. I didn't know what to do, I said, she scared me, I was terrified. Florencia, Napoleon, David, Dressed Like a Man, everybody just stared at me with their mouths open. I felt completely ridiculous, but I didn't know what to do. . . . My brother was unbelievably insulted, you can imagine, forget it. . . . Little Jalisco whispers in my ear, I think it's better for me to go, too, and she gave me a pat, of encouragement, right? Can I read your palm? says Florencia. Sure, I said, sure. . . . I was shaking. The Monk put a spoonful of sugar in my mouth. Feyote and his Grand Combo were singing at the top of their lungs, and the party started picking up a little. . . .

Four hundred and twenty-nine rumbas later, my legs were still shaking. Tito was super nice to me and Florencia too. Unbelievable, both of them. They were about to get married, and they stayed right to the end, after everybody else had gone, all their friends and buddies. Dressed Like a Man says Ay, I think I'll sleep here, it's practically sunrise already, and I can stay here and help you pick up tomorrow morning early. . . . I was delighted. We left my brother gathering up ashtrays and glasses with the remains of cuba libres in them. Everybody drank rum and Coca-colas back then, you remember that? We opened all the windows and went upstairs to go to bed, you know, the usual nightly ritual, the first stiffness, then the images of the day sort of evaporating and then the warm sweet letting-go, the flotation, is that right? Afloat on the river of dreams, as you always say. So I was in that magic world when somebody comes in and goes like this and says Sweetheart, sweetheart. . . . I wake up and it's Alberto. He could come in because he was my doctor, I mean he practically lived at my house. Besides, he'd found my brother dusting the office. So he goes Sweetheart, could you get up a second? Uh-huh, I said, and I put on a robe, and we went to the literary room. The sun wasn't up yet. And so he says I just dropped your friend off, I just dropped her off at her house, and I swear, I swear to God, she hasn't stopped crying for a second. She's crying and crying and crying. It's like her heart is broken. . . . But I've got this problem because I know it's really true, because you could never lie to me. But I don't know what to do, I see you, I see her. So, I yawned, you want me to prove it's true? Yes, he says, could you? Sure I can, I said, find so-and-so's telephone number for me. . . . So he gets the telephone number. All he had to do was open his address book. He'd already gotten the number. So again I said Do you really want me to do this? Yes, he said. . . . So I said Okay, let's call. So the butler answers. It was six o'clock in the morning, this butler or houseboy or whatever answers, and I said I know it's not a very good hour to be calling, but tell so-and-so that it's a matter of life and death, I have to talk to him. . . . Who shall I say is calling, please? So I go Never mind my name, he won't know who I am, just tell him to come to the phone!

So he answers. . . . Nasty, this guy, not even polite. Well! he says. I'm really sorry to call you at this hour, I don't know if you remember me. . . . So he spluttered out a few dirty words. . . . Do you remember about three years ago, a long time ago I went with Big Jalisco to your house for lunch? Yes, yes, I remember, what is it? Suddenly as polite and nice as you could ever ask for. . . . Well, somebody told her fiancé what happened there, who knows who it was, and she called me to ask me to call you and tell you that if Alberto, which is her fiancé's name, should happen to call you and ask you what happened, you should deny everything, tell him it's not true, that you didn't go to bed with her with me in the room with you, that it's not true the three of us had lunch together, none of it's true. You tell him it's not true. None of it, none of it, none of it! . . . And this guy says Poor guy, what we really ought to do is once and for all show him that it *is* true. She's a whore, that wasn't the first time she'd gone to bed with me . . . and not for a hundred pesos, for thirty! Even for twenty once! She'd come over and visit me, and when we finished in here she'd say Can you lend me thirty pesos? Or twenty. . . . Because I mean the poor girl was so common she didn't dare ask for more than thirty pesos. . . . And Alberto, that fine, decent young man, imagine. . . . I feel sorry for him. . . . Who, by the way, was listening in on the extension, he heard every word, every word of it. And this guy keeps on, he says Really, I feel sorry for him because that boy is going to marry that girl and she's such a whore. . . . So listen, thanks for waking me up so early, but . . . So anyway, to make a long story short, he says Give me your telephone number, I'll have to call and find out what happens, and so on and so forth. . . .

So Alberto had heard everything on the phone in the bar. He was there. He came upstairs and the poor thing . . . He practically falls dead at my feet, and he hugs my knees, and he cries and cries and cries. Oh, what am I going to do! I was sitting there, and I say I don't know, I really don't know, really, you wanted me to do this, you wanted to hear it for yourself. . . . I started running my hand over his head. . . . Now you know, so do whatever you have to do. . . .

He married her, of course. He married her. He stopped seeing all his friends, his lifelong friends, from the cradle practically, he stopped seeing everybody, everybody went to the devil. And now he's got kids crawling all over him, he's lousy with kids, and he lives with her. I mean imagine. Incredible, isn't it?, because if it had been me, I mean just for lying, just for the scene she made, I'd have kicked her ass to hell, wouldn't you have? And she was one of my best friends. . . .

("There are days when I feel like I've been kicked, just kicked. . . .")

21

Speaking of the next step
in social evolution . . .

Let me try to remember . . . one time . . . one of the times Alexis
came over. . . . Oh no, we were at The Gondola, uh-huh, at The
Gondola, you know, in the Zona Rosa, and he said he wanted to
talk to me. . . . I thought he was going to break up with me, say
it had been nice and fun or exciting or something, or even un-
forgettable and moving while it lasted, but you know, new com-
mitments, new lifestyles, a little bit of boredom, another little bit
of curiosity about the other side of the fence, well, you know, he
didn't know, . . . and experience had taught me that nobody, not
your girlfriends, or your family, or even worse your worst enemies
could hurt you as much as your lovers. . . . So I figured he was
going to send me to Hell-o operator, as somebody or other used to
say. . . . What else was there for him to talk to me about? We

talked every day. . . . But he said that for eleven years, because he said for a trifling eleven years, or was it the wink of an eye eleven years. Anyway, for all that time he'd been with this woman he'd loved very much. But he was convinced, he said, and he spent a lot of time pronouncing those three words, trying to invest them with profound meaning, you know?, he was completely sure that in those eleven years he'd never loved anybody like he loved me. . . . So he was completely and utterly convinced and decided to get a divorce so he could marry me. My heart went bump. Hahahahaha, why don't you come right out and say what you mean, right? So then he said . . . About then a friend of his comes up, his best friend. Wait a minute. God, what an awful person I am, he really liked me, and I'd forgotten his name, what was his name?, I can't even remember now, God, I'd have to wait for it to come up, why beat my brains out, right? So anyway, his friend comes up, and Alexis goes Tell me what I was telling you this morning when we went to Cuernavaca. . . . Because they'd been to Cuernavaca that day, bright and early. . . . You really want me to? Uh-huh, tell me. . . . This guy had this what do you call it, this twitch, this tic, is it? He blinked his left eye, but to do it he had to get his mouth, his cheek, his eyelid, his nose, his ear, everything, in on the act. So the left side of his face was covered with crow's-feet. . . . Well, says he, and *tic*, you were saying that you were thinking seriously about marrying her, *tic*, I mean, *tic*, getting a divorce and marrying her, the *tic* again, that you loved her and needed her, *tic*, that she's the girl you've always loved, *tic*, blah blah blah, *tic tic tic*. . . . So anyway, to make a long story short, this guy left, and I stood there like this, not saying a word, how grotesque, right? So then Alexis went on, he said I'm getting a divorce so we can get married. . . . I shook the crumbs out of a napkin and put it on my lap like I was about to attack a dangerous *enchilada con mole*, and I said Listen Alexis, what a shame you didn't give me some notice about this and ask me whether I wanted to marry you, I mean, I love you and all, but not like enough to marry you, not to marry you, much less now, because we know each other so well, I mean so so well. . . . We know each other so well, we're so close, and we know so much about each other, we don't have any secrets from each other, and we've discussed so many things you shouldn't discuss with *any*body, that I could never be comfortable living with you. . . . Because you laugh at the guys I go out with, you die laughing, and I'm one of those poor bitches that cry when they look at you, cry with love. . . .

Because he had told me about this one woman that whenever she looked at him she'd say Hello, Stamatis and start crying and crying and crying, and he said he couldn't even talk to her because she was always bawling. . . .

So I said I just couldn't ever be comfortable. . . . And besides I can see how you're living your life, and I don't want to think I'd always live in fear, sitting at home worried you were going to do the same thing to me. So thanks but no thanks. . . . Fortunately we'd already finished dinner, because he was incredibly insulted. Are you sure you know what you're saying? Uh-huh, I'm sure, I'm as sure as I can be. At that the captain, the maître d', right?, brings us over an after-dinner drink, courtesy of the house, and he practically throws it in the guy's face. He asked for the check, paid it, and we went back to the hotel. . . .

We talked about this for hours and hours, and he just couldn't believe his ears. It was hot, so we were in bed naked, but not beside each other like this, he was down at my feet, sitting there, looking at my, you know, my sex, like it was one of those blobs the psychiatrists give you to try to make sense out of, make associations, whatever, like it was my sex that didn't want to marry him. . . . Spread your legs! he said. And he stared at my clitoris like he was hypnotized by this throbbing meat-eating oriental flower. I felt pretty vulnerable in that position, as you can well imagine, completely defenseless. And I couldn't even see him. It was more comfortable to look up at the ceiling, at the way the light reflected on the ceiling. I kept giving him one reason after another, and he didn't so much as touch me, he just stared at my sex. It was making it wet. Until finally he saw that we wouldn't work married, we were better off just like we were, just like we were living now, instead of living with each other. No. . . . Imagine, how could I stand living with him with him the way he was.

Imagine, how could I take knowing he had ten girlfriends, and I was like just the main one! Number one wife, right? Imagine, he'd apologize by saying But you're my main woman! That was the only time in our lives we ever talked about marriage. . . . So anyway, he started with his hands like this, real real slow, and then with just one finger, one white finger, his white fingers and his tongue and his saliva, and I leaned on his hands, and he wrapped his white thighs around my thighs, I was sitting up—and his lips and the rhythm, the bent knees and his stare, and then one of my legs was over his head and the other one stretched out, a little faster now, flying, and his rhythm, his white hands on my breasts, twenty wet lips, our rhythm, my knees bent up to . . . and the sweet back and forth, then astraddle, my tongue, his breathing, my legs tight around his waist, happy with our rhythm, and his white breathing turning to fire, resurrection, and my hair a dance, the air on fire, and sweat turned to marmalade, ringlets of hair—striving, twisting, faster, squeezed together, desperation, faster, soaking wet, incandescent white from his single eye, white white white, me leaning back on the bed with my feet and head and hands, and he was on his knees and white white, a little electric and white and very satisfactory, a languid touch and a long held out sigh . . . How deep! . . .

Love makes you forget your problems, don't you think? Or does it make more of them?

He called me on the telephone lots and lots of times a week, until one day he called, and I was crying and crying because he hadn't called me in four or five days, so I answered the phone crying. He cursed and yelled at me for about an hour and a half, and he told me he was never going to call me again, that I could go out with anybody I felt like, because I lived waiting for him to call, right? To do anything I wanted to with my life, go out, have fun, and he'd call when he damn well felt like it. . . . Then you know what he did? That was when I started having all this trouble at home because he called, and back then I told my mother I had this boyfriend in Acapulco named Salvador Ortíz, in Acapulco of all places. I'd tell my mother all about him, but my mother never, I mean really swallowed the story. So finally, she says Why don't you tell him to come for a visit so I can get to meet him. . . . And so you know what would happen when Alexis called two or three times and I wasn't there? He'd get furious and ask to talk to my mother. She detested him, right? So he'd go *Cómo está Usted, señora*, I'm sorry to bother you, but I'd like to ask you to tell your daughter that Alexis called to invite her out. . . . The second or third time he called he'd ask to speak to her, and he'd say Alexis, just to bug her. Alexis, because he knew I'd get into big trouble that way. Tell her Alexis called. . . . I mean imagine. So anyway, he called once in a while, not every day by a long shot, once a week or twice at the most. When he didn't have anything else to do or he felt horny he'd call. So we'd always see each other, and it would always be the same thing, I swear, we'd never leave the hotel, we almost never did anything else. Until finally I was about to get married. . . .

It was the last modeling job I did in the United States. He caught up to me in San Antonio the day I got there. So we were there together, naked, like always, and I told him I was getting married. I told him all about my husband-to-be, and I told him I hadn't told him about it before because it hadn't made any difference, but now it did, now it did. I said It's for sure, in twelve days. He froze. Then he said Well, I'm very happy for you, because if he's as nice a guy as you say he is, you shouldn't miss this opportunity, you can't let him get away from you, so sure, marry him. Everything was normal, and, uh, how can I explain? We agreed, right? When we got back from San Antonio . . . We were there with this friend of his, the three of us. Listen, Alexis was apparently very liberal, right?, but one day I made him think . . . Anyway, he had this cocaine, and one night I made him think I was sniffing cocaine. I've never seen *anybody* as mad as he got. I'd never seen *him* that angry, for that matter, so mad, so pissed off. . . . You know how I did it? I said I'll be right back, okay? I'm going to the bathroom, and I took the stuff with me because he'd given it to me to hold. And you know where I had it? Where you keep rosaries. You know those special little sacks for keeping rosaries in? Well that's where I had it. So I said I'll be right back, let me have my rosary, please, I have to say a little prayer. When I got up, he pretended he was ignoring me, but naturally he was watching me. So I picked up the little bag, and I said Be right back. . . . And when I came back, I was on a high. . . . I was super happy. I mean noisy, very out of character, going like this, right? When we left the hotel, Alexis was practically having an epileptic attack. He couldn't see straight he was so mad, and he could barely talk. I never thought you'd be capable, he says, never never ever, I never thought you'd do what you did tonight. He was completely disillusioned sounding. But I felt guilty, right? I mean all our memories were going to depend on that one stupid joke. So I laughed. I wanted to see how you'd react, I said. But he didn't believe me. I'm crushed, he said, or some word like that, to try to tell me how disappointed he was. . . .

You know I used to sneak off from him and just put on a tiny little bit of makeup. Then I'd come back, and two minutes later if he hadn't noticed, I'd leave again and put on a tiny little bit of blue eyeshadow, like this, above my eyes. And if he still didn't notice, I'd put on just a little touch of mascara, and that would be it for the night, so he wouldn't notice, because if he noticed, he made me wash my whole face, you have no idea. Horrible, horrible. And strange, too, right? He was shocked that I used makeup. . . . He'd get furious. . . .

So anyway, on the way back, in the plane, who would ever imagine I'd be sitting there with all the little pieces of my broken heart, I was destroyed, I'm not kidding, because I knew this was the end. Why did it have to be that way? I put the little pieces of my heart on a plate. You should have seen my heart! I had told him I was getting married on such and such a day. Perfect, great, and so on and so forth. And do you know he called me that day. I've got wedding pictures with me going like this, when he called me. Ay, you have no idea. . . . I was getting married, and I get called on the telephone. I mean I was in the middle of the ceremony, so naturally I couldn't go to the telephone, right? So he called back a little later. When I answered the phone, he says to me, You're an idiot, you're an absolute idiot because you're getting married, in fact I guess you're already married. I told you I was getting married, I told you! But all of a sudden I got so blue, I collapsed, I just caved in. Look at what I'd come to. Before I got married, while we were in San Antonio, I said to him, I'll make a deal with you, I mean I'll never marry you, but I will do one thing. Think it over, if you really don't want me to get married, get me an apartment, and I'll live with you, I'll live in an apartment with you, but we'll never get married. And he says No, no way, you need to get married, make a life for yourself, be somebody, you have to have your own life, I can't ask you to do that. . . . To be honest, I don't think he ever believed it, I think he thought I was just talking for the sake of talking, without the least conviction, because otherwise he would never have told me I was stupid, why was I getting married, don't you agree? Ay, my heart was wriggling like a lizard with its leg cut off. . . .

So anyway, I hope I'm not skipping around too much for you, anyway, he came to see me several times before I got married in the church. So then I wrote him, we'd come to the conclusion we were never going to be able to break up, so we had to just keep going, our love was this kind of curse, and our bodies depended on each other too much, so we were going to keep seeing each other even if I got married. So I wrote him a letter and told him I think I'm getting married because I'm sure someday I'll have to get a divorce, and from that day on, when I get a divorce, I'll devote myself body and soul to you, only for the moments you want to spend with me, for the days you want to come see me. I remember exactly what I said. I wrote that letter when I was already married in the civil ceremony and I mailed it to him. . . . No, wait, I don't think I ever mailed it. . . .

So then we have this church wedding, and I get more rashes than you ever saw in your life, I kid you not, on my wedding day. I cried, I begged my fiancé for us not to get married, but I finally got pressured into it. In fact, I got married, and this doctor had to go to the airport with me because these sort of red blotches, like bruises?, with green and white spots?, came out all over my backside, like those rashes Dressed Like a Man used to have? So there I am all day, I mean even all through the wedding, going scrtch scrtch scrtch, I didn't even care if people saw, I told you about this, right? Because I was terrified, honestly and truly terrified. . . . But during that period back then, all my friends were getting married, even Handsome to the Maximum. So every day, if it wasn't some civil ceremony, it was this huge ceremony in some little church in Las Lomas de Chapultepec or San Angel. . . .

After the civil wedding, between that and the church one, right?, my husband slept in my parents' bedroom, and my mother and I *tried* to sleep together in my room, but we could never sleep a wink. Because I sleep so light, the slightest thing . . . And my mother watched television till all hours, so when she turned around to look at me to see if I was asleep, just feeling her eyes on me would wake me up. And when I woke up she'd throw a fit. She'd say Shit, like that, Shit, you're impossible, and since she got mad, I'd get mad too. Damn it! So I'd go to the guest bedroom. And so anyway, one day The Monk calls at five o'clock in the morning. He starts talking, and he talked and talked and talked, so my mother finally just hung up on him. I mean I was already married, right?, we'd already had the civil service, but The Monk didn't go. So my mother comes in and shakes me. That idiot you were going out with before is calling, she says. She'd picked up the receiver in the hall, and it was freezing, brrr. . . . So anyway, The Monk says I'm calling you, he says, because I need to see you. I've spent the night waiting for it to be six o'clock, waiting for the sun to come up so I could call you. I've been drinking beer at Vips all night. No kidding, right? I need you. If you don't come right now, I'm coming to get you, and I'll make a scene, you have no idea what I'm capable of. Come over here right now, or I'll come to your house. Imagine! So I jumped in the shower, right? I'll be right there, hold on! My mother says Where are you going! I don't know, Mother, I'm going to talk to The Monk. And what if he wakes up!—referring to my husband. . . . Tell him I went to work, I had a show, I had to go out for a photo session they called at the last minute, tell him anything, I'll be right back, I won't be long. . . . Imagine—come over here right now or I'm going to your house and break all your windows. . . .

I'll be right back, indeed! The Monk locked me in a cabin at

Lion World for three days and two nights! He said that it wasn't so I'd go back to him, not that at all. . . . He said that he was a jerk, that I was the only person who had ever understood him, that had ever made him understand his fellow men, that I had taken away his fear of living. . . . Fear of living? Can you believe that? And with this look on his face. . . . With this mysterious, scary look of a sad dog, he said all these things I couldn't, I mean they were incomprehensible. For the simple reason that he didn't dare face his own true desires. . . .

He was stinking drunk. And the minute we're inside, he locks the door and throws the keys down the toilet. . . . The man talked and talked and talked. . . . He said imagine him, as intelligent as he'd always thought of himself as being, and all he was was a poor jerk, an idiot, an asshole, a moron that couldn't see an inch past his own nose. . . . He'd flopped down on a bed, and he lay there snoring, sort of purring like a cat. . . . He was suffering something awful. . . . He looked like he belonged to some secret society, I didn't recognize him, like one of those fanatics keeping a vow he'd made at some black mass. . . . My heart was going like this. . . . I was so confused. . . .

I looked around for a telephone, but like they're never around when you need them, right? The Monk was lying on a bunk this cabin had with rough filthy sheets. I wrapped him up in a sweater from Chinconcoac. There was this feeling of complicity in that cabin, not like complicity between us, not like that, but this sneaking-around feeling, sort of scary, right?, like those cheap hotels you go to once and never even dare mention again as long as you live. . . . I was trapped! . . . I tried to get out the windows, I tried to knock down the door, I screamed like crazy. . . . The Monk was lying there snoring, and that made it all seem so morbid and depressing. The solitude, you know? He was lying there face down, like a teenager jerking off real real slow and easy, and you could see his reflection in the grimy windows. . . . His obsessions and his fear of living . . . those strange forces, he like projected them into the world, you know?, and they got bigger and bigger, huge, inexplicable, almost suffocating. . . . The drawers of a chest I opened were full of unspeakable things. . . . So then he woke up. I called him every name in the book, I told him he could *chinga* his *madre*, I spit in that camel's face of his three, four times. We were screaming at each other, arguing, and then we punched each other until we both collapsed exhausted. . . . There was all the violence in the world vibrating inside that cabin. . . .

You know, way down deep I kind of liked the idea of being kidnapped. That powerless feeling, that feeling of being available, you know?, *usable*, made me feel feminine, it lubricated me. Although why should I feel powerless with The Monk? I wasn't afraid even there, all locked up. . . . Like this one time in his car, for example, when we were going out together, he was passionately kissing me and all of a sudden, *chíngale*, he bangs his head into the window, I mean his forehead is bleeding and everything, and he starts going Forgive me, forgive me—he looked super hand-some with all this blood running off his forehead down his cheeks, plastering his hair down. Forgive me, he says. So I go What for. I'm a cretin, you have no idea the thoughts that come to my mind, you can't imagine how I was picturing you, you don't know, you don't know. And he kept banging his head like this. I'm a pervert, you don't know what it does to me to have that kind of thoughts about you. . . . And that terrified me. . . .

I tried to read a couple of books that were lying around, I tried to open the door with a knife. . . . I couldn't sleep! This solitude was making me want to go home . . . so much. . . . Fornicating arma-dilloes! All I could think about was how desperate my mother must have been. And my husband—I mean how would he take this? Finally, sleep crept up on me as I watched The Monk sleep-ing. . . . My sleep was full of images. Lindolf was ruthlessly chas-ing Carmelita Longlegs night and day. He traced her through London pubs and restaurants of all kinds, in beauty shops and dance halls and at parties. He kept her under surveillance con-stantly, he followed every move she made, and whenever he could, he gave her the punishments he craved, he burned her body with cigarette butts. He held the cigarettes up for Captain Tarcisio to light, but Captain Tarcisio was jumped by these hoodlums without any faces, who chased him away in his taxi. Then they shaved all Carmelita's hair off and scattered the locks to the winds, like this. . . . Tourists flagged down the Captain's taxi, so he stopped. They had a mountain of luggage, and when they opened the trunk to put it in, there was the naked, beaten, shaved body of Carmelita. A trickle of dried blood ran across the tarantula tattooed on the inside of her thigh. So he slammed the trunk and screeched off to Lindolf's gun shop. But where the armory used to be, there was the Zero Zone. When he got there, he could make out Lindolf's back, Handsome to the Maximum and Gabriel Infante's profiles, Alexis Stamatis' affected laugh, Andrés' moustache, all of them, so he gauged the distance and stepped on the gas. Eighty, ninety, a hundred miles an hour, and he ran up the hill to the Zero Zone and slammed into it with a sound of shattering glass, like some creature from outer space, some intergalactic monster. He fell onto our friends' table. The chairs went slowly, slowly flying through the air. Lindolf sort of bounced off the table and turned in the air like the forward for a soccer team trying to reach some impossible ball. Gabriel and Alexis were flying too, Andrés twisting like a rag doll, and the restaurant collapsed with a deafening crash. . . . I jumped awake. . . .

The sun was just up, and we started fighting and arguing again until our hearts were a little calmer. . . . My clothes were ripped to shreds, and he couldn't bring himself to make love. . . . He wasn't quite so drunk now, so he started philosophizing, looking at me anxiously like he was trying to make out the answer. . . . We were hungry, so he cooked, trying, I think, to restore his own strength, and then afterward, he sat there drinking red wine out of a bottle, as soft and tender as a loaf of white bread. My little philosopher! The cabin reeked of eggs and chorizos, and truly we had nothing else left to talk about. We looked into each other's eyes, studied every line of each other's faces, but pretty soon we were at it again. . . . I moaned, I scratched his back like a cat, and The Monk tried to make me forget that sooner or later I had to leave. . . .

But I wasn't some stray woman, it was too late now to try to hold me, I belonged to another man. . . . Another man? No, no, it wasn't that I was attracted to my husband, no, although deep down, way down deep inside, I knew he was right for me, more

than right. . . . Go to hell! The Monk would scream. Go to fucking hell! and then he'd cry. . . . He lumbered around like a
drunk elephant, like a sad-faced clown in those great big huge
shoes, trying to get as far away from me as he could, staggering
against the boarded-up walls. His hair was down in his eyes, and
his nose had this bright glow. . . .

The second night we desperately held each other. . . . The
sounds from the woods sounded like voices from another time,
and in my dreams I went back to when I was a girl. I was playing
with a little woolly dog, I was pedaling a pearly tricycle through a
foggy garden. . . . And The Monk's arms, the heat from his body
were my mother's. . . . My mother at twenty, beautiful, wearing a
white dress! She smelled like jasmine and teddy bears, warm
milk, talcum powder. My mother loomed up out of the night,
eternal, constant, floating along in a filmy pleated dress, smiling,
her hair bouncing in soft hieroglyphic waves full of sensuality. My
mother . . . And I could hear her voice floating over the grass in
Alameda Park. I could feel her breath, too, close to my face, but
most of all her voice, her voice lightening the weight of so many,
so many memories. Her voice . . .

Stop wiggling so much, my darling. You want me to bring you
here again? Keep still! You want down, sweetheart? But behave
yourself now, princess. There, there . . . Wait. Ay, you're sticking your fingernails in me, sweetheart. Okay now? That's right,
that's right. Be good. . . . How pretty my little princess is! How
pretty! . . . No, don't go that way! Come back! You'll get run
over! Sweetheart! Ay, look at her. . . . Don't run off that way
either! Look where you're going, for heaven's sake. What a bad
little girl! I'm going to have to tie you to me. Come back, come
here now. Are you going to mind me! Do you want me to just
leave you here? Why won't you mind me! Ay, no, now you've got
mud all over yourself, how can you be such a little pig! Look at
what you look like. Oh my God. Heavens, how am I supposed to
pick you up now? You're filthy. Sweetheart, how in the world . . .
Yuck. Yuck! Well, we're going to have to scrub the little piggy
with a bristle brush. What am I ever going to do with you if you
don't mind me! Huh? I'll have to give you to the trash man. I'll

throw you out with the trash! Aw, how could I throw you in the trash! You're so sweet, my pretty little princess. . . .

You're so sweet, my pretty little princess. . . .

If I woke up, I was going to see a smile like a hyena on my mother's face. She pushed me away, she tenderly sprinkled me with sugar and watched for her chance to stick me in the oven, she drove away in a big car with my father and my brother, she threatened to slap me, she was ready to chop off my head at the drop of a hat. I was drenched in sweat, and suddenly I thought the tarantula on Carmelita Longlegs' thigh was coming alive and running to hide in my uterus. I moaned, with my head lying next to The Monk's. It was his hand, that seminarian's hand of his, greedily searching for my clitoris. His pianist's fingers were playing obscene scales. Carmelita Longlegs' tarantula!

I never went out with boys to sleep with them, no way, but at the same time I tried with many, many people to come to some sort of sexual understanding. If I liked a guy, if he turned me on, and I made love with him, then really the important thing to me was, to do everything I could to make him the happiest guy in the world. I always tried to make them as delighted, as satisfied, as *gratified*, as I possibly could. The first time I ever saw a pornographic movie, I was turned on from the ends of my hair all the way to my toenails, you know what I mean? I watched it, and if we'd turned off the projector and said Okay now, to bed, the orgasm would have flooded my whole life. Later on, though, I'd watch them and get the giggles. Do you know, giggles were my defense mechanism. Can you believe I threw giggles over all the parts of the body I'd always seen covered? Or maybe what made us laugh was how ridiculous it all was, how awful the acting was, the complete lack of romance, you know, *mystery*. Or maybe I caught Puritanitis from The Monk, I don't know. And now, the latest times, ugh, I can't stand them. I hate them. I don't get turned on anymore, they even make me mad, I get furious. . . . For example, when I was in Sweden and went to the porno shows and the sex shops and all, I didn't feel a thing, it was like So what. It's that I work a hundred percent on the basis that, on the basis that—it starts with *s*, wait a second—on the basis that I'm *stimulated*. Then I can come a thousand times, a hundred thousand times, I can come half a million times. . . . I can come a lot, I've always been able to. . . .

Hey! Next time I'm going to put a leash on you so you'll be still . . . My mother's voice . . . I'm going to tell your father to spank you for not minding and talking back. Do you hear? Oh, poor thing, where'd you get that sneeze. . . . You shouldn't have gotten wet like that. . . . See what happens when you don't behave? But no, I tell you and tell you and you won't listen to me. . . . My little princess! That's what you get for not minding your mother! Yuck! What am I ever going to do with you if you won't mind me. I'm going to throw you in the garbage truck one of these days! I'm going to tell the garbage man to take you away! No, sweetheart, I was kidding. How could I let them take my little princess away, sweetheart? Don't cry, don't cry, baby. What a pretty baby my little princess is! . . .

At that hour, that dusk, Captain Tarcisio the maître d' was surely coming back home with a sackful of goodies. Carmelita Longlegs, in hot pants to show off the tarantula tattooed on her thigh, would be waiting for him with a big pot of coffee and hot milk, the TV news turned on. . . . Captain Tarcisio's gaze lingered on the tattoo and his most secret organs, stimulated as never before by the perfume of bath salts, the clean cool odor of a woman's skin, the smell of fresh-washed sheets, churned out gallons of hormones. Shit . . .

("Long live the sperm . . . though I perish!")

22

They make a noise like feathers

VLADIMIR: What do they say?
ESTRAGON: They talk about their lives.
VLADIMIR: To have lived is not enough for them.
ESTRAGON: They have to talk about it.
VLADIMIR: To be dead is not enough for them.
ESTRAGON: It is not sufficient.
    Silence.
VLADIMIR: They make a noise like feathers.
ESTRAGON: Like leaves.
VLADIMIR: Like ashes.
ESTRAGON: Like leaves.

Samuel Beckett: *Waiting for Godot*